D0392222

SLEEPING MURDER

&

THE MURDER AT THE VICARAGE

AGATHA CHRISTIE

Sleeping Murder & The Murder at the Vicarage

DODD, MEAD & COMPANY
NEW YORK

Printed in the United States of America

Sleeping Murder

1

A Mouse

GWENDA REED stood, shivering a little, on the quayside.

The docks and the custom sheds and all of England that she could see were gently waving up and down.

And it was in that moment that she made her decision—the decision that was to lead to such very momentous events.

She wouldn't go by the boat train to London as she had planned.

After all, why should she? No one was waiting for her, nobody expected her. She had only just got off that heaving creaking boat (it had been an exceptionally rough three days through the Bay and up to Plymouth) and the last thing she wanted was to get into a heaving, swaying train. She would go to a hotel, a nice firm, steady hotel standing on good solid ground. And she would get into a nice steady bed that didn't creak and roll. And she would go to sleep, and the next morning—why, of course—what a splendid idea! She would hire a car and she would drive slowly and without hurrying herself all through the South of England looking about for a house—a nice house—the house that she and Giles had planned she should find. Yes, that was a splendid idea.

In that way she would see something of England—of the England that Giles had told her about and which she had never seen; although, like most New Zealanders, she called it home. At the moment, England was not looking particularly attractive. It was a grey day with rain imminent and a sharp, irritating wind blowing. Plymouth, Gwenda thought, as she moved forward obediently in the queue for Passports and Customs, was probably not the best of England.

On the following morning, however, her feelings were entirely different. The sun was shining. The view from her window was attractive. And the universe in general was no longer waving and wobbling. It had steadied down. This was England at last and here she was, Gwenda Reed, young married woman of twenty-one, on her travels. Giles's return to England was uncertain. He might follow her in a few weeks. It might be as long as six months. His suggestion had been that Gwenda should precede him to England and should look about for a suitable house. They both thought it would be nice to have, somewhere, a permanency. Giles's job would always entail a certain amount of travelling. Sometimes Gwenda would come too, sometimes the conditions would not be suitable. But they both liked the idea of having a home—some place of their very own. Giles had inherited some furniture from an aunt recently, so that everything combined to make the idea a sensible and practical one.

Since both Gwenda and Giles were reasonably well-off, the prospect presented no difficulties.

Gwenda had demurred at first to choosing a house on her own. "We ought to do it together," she had said. But Giles had said laughingly: "I'm not much of a hand at houses. If *you* like it, *I* shall. A bit of a garden, of course, and not some brand-new horror—and not too big. Somewhere on the south coast was my idea. At any rate, not too far inland."

"Was there any particular place?" Gwenda asked. But Giles said No. He'd been left an orphan young (they were both orphans) and had been passed around to various relations for holidays, and no particular spot had any particular association for him. It was to be Gwenda's house, and as for waiting until they could choose it together, suppose he were held up for six months? What would Gwenda do with herself all that time? Hang about in hotels? No, she was to find a house and get settled in.

"What you mean is," said Gwenda, "do all the work!"

But she liked the idea of finding a home and having it all ready, cosy and lived in, for when Giles came back.

They had been married just three months and she loved him very much.

After sending for breakfast in bed, Gwenda got up and arranged her plans. She spent a day seeing Plymouth, which she enjoyed, and on the following day she hired a comfortable Daimler car and chauffeur and set off on her journey through England.

The weather was good and she enjoyed her tour very much. She saw several possible residences in Devonshire but nothing that she felt was exactly right. There was no hurry. She would go on looking. She learned to read between the lines of the house agents' enthusiastic descriptions and saved herself a certain number of fruitless errands.

It was on a Tuesday evening about a week later that the car came gently down the curving hill road into Dillmouth and on the outskirts of that still charming seaside resort, passed a For Sale board where, through the trees, a glimpse of a small white Victorian villa could be seen.

Immediately Gwenda felt a throb of appreciation—almost of recognition. This was *her* house! Already she was sure of it. She could picture the garden, the long windows—she was sure that the house was just what she wanted.

It was late in the day, so she put up at the Royal Clarence Hotel and went to the house agents whose name she had noted on the board the following morning.

Presently, armed with an order to view, she was standing in the old-fashioned long drawing room with its two French windows giving onto a flagged terrace in front of which a kind of rockery interspersed with flowering shrubs fell sharply to a stretch of lawn below. Through the trees at the bottom of the garden the sea could be seen.

"This is *my* house," thought Gwenda. "It's *home*. I feel already as though I know every bit of it."

The door opened and a tall melancholy woman with a cold in the head entered sniffing. "Mrs. Hengrave? I have an order from Messrs. Galbraith and Penderley. I'm afraid it's rather early in the day—" Mrs. Hengrave, blowing her nose, said sadly that that didn't matter at all. The tour of the house began.

Yes, it was just right. Not too large. A bit old-fashioned, but she and Giles could put in another bathroom or two. The kitchen could be modernized. It already had a stove fortunately. With a new sink and up-to-date equipment—

Through all Gwenda's plans and preoccupations, the voice of Mrs. Hengrave droned thinly on recounting the details of the late Major Hengrave's last illness. Half of Gwenda attended to making the requisite noises of condolence, sympathy and understanding. Mrs. Hengrave's people all lived in Kent—anxious she should come and settle near them . . . the Major had been very fond of Dillmouth, secretary for many years of the golf club, but she herself . . .

"Yes . . . Of course . . . Dreadful for you . . . Most natural . . . Yes, nursing homes *are* like that . . . Of course . . . You must be. . . ."

And the other half of Gwenda raced along in thought:

"Linen cupboard here, I expect . . . Yes. Double room—nice view of the sea—Giles will like that. Quite a useful little room here—Giles might have it as a dressing room . . . Bathroom—I expect the bath has a mahogany surround—Oh yes, it *has!* How lovely—and standing in the middle of the floor! I shan't change *that*—it's a period piece!"

Such an enormous bath!

One could have apples on the surround. And sailboats—and painted ducks. You could pretend you were in the sea . . . "I know, we'll make that dark back spare room into a couple of really up-to-date green and chromium bathrooms—the pipes ought to be all right over the kitchen—and keep this just as it is. . . ."

"Pleurisy," said Mrs. Hengrave. "Turning to double pneumonia on the third day—"

"Terrible," said Gwenda. "Isn't there another bedroom at the end of this passage?"

There was—and it was just the sort of room she had imagined it would be—almost round, with a big bow window. She'd have to do it up, of course. It was in quite good condition, but why were people like Mrs. Hengrave so fond of that mustard-cum-biscuit shade of wall paint?

They retraced their steps along the corridor. Gwenda murmured conscientiously, "Six, no, seven bedrooms, counting the little one and the attic."

The boards creaked faintly under her feet. Already she felt that it was she and not Mrs. Hengrave who lived here! Mrs. Hengrave was an interloper—a woman who did up the rooms in mustard-cum-biscuit colour and liked a frieze of wisteria in her drawing room. Gwenda glanced down at the typewritten paper in her hand on which the details of the property and the price asked were given.

In the course of a few days Gwenda had become fairly conversant with house values. The sum asked was not large—of course the house needed a certain amount of modernization—but even then. . . . And she noted the words "Open to offer." Mrs. Hengrave must be very anxious to go to Kent and live near "her people."

They were starting down the stairs when quite suddenly Gwenda felt a wave of irrational terror sweep over her. It was a sickening sensation, and it passed almost as quickly as it came. Yet it left behind it a new idea.

"The house isn't—haunted, is it?" demanded Gwenda.

Mrs. Hengrave, a step below, and having just got to the moment in her narrative when Major Hengrave was sinking fast, looked up in an affronted manner.

"Not that I am aware of, Mrs. Reed. Why—has anyone—been saying something of the kind?"

"You've never felt or seen anything yourself? Nobody's *died* here?"

Rather an unfortunate question, she thought a split second of a moment too late, because presumably Major Hengrave—

"My husband died in the St. Monica's Nursing Home," said Mrs. Hengrave stiffly.

"Oh, of course. You told me so."

Mrs. Hengrave continued in the same rather glacial manner:

"In a house which was presumably built about a hundred years ago, there would normally be deaths during that period. Miss Elworthy, from whom my dear husband acquired this house seven years ago, was in excellent health, and indeed planning to go abroad and do missionary work, and she did not mention any recent demises in her family."

Gwenda hastened to soothe the melancholy Mrs. Hengrave down. They were now once more in the drawing room. It was a peaceful and charming room, with exactly the kind of atmosphere that Gwenda coveted. Her momentary panic just now seemed quite incomprehensible. What *had* come over her? There was nothing wrong with the house.

Asking Mrs. Hengrave if she could take a look at the garden, she went out through the French windows onto the terrace.

"There should be steps here," thought Gwenda, "going down to the lawn."

But instead there was a vast uprising of forsythia which at this particular place seemed to have got above itself and effectually shut out all view of the sea.

Gwenda nodded to herself. She would alter all that.

Following Mrs. Hengrave, she went along the terrace and down some steps at the far side onto the lawn. She noted that the rockery was neglected and overgrown, and that most of the flowering shrubs needed pruning.

Mrs. Hengrave murmured apologetically that the garden had been rather neglected. Only able to afford a man twice a week. And quite often *he* never turned up.

They inspected the small but adequate kitchen garden and returned to the house. Gwenda explained that she had other houses to see, and that though she liked Hillside (what a commonplace name!) very much, she could not decide immediately.

Mrs. Hengrave parted from her with a somewhat wistful look and a last long-lingering sniff.

Gwenda returned to the agents, made a firm offer subject to the surveyor's report, and spent the rest of the morning walking round Dillmouth. It was a charming and old-fashioned little seaside town. At the far, "modern" end, there were a couple of new-looking hotels and some raw-looking bungalows, but the geographical formation of the coast with the hills behind had saved Dillmouth from undue expansion.

After lunch Gwenda received a telephone call from the agents saying that Mrs. Hengrave accepted her offer. With a mischievous smile on her lips Gwenda made her way to the post office and despatched a cable to Giles.

HAVE BOUGHT A HOUSE. LOVE. GWENDA.

"That'll tickle him up," said Gwenda to herself. "Show him that the grass doesn't grow under *my* feet!"

2

Wallpaper

A MONTH had passed and Gwenda had moved into Hillside. Giles's aunt's furniture had come out of storage and was arranged round the house. It was good-quality old-fashioned stuff. One or two overlarge wardrobes Gwenda had sold, but the rest fitted in nicely and was in harmony with the house. There were small gay papier-mâché tables in the drawing room, inlaid with mother of pearl and painted with castles and roses. There was a prim little worktable with a gathered sack underneath of puce silk, there was a rosewood bureau and a mahogany sofa table.

The so-called easy chairs Gwenda had relegated to various bedrooms and had bought two large squashy wells of comfort for herself and Giles to stand at each side of the fireplace. The large Chesterfield sofa was placed near the windows. For curtains Gwenda had chosen old-fashioned chintz of pale eggshell blue with prim urns of roses and yellow birds on them. The room, she now considered, was exactly right.

She was hardly settled yet, since she had workmen in the house still. They should have been out by now, but Gwenda rightly estimated that until she herself came into residence, they would not go.

The kitchen alterations were finished, the new bathrooms nearly so. For further decorating Gwenda was going to wait a while. She wanted time to savour her new home and decide on the exact colour schemes she wanted for the bedrooms. The house was really in very good order and there was no need to do everything at once.

In the kitchen a Mrs. Cocker was now installed, a lady of condescending graciousness, inclined to repulse Gwenda's overdemocratic friendliness, but who, once Gwenda had been satisfactorily put in her place, was willing to unbend.

On this particular morning Mrs. Cocker deposited a breakfast tray on Gwenda's knees as she sat up in bed.

"When there's no gentleman in the house," Mrs. Cocker affirmed, "a lady prefers her breakfast in bed." And Gwenda had bowed to this supposedly English enactment.

"Scrambled this morning," Mrs. Cocker observed, referring to the eggs. "You said something about finnan haddock, but you wouldn't like it in the bedroom. It leaves a smell. I'm giving it to you for your supper, creamed on toast."

"Oh, thank you, Mrs. Cocker."

Mrs. Cocker smiled graciously and prepared to withdraw.

Gwenda was not occupying the big double bedroom. That could wait until Giles returned. She had chosen instead the end room, the one with the rounded walls and the bow window. She felt thoroughly at home in it and happy.

Looking round her now, she exclaimed impulsively:

"I do like this room."

Mrs. Cocker looked round indulgently.

"It is quaite a naice room, madam, though small. By the bars on the window I should say it had been the nursery at one time."

"I never thought of that. Perhaps it has."

"Ah, well," said Mrs. Cocker, with implication in her voice, and withdrew.

"Once we have a gentleman in the house," she seemed to be saying, "who knows? A nursery *may* be needed."

Gwenda blushed. She looked round the room. A nursery? Yes, it would be a nice nursery. She began furnishing it in her mind. A big doll's house there against the wall. And low cupboards with toys in them. A fire burning cheerfully in the grate and a tall guard round it with things airing on the rail. But not this hideous mustard wall. No, she would have a gay wallpaper. Something bright and cheerful. Little bunches of poppies alternating with bunches of cornflowers. . . . Yes, that would be lovely. She'd try and find a wallpaper like that. She felt sure she had seen one somewhere.

One didn't need much furniture in the room. There were two built-in cupboards, but one of them, a corner one, was locked and the key lost. Indeed the whole thing had been painted over, so that it could not have been opened for many years. She must get the men to open it up before they left. As it was, she hadn't got room for all her clothes.

She felt more at home every day in Hillside. Hearing a throat being ponderously cleared and a short dry cough through the open window, she hurried over her breakfast. Foster, the temperamental jobbing gardener, who was not always reliable in his promises, must be here today as he had said he would be.

Gwenda bathed, dressed, put on a tweed skirt and a sweater and hurried out into the garden. Foster was at work outside the drawing-room window. Gwenda's first action had been to get a path made down through the rockery at this point. Foster had been recalcitrant, pointing out that the forsythia would have to go and the weigela, and them there lilacs, but Gwenda had been adamant, and he was now almost enthusiastic about his task.

He greeted her with a chuckle.

"Looks like you're going back to old times, miss." (He persisted in calling Gwenda "miss.")

"Old times? How?"

Foster tapped with his spade.

"I come on the old steps—see, that's where they went—just as you want 'em now. Then someone planted them over and covered them up."

"It was very stupid of them," said Gwenda. "You want a vista down to the lawn and the sea from the drawing-room window."

Foster was somewhat hazy about a vista—but he gave a cautious and grudging assent.

"I don't say, mind you, that it won't be an improvement. . . . Gives you a view—and them shrubs made it dark in the drawing room. Still they was growing a treat—never seen a healthier lot of forsythia. Lilacs isn't much, but them wiglers costs money—and mind you—they're too old to replant."

"Oh, I know. But this is much, much nicer."

"Well"—Foster scratched his head—"maybe it is."

"It's *right*," said Gwenda, nodding her head. She asked suddenly: "Who lived here before the Hengraves? They weren't here very long, were they?"

"Matter of six years or so. Didn't belong. Afore them? The Miss Elworthys. Very churchy folk. Low church. Missions to the heathen. Once had a black clergyman staying here, they did. Four of 'em there was, and their brother—but he didn't get much of a look-in with all those women. Before them—now let me see, it was Mrs. Findeyson—ah! she was the real gentry, she was. She belonged. Was living here afore I was born."

"Did she die here?" asked Gwenda.

"Died out in Egypt or some such place. But they brought her home. She's buried up to churchyard. She planted that magnolia and those labiurnams. And those pittispores. Fond of shrubs, she was."

Foster continued:

"Weren't none of those new houses built up along the hill then. Countrified it was. No cinema then. And none of them new shops. Or that there parade on the front." His tone held the disapproval of the aged for all innovations. "Changes," he said with a snort. "Nothing but changes."

"I suppose things are bound to change," said Gwenda. "And after all, there are lots of improvements nowadays, aren't there?"

"So they say. I ain't noticed them. Changes!" He gestured towards the macrocarpa hedge on the left through which the gleam of a building showed. "Used to be the Cottage Hospital, that used," he said. "Nice place and handy. Then they goes and builds a great place near to a mile out of town. Twenty minutes' walk if you want to get there on a visiting day—or threepence on the bus." He gestured once more towards the hedge. "It's a girls' school now. Moved in ten years ago. Changes all the time. People takes a house nowadays and lives in it ten or twelve years and then off they goes. Restless. What's the good of that? You can't do any proper planting unless you can look well ahead."

Gwenda looked affectionately at the magnolia.

"Like Mrs. Findeyson," she said.

"Ah. She was the proper kind. Come here as a bride, she did. Brought up her children and married them, buried her husband, had her grandchildren down in the summers, and took off in the end when she was nigh on eighty."

Foster's tone held warm approval.

Gwenda went back into the house smiling a little.

She interviewed the workmen, and then returned to the drawing room, where she sat down at the desk and wrote some letters. Amongst the correspondence that remained to be answered was a letter from some cousins of Giles's who lived in London. Any time she wanted to come to London, they begged her to come and stay with them at their house in Chelsea.

Raymond West was a well-known (rather than popular) novelist and his wife Joan, Gwenda knew, was a painter. It would be fun to go and stay with them, though probably they would think she was a most terrible Philistine. "Neither Giles nor I are a bit highbrow," reflected Gwenda.

A sonorous gong boomed pontifically from the hall. Surrounded by a great deal of carved and tortured black wood, the gong had been one of Giles's aunt's prized possessions. Mrs. Cocker herself appeared to derive distinct pleasure from sounding it, and always gave full measure. Gwenda put her hands to her ears and got up.

She walked quickly across the drawing room to the wall by the far window and then brought herself up short with an exclamation of annoyance. It was the third time she'd done that. She always seemed to expect to be able to walk through solid wall into the dining room next door.

She went back across the room and out into the front hall and then round the angle of the drawing-room wall and so along to the dining room. It was a long way round, and it would be annoying in winter, for the front hall was draughty and the only central heating was in the drawing room and dining room and two bedrooms upstairs.

"I don't see," thought Gwenda to herself as she sat down at the charming Sheraton dining table which she had just bought at vast expense in lieu of Aunt Lavender's massive square mahogany one, "I don't see why I shouldn't have a doorway made through from the drawing room to the dining room. I'll talk to Mr. Sims about it when he comes this afternoon."

Mr. Sims was the builder and decorator, a persuasive middle-aged man with a husky voice and a little notebook which he always held at the ready to jot down any expensive idea that might occur to his patrons.

Mr. Sims, when consulted, was keenly appreciative.

"Simplest thing in the world, Mrs. Reed—and a great improvement, if I may say so."

"Would it be very expensive?" Gwenda was by now a little doubtful of Mr. Sims's assents and enthusiasms. There had been a little unpleasantness over various extras not included in Mr. Sims's original estimate.

"A mere trifle," said Mr. Sims, his husky voice indulgent and reassuring. Gwenda looked more doubtful than ever. It was Mr. Sims's trifles that she had learnt to distrust. His straightforward estimates were studiously moderate.

"I'll tell you what, Mrs. Reed," said Mr. Sims coaxingly, "I'll get Taylor to have a look when he's finished with the dressing room this afternoon, and then I can give you an exact idea. Depends what the wall's like."

Gwenda assented. She wrote to Joan West thanking her for her invitation, but saying that she would not be leaving Dillmouth at present since she wanted to keep an eye on the workmen. Then she went out for a walk along the front and enjoyed the sea breeze. She came back into the drawing room, and Taylor, Mr. Sims's leading workman, straightened up from the corner and greeted her with a grin.

"Won't be no difficulty about this, Mrs. Reed," he said. "Been a door here before, there has. Somebody as didn't want it has just had it plastered over."

Gwenda was agreeably surprised. "How extraordinary," she thought, "that I've always seemed to feel there was a door there." She remembered the confident way she had walked to it at lunchtime. And remembering it, quite suddenly, she felt a tiny shiver of uneasiness. When you came to think of it, it was really rather odd. . . . Why should she have felt so sure that there was a door there? There was no sign of it on the outside wall. How had she guessed—known—that there was a door just there? Of course it would be convenient to have a door through to the dining room, but why had she always gone so unerringly to that one particular spot? Anywhere on the dividing wall would have done equally well, but she had always gone automatically, thinking of other things, to the one place where a door had actually been:

"I hope," thought Gwenda uneasily, "that I'm not clairvoyant or anything. . . ."

There had never been anything in the least psychic about her. She wasn't that kind of person. Or was she? That path outside from the terrace down through the shrubbery to the lawn. Had she in some way known it was there when she was so insistent on having it made in that particular place?

"Perhaps I am a bit psychic," thought Gwenda uneasily. "Or is it something to do with the house?"

Why had she asked Mrs. Hengrave that day if the house was haunted?

It wasn't haunted! It was a darling house! There couldn't be anything wrong with the house. Why, Mrs. Hengrave had seemed quite surprised by the idea.

Or had there been a trace of reserve, of wariness, in her manner?

"Good heavens, I'm beginning to imagine things," thought Gwenda.

She brought her mind back with an effort to her discussion with Taylor.

"There's one other thing," she added. "One of the cupboards in my room upstairs is stuck. I want to get it opened."

The man came up with her and examined the door.

"It's been painted over more than once," he said. "I'll get the men to get it open for you tomorrow, if that will do."

Gwenda acquiesced and Taylor went away.

That evening Gwenda felt jumpy and nervous. Sitting in the drawing room and trying to read, she was aware of every creak of the furniture. Once or twice she looked over her shoulder and shivered. She told herself repeatedly that there was nothing in the incident of the door and the path. They were just coincidences. In any case they were the result of plain common sense.

Without admitting it to herself, she felt nervous about going up to bed. When she finally got up and turned off the lights and opened the door into the hall, she found herself dreading to go up the stairs. She almost ran up them in her haste, hurried along the passage and opened the door of her room. Once inside she at once felt her fears calmed and appeased. She looked round the room affectionately. She felt safe in here—safe and happy. Yes, now she was here, she was safe. ("Safe from what, you idiot?" she asked herself.) She looked at her pyjamas spread out on the bed and her bedroom slippers below them.

"Really, Gwenda, you might be six years old! You ought to have bunny shoes, with rabbits on them."

She got into bed with a sense of relief and was soon asleep.

The next morning she had various matters to see to in the town. When she came back, it was lunchtime.

"The men have got the cupboard open in your bedroom, madam," said Mrs. Cocker as she brought in the delicately fried sole, the mashed potatoes and the creamed carrots.

"Oh, good," said Gwenda.

She was hungry and enjoyed her lunch. After having coffee in the drawing room, she went upstairs to her bedroom. Crossing the room, she pulled open the door of the corner cupboard.

Then she uttered a sudden frightened little cry and stood staring.

The inside of the cupboard revealed the original papering of the wall, which elsewhere had been done over in the yellowish wall paint. The room had once been gaily papered in a floral design, a design of little bunches of scarlet poppies alternating with bunches of blue cornflowers. . . .

Gwenda stood there staring a long time, then she went shakily over to the bed and sat down on it.

Here she was in a house she had never been in before, in a country she had never visited—and only two days ago she had lain in bed imagining a paper for this very room—and the paper she had imagined corresponded exactly with the paper that had once hung on the walls.

Wild fragments of explanation whirled round in her head. Donne, Experiment with Time—seeing forward instead of back . . .

She could explain the garden path and the connecting door as coincidence—but there couldn't be coincidence about this—you couldn't conceivably imagine a wallpaper of such a distinctive design and then find one exactly as you had imagined it. . . . No, there was some explanation that eluded her and that—yes, frightened her. Every now and then she was seeing, not forward, but back—back to some former state of the house. Any moment she might see something more—something she didn't want to see. . . . The house frightened her. . . . But was it the house or *herself?* She didn't want to be one of those people who *saw* things. . . .

She drew a long breath, put on her hat and coat and slipped quickly out of the house. At the post office she sent the following telegram:

WEST, 19 ADDWAY SQUARE CHELSEA LONDON. MAY I CHANGE MY MIND AND COME TO YOU TOMORROW. GWENDA.

She sent it reply paid.

3

"Cover her face; mine eyes dazzle: she died young"

RAYMOND WEST and his wife did all they could to make young Giles's wife feel welcome. It was not their fault that Gwenda found them secretly rather alarming. Raymond, with his odd appearance, rather like a pouncing raven, his sweep of hair and his sudden crescendos of quite incomprehensible conversation, left Gwenda round-eyed and nervous. Both he and Joan seemed to talk a language of their own. Gwenda had never been plunged in a highbrow atmosphere before and practically all its terms were strange.

"We've planned to take you to a show or two," said Raymond while Gwenda was drinking gin and rather wishing she could have had a cup of tea after her journey.

Gwenda brightened up immediately.

"The ballet tonight at Sadler's Wells, and tomorrow we've got a birthday party on for my quite incredible Aunt Jane—*The Duchess of Malfi* with Gielgud, and on Friday you simply must see *They Walked Without Feet*. Translated from the Russian—absolutely the most significant piece of drama for the last twenty years. It's at the little Witmore Theatre."

Gwenda expressed herself grateful for these plans for her entertainment. After all, when Giles came home, they would go together to the musical shows and all that. She flinched slightly at the prospect of *They Walked Without Feet*, but supposed she might enjoy it—only the point about "significant" plays was that you usually didn't.

"You'll adore my Aunt Jane," said Raymond. "She's what I should describe as a perfect Period Piece. Victorian to the core. All her dressing tables have their legs swathed in chintz. She lives in a village, the kind of village where nothing ever happens, exactly like a stagnant pond."

"Something did happen there once," his wife said drily.

Raymond waved his hand.

"A mere drama of passion—crude—no subtlety to it."

"You enjoyed it frightfully at the time," Joan reminded him with a slight twinkle.

"I sometimes enjoy playing village cricket," said Raymond with dignity.

"Anyway, Aunt Jane distinguished herself over that murder."

"Oh, she's no fool. She adores problems."

"Problems?" said Gwenda, her mind flying to arithmetic.

Raymond waved a hand.

"Any kind of problems. Why the grocer's wife took her umbrella to the church social on a fine evening. Why a gill of pickled shrimps was found where it was. What happened to the vicar's surplice. All grist to my Aunt Jane's mill. So if you've any problem in your life, put it to her, Gwenda. She'll tell you the answer."

He laughed and Gwenda laughed too, but not very heartily. She was introduced to Aunt Jane, otherwise Miss Marple, on the following day. Miss Marple was an attractive old lady, tall and thin, with pink cheeks and blue eyes, and a gentle, rather fussy manner. Her blue eyes often had a little twinkle in them.

After an early dinner at which they drank Aunt Jane's health, they all went off to His Majesty's theatre. Two extra men, an elderly artist and a young barrister, were in the party. The elderly artist devoted himself to Gwenda and the young barrister divided his attentions between Joan and Miss Marple, whose remarks he seemed to enjoy very much. At the theatre, however, this arrangement was reversed. Gwenda sat in the middle of the row between Raymond and the barrister.

The lights went down and the play began.

It was superbly acted and Gwenda enjoyed it very much. She had not seen very many first-rate theatrical productions.

The play drew to a close, came to that supreme moment of horror. The actor's voice came over the footlights filled with the tragedy of a warped and perverted mentality.

"Cover her face; mine eyes dazzle: she died young."

Gwenda screamed.

She sprang up from her seat, pushed blindly past the others out into the aisle, through the exit and up the stairs and so to the street. She did not stop, even then, but half walked, half ran, in a blind panic up the Haymarket.

It was not until she had reached Piccadilly that she noticed a free taxi cruising along, hailed it and, getting in, gave the address of the Chelsea house. With fumbling fingers she got out money, paid the taxi and went up the steps. The servant who let her in glanced at her in surprise.

"You've come back early, miss. Didn't you feel well?"

"I—no, yes—I—I felt faint."

"Would you like anything, miss? Some brandy?"

"No, nothing. I'll go straight up to bed."

She ran up the stairs to avoid further questions.

She pulled off her clothes, left them on the floor in a heap and got into bed. She lay there shivering, her heart pounding, her eyes staring at the ceiling.

She did not hear the sound of fresh arrivals downstairs, but after about five minutes the door opened and Miss Marple came in. She had two hot-water bottles tucked under her arm and a cup in her hand.

Gwenda sat up in bed, trying to stop her shivering.

"Oh, Miss Marple, I'm frightfully sorry. I don't know what— It was awful of me. Are they very annoyed with me?"

"Now don't worry, my dear child," said Miss Marple. "Just tuck yourself up warmly with these hot-water bottles."

"I don't really need a hot-water bottle."

"Oh yes, you do. That's right. And now drink this cup of tea."

It was hot and strong and far too full of sugar, but Gwenda drank it obediently. The shivering was less acute now.

"Just lie down now and go to sleep," said Miss Marple. "You've had a shock, you know. We'll talk about it in the morning. Don't worry about anything. Just go to sleep."

She drew the covers up, smiled, patted Gwenda and went out.

Downstairs Raymond was saying irritably to Joan:

"What on earth was the matter with the girl? Did she feel ill, or what?"

"My dear Raymond, I don't know, she just screamed! I suppose the play was a bit too macabre for her."

"Well, of course Webster is a bit grisly. But I shouldn't have thought—" He broke off as Miss Marple came into the room. "Is she all right?"

"Yes, I think so. She'd had a bad shock, you know."

"Shock? Just seeing an Elizabethan drama?"

"I think there must be a little more to it than that," said Miss Marple thoughtfully.

Gwenda's breakfast was sent up to her. She drank some coffee and nibbled a little piece of toast. When she got up and came downstairs, Joan had gone to her studio, Raymond was shut up in his workroom, and only Miss Marple was sitting by the window which had a view over the river; she was busily engaged in knitting.

She looked up with a placid smile as Gwenda entered.

"Good morning, my dear. You're feeling better, I hope."

"Oh yes, I'm quite all right. How could I make such an utter *idiot* of myself last night, I don't know. Are they—are they very mad with me?"

"Oh no, my dear. They quite understand."

"Understand what?"

Miss Marple glanced up over her knitting.

"That you had a bad shock last night." She added gently: "Hadn't you better tell me all about it?"

Gwenda walked restlessly up and down.

"I think I'd better go and see a psychiatrist or someone."

"There are excellent mental specialists in London, of course. But are you sure it is necessary?"

"Well—I think I'm going mad. . . . I *must* be going mad."

An elderly parlourmaid entered the room with a telegram on a salver which she handed to Gwenda.

"The boy wants to know if there's an answer, m'am?"

Gwenda tore it open. It had been retelegraphed on from Dillmouth. She stared at it for a moment or two uncomprehendingly, then screwed it into a ball.

"There's no answer," she said mechanically.

The maid left the room.

"Not bad news, I hope, dear?"

"It's Giles—my husband. He's flying home. He'll be here in a week."

Her voice was bewildered and miserable. Miss Marple gave a gentle little cough.

"Well—surely—that is very nice, isn't it?"

"Is it? When I'm not sure if I'm mad or not? If I'm mad, I ought never to have married Giles. And the house and everything. I can't go back there. Oh, I don't know what to do."

Miss Marple patted the sofa invitingly.

"Now suppose you sit down here, dear, and just tell me all about it."

It was with a sense of relief that Gwenda accepted the invitation. She poured out the whole story, starting with her first view of Hillside and going on to the incidents that had first puzzled her and then worried her.

"And so I got rather frightened," she ended. "And I thought I'd come up to London—get away from it all. Only, you see, I couldn't get away from it. It followed me. Last night—" She shut her eyes and gulped reminiscently.

"Last night?" prompted Miss Marple.

"I daresay you won't believe this," said Gwenda, speaking very fast. "You'll think I'm hysterical or queer or something. It happened quite suddenly, right at the end. I'd enjoyed the play. I'd never thought once of the house. And then it came—out of the blue—when he said those words—"

She repeated in a low, quivering voice:

"*Cover her face; mine eyes dazzle: she died young.*"

"I was back there—on the stairs, looking down on the hall through the banisters, and I saw her lying there. Sprawled out—dead. Her hair all golden and her face all—all *blue!* She was dead, strangled, and someone was saying those words in that same horrible, gloating way—and I saw his hands—grey, wrinkled—not hands—monkey's paws. . . . It was horrible, I tell you. She was dead. . . ."

Miss Marple asked gently:

"Who was dead?"

The answer came back quick and mechanical:

"Helen. . . ."

4

Helen?

FOR A MOMENT Gwenda stared at Miss Marple, then she pushed back the hair from her forehead.

"Why did I say that?" she said. "Why did I say Helen? I don't know any Helen!"

She dropped her hands with a gesture of despair.

"You see," she said, "I'm mad! I imagine things! I go about seeing things that aren't there. First it was only wallpapers—but now it's dead bodies. So I'm getting worse."

"Now don't rush to conclusions, my dear—"

"Or else it's the *house*. The house is haunted—or bewitched or something. . . . I see things that have happened there—or else I see things that are going to happen there—and that would be worse. Perhaps a woman called Helen is going to be murdered there. . . . Only I don't see if it's the *house* that's haunted why I should see these awful things when I am away from it. So I think really that it must be me that's going queer. And I'd better go and see a psychiatrist *at once*—this morning."

"Well, of course, Gwenda dear, you can always do that when you've exhausted every other line of approach, but I always think myself that it's better to examine the simplest and most commonplace explanations first. Let me get the facts quite clear. There were three definite incidents that upset you. A path in the garden that had been planted over but that you felt was there, a door that had been bricked up, and a wallpaper which you imagined correctly and in detail without having seen it? Am I right?"

"Yes."

"Well, the easiest, the most natural explanation would be that you *had* seen them before."

"In another life, you mean?"

"Well, no, dear. I meant in *this* life. I mean that they might be actual *memories*."

"But I've never been in England until a month ago, Miss Marple."

"You are quite sure of that, my dear?"

"Of course I'm sure. I've lived near Christchurch in New Zealand all my life."

"Were you born there?"

"No, I was born in India. My father was a British Army officer. My mother died a year or two after I was born and he sent me back to her people in New Zealand to bring up. Then he himself died a few years later."

"You don't remember coming from India to New Zealand?"

"Not really. I do remember, frightfully vaguely, being on a boat. A round window thing—a porthole, I suppose. And a man in white uniform with a red face and blue eyes and a mark on his chin—a scar, I suppose. He used to toss me up in the air and I remember being half frightened and half loving it. But it's all very fragmentary."

"Do you remember a nurse—or an ayah?"

"Not an ayah—Nannie. I remember Nannie because she stayed for some time—until I was five years old. She cut ducks out of paper. Yes, she was on the boat. She scolded me when I cried because the captain kissed me and I didn't like his beard."

"Now that's very interesting, dear, because you see you are mixing up two different voyages. In one, the captain had a beard and in the other he had a red face and a scar on his chin."

"Yes," Gwenda considered, "I suppose I must be."

"It seems possible to me," said Miss Marple, "that when your mother died, your father brought you to *England* with him first, and that you actually lived at this house, Hillside. You've told me, you know, that the house felt like home to you as soon as you got inside it. And that room you chose to sleep in, it was probably your nursery—"

"It *was* a nursery. There were bars on the windows."

"You see? It had this pretty gay paper of cornflowers and poppies. Children remember their nursery walls very well. I've always remembered the mauve irises on my nursery walls and yet I believe it was repapered when I was only three."

"And that's why I thought at once of the toys, the doll's house and the toy cupboards?"

"Yes. And the bathroom. The bath with the mahogany surround. You told me that you thought of sailing ducks in it as soon as you saw it."

Gwenda said thoughtfully:

"It's true that I seemed to know right away just where everything was—the kitchen and the linen cupboard. And that I kept thinking there was a door through from the drawing room to the dining room. But surely it's quite impossible that I should come to England and actually buy the identical house I'd lived in long ago?"

"It's not *impossible*, my dear. It's just a very remarkable coincidence—and remarkable coincidences do happen. Your husband wanted a house on the south coast, you were looking for one, and you passed a house that stirred memories, and attracted you. It was the right size and a reasonable price and so you bought it. No, it's not too wildly improbable. Had the house been merely what is called (perhaps rightly) a haunted house, you would have reacted quite differently, I think. But you had no feeling of violence or repulsion except, so you have told me, at one very definite moment, and that was when you were just starting to come down the staircase and looking down into the hall."

Some of the scared expression came back into Gwenda's eyes. She said:

"You mean—that—that Helen—that *that's* true too?"

Miss Marple said very gently:

"Well, I think so, my dear. . . . I think we must face the position that if the other things are memories, *that* is a memory too. . . ."

"That I really saw someone killed—strangled—and lying there dead?"

"I don't suppose you knew consciously that she was strangled. That was suggested by the play last night and fits in with your adult recognition of what a blue convulsed face must mean. I think a very young child, creeping down the stairs, would realize violence and death and evil and associate them with a certain series of words—for I think there's no doubt that the murderer actually *said* those words. It would be a very severe shock to a child. Children are odd little creatures. If they are badly frightened, especially by something they don't understand, they don't talk about it. They bottle it up. Seemingly, perhaps, they forget it. But the memory is still there deep down."

Gwenda drew a deep breath.

"And you think that's what happened to me? But why don't I remember it all *now?*"

"One can't remember to order. And often when one tries to, the memory goes farther away. But I think there are one or two indications that that is what did happen. For instance when you told me just now about your experience in the theatre last night, you used a very revealing turn of words. You said you seemed to be looking '*through* the banisters'—but normally, you know, one doesn't look down into a hall *through* the banisters but *over* them. Only a child would look *through*."

"That's clever of you," said Gwenda appreciatively.

"These little things are very significant."

"But who was Helen?" asked Gwenda in a bewildered way.

"Tell me, my dear, are you still quite sure it was Helen?"

"Yes. . . . It's frightfully odd, because I don't know who 'Helen' is—but at the same time I do know—I mean I know that it was 'Helen' lying there. . . . How am I going to find out more?"

"Well, I think the obvious thing to do is to find out definitely if you ever were in England as a child, or if you could have been. Your relations—"

Gwenda interrupted. "Aunt Alison. She would know, I'm sure."

"Then I should write to her by airmail. Or send a night mail letter. Tell her circumstances have arisen which make it imperative for you to know if you have ever been in England. You would probably get an answer by airmail by the time your husband arrives."

"Oh, thank you, Miss Marple. You've been frightfully kind. And I do hope what you've suggested is true. Because if so, well, it's quite all right. I mean, it won't be anything supernatural."

Miss Marple smiled.

"I hope it turns out as we think. I am going to stay with some old friends of mine in the North of England the day after tomorrow. I shall be passing back through London in about ten days. If you and your husband are here then, or if you have received an answer to your letter, I should be very curious to know the result."

"Of course, dear Miss Marple! Anyway, I want you to meet Giles. He's a perfect pet. And we'll have a good powwow about the whole thing."

Gwenda's spirits were fully restored by now.

Miss Marple, however, looked thoughtful.

5

Murder in Retrospect

IT WAS some ten days later that Miss Marple entered a small hotel in Mayfair, and was given an enthusiastic reception by young Mr. and Mrs. Reed.

"This is my husband, Miss Marple. Giles, I can't tell you how kind Miss Marple was to me."

"I'm delighted to meet you, Miss Marple. I hear Gwenda nearly panicked herself into a lunatic asylum."

Miss Marple's gentle blue eyes summed up Giles Reed favourably. A very likeable young man, tall and fair, with a disarming way of blinking every now and then out of a natural shyness. She noted his determined chin and the set of his jaw.

"We'll have tea in the little writing room, the dark one," said Gwenda. "Nobody ever comes there. And then we can show Miss Marple Aunt Alison's letter.

"Yes," she added, as Miss Marple looked up sharply. "It's come, and it's almost exactly what you thought."

Tea over, the airmail letter was spread out and read.

Dearest Gwenda, [Miss Danby had written]

I was much disturbed to hear that you had had some worrying experience. To tell you the truth, it had really entirely escaped my memory that you had actually resided for a short time in England as a young child.

Your mother, my sister Megan, met your father, Major Halliday, when she was on a visit to some friends of ours at that time stationed in India. They were married and you were born there. About two years after your birth your mother died. It was a great shock to us and we wrote to your father, with whom we had corresponded, but whom actually we had never seen, begging him to entrust you to our care, as we would be only too glad to have you, and it might be difficult for an Army man stranded with a young child. Your father, however, refused, and told us he was resigning from the Army and taking you back with him to England. He said he hoped we would at some time come over and visit him there.

I understand that on the voyage home, your father met a young woman, became engaged to her, and married her as soon as he got to England. The marriage was not, I gather, a happy one, and I understand they parted about a year later. It was then that your father wrote to us and asked if we were still willing to give you a home. I need hardly tell you, my dear, how happy we were to do so. You were sent out to us in charge of an English nurse, and at the same time your father settled the bulk of his estate upon you and suggested that you might legally adopt our name. This, I may say, seemed a little curious to us, but we felt that it was kindly meant—and intended to make you more one of the family—we did not, however, adopt that suggestion. About a year later your father died in a nursing home. I surmise that he had already received bad news about his health at the time when he sent you out to us.

I'm afraid I cannot tell you where you lived while with your father in England. His letter naturally had the address on it at the time, but that is now eighteen years ago and I'm afraid one doesn't remember such details. It was in the South of England, I know—and I fancy Dillmouth is correct. I had a vague idea it was Dartmouth, but the two names are not unlike. I believe your stepmother married again, but I have no recollection of her name, not even of her unmarried name, though your father had mentioned it in the original letter telling of his remarriage. We were, I think, a little resentful of his marrying again so soon, but of course one knows that on board ship the influence of propinquity is very great—and he may also have thought that it would be a good thing on your account.

It seems stupid of me not to have mentioned to you that you had been in England even if you didn't remember the fact, but, as I say, the whole thing had faded from my mind. Your mother's death in India and your subsequently coming to live with us always seemed the important points.

I hope this is all cleared up now?

I do trust Giles will soon be able to join you. It is hard for you both being parted at this early stage.

All my news in my next letter, as I am sending this off hurriedly in answer to your wire.

Your loving aunt,
Alison Danby.

P.S. You do not say what your worrying experience was?

"You see," said Gwenda. "It's almost exactly as you suggested."

Miss Marple smoothed out the flimsy sheet.

"Yes—yes, indeed. The common-sense explanation. I've found, you know, that that is so often right."

"Well, I'm very grateful to you, Miss Marple," said Giles. "Poor Gwenda was thoroughly upset, and I must say I'd have been rather worried myself to think that Gwenda was clairvoyant or psychic or something."

"It might be a disturbing quality in a wife," said Gwenda. "Unless you've always led a thoroughly blameless life."

"Which I have," said Giles.

"And the house? What do you feel about the house?" asked Miss Marple.

"Oh, that's all right. We're going down tomorrow. Giles is dying to see it."

"I don't know whether you realize it, Miss Marple," said Giles, "but what it amounts to is that we've got a first-class murder mystery on our hands. Actually on our very doorstep—or more accurately in our front hall."

"I *had* thought of that, yes," said Miss Marple slowly.

"And Giles simply loves detective stories," said Gwenda.

"Well, I mean, it *is* a detective story. Body in the hall of a beautiful strangled woman. Nothing known of her but her Christian name. Of course I know it's nearly twenty years ago. There can't be any clues after all this time, but one can at least cast about, and try to pick up some of the threads. Oh! I daresay one won't succeed in solving the riddle—"

"I think you might," said Miss Marple. "Even after eighteen years. Yes, I think you might."

"But at any rate it won't do any harm to have a real good try?"

Giles paused, his face beaming.

Miss Marple moved uneasily, her face was grave—almost troubled.

"But it might do a great deal of harm," she said. "I would advise you both—oh yes, I really would advise it very strongly—to leave the whole thing alone."

"Leave it alone? Our very own murder mystery—if it *was* murder?"

"It was murder, I think. And that's just why I should leave it alone. Murder isn't—it really isn't—a thing to tamper with lightheartedly."

Giles said:

"But, Miss Marple, if everybody felt like that—"

She interrupted him.

"Oh, I know. There are times when it is one's *duty*—an innocent person accused—suspicion resting on various other people—a dangerous criminal at large who may strike again. But you must realize that this murder is very much in the *past*. Presumably it wasn't known for murder. If so, you would have heard fast enough from your old gardener or someone down there. A murder, however long ago, is always news. No, the body must have been disposed of somehow, and the whole thing never suspected. Are you sure—are you really sure—that you are wise to dig it all up again?"

"Miss Marple," cried Gwenda, "you sound really concerned?"

"I am, my dear. You are two very nice and charming young people (if you will allow me to say so). You are newly married and happy together. Don't, I beg of you, start to uncover things that may—well, that may—how shall I put it?—that may *upset* and *distress* you."

Gwenda stared at her. "You're thinking of something special—of something— What is it you're hinting at?"

"Not hinting, dear. Just advising you (because I've lived a long time and know how very upsetting human nature can be) to let well alone. That's *my* advice, *let well alone.*"

"But it isn't letting well alone." Giles's voice held a different note, a sterner note. "Hillside is our house, Gwenda's and mine, and someone was murdered in that house, or so we believe. I'm not going to stand for murder in my house and do nothing about it, even if it *is* eighteen years ago!"

Miss Marple sighed. "I'm sorry," she said. "I imagine that most young men of spirit would feel like that. I even sympathize and almost admire you for it. But I wish—oh, I do wish—that you wouldn't do it."

II

On the following day, news went round the village of St. Mary Mead that Miss Marple was at home again. She was seen in the High Street at eleven o'clock. She called at the vicarage at ten minutes to twelve. That afternoon three of the gossipy ladies of the village called upon her and obtained her impressions of the gay Metropolis and, this tribute to politeness over, themselves plunged into details of an approaching battle over the fancywork stall at the fete and the position of the tea tent.

Later that evening Miss Marple could be seen as usual in her garden, but for once her activities were more concentrated on the depredations of weeds than on the activities of her neighbours. She was *distraite* at her frugal evening meal, and hardly appeared to listen to her little maid Evelyn's spirited account of the goings-on of the local chemist. The next day she was still *distraite*, and one or two people, including the vicar's wife, remarked upon it. That evening Miss Marple said that she did not feel very well and took to her bed. The following morning she sent for Dr. Haydock.

Dr. Haydock had been Miss Marple's physician, friend and ally for many years. He listened to her account of her symptoms, gave her an examination, then sat back in his chair and waggled his stethoscope at her.

"For a woman of your age," he said, "and in spite of that misleading frail appearance, you're in remarkably good fettle."

"I'm sure my general health is sound," said Miss Marple. "But I confess I do feel a little overtired—a little run-down."

"You've been gallivanting about. Late nights in London."

"That, of course. I do find London a little tiring nowadays. And the air—so used-up. Not like fresh seaside air."

"The air of St. Mary Mead is nice and fresh."

"But often damp and rather muggy. Not, you know, exactly *bracing*."

Dr. Haydock eyed her with a dawning of interest.

"I'll send you round a tonic," he said obligingly.

"Thank you, Doctor. Easton's syrup is always very helpful."

"There's no need for you to do my prescribing for me, woman."

"I wondered if, perhaps, a change of air—?"

Miss Marple looked questioningly at him with guileless blue eyes.

"You've just been away for three weeks."

"I know. But to London which, as you say, is enervating. And then up North—a manufacturing district. Not like bracing sea air."

Dr. Haydock packed up his bag. Then he turned round, grinning.

"Let's hear why you sent for me," he said. "Just tell me what it's to be and I'll repeat it after you. You want my professional opinion that what you need is sea air—"

"I knew you'd understand," said Miss Marple gratefully.

"Excellent thing, sea air. You'd better go to Eastbourne right away, or your health may suffer seriously."

"Eastbourne, I think, is rather cold. The downs, you know."

"Bournemouth, then, or the Isle of Wight."

Miss Marple twinkled at him.

"I always think a small place is much pleasanter."

Dr. Haydock sat down again.

"My curiosity is roused. What small seaside town are you suggesting?"

"Well, I *had* thought of Dillmouth."

"Pretty little place. Rather dull. Why Dillmouth?"

For a moment or two Miss Marple was silent. The worried look had returned to her eyes. She said:

"Supposing that one day, by accident, you turned up a fact that seemed to indicate that many years ago—nineteen or twenty—a murder had occurred. That fact was known to you alone, nothing of the kind had ever been suspected or reported. What would you do about it?"

"Murder in retrospect, in fact?"

"Just exactly that."

Haydock reflected for a moment.

"There had been no miscarriage of justice? Nobody had suffered as a result of this crime?"

"As far as one can see, no."

"Hm. Murder in retrospect. Sleeping murder. Well, I'll tell you. I'd let sleeping murder lie—that's what I'd do. Messing about with murder is dangerous. It could be *very* dangerous."

"That's what I'm afraid of."

"People say a murderer always repeats his crimes. That's not true. There's a type who commits a crime, manages to get away with it, and is darned careful never to stick a neck out again. I won't say they live happily ever after—I don't believe that's true—there are many kinds of retribution. But outwardly at least all goes well. Perhaps that was so in the case of Madeleine Smith or again in the case of Lizzie Borden. It was nonproven in the case of Madeleine Smith, and Lizzie was acquitted—but many people believe both of those women were guilty. I could name you others. They never repeated their crimes—one crime gave them what they wanted and they were content. But suppose some danger had menaced them? I take it your killer, whoever he or she is, was one of that kind. He committed a crime and got away with it and nobody suspected. But supposing somebody goes poking about, digging into things, turning up stones and exploring avenues and finally, perhaps, hitting the target? What's your killer going to do about it? Just stay there smiling while the hunt comes nearer and nearer? No, if there's no principle involved, I'd say let it alone." He repeated his former phrase: "Let sleeping murder lie."

He added firmly:

"And those are my orders to *you. Let the whole thing alone.*"

"But it's not I who am involved. It's two very delightful children. Let me tell you!"

She told him the story and Haydock listened.

"Extraordinary," he said when she had finished. "Extraordinary coincidence. Extraordinary business altogether. I suppose you see what the implications are?"

"Oh, of course. But I don't think it's occurred to *them* yet."

"It will mean a good deal of unhappiness and they'll wish they'd never meddled with the thing. Skeletons should be kept in their cupboards. Still, you know, I can quite see young Giles's point of view. Dash it all, I couldn't leave the thing alone myself. Even now, I'm curious. . . ."

He broke off and directed a stern glance at Miss Marple.

"So that's what you're doing with your excuses to get to Dillmouth. Mixing yourself up in something that's no concern of yours."

"Not at all, Dr. Haydock. But I'm worried about those two. They're very young and inexperienced and much too trusting and credulous. I feel I ought to be there to look after them."

"So that's why you're going. To look after them! Can't you *ever* leave murder alone, woman? Even murder in retrospect?"

Miss Marple gave a small prim smile.

"But you do think, don't you, that a few weeks at Dillmouth would be beneficial to my health?"

"More likely to be the end of you," said Dr. Haydock. "But you won't listen to me!"

III

On her way to call upon her friends, Colonel and Mrs. Bantry, Miss Marple met Colonel Bantry coming along the drive, his gun in his hand and his spaniel at his heels. He welcomed her cordially.

"Glad to see you back again. How's London?"

Miss Marple said that London was very well. Her nephew had taken her to several plays.

"Highbrow ones, I bet. Only care for a musical comedy myself."

Miss Marple said that she had been to a Russian play that was very interesting, though perhaps a little too long.

"Russians!" said Colonel Bantry explosively. He had once been given a novel by Dostoevski to read in a nursing home.

He added that Miss Marple would find Dolly in the garden.

Mrs. Bantry was almost always to be found in the garden. Gardening was her passion. Her favourite literature was bulb catalogues and her conversation dealt with primulas, bulbs, flowering shrubs and alpine novelties. Miss Marple's first view of her was a substantial posterior clad in faded tweed.

At the sound of approaching steps, Mrs. Bantry reassumed an erect position with a few creaks and winces, her hobby had made her rheumaticky, wiped her hot brow with an earth-stained hand and welcomed her friend.

"Heard you were back, Jane," she said. "Aren't my new delphiniums doing well? Have you seen these new little gentians? I've had a bit of trouble with them, but I think they're all set now. What we need is rain. It's been terribly dry." She added, "Esther told me you were ill in bed." Esther was Mrs. Bantry's cook and liaison officer with the village. "I'm glad to see it's not true."

"Just a little overtired," said Miss Marple. "Dr. Haydock thinks I need some sea air. I'm rather run-down."

"Oh, but you couldn't go away *now*," said Mrs. Bantry. "This is absolutely the best time of the year in the garden. Your border must be just coming into flower."

"Dr. Haydock thinks it would be advisble."

"Well, Haydock's not such a fool as some doctors," admitted Mrs. Bantry grudgingly.

"I was wondering, Dolly, about that cook of yours."

"Which cook? Do you want a cook? You don't mean that woman who drank, do you?"

"No, no, no. I mean the one who made such delicious pastry. With a husband who was the butler."

"Oh, you mean the Mock Turtle," said Mrs. Bantry with immediate recognition. "Woman with a deep mournful voice who always sounded as though she was just going to burst into tears. She *was* a good cook. Husband was a fat, rather lazy man. Arthur always said he watered the whisky. I don't know. Pity there's always onc of a couple that's unsatisfactory. They got left a legacy by some former employer and they went off and opened a boarding house on the South coast."

"That's just what I thought. Wasn't it at Dillmouth?"

"That's right. Fourteen Sea Parade, Dillmouth."

"I was thinking that as Dr. Haydock has suggested the seaside, I might go to—was their name Saunders?"

"Yes. That's an excellent idea, Jane. You couldn't do better. Mrs. Saunders will look after you well, and as it's out of the season, they'll be glad to get you and won't charge very much. With good cooking and sea air you'll soon pick up."

"Thank you, Dolly," said Miss Marple, "I expect I shall."

6

Exercise in Detection

"WHERE do you think the body was? About here?" asked Giles.

He and Gwenda were standing in the front hall of Hillside. They had arrived back the night before, and Giles was now in full cry. He was as pleased as a small boy with his new toy.

"Just about," said Gwenda. She retreated up the stairs and peered down critically. "Yes—I think that's about it."

"Crouch down," said Giles. "You're only about three years old, you know."

Gwenda crouched obligingly.

"You couldn't actually see the man who said the words?"

"I can't remember seeing him. He must have been just a bit farther back—yes, there. I could only see his paws."

"*Paws.*" Giles frowned.

"They *were* paws. Grey paws—not human."

"But look here, Gwenda. This isn't a kind of Murder in the Rue Morgue. A man doesn't have paws."

"Well, *he* had paws."

Giles looked doubtfully at her.

"You must have imagined that bit afterwards."

Gwenda said slowly:

"Don't you think I may have imagined the whole thing? You know, Giles, I've been thinking. It seems to me far more probable that the whole thing was a *dream*. It might have been. It was the sort of dream a child might have, and be terribly frightened, and go on remembering about. Don't you think really that's the proper explanation? Because nobody in Dillmouth seems to have the faintest idea that there was ever a murder, or a sudden death, or a disappearance or *anything* odd about this house."

Giles looked like a different kind of little boy—a little boy who has had his nice new toy taken away from him.

"I suppose it might have been a nightmare," he admitted grudgingly. Then his face cleared suddenly.

"No," he said. "I don't believe it. You could have dreamt about monkeys' paws and someone dead—but I'm damned if you could have dreamt that quotation from *The Duchess of Malfi*."

"I could have heard someone say it and then dreamt about it afterwards."

"I don't think any child could do that. Not unless you heard it in conditions of great stress—and if that was the case we're back again where we were—hold on, I've got it. It was the *paws* you dreamt. You saw the body and heard the words and you were scared stiff and then you had a nightmare about it, and there were waving monkeys' paws too—probably you were frightened of monkeys."

Gwenda looked slightly dubious—she said slowly:

"I suppose that *might* be it. . . ."

"I wish you could remember a bit more. . . . Come down here in the hall. Shut your eyes. Think . . . Doesn't anything more come back to you?"

"No, it doesn't, Giles. . . . The more I think, the further it all goes away. . . . I mean I'm beginning to doubt now if I ever really saw anything at all. Perhaps the other night I just had a brainstorm in the theatre."

"No. There *was* something. Miss Marple thinks so, too. What about 'Helen'? Surely you must remember something about Helen?"

"I don't remember anything at all. It's just a name."

"It mightn't even be the right name."

"Yes, it was. It *was* Helen."

Gwenda looked obstinate and convinced.

"Then if you're so sure it was Helen, you must know something about her," said Giles reasonably. "Did you know her well? Was she living here? Or just staying here?"

"I tell you I don't *know*." Gwenda was beginning to look strained and nervy.

Giles tried another tack.

"Who else can you remember? Your father?"

"No. I mean, I can't tell. There was always his photograph, you see. Aunt Alison used to say: 'That's your Daddy.' I don't remember him *here*, in this house. . . ."

"And no servants—nurses—anything like that?"

"No—no. The more I try and remember, the more it's all a blank. The things I know are all underneath—like walking to that door automatically. I didn't *remember* a door there. Perhaps if you wouldn't worry me so much, Giles, things would come back more. Anyway, trying to find out about it all is hopeless. It's so long ago."

"Of course it's not hopeless—even old Miss Marple admitted that."

"She didn't help us with any ideas of how to set about it," said Gwenda. "And yet I feel, from the glint in her eye, that she had a few. I wonder how *she* would have gone about it."

"I don't suppose she would be likely to think of ways that we wouldn't," said Giles positively. "We must stop speculating, Gwenda, and set about things in a systematic way. We've made a beginning—I've looked through the parish registers of deaths. There's no 'Helen' of the right age among them. In fact there doesn't seem to be a Helen at all in the period I covered. Ellen Pugg, ninety-four, was the nearest. Now we must think of the next profitable approach. If your father, and presumably your stepmother, lived in this house, they must either have bought it or rented it."

"According to Foster, the gardener, some people called Elworthy had it before the Hengraves and before them Mrs. Findeyson. Nobody else."

"Your father might have bought it and lived in it for a very short time—and then sold it again. But I think that it's much more likely that he rented it—probably rented it furnished. If so, our best bet is to go round the house agents."

Going round the house agents was not a prolonged labour. There were only two house agents in Dillmouth. Messrs. Wilkinson were a comparatively new arrival. They had only opened their premises eleven years ago. They dealt mostly with the small bungalows and new houses at the far end of the town. The other agents, Messrs. Galbraith and Penderley, were the ones from whom Gwenda had bought the house. Calling upon them, Giles plunged into his story. He and his wife were delighted with Hillside and with Dillmouth generally. Mrs. Reed had only just discovered that she had actually lived in Dillmouth as a small child. She had some very faint memories of the place, and had an idea that Hillside was actually the house in which she had lived but could not be quite certain about it. Had they any record of the house being let to a Major Halliday? It would be about eighteen or nineteen years ago. . . .

Mr. Penderley stretched out apologetic hands.

"I'm afraid it's not possible to tell you, Mr. Reed. Our records do not go back that far—not, that is, of furnished or short-period lets. Very sorry I can't help you, Mr. Reed. As a matter of fact, if our old head clerk, Mr. Narracott, had still been alive—he died last winter—he might have been able to assist you. A most remarkable memory, really quite remarkable. He had been with the firm for nearly thirty years."

"There's no one else who would possibly remember?"

"Our staff is all on the comparatively young side. Of course there is old Mr. Galbraith himself. He retired some years ago."

"Perhaps I could ask him?" said Gwenda.

"Well, I hardly know about that. . . ." Mr. Penderley was dubious. "He had a stroke last year. His faculties are sadly impaired. He's over eighty, you know."

"Does he live in Dillmouth?"

"Oh yes. At Calcutta Lodge. A very nice little property on the Scaton road. But I really don't think—"

II

"It's rather a forlorn hope," said Giles to Gwenda. "But you never know. I don't think we'll write. We'll go there together and exert our personality."

Calcutta Lodge was surrounded by a neat trim garden, and the sitting room into which they were shown was also neat if slightly overcrowded. It smelt of beeswax and Ronuk. Its brasses shone. Its windows were heavily festooned.

A thin middle-aged woman with suspicious eyes came into the room.

Giles explained himself quickly, and the expression of one who expects to have a vacuum cleaner pushed at her left Miss Galbraith's face.

"I'm sorry, but I really don't think I can help you," she said. "It's so long ago, isn't it?"

"One does sometimes remember things," said Gwenda.

"Of course I shouldn't know anything myself. I never had any connection with the business. A Major Halliday, you said? No, I never remember coming across anyone in Dillmouth of that name."

"Your father might remember, perhaps," said Gwenda.

"Father?" Miss Galbraith shook her head. "He doesn't take much notice nowadays, and his memory's very shaky."

Gwenda's eyes were resting thoughtfully on a Benares brass table and they shifted to a procession of ebony elephants marching along the mantelpiece.

"I thought he might remember, perhaps," she said, "because my father had just come from India. Your house is called Calcutta Lodge?"

She paused interrogatively.

"Yes," said Miss Galbraith. "Father was out in Calcutta for a time. In business there. Then the war came and in nineteen twenty he came into the firm here, but would have liked to go back, he always says. But my mother didn't fancy foreign parts—and of course you can't say the climate's really healthy. Well, I don't know—perhaps you'd like to see my father. I don't know that it's one of his good days—"

She led them into a small back study. Here, propped up in a big shabby leather chair, sat an old gentleman with a white walrus moustache. His face was pulled slightly sideways. He eyed Gwenda with distinct approval as his daughter made the introductions.

"Memory's not what it used to be," he said in a rather indistinct voice. "Halliday, you say? No, I don't remember the name. Knew a boy at school in Yorkshire—but that's seventy-odd years ago."

"He rented Hillside, we think," said Giles.

"Hillside? Was it called Hillside then?" Mr. Galbraith's one movable eyelid snapped shut and open. "Findeyson lived there. Fine woman."

"My father might have rented it furnished. . . . He'd just come from India."

"India? India, d'you say? Remember a fellow—Army man. Knew that old rascal Mohammed Hassan who cheated me over some carpets. Had a young wife—and a baby—little girl."

"That was me," said Gwenda firmly.

"In-deed—you don't say so! Well, well, time flies. Now what *was* his name? Wanted a place furnished—yes— Mrs. Findeyson had been ordered to Egypt or some such place for the winter—all tomfoolery. Now what was his name?"

"Halliday," said Gwenda.

"That's right, my dear—Halliday. Major Halliday. Nice fellow. Very pretty wife—quite young—fair-haired, wanted to be near her people or something like that. Yes, very pretty."

"Who were her people?"

"No idea at all. No idea. You don't look like her."

Gwenda nearly said: "She was only my stepmother," but refrained from complicating the issue. She said: "What did she look like?"

Unexpectedly Mr. Galbraith replied:

"Looked worried. That's what she looked—worried. Yes, very nice fellow, that Major chap. Interested to hear I'd been out in Calcutta. Not like these chaps that have never been out of England. Narrow—that's what they are. Now *I've* seen the world. What was his name, that Army chap—wanted a furnished house?"

He was like a very old gramophone, repeating a worn record.

"St. Catherine's. That's it. Took St. Catherine's—six guineas a week—while Mrs. Findeyson was in Egypt. Died there, poor soul. House was put up for auction—who bought it now? Elworthys—that's it—pack of women—sisters. Changed the name—said St. Catherine's was popish. Very down on anything popish. Used to send out tracts. Plain women, all of 'em— Took an interest in the natives—Sent 'em out trousers and Bibles. Very strong on converting the heathen."

He sighed suddenly and leant back.

"Long time ago," he said fretfully. "Can't remember names. Chap from India—nice chap. . . . I'm tired, Gladys. I'd like my tea."

Giles and Gwenda thanked him, thanked his daughter, and came away.

"So that's proved," said Gwenda. "My father and I were at Hillside. What do we do next?"

"I've been an idiot," said Giles. "Somerset House."

"What's Somerset House?" asked Gwenda.

"It's a record office where you can look up marriages. I'm going there to look up your father's marriage. According to your aunt, your father was married to his second wife immediately on arriving in England. Don't you see, Gwenda—it ought to have occurred to us before—it's perfectly possible that 'Helen' may have been a relation of your stepmother's—a young sister, perhaps. Anyway, once we know what her surname was, we may be able to get onto someone who knows about the general setup at Hillside. Remember the old boy said they wanted a house in Dillmouth to be near Mrs. Halliday's people. If her people live near here, we may get something."

"Giles," said Gwenda. "I think you're wonderful."

III

Giles did not, after all, find it necessary to go to London. Though his energetic nature always made him prone to rush hither and thither and try to do everything himself, he admitted that a purely routine inquiry could be delegated.

He put through a trunk call to his office.

"Got it," he exclaimed enthusiastically, when the expected reply arrived.

From the covering letter he extracted a certified copy of a marriage certificate.

"Here we are, Gwenda. Friday, August seventh, Kensington Registry Office. Kelvin James Halliday to Helen Spenlove Kennedy."

Gwenda cried out sharply:

"*Helen?*"

They looked at each other.

Giles said slowly:

"But—but—it can't be *her*. I mean—they separated, and she married again—and went away."

"We don't know," said Gwenda, "that she went away . . ."

She looked again at the plainly written name: *Helen Spenlove Kennedy.*

Helen . . .

7

Dr. Kennedy

A FEW DAYS later Gwenda, walking along the esplanade in a sharp wind, stopped suddenly beside one of the glass shelters which a thoughtful corporation had provided for the use of its visitors.

"Miss Marple?" she exclaimed in lively surprise.

For indeed Miss Marple it was, nicely wrapped up in a thick fleecy coat and well wound round with scarves.

"Quite a surprise to you, I'm sure, to find me here," said Miss Marple briskly. "But my doctor ordered me away to the seaside for a little change, and your description of Dillmouth sounded so attractive that I decided to come here—especially as the cook and butler of a friend of mine take in boarders."

"But why didn't you come and see us?" demanded Gwenda.

"Old people can be rather a nuisance, my dear. Newly married young couples should be left to themselves." She smiled at Gwenda's protest. "I'm sure you'd have made me very welcome. And how are you both? And are you progressing with your mystery?"

"We're hot on the trail," Gwenda said, sitting beside her.

She detailed their various investigations up to date.

"And now," she ended, "we've put an advertisement in lots of papers—local ones and the *Times* and the other big dailies. We've just said will anyone with any knowledge of Helen Spenlove Halliday, née Kennedy, communicate, et cetera. I should think, don't you, that we're bound to get *some* answers?"

"I should think so, my dear—yes, I should think so."

Miss Marple's tone was placid as ever, but her eyes looked troubled. They flashed a quick appraising glance at the girl sitting beside her. That tone of determined heartiness did not ring quite true. Gwenda, Miss Marple thought, looked worried. What Dr. Haydock had called "the implications" were, perhaps, beginning to occur to her. Yes, but now it was too late to go back. . . .

Miss Marple said gently and apologetically:

"I have really become most interested in all this. My life, you know, has so *few* excitements. I hope you won't think me *very* inquisitive if I ask you to let me know how you progress?"

"Of course we'll let you know," said Gwenda warmly. "You shall be in on everything. Why, but for you, I should be urging doctors to shut me up in a loony bin. Tell me your address here, and then you must come and have a drink—I mean, have tea with us, and see the house. You've got to see the scene of the crime, haven't you?"

She laughed, but there was a slightly nervy edge to her laugh.

When she had gone on her way, Miss Marple shook her head very gently and frowned.

II

Giles and Gwenda scanned the mail eagerly every day, but at first their hopes were disappointed. All they got was two letters from private inquiry agents who pronounced themselves willing and skilled to undertake investigations on their behalf.

"Time enough for them later," said Giles. "And if we do have to employ some agency, it will be a thoroughly first-class firm, not one that touts through the mail. But I don't really see what they could do that we aren't doing."

His optimism (or self-esteem) was justified a few days later. A letter arrived, written in one of those clear and yet somewhat illegible handwritings that stamp the professional man.

Galls Hill
Woodleigh Bolton.
Dear Sir,

In answer to your advertisement in the *Times*, Helen Spenlove Kennedy is my sister. I have lost touch with her for many years and should be glad to have news of her.

Yours faithfully,
James Kennedy, M.D.

"Woodleigh Bolton," said Giles. "That's not too far away. Woodleigh Camp is where they go for picnics. Up on the moorland. About thirty miles from here. We'll write and ask Dr. Kennedy if we may come and see him, or if he would prefer to come to us."

A reply was received that Dr. Kennedy would be prepared to receive them on the following Wednesday; and on that day they set off.

Woodleigh Bolton was a straggling village set along the side of a hill. Galls Hill was the highest house just at the top of the rise, with a view over Woodleigh Camp and the moors towards the sea.

"Rather a bleak spot," said Gwenda, shivering.

The house itself was bleak and obviously Dr. Kennedy scorned such modern innovations as central heating. The woman who opened the door was dark and rather forbidding. She led them across the rather bare hall and into a study where Dr. Kennedy rose to receive them. It was a long, rather high room, lined with well-filled bookshelves.

Dr. Kennedy was a grey-haired elderly man with shrewd eyes under tufted brows. His gaze went sharply from one to the other of them.

"Mr. and Mrs. Reed? Sit here, Mrs. Reed. It's probably the most comfortable chair. Now, what's all this about?"

Giles went fluently into their prearranged story.

He and his wife had been recently married in New Zealand. They had come to England, where his wife had lived for a short time as a child, and she was trying to trace old family friends and connections.

Dr. Kennedy remained stiff and unbending. He was polite but obviously irritated by colonial insistence on sentimental family ties.

"And you think my sister—my half-sister—and possibly myself—are connections of yours?" he asked Gwenda civilly, but with slight hostility.

"She was my stepmother," said Gwenda. "My father's second wife. I can't really remember her properly, of course. I was so small. My maiden name was Halliday."

He stared at her—and then suddenly a smile illuminated his face. He became a different person, no longer aloof.

"Good Lord," he said. "Don't tell me that you're Gwennie!"

Gwenda nodded eagerly. The pet name, long forgotten, sounded in her ears with reassuring familiarity.

"Yes," she said. "I'm Gwennie."

"God bless my soul. Grown-up and married. How time flies! It must be—what—fifteen years—no, of course, much longer than that. You don't remember me, I suppose?"

Gwenda shook her head.

"I don't even remember my father. I mean it's all a vague kind of blur."

"Of course—Halliday's first wife came from New Zealand—I remember his telling me so. A fine country, I should think."

"It's the loveliest country in the world—but I'm quite fond of England, too."

"On a visit—or settling down here?" He rang the bell. "We must have tea."

When the tall woman came, he said, "Tea, please—and—er—hot buttered toast, or—or cake, or something."

The respectable housekeeper looked venomous, but said "Yes, sir," and went out.

"I don't usually go in for tea," said Dr. Kennedy vaguely. "But we must celebrate."

"It's very nice of you," said Gwenda. "No, we're not on a visit. We've bought a house." She paused and added, "Hillside."

Dr. Kennedy said vaguely:

"Oh yes. In Dillmouth. You wrote from there."

"It's the most extraordinary coincidence," said Gwenda. "Isn't it, Giles?"

"I should say so," said Giles. "Really quite staggering."

"It was for sale, you see," said Gwenda, and added in face of Dr. Kennedy's apparent noncomprehension, "It's the same house where we used to live long ago."

Dr. Kennedy frowned. "Hillside? But surely— Oh yes, I did hear they'd changed the name. Used to be St. something or other —if I'm thinking of the right house—on the Leahampton road, coming down into the town, on the right-hand side?"

"Yes."

"That's the one. Funny how names go out of your head. Wait a minute. St. Catherine's—that's what it used to be called."

"And I did live there, didn't I?" Gwenda said.

"Yes, of course you did." He stared at her, amused. "Why did you want to come back there? You can't remember much about it, surely?"

"No. But somehow—it felt like home."

"It felt like home," the doctor repeated. There was no expression in the words, but Giles wondered suddenly what he was thinking about.

"So you see," said Gwenda, "I hoped you'd tell me about it all —about my father and Helen and—" she ended lamely—"and everything. . . ."

He looked at her reflectively.

"I suppose they didn't know very much—out in New Zealand. Why should they? Well, there isn't much to tell. Helen—my sister—was coming back from India on the same boat with your father. He was a widower with a small daughter. Helen was sorry for him or fell in love with him. He was lonely, or fell in love with her. Difficult to know just the way things happen. They were married in London on arrival, and came down to Dillmouth to me. I was in practice there then. Kelvin Halliday seemed a nice chap, rather nervy and run-down—but they seemed happy enough together—then."

He was silent for a moment before he said:

"However, in less than a year, she ran away with someone else. You probably know that?"

"Who did she run away with?" asked Gwenda.

He bent his shrewd eyes upon her.

"She didn't tell me," he said, "I wasn't in her confidence. I'd seen—couldn't help seeing—that there was friction between her and Kelvin. I didn't know why. I was always a strait-laced sort of fellow—a believer in marital fidelity. Helen wouldn't have wanted me to know what was going on. I'd heard rumours—one does—but there was no mention of any particular name. They often had guests staying with them who came from London or from other parts of England. I imagined it was one of them."

"There wasn't a divorce, then?"

"Helen didn't want a divorce. Kelvin told me that. That's why I imagined, perhaps wrongly, that it was a case of some married man. Someone whose wife was an R.C. perhaps."

"And my father?"

"He didn't want a divorce either."

Dr. Kennedy spoke rather shortly.

"Tell me about my father," said Gwenda. "Why did he decide suddenly to send me out to New Zealand?"

Kennedy paused a moment before saying:

"I gather your people out there had been pressing him. After the breakup of his second marriage, he probably thought it was the best thing."

"Why didn't he take me out there himself?"

Dr. Kennedy looked along the mantelpiece, searching vaguely for a pipe cleaner.

"Oh, I don't know. . . . He was in rather poor health."

"What was the matter with him? What did he die of?"

The door opened and the scornful housekeeper appeared with a laden tray.

There was buttered toast and some jam, but no cake. With a vague gesture Dr. Kennedy motioned Gwenda to pour out. She did so. When the cups were filled and handed round and Gwenda had taken a piece of toast, Dr. Kennedy said with rather forced cheerfulness:

"Tell me what you've done to the house? Made a lot of changes and improvements? I don't suppose I'd recognize it now—after you two have finished with it."

"We're having a little fun with bathrooms," admitted Giles.

Gwenda, her eyes on the doctor, said:

"What did my father die of?"

"I couldn't really tell you, my dear. As I say, he was in rather poor health for a while, and he finally went into a sanatorium—somewhere on the East coast. He died about two years later."

"Where was this sanatorium exactly?"

"I'm sorry. I can't remember now. As I say, I have an impression it was on the East coast."

There was definite evasion now in his manner. Giles and Gwenda looked at each other for a brief second.

Giles said:

"At least, sir, you can tell us where he's buried? Gwenda is—naturally—very anxious to visit his grave."

Dr. Kennedy bent over the fireplace, scraping in the bowl of his pipe with a penknife.

"Do you know," he said rather indistinctly, "I don't really think I should dwell too much on the past. All this ancestor worship—it's a mistake. The future is what matters. Here you are, you two, young and healthy, with the world in front of you. Think forward. No use going about putting flowers on the grave of someone whom, for all practical purposes, you hardly knew."

Gwenda said mutinously:

"I should like to see my father's grave."

"I'm afraid I can't help you." Dr. Kennedy's tones were pleasant but cold. "It's a long time ago, and my memory isn't what it was. I lost touch with your father after he left Dillmouth. I think he wrote to me once from the sanatorium and, as I say, I have an impression it was on the East coast—but I couldn't really be sure even of that. And I've no idea at all of where he is buried."

"How very odd," said Giles.

"Not really. The link between us, you see, was Helen. I was always very fond of Helen. She's my half-sister and very many years younger than I am, but I tried to bring her up as well as I could.

The right schools and all that. But there's no gainsaying that Helen—well, that she never had a stable character. There was trouble when she was quite young with a very undesirable young man. I got her out of that safely. Then she elected to go out to India and marry Walter Fane. Well, that was all right, nice lad, son of Dillmouth's leading solicitor, but frankly, dull as ditch-water. He'd always adored her, but she never looked at him. Still, she changed her mind and went out to India to marry him. When she saw him again, it was all off. She wired to me for money for her passage home. I sent it. On the way back, she met Kelvin. They were married before I knew about it. I've felt, shall we say, apologetic for that sister of mine. It explains why Kelvin and I didn't keep up the relationship after she went away." He added suddenly: "Where's Helen now? Can you tell me? I'd like to get in touch with her."

"But we don't know," said Gwenda. "We don't know at all."

"Oh! I thought from your advertisement—" He looked at them with sudden curiosity. "Tell me, why did you advertise?"

Gwenda said:

"We wanted to get in touch—" and stopped.

"With someone you can hardly remember?" Dr. Kennedy looked puzzled.

Gwenda said quickly:

"I thought—if I could get in touch with her—she'd tell me—about my father."

"Yes—yes—I see. Sorry I can't be of much use. Memory not what it was. And it's a long time ago."

"At least," said Giles, "you know what kind of a sanatorium it was? Tubercular?"

Dr. Kennedy's face again looked suddenly wooden.

"Yes—yes, I rather believe it was."

"Then we ought to be able to trace that quite easily," said Giles. "Thank you very much, sir, for all you've told us."

He got up and Gwenda followed suit.

"Thank you very much," she said. "And do come and see us at Hillside."

They went out of the room and Gwenda, glancing back over her shoulder, had a final view of Dr. Kennedy standing by the mantelpiece, pulling his grizzled moustache and looking troubled.

"He knows something he won't tell us," said Gwenda, as they got into the car. "There's *something*—oh, Giles! I wish—I wish now that we'd never started. . . ."

They looked at each other, and in each mind, unacknowledged to the other, the same fear sprang.

"Miss Marple was right," said Gwenda. "We should have left the past alone."

"We needn't go any further," said Giles uncertainly. "I think perhaps, Gwenda darling, we'd better not."

Gwenda shook her head.

"No, Giles, we can't stop now. We should always be wondering and imagining. No, we've got to go on. . . . Dr. Kennedy wouldn't tell us because he wanted to be kind—but that sort of kindness is no good. We'll have to go on and find out what really happened. Even if—even if—it was my father who . . ." But she couldn't go on.

8

Kelvin Halliday's Delusion

THEY WERE in the garden on the following morning when Mrs. Cocker came out and said:

"Excuse me, sir. There's a Dr. Kennedy on the telephone."

Leaving Gwenda in consultation with old Foster, Giles went into the house and picked up the telephone receiver.

"Giles Reed here."

"This is Dr. Kennedy. I've been thinking over our conversation yesterday, Mr. Reed. There are certain facts which I think perhaps you and your wife ought to know. Will you be at home if I come over this afternoon?"

"Certainly we shall. What time?"

"Three o'clock?"

"Suits us."

In the garden old Foster said to Gwenda:

"Is that Dr. Kennedy as used to live over at West Cliff?"

"I expect so. Did you know him?"

"'E was allus reckoned to be the best doctor here—not but what Dr. Lazenby wasn't more popular. Always had a word and a laugh to jolly you along, Dr. Lazenby did. Dr. Kennedy was always short and a bit dry-like—but he knew his job."

"When did he give up his practice?"

"Long time ago now. Must be fifteen years or so. His health broke down, so they say."

Giles came out of the window and answered Gwenda's unspoken question.

"He's coming over this afternoon."

"Oh." She turned once more to Foster. "Did you know Dr. Kennedy's sister at all?"

"Sister? Not as I remember. She was only a bit of a lass. Went away to school, and then abroad, though I heard she come back here for a bit after she married. But I believe she run off with some chap—always wild she was, they said. Don't know as I ever laid eyes on her myself. I was in a job over to Plymouth for a while, you know."

Gwenda said to Giles as they walked to the end of the terrace:

"Why is he coming?"

"We'll know at three o'clock."

Dr. Kennedy arrived punctually. Looking round the drawing room, he said: "Seems odd to be here again."

Then he came to the point without preamble.

"I take it that you two are quite determined to track down the sanatorium where Kelvin Halliday died and learn all the details you can about his illness and death?"

"Definitely," said Gwenda.

"Well, you can manage that quite easily, of course. So I've come to the conclusion that it will be less shock to you to hear the facts from me. I'm sorry to have to tell you for it won't do you or anybody else a bit of good, and it will probably cause *you*, Gwennie, a good deal of pain. But there it is. Your father wasn't suffering from tuberculosis and the sanatorium in question was a mental home."

"A mental home? Was he out of his mind, then?"

Gwenda's face had gone very white.

"He was never certified. And in my opinion he was not insane in the general meaning of the term. He had had a very severe nervous breakdown and suffered from certain delusional obsessions. He went into the nursing home of his own will and volition and could, of course, have left it at any time he wanted to. His condition did not improve, however, and he died there."

"Delusional obsessions?" Giles repeated the words questioningly. "What kind of delusions?"

Dr. Kennedy said drily:

"He was under the impression that he had strangled his wife."

Gwenda gave a stifled cry. Giles stretched out a hand quickly and took her cold hand in his.

Giles said:

"And—and had he?"

"Eh?" Dr. Kennedy stared at him. "No, of course he hadn't. No question of such a thing."

"But—but how do you know?" Gwenda's voice came uncertainly.

"My dear child! There was never any question of such a thing. Helen left him for another man. He'd been in a very unbalanced condition for some time; nervous dreams, sick fancies. The final shock sent him over the edge. I'm not a psychologist myself. They have their explanations for such matters. If a man would rather his wife was dead than unfaithful, he can manage to make himself believe that she is dead—even that he has killed her."

Warily, Giles and Gwenda exchanged a warning glance.

Giles said quietly:

"So you are quite sure that there was no question of his having actually done what he said he had done?"

"Oh, quite sure. I had two letters from Helen. The first one from France about a week after she went away and one about six months later. Oh no, the whole thing was a delusion pure and simple."

Gwenda drew a deep breath.

"Please," she said. "Will you tell me all about it?"

"I'll tell you everything I can, my dear. To begin with, Kelvin had been in a rather peculiar neurotic state for some time. He came to me about it. Said he had had various disquieting dreams.

These dreams, he said, were always the same, and they ended in the same way—with his throttling Helen. I tried to get at the root of the trouble—there must, I think, have been some conflict in early childhood. His father and mother apparently were not a happy couple. . . . Well, I won't go into all that. That's only interesting to a medical man. I actually suggested that Kelvin should consult a psychologist, there are several first-class chaps—but he wouldn't hear of it—thought that kind of thing was all nonsense.

"I had an idea that he and Helen weren't getting along too well, but he never spoke about that, and I didn't like to ask questions. The whole thing came to a head when he walked into my house one evening—it was a Friday, I remember, I'd just come back from the hospital and found him waiting for me in the consulting room; he'd been there about a quarter of an hour. As soon as I came in, he looked up and said:

"*'I've killed Helen.'*

"For a moment I didn't know what to think. He was so cool and matter-of-fact. I said: 'You mean—you've had another dream?' He said: 'It isn't a dream this time. It's true. She's lying there strangled. I strangled her.'

"Then he said—quite coolly and reasonably: 'You'd better come back with me to the house. Then you can ring up the police from there.' I didn't know what to think. I got out the car again, and we drove along here. The house was quiet and dark. We went up to the bedroom—"

Gwenda broke in: "*The bedroom?*" Her voice held pure astonishment.

Dr. Kennedy looked faintly surprised.

"Yes, yes, that's where it all happened. Well, of course when we got up there—there was nothing at all! No dead woman lying across the bed. Nothing disturbed—the coverlets not even rumpled. The whole thing had been pure hallucination."

"But what did my father say?"

"Oh, he persisted in his story, of course. He really believed it, you see. I persuaded him to let me give him a sedative and I put him to bed in the dressing room. Then I had a good look round. I found a note that Helen had left crumpled up in the waste-paper basket in the drawing room. It was quite clear. She had written something like this: 'This is good-bye. I'm sorry—but our marriage has been a mistake from the beginning. I'm going away with the only man I've ever loved. Forgive me if you can. Helen.'

"Evidently Kelvin had come in, read her note, gone upstairs, had a kind of emotional brainstorm and had then come over to me persuaded that he had killed Helen.

"Then I questioned the housemaid. It was her evening out and she had come in late. I took her into Helen's room and she went through Helen's clothes. It was all quite clear. Helen had packed a suitcase and a bag and had taken them away with her. I searched the house, but there was no trace of anything unusual—certainly no sign of a strangled woman.

"I had a very difficult time with Kelvin in the morning, but he realized at last that it was a delusion—or at least he said he did, and he consented to go into a nursing home for treatment.

"A week later I got, as I say, a letter from Helen. It was posted from Biarritz, but she said she was going on to Spain. I was to tell Kelvin that she did not want a divorce. He had better forget her as soon as possible.

"I showed the letter to Kelvin. He said very little. He was going ahead with his plans. He wired out to his first wife's people in New Zealand, asking them to take the child. He settled up his affairs and he then entered a very good private mental home and consented to have appropriate treatment. That treatment, however, did nothing to help him. He died there two years later. I can give you the address of the place. It's in Norfolk. The present superintendent was a young doctor there at the time, and will probably be able to give you full details of your father's case."

Gwenda said:

"And you got another letter from your sister—after that again?"

"Oh yes. About six months later. She wrote from Florence—gave an address poste restante as 'Miss Kennedy.' She said she realized that perhaps it was unfair to Kelvin not to have a divorce—though she herself did not want one. If he wanted a divorce and I would let her know, she would see that he had the necessary evidence. I took the letter to Kelvin. He said at once that he did not want a divorce. I wrote to her and told her so. Since then I have never heard any more. I don't know where she is living, or indeed if she is alive or dead. That is why I was attracted by your advertisement and hoped that I should get news of her."

He added gently:

"I'm very sorry about this, Gwennie. But you had to know. I only wish you could have left well alone. . . ."

9

Unknown Factor?

When Giles came back from seeing Dr. Kennedy off, he found Gwenda sitting where he had left her. There was a bright red patch on each of her cheeks, and her eyes looked feverish. When she spoke, her voice was harsh and brittle.

"What's the old catch phrase? Death or madness either way? That's what this is—death or madness."

"Gwenda—darling." Giles went to her—put his arm round her. Her body felt hard and stiff.

"Why didn't we leave it all alone? Why didn't we? It was my own father who strangled her. And it was my own father's voice I heard saying those words. No wonder it all came back—no wonder I was so frightened. My own father."

"Wait, Gwenda—wait. We don't really know—"

"Of course we know! He told Dr. Kennedy he had strangled his wife, didn't he?"

"But Kennedy is quite positive he didn't—"

"Because he didn't find a body. But there *was* a body—and I *saw* it."

"You saw it in the hall—not the bedroom."

"What difference does that make?"

"Well, it's queer, isn't it? Why should Halliday say he strangled his wife in the bedroom if he actually strangled her in the hall?"

"Oh, I don't know. That's just a minor detail."

"I'm not so sure. Pull your socks up, darling. There are some very funny points about the whole setup. We'll take it, if you like, that your father *did* strangle Helen. In the hall. What happened next?"

"He went off to Dr. Kennedy."

"And told him he had strangled his wife in the bedroom, brought him back with him and there was no body in the hall—*or* in the bedroom. Dash it all, there can't be a murder without a body. What had he done with the body?"

"Perhaps there was one and Dr. Kennedy helped him and hushed it all up—only of course he couldn't tell *us* that."

Giles shook his head.

"No, Gwenda—I don't see Kennedy acting that way. He's a hardheaded, shrewd unemotional Scotsman. You're suggesting that he'd be willing to put himself in jeopardy as an accessory after the fact. I don't believe he would. He'd do his best for Halliday by giving evidence as to his mental state—that, yes. But why should he stick his neck out to hush the whole thing up? Kelvin Halliday wasn't any relation to him, nor a close friend. It was his own sister who had been killed and he was clearly fond of her —even if he did show slight Victorian disapproval of her gay ways. It's not, even, as though *you* were his sister's child. No, Kennedy wouldn't connive at concealing murder. If he did, there's only one possible way he could have set about it, and that would be deliberately to give a death certificate that she had died of heart failure or something. I suppose he *might* have got away with that—but we know definitely that he didn't do that. Because there's no record of her death in the parish registers, and if he had done it, he would have told us that his sister had died. So go on from there and explain, if you can, what happened to the body."

"Perhaps my father buried it somewhere—in the garden?"

"And *then* went to Kennedy and told him he'd murdered his wife? Why? Why not rely on the story that she'd 'left him?' "

Gwenda pushed back her hair from her forehead. She was less stiff and rigid now, and the patches of sharp colour were fading.

"I don't know," she admitted. "It does seem a bit screwy now you've put it that way. Do you think Dr. Kennedy was telling us the truth?"

"Oh yes—I'm pretty sure of it. From his point of view it's a perfectly reasonable story. Dreams, hallucinations—finally a major hallucination. He's got no doubt that it was a hallucination because, as we've just said, you can't have a murder without a body. That's where we're in a different position from him. We know that there was a body."

He paused and went on.

"From his point of view, everything fits in. Missing clothes and suitcase, the farewell note. And later, two letters from his sister."

Gwenda stirred.

"Those letters. How do we explain those?"

"We don't—but we've got to. If we assume that Kennedy was telling us the truth (and as I say, I'm pretty sure that he was), we've got to explain those letters."

"I suppose they really were in his sister's handwriting? He recognized it?"

"You know, Gwenda, I don't believe that point would arise. It's not like a signature on a doubtful check. If those letters were written in a reasonably close imitation of his sister's writing, it wouldn't occur to him to doubt them. He's already got the preconceived idea that she's gone away with someone. The letters just confirmed that belief. If he had never heard from her at all—why, then he *might* have got suspicious. All the same, there are certain curious points about those letters that wouldn't strike him, perhaps, but do strike me. They're strangely anonymous. No address except a poste restante. No indication of who the man in the case was. A clearly stated determination to make a clean break with all old ties. What I mean is, they're exactly the kind of letters a *murderer* would devise if he wanted to allay any suspicions on the part of his victim's family. It's the old Crippen touch again. To get the letters posted from abroad would be easy."

"You think my father—"

"*No*—that's just it—I *don't*. Take a man who's deliberately decided to get rid of his wife. He spreads rumours about her possible unfaithfulness. He stages the departure—note left behind, clothes packed and taken. Letters will be received from her at carefully spaced intervals from somewhere abroad. Actually he has murdered her quietly and put her, say, under the cellar floor. That's one pattern of murder—and it's often been done. But what that type of murderer *doesn't* do is to rush to his brother-in-law and say he's murdered his wife and hadn't they better go to the police? On the other hand, if your father was the emotional type of killer, and was terribly in love with his wife and strangled her in a fit of frenzied jealousy—Othello fashion (and that fits in with the words you heard)—he certainly doesn't pack clothes and arrange for letters to come, before he rushes off to broadcast his crime to a man who isn't the type likely to hush it up. It's all wrong, Gwenda. The whole pattern is wrong."

"Then what are you trying to get at, Giles?"

"I don't know. . . . It's just that throughout it all, there seems to be an unknown factor—call him X. Someone who hasn't appeared as yet. But one gets glimpses of his technique."

"X?" said Gwenda wonderingly. Then her eyes darkened. "You're making that up, Giles. To comfort me."

"I swear I'm not. Don't you see yourself that you can't make a satisfactory outline to fit all the facts. We know that Helen Halliday was strangled because you saw—"

He stopped.

"Good Lord. I've been a fool. I see it now. It covers everything. You're right. And Kennedy's right, too. Listen, Gwenda. Helen's preparing to go away with a lover—who that is, we don't know."

"X?"

Giles brushed her interpolation aside impatiently.

"She's written her note to her husband—but at that moment he comes in, reads what she's writing and goes haywire. He crumples up the note, slings it into the wastebasket, and goes for her. She's terrified, rushes out into the hall—he catches up with her, throttles her—she goes limp and he drops her. And then, standing a little way from her, he quotes those words from *The Duchess of Malfi* just as the child upstairs has reached the banisters and is peering down."

"And after that?"

"The point is, *that she isn't dead.* He may have thought she was dead—but she's merely semi-suffocated. Perhaps her lover comes round—after the frantic husband has started for the doctor's house on the other side of the town, or perhaps she regains consciousness by herself. Anyway, as soon as she has come to, she beats it. Beats it quickly. And that explains everything. Kelvin's belief that he has killed her. The disappearance of the clothes; packed and taken away earlier in the day. And the subsequent letters *which are perfectly genuine*. There you are—that explains everything."

Gwenda said slowly:

"It doesn't explain why Kelvin said he had strangled her in the bedroom."

"He was so het-up he couldn't quite remember where it had all happened."

Gwenda said:

"I'd like to believe you. I want to believe. . . . But I go on feeling sure—quite sure—that when I looked down, she was dead—quite dead."

"But how could you possibly tell? A child of barely three."

She looked at him queerly.

"I think one can tell—better then than if one was older. It's like dogs—they know death and throw back their heads and howl. I think children—know death. . . ."

"That's nonsense—that's fantastic."

The ring of the front doorbell interrupted him. He said:

"Who's that, I wonder?"

Gwenda looked dismayed.

"I quite forgot. It's Miss Marple. I asked her to tea today. Don't let's say anything about all this to her."

II

Gwenda was afraid that tea might prove a difficult meal—but Miss Marple fortunately seemed not to notice that her hostess talked a little too fast and too feverishly, and that her gaiety was somewhat forced. Miss Marple herself was gently garrulous—she was enjoying her stay in Dillmouth so much and—wasn't it exciting?—some friends of friends of hers had written to friends of theirs in Dillmouth, and as a result she had received some very pleasant invitations from the local residents.

"One feels so much less of an outsider, if you know what I mean, my dear, if one gets to know some of the people who have been established here for years. For instance, I am going to tea with Mrs. Fane—she is the widow of the senior partner in the best firm of solicitors here. Quite an old-fashioned family firm. Her son is carrying it on now."

The gentle gossiping voice went on. Her landlady was so kind—and made her so comfortable—"and really delicious cooking, she was for some years with my old friend Mrs. Bantry—although she does not come from this part of the world herself—her aunt lived here for many years and she and her husband used to come here for holidays—so she knows a great deal of the local gossip. Do you find your gardener satisfactory, by the way? I hear that he is considered locally as rather a *scrimshanker*—more talk than work."

"Talk and tea is his speciality," said Giles. "He has about five cups of tea a day. But he works splendidly when we are looking."

"Come out and see the garden," said Gwenda.

They showed her the house and the garden, and Miss Marple made the proper comments. If Gwenda had feared her shrewd observation of something amiss, then Gwenda was wrong. For Miss Marple showed no cognizance of anything unusual.

Yet, strangely enough, it was Gwenda who acted in an unpredictable manner. She interrupted Miss Marple in the midst of a little anecdote about a child and a seashell to say breathlessly to Giles:

"I don't care—I'm going to tell her. . . ."

Miss Marple turned her head attentively. Giles started to speak, then stopped. Finally he said: "Well, it's your funeral, Gwenda."

And so Gwenda poured it all out. Their call on Dr. Kennedy and his subsequent call on them and what he had told them.

"That was what you meant in London, wasn't it?" Gwenda asked breathlessly. "You thought, then, that—that my father might be involved?"

Miss Marple said gently:

"It occurred to me as a possibility—yes. 'Helen' might very well be a young stepmother—and in a case of—er—strangling, it is so often a husband who is involved."

Miss Marple spoke as one who observes natural phenomena without surprise or emotion.

"I do see why you urged us to leave it alone," said Gwenda. "Oh, and I wish now we had. But one can't go back."

"No," said Miss Marple, "one can't go back."

"And now you'd better listen to Giles. He's been making objections and suggestions."

"All I say is," said Giles, "that it doesn't fit."

And lucidly, clearly, he went over the points as he had previously outlined them to Gwenda.

Then he particularized his final theory.

"If you'll only convince Gwenda that that's the only way it could have been."

Miss Marple's eyes went from him to Gwenda and back again.

"It is a perfectly reasonable hypothesis," she said. "But there is always, as you yourself pointed out, Mr. Reed, the possibility of X."

"X!" said Gwenda.

"The unknown factor," said Miss Marple. "Someone, shall we say, who hasn't appeared yet—but whose presence, behind the obvious facts, can be deduced."

"We're going to the sanatorium in Norfolk where my father died," said Gwenda. "Perhaps we'll find out something there."

10

A Case History

SALTMARSH HOUSE was set pleasantly about six miles inland from the coast. It had a good train service to London from the five-mile-distant town of South Benham.

Giles and Gwenda were shown into a large airy sitting room with cretonne covers patterned with flowers. A very charming-looking old lady with white hair came into the room holding a glass of milk. She nodded to them and sat down near the fireplace. Her eyes rested thoughtfully on Gwenda and presently she leaned forward towards her and spoke in what was almost a whisper.

"Is it your poor child, my dear?"

Gwenda looked slightly taken aback. She said doubtfully:

"No—no. It isn't."

"Ah, I wondered." The old lady nodded her head and sipped her milk. Then she said conversationally:

"Half-past ten—that's the time. It's always at half-past ten. Most remarkable." She lowered her voice and leaned forward again.

"Behind the fireplace," she breathed. "But don't say *I* told you."

At this moment, a white-uniformed maid came into the room and requested Giles and Gwenda to follow her.

They were shown into Dr. Penrose's study, and Dr. Penrose rose to greet them.

Dr. Penrose, Gwenda could not help thinking, looked a little mad himself. He looked, for instance, much madder than the nice old lady in the drawing room—but perhaps psychiatrists always looked a little mad.

"I had your letter, and Dr. Kennedy's," said Dr. Penrose. "And I've been looking up your father's case history, Mrs. Reed. I remembered his case quite well, of course, but I wanted to refresh my memory so that I should be in a position to tell you everything you wanted to know. I understand that you have only recently become aware of the facts?"

Gwenda explained that she had been brought up in New Zealand by her mother's relations and that all she had known about her father was that he had died in a nursing home in England.

Dr. Penrose nodded. "Quite so. Your father's case, Mrs. Reed, presented certain rather peculiar features."

"Such as?" Giles asked.

"Well, the obsession—or delusion—was very strong. Major Halliday, though clearly in a very nervous state, was most emphatic and categorical in his assertion that he had strangled his second wife in a fit of jealous rage. A great many of the usual signs in these cases were absent, and I don't mind telling you frankly, Mrs. Reed, that had it not been for Dr. Kennedy's assurance that Mrs. Halliday was actually alive, I should have been prepared, at that time, to take your father's assertion at its face value."

"You formed the impression that he had actually killed her?" Giles asked.

"I said 'At that time.' Later, I had cause to revise my opinion, as Major Halliday's character and mental makeup became more familiar to me. Your father, Mrs. Reed, was most definitely *not* a paranoiac type. He had no delusions of persecution, no impulses of violence. He was a gentle, kindly, and well-controlled individual. He was neither what the world calls mad, nor was he dangerous to others. But he did have this obstinate fixation about Mrs. Halliday's death, and to account for its origin I am quite convinced we have to go back a long way—to some childish experience. But I admit that all methods of analysis failed to give us the right clue. Breaking down a patient's resistance to analysis is sometimes a very long business. It may take several years. In your father's case, the time was insufficient."

He paused, and then, looking up sharply, said:

"You know, I presume, that Major Halliday committed suicide."

"Oh *no!*" cried Gwenda.

"I'm sorry, Mrs. Reed. I thought you knew that. You are entitled, perhaps, to attach some blame to us on that account. I admit that proper vigilance would have prevented it. But frankly I saw no sign of Major Halliday's being a suicidal type. He showed no tendency to melancholia—no brooding or despondency. He complained of sleeplessness and my colleague allowed him a certain amount of sleeping tablets. While pretending to take them, he actually kept them until he had accumulated a sufficient amount and—"

He spread out his hands.

"Was he so dreadfully unhappy?"

"No. I do not think so. It was more, I should judge, a guilt complex, a desire for a penalty to be exacted. He had insisted at first, you know, on calling in the police, and though persuaded out of that, and assured that he had actually committed no crime at all, he obstinately refused to be wholly convinced. Yet it was proved to him over and over again, and he had to admit that he had no recollection of committing the actual act." Dr. Penrose ruffled over the papers in front of him. "His account of the evening in question never varied. He came into the house, he said, and it was dark. The servants were out. He went into the dining room, as he usually did, poured himself out a drink and drank it, then went through the connecting door into the drawing room.

After that he remembered nothing—nothing at all, until he was standing in his bedroom looking down at his wife, who was dead —strangled. He knew he had done it—"

Giles interrupted:

"Excuse me, Dr. Penrose, but *why* did he know he had done it?"

"There was no doubt in his mind. For some months past he had found himself entertaining wild and melodramatic suspicions. He told me, for instance, that he had been convinced his wife was administering drugs to him. He had, of course, lived in India, and the practice of wives driving their husbands insane by datura poisoning often comes up there in the native courts. He had suffered fairly often from hallucinations, with confusion of time and place. He denied strenuously that he suspected his wife of infidelity, but nevertheless I think that that was the motivating power. It seems that what actually occurred was that he went into the drawing room, read the note his wife left saying she was leaving him, and that his way of eluding this fact was to prefer to 'kill' her. Hence the hallucination."

"You mean he cared for her very much?" asked Gwenda.

"Obviously, Mrs. Reed."

"And he never—recognized—that it was a hallucination?"

"He had to acknowledge that it *must* be—but his inner belief remained unshaken. The obsession was too strong to yield to reason. If we could have uncovered the underlying childish fixation—"

Gwenda interrupted. She was uninterested in childish fixations.

"But *you*'re quite sure, you say, that he—that he didn't do it?"

"Oh, if that is what is worrying you, Mrs. Reed, you can put it right out of your head. Kelvin Halliday, however jealous he may have been of his wife, was emphatically not a killer."

Dr. Penrose coughed and picked up a small shabby black book.

"If you would like this, Mrs. Reed, you are the proper person to have it. It contains various jottings set down by your father during the time he was here. When we turned over his effects to his executor (actually a firm of solicitors), Dr. McGuire, who was then superintendent, retained this as part of the case history. Your father's case, you know, appears in Dr. McGuire's book—only under initials, of course. Mr. K. H. If you would like this diary—"

Gwenda stretched out her hand eagerly.

"Thank you," she said. "I should like it very much."

II

In the train on the way back to London, Gwenda took out the shabby little black book and began to read.

She opened it at random.

Kelvin Halliday had written:

I suppose these doctor wallahs know their business. . . . It all sounds such poppycock. Was I in love with my mother? Did I hate my father? I don't believe a word of it. . . . I can't help feeling this is a simple police case—criminal court—not a crazy loony bin matter. And yet—some of these people here—so natural, so reasonable—just like everyone else—except when you suddenly come across the kink. Very well, then, it seems that I, too, have a kink. . . .

I've written to James . . . urged him to communicate with Helen. . . . Let her come and see me in the flesh if she's alive. . . . He says he doesn't know where she is . . . that's because he knows that she's dead and that I killed her . . . he's a good fellow, but I'm not deceived. . . . Helen is dead. . . .

When did I begin to suspect her? A long time ago . . . Soon after we came to Dillmouth . . . Her manner changed . . . She was concealing something . . . I used to watch her . . . Yes, and *she* used to watch *me*. . . .

Did she give me drugs in my food? Those queer awful nightmares. Not ordinary dreams . . . living nightmares . . . I know it was drugs. . . . Only *she* could have done that. . . . Why? . . . There's some man . . . Some man she was afraid of. . . .

Let me be honest. I suspected, didn't I, that she had a lover? There was someone—I know there was someone—She said as much to me on the boat. . . . Someone she loved and couldn't marry. . . . It was the same for both of us . . . I couldn't forget Megan . . . How like Megan little Gwennie looks sometimes. Helen played with Gwennie so sweetly on the boat . . . Helen . . . You are so lovely, Helen. . . .

Is Helen alive? Or did I put my hands round her throat and choke the life out of her? I went through the dining-room door and I saw the note—propped up on the desk, and then—and then—all black—just blackness. But there's no doubt about it. . . . I killed her. . . . Thank God Gwennie's all right in New Zealand. They're good people. They'll love her for Megan's sake. Megan—Megan, how I wish you were here. . . .

It's the best way . . . No scandal . . . The best way for the child. I can't go on. Not year after year. I must take the short way out. Gwennie will never know anything about all this. She'll never know her father was a murderer. . . .

Tears blinded Gwenda's eyes. She looked across at Giles, sitting opposite her. But Giles's eyes were riveted on the opposite corner.

Aware of Gwenda's scrutiny, he motioned faintly with his head.

Their fellow passenger was reading an evening paper. On the outside of it, clearly presented to their view, was a melodramatic caption—

WHO WERE THE MEN IN HER LIFE?

Slowly, Gwenda nodded her head. She looked down again at the diary.

There was someone—I know there was someone—

11

The Men in Her Life

Miss Marple crossed Sea Parade and walked along Fore Street, turning up the hill by the arcade. The shops here were the old-fashioned ones. A wool and art needlework shop, a confectioner, a Victorian-looking Ladies' Outfitter and Draper and others of the same kind.

Miss Marple looked in at the window of the art needlework shop. Two young assistants were engaged with customers, but an elderly woman at the back of the shop was free.

Miss Marple pushed open the door and went in. She seated herself at the counter and the assistant, a pleasant woman with grey hair, asked, "What can I do for you, madam?"

Miss Marple wanted some pale blue wool to knit a baby's

jacket. The proceedings were leisurely and unhurried. Patterns were discussed, Miss Marple looked through various children's knitting books and in the course of it discussed her great-nephews and nieces. Neither she nor the assistant displayed impatience. The assistant had attended to customers such as Miss Marple for many years. She preferred those gentle gossipy rambling old ladies to the impatient rather impolite young mothers who didn't know what they wanted and had an eye for the cheap and showy.

"Yes," said Miss Marple. "I think that will be very nice indeed. And I always find Storkleg so reliable. It really doesn't shrink. I think I'll take an extra two ounces."

The assistant remarked that the wind was very cold today, as she wrapped up the parcel.

"Yes, indeed, I noticed it as I was coming along the front. Dillmouth has changed a good deal. I have not been here for, let me see, nearly nineteen years."

"Indeed, madam? Then you will find a lot of changes. The Superb wasn't built then, I suppose, nor the Southview Hotel?"

"Oh no, it was quite a small place. I was staying with friends. . . . A house called St. Catherine's—perhaps you know it? On the Leahampton road."

But the assistant had only been in Dillmouth a matter of ten years.

Miss Marple thanked her, took the parcel, and went into the draper's next door. Here, again, she selected an elderly assistant. The conversation ran much on the same lines, to an accompaniment of summer vests. This time, the assistant responded promptly.

"That would be Mrs. Findeyson's house."

"Yes—yes. Though the friends I knew had it furnished. A Major Halliday and his wife and a baby girl."

"Oh yes, madam. They had it for about a year, I think."

"Yes. He was home from India. They had a very good cook—she gave me a wonderful recipe for baked apple pudding—and also, I think, for gingerbread. I often wonder what became of her."

"I expect you mean Edith Pagett, madam. She's still in Dillmouth. She's in service now—at Windrush Lodge."

"Then there were some other people—the Fanes. A lawyer, I think he was!"

"Old Mr. Fane died some years ago—young Mr. Fane, Mr. Walter Fane, lives with his mother. Mr. Walter Fane never married. He's the senior partner now."

"Indeed? I had an idea Mr. Walter Fane had gone out to India —tea planting or something."

"I believe he did, madam. As a young man. But he came home and went into the firm after about a year or two. They do all the best business round here—they're very highly thought of. A very nice quiet gentleman, Mr. Walter Fane. Everybody likes him."

"Why, of course," exclaimed Miss Marple. "He was engaged to Miss Kennedy, wasn't he? And then she broke it off and married Major Halliday."

"That's right, madam. She went out to India to marry Mr. Fane, but it seems as she changed her mind and married the other gentleman instead."

A faintly disapproving note had entered the assistant's voice.

Miss Marple leaned forward and lowered her voice.

"I was always so sorry for poor Major Halliday (I knew his mother) and his little girl. I understand his second wife left him. Ran away with someone. A rather flighty type, I'm afraid."

"Regular flibbertigibbet, she was. And her brother, the doctor, such a nice man. Did my rheumatic knee a world of good."

"Whom did she run away with? I never heard."

"That I couldn't tell you, madam. Some said it was one of the summer visitors. But I know Major Halliday was quite broken up. He left the place and I believe his health gave way. Your change, madam."

Miss Marple accepted her change and her parcel.

"Thank you so much," she said. "I wonder if—Edith Pagett, did you say—still has that nice recipe for gingerbread? I lost it—or rather my careless maid lost it—and I'm so fond of good gingerbread."

"I expect so, madam. As a matter of fact her sister lives next door here, married to Mr. Mountford, the confectioner. Edith usually comes there on her days out and I'm sure Mrs. Mountford would give her a message."

"That's a very good idea. Thank you *so much* for all the trouble you've taken."

"A pleasure, madam, I assure you."

Miss Marple went out into the street.

"A nice old-fashioned firm," she said to herself. "And those vests are really very nice, so it isn't as though I had wasted any money." She glanced at the pale blue enamel watch that she wore pinned to one side of her dress. "Just five minutes to go before meeting those two young things at the Ginger Cat. I hope they didn't find things too upsetting at the sanatorium."

II

Giles and Gwenda sat together at a corner table at the Ginger Cat. The little black notebook lay on the table between them.

Miss Marple came in from the street and joined them.

"What will you have, Miss Marple? Coffee?"

"Yes, thank you—no, not cakes, just a scone and butter."

Giles gave the order, and Gwenda pushed the little black book across to Miss Marple.

"First you must read that," she said, "and then we can talk. It's what my father—what he wrote himself when he was at the nursing home. Oh, but first of all, just tell Miss Marple exactly what Dr. Penrose said, Giles."

Giles did so. Then Miss Marple opened the little black book and the waitress brought three cups of weak coffee, and a scone and butter, and a plate of cakes. Giles and Gwenda did not talk. They watched Miss Marple as she read.

Finally she closed the book and laid it down. Her expression was difficult to read. There was, Gwenda thought, anger in it. Her lips were pressed tightly together, and her eyes shone very brightly, unusually so, considering her age.

"Yes, indeed," she said. "Yes, indeed!"

Gwenda said:

"You advised us once—do you remember—not to go on? I can see why you did. But we did go on—and this is where we've got to. Only now, it seems as though we'd got to another place where one could—if one liked—stop. . . . Do you think we ought to stop? Or not?"

Miss Marple shook her head slowly. She seemed worried, perplexed.

"I don't know," she said. "I really don't know. It might be better to do so, much better to do so. Because after this lapse of time there is nothing that you can do—nothing, I mean, of a constructive nature."

"You mean that after this lapse of time, there is nothing we can find out?" asked Giles.

"Oh no," said Miss Marple. "I didn't mean that at all. Nineteen years is not such a long time. There are people who would remember things, who could answer questions—quite a lot of people. Servants, for instance. There must have been at least *two* servants in the house at the time, *and* a nurse, and probably a gardener. It will only take time and a little trouble to find and talk to these people. As a matter of fact, I've found *one* of them already. The cook. No, it wasn't that. It was more the question of what practical *good* you can accomplish, and I'd be inclined to say to that—None. And yet—"

She stopped: "There *is* a yet . . . I'm a little slow in thinking things out, but I have a feeling that there is something—something perhaps not very tangible—that would be worth taking risks for—even that one *should* take risks for—but I find it difficult to say just what that is. . . ."

Giles began:

"It seems to me—" and stopped.

Miss Marple turned to him gratefully.

"Gentlemen," she said, "always seem to be able to tabulate things so clearly. I'm sure you have thought things out."

"I have been thinking things out," said Giles. "And it seems to me that there are just two conclusions one can come to. One is the same as I suggested before. Helen Halliday wasn't dead when Gwennie saw her lying in the hall. She came to and went away with her lover, whoever he was. That would still fit the facts as we know them. It would square with Kelvin Halliday's rooted belief that he had killed his wife, and it would square with the missing suitcase and clothes and with the note that Dr. Kennedy found. But it leaves certain points unaccounted for. It doesn't explain why Kelvin was convinced he strangled his wife in the *bedroom*. And it doesn't cover the one, to my mind, really staggering question— *Where is Helen Halliday now?* Because it seems to me against all reason that Helen should never have been heard of or from again. Grant that the two letters she wrote are genuine, what happened *after* that? Why did she never write again? She was on affectionate terms with her brother, he's obviously deeply attached to her and always has been. He might disapprove of her conduct, but that doesn't mean that he expected never to hear from her again. And if you ask me, that point has obviously been worrying Kennedy himself. Let's say he accepted at the time absolutely the story he's told us. His sister's going off and Kelvin's breakdown. But he didn't expect never to hear from his sister again. I think, as the years went on, and he didn't hear, and Kelvin Halliday persisted in his delusion and finally committed suicide, that a terrible doubt began to creep up in his mind. Supposing that Kelvin's story was *true?* That he actually *had* killed Helen? There's no word from her—and surely if she had died somewhere abroad, word would have come to him? I think that explains his eagerness when he saw our advertisement. He hoped that it might lead to some account of where she was or what she had been doing. I'm sure it's absolutely unnatural for someone to disappear as—as completely as Helen seems to have done. That, in itself, is highly suspicious."

"I agree with you," said Miss Marple. "But the alternative, Mr. Reed?"

Giles said slowly:

"I've been thinking out the alternative. It's pretty fantastic, you know, and even rather frightening. Because it involves—how can I put it?—a kind of *malevolence. . . .*"

"Yes," said Gwenda. "Malevolence is just right. Even, I think, something that isn't quite sane. . . ." She shivered.

"That *is* indicated, I think," said Miss Marple. "You know, there's a great deal of—well, *queerness* about—more than people imagine. I have seen some of it. . . ."

Her face was thoughtful.

"There can't be, you see, any *normal* explanation," said Giles. "I'm taking now the fantastic hypothesis that Kelvin Halliday *didn't* kill his wife, but genuinely *thought* he had done so. That's what Dr. Penrose, who seems a decent sort of bloke, obviously wants to think. His first impression of Halliday was that here was a man who had killed his wife and wanted to give himself up to the police. Then he had to take Kennedy's word for it that that wasn't so, so he had perforce to believe that Halliday was a victim of a complex or a fixation or whatever the jargon is—but he didn't really *like* that solution. He'd had a good experience of the type and Halliday didn't square with it. However, on knowing Halliday better, he became quite genuinely sure that Halliday was not the type of man who would strangle a woman under any provocation. So he accepted the fixation theory, but with misgivings. And that really means that only one theory will fit the case—Halliday was induced to believe that he had killed his wife, *by someone else*. In other words, we've come to X.

"Going over the facts very carefully, I'd say that that hypothesis is at least possible. According to his own account, Halliday came into the house that evening, went into the dining room, took a drink *as he usually did*—and then went into the next room, saw a note on the desk and had a blackout—"

Giles paused and Miss Marple nodded her head in approval. He went on:

"Say it wasn't a blackout—that it was just simply dope—knockout drops in the whisky. The next step is quite clear, isn't it? X had strangled Helen in the hall, but afterwards he took her upstairs and arranged her artistically as a *crime passionnel* on the bed, and that's where Kelvin is when he comes to; and the poor devil, who may have been suffering from jealousy where she's concerned, *thinks that he's done it*. What does he do next? Goes off to find his brother-in-law—on the other side of the town and on foot. And that gives X time to do his next trick. Pack and remove a suitcase of clothes and also remove the body—though what he did with the body," Giles ended vexedly, "beats me completely."

"It surprises me you should say *that*, Mr. Reed," said Miss Marple. "I should say that that problem would present few difficulties. But do please go on."

" 'Who were the men in her life?' " quoted Giles. "I saw that in a newspaper as we came back in the train. It set me wondering, because that's really the crux of the matter, isn't it? If there *is* an X, as we believe, all we know about him is that he must have been crazy about her—literally crazy about her."

"And so he hated my father," said Gwenda. "And he wanted him to suffer."

"So that's where we come up against it," said Giles. "We know what kind of a girl Helen was—" He hesitated.

"Man mad," supplied Gwenda.

Miss Marple looked up suddenly as though to speak, and then stopped.

"—and that she was beautiful. But we've no clue to what other men there were in her life besides her husband. There may have been any number."

Miss Marple shook her head.

"Hardly that. She was quite young, you know. But you are not quite accurate, Mr. Reed. We do know something about what you have termed 'the men in her life.' There was the man she was going out to marry—"

"Ah yes—the lawyer chap? What was his name?"

"Walter Fane," said Miss Marple.

"Yes. But you can't count him. He was out in Malaya or India or somewhere."

"But was he? He didn't remain a tea planter, you know," Miss Marple pointed out. "He came back here and went into the firm, and is now the senior partner."

Gwenda exclaimed:

"Perhaps he followed her back here?"

"He may have done. We don't know."

Giles was looking curiously at the old lady.

"How did you find all this out?"

Miss Marple smiled apologetically.

"I've been gossiping a little. In shops—and waiting for buses. Old ladies are supposed to be inquisitive. Yes, one can pick up quite a lot of local news."

"Walter Fane," said Giles thoughtfully. "Helen turned him down. That may have rankled quite a lot. Did he ever marry?"

"No," said Miss Marple. "He lives with his mother. I'm going to tea there at the end of the week."

"There's someone else we know about, too," said Gwenda suddenly. "You remember there was somebody she got engaged to, or entangled with, when she left school—someone undesirable, Dr. Kennedy said. I wonder just *why* he was undesirable. . . ."

"That's two men," said Giles. "Either of them may have had a grudge, may have brooded. . . . Perhaps the first young man may have had some unsatisfactory mental history."

"Dr. Kennedy could tell us that," said Gwenda. "Only it's

going to be a little difficult asking him. I mean it's all very well for me to go along and ask for news of my stepmother whom I barely remember. But it's going to take a bit of explaining if I want to know about her early love affairs. It seems rather excessive interest in a stepmother you hardly knew."

"There are probably other ways of finding out," said Miss Marple. "Oh yes, I think with time and patience, we can gather the information we want."

"Anyway, we've got two possibilities," said Giles.

"We might, I think, infer a third," said Miss Marple. "It would be, of course, a pure hypothesis, but justified, I think, by the turn of events."

Gwenda and Giles looked at her in slight surprise.

"It is just an inference," said Miss Marple, turning a little pink. "Helen Kennedy went out to India to marry young Fane. Admittedly she was not wildly in love with him, but she must have been fond of him, and quite prepared to spend her life with him. Yet as soon as she gets there, she breaks off the engagement and wires her brother to send her money to get home. Now why?"

"Changed her mind, I suppose," said Giles.

Both Miss Marple and Gwenda looked at him in mild contempt.

"Of course she changed her mind," said Gwenda. "We know that. What Miss Marple means is—why?"

"I suppose girls do change their minds," said Giles vaguely.

"*Under certain circumstances*," said Miss Marple.

Her words held all the pointed innuendo that elderly ladies are able to achieve with the minimum of actual statement.

"Something he did—" Giles was suggesting vaguely, when Gwenda chipped in sharply.

"Of course," she said. "Another man!"

She and Miss Marple looked at each other with the assurance of those admitted to a freemasonry from which men were excluded.

Gwenda added with certainty:

"On the boat! Going out!"

"Propinquity," said Miss Marple.

"Moonlight on the boat deck," said Gwenda. "All that sort of thing. Only—it must have been serious—not just a flirtation."

"Oh yes," said Miss Marple, "I think it was serious."

"If so, why didn't she marry the chap?" demanded Giles.

"Perhaps he didn't really care for her," Gwenda said slowly. Then shook her head. "No, I think in that case she would still have married Walter Fane. Oh, of course, I'm being stupid. Married man."

She looked triumphantly at Miss Marple.

"Exactly," said Miss Marple. "That's how I should reconstruct it. They fell in love, probably desperately in love. But if he was a married man—with children, perhaps—and probably an honourable type—well, that would be the end of it."

"Only she couldn't go on and marry Walter Fane," said Gwenda. "So she wired her brother and went home. Yes, that all fits. And on the boat home, she met my father . . ."

She paused, thinking it out.

"Not wildly in love," she said. "But attracted . . . and then there was me. They were both unhappy . . . and they consoled each other. My father told her about my mother, and perhaps she told him about the other man . . . Yes—of course—" She flicked over the pages of the diary. "*I know there was someone— She said as much to me on the boat . . . Someone she loved and couldn't marry*. Yes—that's it. Helen and my father felt they were alike—and there was me to be looked after, and she thought she could make him happy—and she even thought, perhaps, that she'd be quite happy herself in the end."

She stopped, nodded violently at Miss Marple, and said brightly:

"That's it."

Giles was looking exasperated.

"Really, Gwenda, you make a whole lot of things up and pretend that they actually happened."

"They did happen. They must have happened. And that gives us a third person for X."

"You mean—?"

"The married man. We don't know what he was like. He mayn't have been nice at all. He may have been a little mad. He may have followed her here—"

"You've just placed him as going out to India."

"Well, people can come back from India, can't they? Walter

Fane did. It was nearly a year later. I don't say this man *did* come back, but I say he's a possibility. You keep harping on who the men were in her life. Well, we've got three of them. Walter Fane, and some young man whose name we don't know, and a married man—"

"Whom we don't know exists," finished Giles.

"We'll find out," said Gwenda. "Won't we, Miss Marple?"

"With time and patience," said Miss Marple, "we may find out a great deal. Now for my contribution. As a result of a very fortunate little conversation in the draper's today, I have discovered that Edith Pagett, who was cook at St. Catherine's at the time we are interested in, is still in Dillmouth. Her sister is married to a confectioner here. I think it would be quite natural, Gwenda, for you to want to see her. She may be able to tell us a good deal."

"That's wonderful," said Gwenda. "I've thought of something else," she added. "I'm going to make a new will. Don't look so grave, Giles. I shall still leave my money to you. But I shall get Walter Fane to do it for me."

"Gwenda," said Giles. "Do be careful."

"Making a will," said Gwenda, "is a most normal thing to do. And the line of approach I've thought up is quite good. Anyway, I want to see him. I want to see what he's like, and if I think that possibly—"

She left the sentence unfinished.

"What surprises me," said Giles, "is that no one else answered that advertisement of ours—this Edith Pagett, for example—"

Miss Marple shook her head.

"People take a long time to make up their minds about a thing like that in these country districts," she said. "They're suspicious. They like to think things over."

12

Lily Kimble

Lily Kimble spread a couple of old newspapers on the kitchen table in readiness for draining the chipped potatoes which were hissing in the pan. Humming tunelessly a popular melody of the day, she leaned forward, aimlessly studying the newsprint spread out before her.

Then suddenly she stopped humming and called:

"Jim—Jim. Listen here, will you?"

Jim Kimble, an elderly man of few words, was washing at the scullery sink. To answer his wife, he used his favourite monosyllable.

"Ar?" said Jim Kimble.

"It's a piece in the paper. 'Will anyone with any knowledge of Helen Spenlove Halliday, née Kennedy, communicate with Messrs. Reed and Hardy, Southampton Row!' Seems to me they might be meaning Mrs. Halliday as I was in service with at St. Catherine's. Took it from Mrs. Findeyson, they did, she and 'er 'usband. *Her* name was Helen right enough— Yes, and she was sister to Dr. Kennedy, him as always said I ought to have had my adenoids out."

There was a momentary pause as Mrs. Kimble adjusted the frying chips with an expert touch. Jim Kimble was snorting into the roller towel as he dried his face.

"Course it's an old paper, this," resumed Mrs. Kimble. She studied its date. "Nigh on a week or more old. Wonder what it's all about? Think as there's any money in it, Jim?"

Mr. Kimble said "Ar" noncommittally.

"Might be a will or something," speculated his wife. "Powerful lot of time ago."

"Ar."

"Eighteen years or more, I shouldn't wonder. . . . Wonder what they're raking it all up for now? You don't think it could be *police*, do you, Jim?"

"Whatever?" asked Mr. Kimble.

"Well, you know what I always thought," said Mrs. Kimble mysteriously. "Told you at the time, I did, when we was walking out. Pretending that she'd gone off with a feller. That's what they say, husbands, when they do their wives in. Depend upon it, it was murder. That's what I said to you and what I said to Edie, but Edie she wouldn't have it at any price. Never no imagination, Edie hadn't. Those clothes she was supposed to have took away with her—well, they weren't right, if you know what I mean. There was a suitcase gone and a bag, and enough clothes to fill 'em, but they wasn't right, those clothes. And that's when I said to Edie, 'Depend upon it,' I said, 'the master's murdered her and put her in the cellar.' Only not really the cellar, because that Layonee, the Swiss nurse, she saw something. Out of the window. Come to the cinema along of me, she did, though she wasn't supposed to leave the nursery—but there, I said, the child never wakes up—good as gold she was, always, in her bed at night. 'And Madam never comes up to the nursery in the evening,' I says. 'Nobody will know if you slip out with me.' So she did. And when we got in, there was ever such a schemozzle going on. Doctor was there and the master ill and sleeping in the dressing room, and the doctor looking after him, and it was then he asked me about the clothes, and it seemed all right at the time. I thought she'd gone off all right with that fellow she was so keen on—and him a married man, too—and Edie said she did hope and pray we wouldn't be mixed up in any divorce case. What was his name now? I can't remember. Began with an M—or was it an R? Bless us, your memory does go."

Mr. Kimble came in from the scullery and, ignoring all matters of lesser moment, demanded if his supper was ready.

"I'll just drain the chips. . . . Wait, I'll get another paper. Better keep this one. 'Twouldn't be likely to be police—not after all this time. Maybe it's lawyers—and money in it. It doesn't *say* something to your advantage . . . but it might be all the same. . . . Wish I knew who I could ask about it. It says write to some address in London—but I'm not sure I'd like to do a thing like that . . . not to a lot of people in London. . . . What do you say, Jim?"

"Ar," said Mr. Kimble, hungrily eyeing the fish and chips.

The discussion was postponed.

13

Walter Fane

GWENDA LOOKED across the broad mahogany desk at Mr. Walter Fane.

She saw a rather tired-looking man of about fifty, with a gentle nondescript face. The sort of man, Gwenda thought, that you would find it a little difficult to recollect if you had just met him casually. . . . A man who, in modern phrase, lacked personality. His voice, when he spoke, was slow and careful and pleasant. Probably, Gwenda decided, a very sound lawyer.

She stole a glance round the office—the office of the senior partner of the firm. It suited Walter Fane, she decided. It was definitely old-fashioned, the furniture was shabby, but was made of good solid Victorian material. There were deed boxes piled up against the walls—boxes with respectable county names on them. Sir John Vavasour-Trench. Lady Jessup. Arthur ffoulkes Esq. Deceased.

The big sash window, the panes of which were rather dirty, looked into a square backyard flanked by the solid walls of a seventeenth-century adjoining house. There was nothing smart or up-to-date anywhere, but there was nothing sordid either. It was superficially an untidy office with its piled-up boxes, and its littered desk, and its row of lawbooks leaning crookedly on a shelf—but it was actually the office of someone who knew exactly where to lay his hand upon anything he wanted.

The scratching of Walter Fane's pen ceased. He smiled his slow pleasant smile.

"I think that's all quite clear, Mrs. Reed," he said. "A very simple will. When would you like to come in and sign it?"

Gwenda said whenever he liked. There was no particular hurry.

"We've got a house down here, you know," she said. "Hillside."

Walter Fane said, glancing down at his notes:

"Yes, you gave me the address. . . ."

There was no change in the even tenor of his voice.

"It's a very nice house," said Gwenda. "We love it."

"Indeed?" Walter Fane smiled. "Is it on the sea?"

"No," said Gwenda. "I believe the name as been changed. It used to be St. Catherine's."

Mr. Fane took off his pince-nez. He polished them with a silk handkerchief, looking down at the desk.

"Oh yes," he said. "On the Leahampton road?"

He looked up and Gwenda thought how different people who habitually wear glasses look without them. His eyes, a very pale grey, seemed strangely weak and unfocussed.

"It makes his whole face look," thought Gwenda, "as though he isn't really there."

Walter Fane put on the pince-nez again. He said in his precise lawyer's voice:

"I think you said you did make a will on the occasion of your marriage?"

"Yes. But I'd left things in it to various relatives in New Zealand who have died since, so I thought it would be simpler really to make a new one altogether—especially as we mean to live permanently in this country."

Walter Fane nodded.

"Yes, quite a sound view to take. Well, I think this is all quite clear, Mrs. Reed. Perhaps if you come in the day after tomorrow? Will eleven o'clock suit you?"

"Yes, that will be quite all right."

Gwenda rose to her feet and Walter Fane rose also.

Gwenda said, with exactly the little rush she had rehearsed beforehand:

"I—I asked specially for you, because I think—I mean I believe —that you once knew my—my mother."

"Indeed?" Walter Fane put a little additional social warmth into his manner. "What was her name?"

"Halliday. Megan Halliday. I think—I've been told—that you were once engaged to her?"

A clock on the wall ticked. One two, one two, one two.

Gwenda suddenly felt her heart beating a little faster. What a very *quiet* face Walter Fane had. You might see a house like that —a house with all the blinds pulled down. That would mean a house with a dead body in it. ("What idiotic thoughts you do have, Gwenda!")

Walter Fane, his voice unchanged, unruffled, said:

"No, I never knew your mother, Mrs. Reed. But I was once engaged, for a short period, to Helen Kennedy, who afterwards married Major Halliday as his second wife."

"Oh, I see. How stupid of me. I've got it all wrong. It was Helen—my stepmother. Of course it's all long before I remember. I was only a child when my father's second marriage broke up. But I heard someone say that you'd once been engaged to Mrs. Halliday in India—and I thought of course it was my own mother —because of India, I mean. . . . My father met her in India."

"Helen Kennedy came out to India to marry me," said Walter Fane. "Then she changed her mind. On the boat going home she met your father."

It was a plain unemotional statement of fact. Gwenda still had the impression of a house with the blinds down.

"I'm so sorry," she said. "Have I put my foot in it?"

Walter Fane smiled—his slow pleasant smile. The blinds were up.

"It's nineteen or twenty years ago, Mrs. Reed," he said. "One's youthful troubles and follies don't mean much after that space of time. So you are Halliday's baby daughter. You know, don't you, that your father and Helen actually lived here in Dillmouth for a while?"

"Oh yes," said Gwenda, "that's really why we came here. I didn't remember it properly, of course, but when we had to decide where we'd live in England, I came to Dillmouth first of all, to see what it was really like, and I thought it was such an attractive place that I decided that we'd park ourselves right here and nowhere else. And wasn't it luck? We've actually got the same house that my people lived in long ago."

"I remember the house," said Walter Fane. Again he gave that slow pleasant smile. "You may not remember me, Mrs. Reed, but I rather imagine I used to give you piggybacks once."

Gwenda laughed.

"Did you really? Then you're quite an old friend, aren't you? I can't pretend I remember you—but then I was only about two and a half or three, I suppose. . . . Were you back on leave from India or something like that?"

"No, I'd chucked India for good. I went out to try tea planting —but the life didn't suit me. I was cut out to follow in my father's footsteps and be a prosy unadventurous country solicitor. I'd passed all my law exams earlier, so I simply came back and went straight into the firm." He paused and said: "I've been here ever since."

Again there was a pause and he repeated in a lower voice:

"Yes—ever since. . . ."

But eighteen years, thought Gwenda, isn't really such a long time as all that. . . .

Then, with a change of manner, he shook hands with her and said:

"Since we seem to be old friends, you really must bring your husband to tea with my mother one day. I'll get her to write to you. In the meanwhile, eleven o'clock on Thursday?"

Gwenda went out of the office and down the stairs. There was a cobweb in the angle of the stairway. In the middle of the web was a pale, rather nondescript spider. It didn't look, Gwenda thought, like a real spider. Not the fat juicy kind of spider who caught flies and ate them. It was more like a ghost of a spider. Rather like Walter Fane, in fact.

II

Giles met his wife on the seafront.

"Well?" he asked.

"He was here in Dillmouth at the time," said Gwenda. "Back from India, I mean. Because he gave me piggybacks. But he couldn't have murdered anyone—not possibly. He's much too quiet and gentle. Very nice, really, but the kind of person you never really notice. You know, they come to parties, but you never notice when they leave. I should think he was frightfully upright and all that, and devoted to his mother, and with a lot of virtues. But from a woman's point of view, terribly *dull.* I can see why he didn't cut any ice with Helen. You know, a nice safe person to marry—but you don't really want to."

"Poor devil," said Giles. "And I suppose he was just crazy about her."

"Oh, I don't know. . . . I shouldn't think so, really. Anyway, I'm sure he wouldn't be our malevolent murderer. He's not my idea of a murderer at all."

"You don't really know a lot about murderers, though, do you, my sweet?"

"What do you mean?"

"Well—I was thinking about quiet Lizzie Borden—only the jury said she didn't do it. And Wallace, a quiet man whom the jury insisted did kill his wife, though the sentence was quashed on appeal. And Armstrong, who everybody said for years was such a kind unassuming fellow. I don't believe murderers are ever a special type."

"I really can't believe that Walter Fane—"

Gwenda stopped.

"What is it?"

"Nothing."

But she was remembering Walter Fane polishing his eyeglasses and the queer blind stare of his eyes when she had first mentioned St. Catherine's.

"Perhaps," she said uncertainly, "he *was* crazy about her. . . ."

14

Edith Pagett

Mrs. Mountford's back parlour was a comfortable room. It had a round table covered with a cloth, and some old-fashioned armchairs and a stern-looking but unexpectedly well-sprung sofa against the wall. There were china dogs and other ornaments on the mantelpiece, and a framed coloured representation of the Princesses Elizabeth and Margaret Rose. On another wall was the King in Naval uniform, and a photograph of Mr. Mountford in a group of other bakers and confectioners. There was a picture made with shells and a watercolour of a very green sea at Capri. There were a great many other things, none of them with any pretensions to beauty or the higher life; but the net result was a happy, cheerful room where people sat round and enjoyed themselves whenever there was time to do so.

Mrs. Mountford, née Pagett, was short and round and dark-haired, with a few grey streaks in the dark. Her sister, Edith Pagett, was tall and dark and thin. There was hardly any grey in her hair though she was at a guess round about fifty.

"Fancy now," Edith Pagett was saying. "Little Miss Gwennie. You must excuse me, m'am, speaking like that, but it does take one back. You used to come into my kitchen, as pretty as could be. 'Winnies' you used to say. 'Winnies,' and what you meant was raisins—though why you called them winnies is more than I can say. But raisins was what you meant and raisins it was I used to give you, sultanas, that is, on account of the stones."

Gwenda stared hard at the upright figure and the red cheeks and black eyes, trying to remember—to remember—but nothing came. Memory was an inconvenient thing.

"I wish I could remember—" she began.

"It's not likely that you would. Just a tiny little mite, that's all you were. Nowadays nobody seems to want to go in a house where there's children. I can't see it myself. Children give life to a house, that's what I feel. Though nursery meals are always liable to cause a bit of trouble. But if you know what I mean, m'am, that's the nurse's fault, not the child's. Nurses are nearly always difficult—trays and waiting upon and one thing and another. Do you remember Layonee at all, Miss Gwennie? Excuse me, Mrs. Reed, I should say?"

"Leonie? Was she my nurse?"

"Swiss girl, she was. Didn't speak English very well, and very sensitive in her feelings. Used to cry a lot if Lily said something to upset her. Lily was house-parlourmaid. Lily Abbott. A young girl and pert in her ways and a bit flighty. Many a game Lily used to have with you, Miss Gwennie. Play peepbo through the stairs."

Gwenda gave a quick uncontrollable shiver.

The stairs . . .

Then she said suddenly:

"I remember Lily. She put a bow on the cat."

"There now, fancy you remembering that! On your birthday it was, and Lily she was all for it, Thomas must have a bow on. Took one off the chocolate box, and Thomas was mad about it. Ran off into the garden and rubbed through the bushes until he got it off. Cats don't like tricks being played on them."

"A black and white cat."

"That's right. Poor old Tommy. Caught mice something beautiful. A real proper mouser." Edith Pagett paused and coughed primly. "Excuse me running on like this, m'am. But talking brings the old days back. You wanted to ask me something?"

"I like hearing you talk about the old days," said Gwenda. "That's just what I want to hear about. You see I was brought up by relations in New Zealand and of course they could never tell me anything about—about my father, and my stepmother. She—she was nice, wasn't she?"

"Very fond of you, she was. Oh yes, she used to take you down to the beach and play with you in the garden. She was quite young herself, you understand. Nothing but a girl, really. I often used to think she enjoyed the games as much as you did. You see she'd been an only child, in a manner of speaking. Dr. Kennedy, her brother, was years and years older and always shut up with his books. When she wasn't away at school, she had to play by herself. . . ."

Miss Marple, sitting back against the wall, asked gently:

"You've lived in Dillmouth all your life, haven't you?"

"Oh yes, madam, Father had the farm up behind the hill—Rylands it was always called. He'd no sons, and Mother couldn't carry on after he died, so she sold it and bought the little fancy shop at the end of the High Street. Yes, I've lived here all my life."

"And I suppose you know all about everyone in Dillmouth?"

"Well, of course it used to be a small place then. Though there used always to be a lot of summer visitors as long as I can remember. But nice quiet people who came here every year, not these trippers and charabancs we have nowadays. Good families they were, who'd come back to the same rooms year after year."

"I suppose," said Giles, "that you knew Helen Kennedy before she was Mrs. Halliday?"

"Well, I knew *of* her, so to speak, and I may have seen her about. But I didn't know her proper until I went into service there."

"And you liked her," said Miss Marple.

Edith Pagett turned towards her.

"Yes, madam, I did," she said. There was a trace of defiance in her manner. "No matter what anybody says. She was as nice as could be to me always. I'd never have believed she'd do what she did do. Took my breath away, it did. Although, mind you, there *had* been talk—"

She stopped rather abruptly and gave a quick apologetic glance at Gwenda.

Instinctively Gwenda spoke impulsively.

"I want to know," she said. "Please don't think I shall mind anything you say. She wasn't my own mother—"

"That's true enough, m'am."

"And you see, we are very anxious to—to find her. She went away from here—and she seems to have been quite lost sight of. We don't know where she is living now, or even if she is alive. And there are reasons—"

She hesitated and Giles said quickly:

"Legal reasons. We don't know whether to presume death or—or what."

"Oh, I quite understand, sir. My cousin's husband was missing—after Ypres it was—and there was a lot of trouble about presuming death and that. Real vexing it was for her. Naturally, sir, if there is anything I can tell you that will help in any way—it isn't as if you were strangers. Miss Gwenda and her 'winnies.' So funny you used to say it."

"That's very kind of you," said Giles. "So, if you don't mind, I'll just fire away. Mrs. Halliday left home quite suddenly, I understand?"

"Yes, sir, it was a great shock to all of us—and especially to the Major, poor man. He collapsed completely."

"I'm going to ask you right out—have you any idea who the man was she went away with?"

Edith Pagett shook her head.

"That's what Dr. Kennedy asked me—and I couldn't tell him. Lily couldn't either. And of course that Layonee, being a foreigner, didn't know a thing about it."

"You didn't *know*," said Giles. "But could you make a guess? Now that it's all so long ago, it wouldn't matter—even if the guess is all wrong. You must, surely, have had some suspicion."

"Well, we had our suspicions . . . but mind you, it wasn't more than suspicions. And as far as I'm concerned, I never saw anything at all. But Lily who, as I told you, was a sharp kind of girl, Lily had her ideas—had had them for a long time. 'Mark my words,' she used to say. 'That chap's sweet on her. Only got to see him looking at her as she pours out the tea. And does his wife look daggers!' "

"I see. And who was the—er—chap?"

"Now I'm afraid, sir, I just don't remember his name. Not after all these years. A Captain—Esdale—no, that wasn't it—Emery—no. I have a kind of feeling it began with an E. Or it might have been H. Rather an unusual kind of name. But I've never even thought of it for sixteen years. He and his wife were staying at the Royal Clarence."

"Summer visitors?"

"Yes, but I think that he—or maybe both of them—had known Mrs. Halliday before. They came to the house quite often. Anyway, according to Lily he was sweet on Mrs. Halliday."

"And his wife didn't like it."

"No, sir. . . . But mind you, I never believed for a moment that there was anything wrong about it. And I still don't know what to think."

Gwenda asked:

"Were they still here—at the Royal Clarence—when—when Helen—my stepmother went away?"

"As far as I recollect they went away just about the same time, a day earlier or a day later—anyway, it was close enough to make people talk. But I never heard anything definite. It was all kept very quiet if it *was* so. Quite a nine days' wonder Mrs. Halliday going off like that, so sudden. But people did say she'd always been flighty—not that I ever saw anything of the kind myself. I wouldn't have been willing to go to Norfolk with them if I'd thought that."

For a moment three people stared at her intently. Then Giles said:

"Norfolk? Were they going to Norfolk?"

"Yes, sir. They'd bought a house there. Mrs. Halliday told me about three weeks before—before all this happened. She asked me if I'd come with them when they moved, and I said I would. After all, I'd never been away from Dillmouth, and I thought perhaps I'd like a change—seeing as I liked the family."

"I never heard they had bought a house in Norfolk," said Giles.

"Well, it's funny you should say that, sir, because Mrs. Halliday seemed to want it kept very quiet. She asked me not to speak about it to anyone at all—so of course I didn't. But she'd been wanting to go away from Dillmouth for some time. She'd been pressing Major Halliday to go, but he liked it at Dillmouth. I even believe he wrote to Mrs. Findeyson, whom St. Catherine's belonged to, asking if she'd consider selling it. But Mrs. Halliday was dead against it. She seemed to have turned right against Dillmouth. It's almost as though she was afraid to stop there."

The words came out quite naturally, yet at the sound of them the three people listening again stiffened to attention.

Giles said:

"You don't think she wanted to go to Norfolk to be near this—this man whose name you can't remember?"

Edith Pagett looked distressed.

"Oh, indeed, sir, I wouldn't like to think *that*. And I don't think it, not for a moment. Besides, I don't think that—I remember now—they came from up North somewhere, that lady and gentleman did. Northumberland, I think it was. Anyway, they liked coming south for a holiday because it was so mild down here."

Gwenda said:

"She was afraid of something, wasn't she? Or of someone? My stepmother, I mean."

"I do remember—now that you say that—"

"Yes?"

"Lily came into the kitchen one day. She'd been dusting the stairs, and she said, 'Ructions!' she said. She had a very common way of talking sometimes, Lily had, so you must excuse me.

"So I asked her what she meant and she said that the missus

had come in from the garden with the master into the drawing room and the door to the hall being open, Lily'd heard what they said.

"'*I'm afraid of you,*' that's what Mrs. Halliday had said.

"'And she sounded scared too,' Lily said. '*I've been afraid of you for a long time. You're mad. You're not normal. Go away and leave me alone.* You must *leave me alone. I'm frightened. I think, underneath, I've always been frightened of you. . . .*'

"Something of that kind—of course I can't say now to the exact words. But Lily, she took it very seriously, and that's why, after it all happened, she—"

Edith Pagett stopped dead. A curious frightened look came over her face.

"I didn't mean, I'm sure—" she began. "Excuse me, madam, my tongue runs away with me."

Giles said gently:

"Please tell us, Edith. It's really important, you see, that we should know. It's all a long time ago now, but we've got to *know.*

"I couldn't say, I'm sure," said Edith helplessly.

Miss Marple asked:

"What was it Lily didn't believe—or did believe?"

Edith Pagett said apologetically:

"Lily was always one to get ideas in her head. I never took no notice of them. She was always one for going to the pictures and she got a lot of silly melodramatic ideas that way. She was out at the pictures the night it happened—and what's more she took Layonee with her—and very wrong *that* was, and I told her so. 'Oh, that's all right,' she said. 'It's not leaving the child alone in the house. You're down in the kitchen and the master and the missus will be in later and anyway that child never wakes once she's off to sleep.' But it was wrong, and I told her so, though of course I never knew about Layonee going till afterwards. If I had, I'd have run up to see she—you, I mean, Miss Gwenda—were quite all right. You can't hear a thing from the kitchen when the baize door's shut."

Edith Pagett paused and then went on.

"I was doing some ironing. The evening passed ever so quick and the first thing I knew, Dr. Kennedy came out in the kitchen and asked me where Lily was and I said it was her night off but she'd be in any minute now, and sure enough she came in that very minute and he took her upstairs to the mistress's room. Wanted to know if she'd taken any clothes away with her and what? So Lily looked about and told him and then she come down to me. All agog she was. 'She's hooked it,' she said. 'Gone off with someone. The master's all in. Had a stroke or something. Apparently it's been a terrible shock to him. More fool he. He ought to have seen it coming.' 'You shouldn't speak like that,' I said. 'How do you know she's gone off with anybody. Maybe she had a telegram from a sick relation.' 'Sick relation my foot,' Lily says (always a common way of speaking, as I said). 'She left a note.' 'Who's she gone off with?' I said. 'Who do you think?' Lily said. 'Not likely to be Mr. Sobersides Fane, for all his sheep's eyes and the way he follows her round like a dog.' So I said, 'You think it's Captain—whatever his name was.' And she said, 'He's my bet. Unless it's our mystery man in the flashy car.' (That's just a silly joke we had.) And I said, 'I don't believe it. Not Mrs. Halliday. She wouldn't do a thing like that.' And Lily says, 'Well, it seems she's done it.'

"All this was at first, you understand. But later on, up in our bedroom—Lily woke me up. 'Look here,' she says. 'It's all wrong.' 'What's wrong?' I said. And she said, 'Those clothes.' 'Whatever are you talking about?' I said. 'Listen, Edie,' she said. 'I went through her clothes because the doctor asked me to. And there's a suitcase gone and enough things to fill it—but they're the *wrong* things.' 'What do you mean?' I said. And Lily said, 'She took an evening dress, her grey and silver—but she didn't take her evening belt and brassiere, nor the slip that goes with it, and she took her gold brocade evening shoes, not the silver strap ones. And she took her green tweed—which she never wears until late on in the autumn, but she didn't take that fancy pullover, and she took her lace blouses that she only wears with a town suit. Oh, and her undies, too, they were a job lot. You mark my words, Edie,' Lily said. 'She's not gone away at all. The master's done her in.'

"Well, that made me wide awake. I sat right up and asked her what on earth she was talking about.

"'Just like it was in the *News of the World* last week,' Lily says. 'The master found she'd been carrying on and he killed her and put her down in the cellar and buried her under the floor.

You'd never hear anything because it's under the front hall. That's what he's done, and then he packed a suitcase to make it look as though she'd gone away. But that's where she is—under the cellar floor. *She never left this house alive.*' I gave her a piece of my mind then, saying such awful things. But I'll admit I slipped down to the cellar the next morning. But there, it was all just as usual and nothing disturbed and no digging been done—and I went and told Lily she'd just been making a fool of herself, but she stuck to it as the master had done her in. 'Remember,' she says, 'she was scared to death of him. I heard her telling him so.' 'And that's just where you're wrong, my girl,' I said, 'because it wasn't the master at all. Just after you'd told me that day, I looked out of the window and there was the master coming down the hill with his golf clubs, so it couldn't have been him who was with the mistress in the drawing room. It was someone else.'"

The words echoed lingeringly in the comfortable commonplace sitting room.

Giles said softly under his breath:

"It was someone else. . . ."

15

An Address

THE ROYAL CLARENCE was the oldest hotel in the town. It had a mellow bowfronted façade and an old-world atmosphere. It still catered to the type of family who came for a month to the seaside.

Miss Narracott, who presided behind the reception desk, was a full-bosomed lady of forty-seven with an old-fashioned style of hairdressing.

She unbent to Giles whom her accurate eye summed up as "one of our nice people." And Giles, who had a ready tongue and a persuasive way with him when he liked, spun a very good tale. He had a bet on with his wife—about her godmother—and whether she had stayed at the Royal Clarence eighteen years ago. His wife had said that they could never settle the dispute because of course all the old registers would be thrown away by this time, but he had said "Nonsense." An establishment like the Royal Clarence would keep its registers. They must go back for a hundred years.

"Well, not quite that, Mr. Reed. But we do keep all our old Visitors' Books, as we prefer to call them. Very interesting names in them, too. Why, the King stayed here once when he was Prince of Wales, and Princess Adlemar of Holstein Retz used to come every winter with her lady-in-waiting. And we've had some very famous novelists, too, and Mr. Dovery, the portrait painter."

Giles responded in suitable fashion with interest and respect and in due course the sacred volume for the year in question was brought out and exhibited to him.

Having first had various illustrious names pointed out to him, he turned the pages to the month of August.

Yes, here surely was the entry he was seeking.

Captain and Mrs. Richard Erskine, Anstell Manor, Daith, Northumberland, July 27th—August 17th.

"If I may copy this out?"

"Of course, Mr. Reed. Paper and ink— Oh, you have your pen. Excuse me, I must just go back to the outer office."

She left him with the open book, and Giles set to work.

On his return to Hillside he found Gwenda in the garden bending over the herbaceous border.

She straightened herself and gave him a quick glance of interrogation.

"Any luck?"

"Yes, I think this must be it."

Gwenda said softly, reading the words:

"Anstell Manor, Daith, Northumberland. Yes, Edith Pagett said Northumberland. I wonder if they're still living there—"

"We'll have to go and see."

"Yes—yes, it would be better to go— When?"

"As soon as possible. Tomorrow? We'll take the car and drive up. It will show you a little more of England."

"Suppose they're dead—or gone away and somebody else is living there?"

Giles shrugged his shoulders.

"Then we come back and go on with our other leads. I've written to Kennedy, by the way, and asked him if he'll send me those letters Helen wrote after she went away—if he's still got them—*and* a specimen of her handwriting."

"I wish," said Gwenda, "that we could get in touch with the other servant—with Lily—the one who put the bow on Thomas—"

"Funny your suddenly remembering that, Gwenda."

"Yes, wasn't it? I remember Tommy, too. He was black with white patches and he had three lovely kittens."

"What? Thomas?"

"Well, he was called Thomas—but actually he turned out to be Thomasina. You know what cats are. But about Lily—I wonder what's become of her? Edith Pagett seems to have lost sight of her entirely. She didn't come from round here—and after the breakup at St. Catherine's she took a place in Torquay. She wrote once or twice but that was all. Edith said she'd heard she'd got married but she didn't know who to. If we could get hold of her, we might learn a lot more."

"And from Leonie, the Swiss girl."

"Perhaps—but she was a foreigner and wouldn't catch on to much of what went on. You know, I don't remember her at all. No—it's Lily I feel would be useful. Lily was the sharp one. . . . I know, Giles, let's put in another advertisement—an advertisement for her—Lily Abbott, her name was."

"Yes," said Giles. "We might try that. And we'll definitely go north tomorrow and see what we can find out about the Erskines."

16

Mother's Son

"Down, Henry," said Mrs. Fane to an asthmatic spaniel whose liquid eyes burned with greed. "Another scone, Miss Marple, while they're hot?"

"Thank you. Such delicious scones. You have an excellent cook."

"Louisa is not bad, really. Forgetful, like all of them. And no variety in her puddings. Tell me, how is Dorothy Yarde's sciatica nowadays? She used to be a martyr to it. Largely nerves, I suspect."

Miss Marple hastened to oblige with details of their mutual acquaintance's ailments. It was fortunate, she thought, that among her many friends and relations scattered over England, she had managed to find a woman who knew Mrs. Fane and who had written explaining that a Miss Marple was at present in Dillmouth and would dear Eleanor be very kind and ask her to something.

Eleanor Fane was a tall, commanding woman with a steely grey eye, crisp white hair, and a baby pink and white complexion which masked the fact that there was no babylike softness whatever about her.

They discussed Dorothy's ailments or imagined ailments and went on to Miss Marple's health, the air of Dillmouth, and the general poor condition of most of the younger generation.

"Not made to eat their crusts as children," Mrs. Fane pronounced. "None of that allowed in *my* nursery."

"You have more than one son?" asked Miss Marple.

"Three. The eldest, Gerald, is in Singapore in the Far East Bank. Robert is in the Army." Mrs. Fane sniffed. "Married a Roman Catholic," she said with significance. "You know what *that* means! All the children brought up as Catholics. What Robert's father would have said, I don't know. My husband was very Low Church. I hardly ever hear from Robert nowadays. He takes exception to some of the things I have said to him purely for his own good. I believe in being sincere and saying exactly what one thinks. His marriage was, in my opinion, a great misfortune. He may pretend to be happy, poor boy—but I can't feel that it is at all satisfactory."

"Your youngest son is not married, I believe?"

Mrs. Fane beamed.

"No, Walter lives at home. He is slightly delicate—always was from a child—and I have always had to look after his health very carefully. (He will be in presently.) I can't tell you what a thoughtful and devoted son he is. I am really a very lucky woman to have such a son."

"And he has never thought of marrying?" inquired Miss Marple.

"Walter always says he really cannot be bothered with the modern young woman. They don't appeal to him. He and I have so much in common that I'm afraid he doesn't go out as much as he should. He reads Thackeray to me in the evenings, and we usually have a game of piquet. Walter is a real home bird."

"How very nice," said Miss Marple. "Has he always been in the firm? Somebody told me that you had a son who was out in Ceylon as a tea planter, but perhaps they got it wrong."

A slight frown came over Mrs. Fane's face. She urged walnut cake upon her guest and explained.

"That was as a very young man. One of those youthful impulses. A boy always longs to see the world. Actually, there was a girl at the bottom of it. Girls can be *so* unsettling."

"Oh yes, indeed. My own nephew, I remember—"

Mrs. Fane swept on, ignoring Miss Marple's nephew. She held the floor and was enjoying the opportunity to reminisce to this sympathetic friend of dear Dorothy's.

"A *most* unsuitable girl—as seems always to be the way. Oh, I don't mean an *actress* or anything like that. The local doctor's sister—more like his daughter, really, years younger—and the poor man with no idea how to bring her up. Men are so helpless, aren't they? She ran quite wild, entangled herself first with a young man in the office—a mere clerk—and a very unsatisfactory character, too. They had to get rid of him. Repeated confidential information. Anyway, this girl, Helen Kennedy, was, I suppose, very pretty. *I* didn't think so. I always thought her hair was touched up. But Walter, poor boy, fell very much in love with her. As I say, quite unsuitable, no money and no prospects, and not the kind of girl one wanted as a daughter-in-law. Still, what can a mother do? Walter proposed to her and she refused him, and then he got this silly idea into his head of going out to India and being a tea planter. My husband said: 'Let him go,' though of course he was very disappointed. He had been looking forward to having Walter with him in the firm and Walter had passed all his law exams and everything. Still, there it was. Really, the havoc these young women cause!"

"Oh, I know. My nephew—"

Once again Mrs. Fane swept over Miss Marple's nephew.

"So the dear boy went out to Assam or was it Bangalore—really, I can't remember after all these years. And I felt most upset because I knew his health wouldn't stand it. And he hadn't been out there a year (doing very well, too; Walter does everything well) than would you believe it, this impudent chit of a girl changes her mind and writes out that she'd like to marry him after all."

"Dear, dear." Miss Marple shook her head.

"Gets together her trousseau, books her passage—and what do you think the next move is?"

"I can't imagine!"

Miss Marple leaned forward in rapt attention.

"Has a love affair with a married man, if you please. On the boat going out. A married man with three children, I believe. Anyway there is Walter on the quay to meet her and the first thing she does is to say she can't marry him after all. Don't you call that a wicked thing to do?"

"Oh, I do indeed. It might have completely destroyed your son's faith in human nature."

"It should have shown her to him in her true colours. But there, that type of woman gets away with anything."

"He didn't—" Miss Marple hesitated—"*resent* her action? Some men would have been terribly angry."

"Walter has always had wonderful self-control. However upset and annoyed Walter may be over anything, he never shows it."

Miss Marple peered at her speculatively.

Hesitantly, she put out a feeler.

"That is because it goes really deep, perhaps? One is really astonished sometimes, with children. A sudden outburst from some child that one has thought didn't care at all. A sensitive nature that can't express itself until it's driven absolutely beyond endurance."

"Ah, it's very curious you should say that, Miss Marple. I remember so well. Gerald and Robert, you know, both hot-tempered and always apt to *fight*. Quite natural, of course, for healthy boys—"

"Oh, quite natural."

"And dear Walter, always so quiet and patient. And then, one day, Robert got hold of his model aeroplane—he'd built it up himself with days of work—so patient and clever with his fingers—and Robert, who was a dear, high-spirited boy but careless, smashed it. And when I came into the schoolroom, there was Robert down on the floor and Walter attacking him with the poker, he'd practically knocked him out—and I simply had all I could do to drag Walter off him. He kept repeating: 'He did it on purpose—he did it on purpose. I'm going to kill him. . . .' You know, I was quite frightened. Boys feel things so intensely, do they not?"

"Yes, indeed," said Miss Marple. Her eyes were thoughtful.

She reverted to the former topic.

"And so the engagement was finally broken off. What happened to the girl?"

"She came home. Had another love affair on the way back, and this time married the man. A widower with one child. A man who has just lost his wife is always a fair target—helpless, poor fellow. She married him and they settled down here in a house the other side of the town—St. Catherine's—next door to the hospital. It didn't last, of course—she left him within the year. Went off with some man or other."

"Dear, dear!" Miss Marple shook her head. "What a lucky escape your son had!"

"That's what I always tell him."

"And did he give up tea planting because his health wouldn't stand it?"

A slight frown appeared on Mrs. Fane's brow.

"The life wasn't really congenial to him," she said. "He came home about six months after the girl did."

"It must have been rather awkward," ventured Miss Marple. "If the young woman was actually living here. In the same town—"

"Walter was wonderful," said Walter's mother. "He behaved exactly as though nothing had happened. I should have thought myself (indeed I said so at the time) that it would be advisable to make a clean break—after all, meetings could only be awkward for both parties. But Walter insisted on going out of his way to be friendly. He used to call at the house in the most informal fashion, and play with the child— Rather curious, by the way, the child's come back here. She's grown-up now, with a husband. Came into Walter's office to make her will the other day. Reed, that's her name now. Reed."

"Mr. and Mrs. Reed? I know them. Such a nice unaffected young couple. Fancy that now—and she is actually the child—"

"The first wife's child. The first wife died out in India. Poor Major—I've forgotten his name—Hallway—something like that—was completely broken up when that minx left him. Why the worst women should always attract the best men is something hard to fathom!"

"And the young man who was originally entangled with her? A clerk, I think you said, in your son's office. What happened to him?"

"Did very well for himself. He runs a lot of these coach tours. Daffodil Coaches. Afflick's Daffodil Coaches. Painted bright yellow. It's a vulgar world nowadays."

"Afflick?" said Miss Marple.

"Jackie Afflick. A nasty pushing fellow. Always determined to get on, I imagine. Probably why he took up with Helen Kennedy in the first place. Doctor's sister and all that—thought it would better his social position."

"And this Helen has never come back again to Dillmouth?"

"No. Good riddance. Probably gone completely to the bad by now. I was sorry for Dr. Kennedy. Not his fault. His father's second wife was a fluffy little thing, years younger than he was. Helen inherited her wild blood from her, I expect. I've always thought—"

Mrs. Fane broke off.

"Here is Walter." Her mother's ear had distinguished certain well-known sounds in the hall. The door opened and Walter Fane came in.

"This is Miss Marple, my son. Ring the bell, son, and we'll have some fresh tea."

"Don't bother, Mother. I had a cup."

"Of course we will have fresh tea—and some scones, Beatrice," she added to the parlourmaid who had appeared to take the teapot.

"Yes, madam."

With a slow likeable smile Walter Fane said:

"My mother spoils me, I'm afraid."

Miss Marple studied him as she made a polite rejoinder.

A gentle quiet-looking person, slightly diffident and apologetic in manner—colourless. A very nondescript personality. The devoted type of young man whom women ignore and only marry because the man they love does not return their affection. Walter, who is Always There. Poor Walter, his mother's darling . . . Little Walter Fane, who had attacked his older brother with a poker and had tried to kill him. . . .

Miss Marple wondered.

17

Richard Erskine

ANSTELL MANOR had a bleak aspect. It was a white house, set against a background of bleak hills. A winding drive led up through dense shrubbery.

Giles said to Gwenda:

"Why have we come? What can we possibly say?"

"We've got it worked out."

"Yes—so far as that goes. It's lucky that Miss Marple's cousin's sister's aunt's brother-in-law or whatever it was lives near here. . . . But it's a far step from a social call to asking your host about his bygone love affairs."

"And such a long time ago. Perhaps—perhaps he doesn't even remember her."

"Perhaps he doesn't. And perhaps there never was a love affair."

"Giles, are we making unutterable fools of ourselves?"

"I don't know. . . . Sometimes I feel that. I don't see why we're concerning ourselves with all this. What does it matter now?"

"So long after . . . Yes, I know. . . . Miss Marple and Dr. Kennedy both said: 'Leave it alone.' Why don't we, Giles? What makes us go on? Is it *her?*"

"Her?"

"Helen. Is that why I remember? Is my childish memory the only link she's got with life—with truth? Is it Helen who's using me—and you—so that the truth will be known?"

"You mean, because she died a violent death—?"

"Yes. They say—books say—that sometimes they can't rest. . . ."

"I think you're being fanciful, Gwenda."

"Perhaps I am. Anyway, we can—choose. This is only a social call. There's no need for it to be anything more—unless we want it to be—"

Giles shook his head.

"We shall go on. We can't help ourselves."

"Yes—you're right. All the same, Giles, I think I'm rather frightened—"

II

"Looking for a house, are you?" said Major Erskine.

He offered Gwenda a plate of sandwiches. Gwenda took one, looking up at him. Richard Erskine was a small man, five foot nine or so. His hair was grey and he had tired, rather thoughtful eyes. His voice was low and pleasant with a slight drawl. There was nothing remarkable about him, but he was, Gwenda thought, definitely attractive. . . . He was actually not nearly as good-looking as Walter Fane, but whereas most women would pass Fane without a second glance, they would not pass Erskine. Fane was nondescript. Erskine, in spite of his quietness, had personality. He talked of ordinary things in an ordinary manner, but there was *something*—that something that women are quick to recognize and to which they react in a purely female way. Almost unconsciously Gwenda adjusted her skirt, tweaked at a side curl, retouched her lips. Nineteen years ago Helen Kennedy could have fallen in love with this man. Gwenda was quite sure of that.

She looked up to find her hostess's eyes full upon her, and involuntarily she flushed. Mrs. Erskine was talking to Giles, but she was watching Gwenda, and her glance was both appraising and suspicious. Janet Erskine was a tall woman, her voice was deep—almost as deep as a man's. Her build was athletic; she wore a well-cut tweed with big pockets. She looked older than her husband, but, Gwenda decided, well might not be so. There was a certain haggardness about her face. An unhappy hungry woman, thought Gwenda.

"I bet she gives him hell," she said to herself.

Aloud she continued the conversation.

"House hunting is terribly discouraging," she said. "House agents' descriptions are always glowing—and then, when you actually get there, the place is quite unspeakable."

"You're thinking of settling down in this neighbourhood?"

"Well—this is one of the neighbourhoods we thought of. Really because it's near Hadrian's Wall. Giles has always been fascinated by Hadrian's Wall. You see—it sounds rather odd, I expect, to you—but almost anywhere in England is the same to us. My own home is in New Zealand and I haven't any ties here. And Giles was taken in by different aunts for different holidays and so hasn't any particular ties either. The one thing we don't want is to be too near London. We want the real country."

Erskine smiled.

"You'll certainly find it real country all round here. It's completely isolated. Our neighbours are few and far between."

Gwenda thought she detected an undercurrent of bleakness in the pleasant voice. She had a sudden glimpse of a lonely life—of short dark winter days with the wind whistling in the chimneys—the curtains drawn—shut in—shut in with that woman with the hungry unhappy eyes—and neighbours few and far between.

Then the vision faded. It was summer again, with the French windows open to the garden—with the scent of roses and the sounds of summer drifting in.

She said:

"This is an old house, isn't it?"

Erskine nodded.

"Queen Anne. My people have lived here for nearly three hundred years."

"It's a lovely house. You must be very proud of it."

"It's rather a shabby house now. Taxation makes it difficult to keep anything up properly. However, now the children are out in the world, the worst strain is over."

"How many children have you?"

"Two boys. One's in the Army. The other's just come down from Oxford. He's going into a publishing firm."

His glance went to the mantelpiece and Gwenda's eyes followed his. There was a photograph there of two boys—presumably about eighteen and nineteen, taken a few years ago, she judged. There was pride and affection in his expression.

"They're good lads," he said, "though I say it myself."

"They look awfully nice," said Gwenda.

"Yes," said Erskine. "I think it's worth it—really. Making sacrifices for one's children, I mean," he added in answer to Gwenda's inquiring look.

"I suppose—often—one has to give up a good deal," said Gwenda.

"A great deal sometimes. . . ."

Again she caught a dark undercurrent, but Mrs. Erskine broke in, saying in her deep authoritative voice:

"And you are really looking for a house in this part of the world? I'm afraid I don't know of anything at all suitable round here."

"And wouldn't tell me if you did," thought Gwenda, with a faint spurt of mischief. "That foolish old woman is actually jealous," she thought. "Jealous because I'm talking to her husband and because I'm young and attractive!"

"It depends how much of a hurry you're in," said Erskine.

"No hurry at all really," said Giles cheerfully. "We want to be sure of finding something we really like. At the moment we've got a house in Dillmouth—on the South coast."

Major Erskine turned away from the tea table. He went to get a cigarette box from a table by the window.

"Dillmouth," said Mrs. Erskine. Her voice was expressionless. Her eyes watched the back of her husband's head.

"Pretty little place," said Giles. "Do you know it at all?"

There was a moment's silence, then Mrs. Erskine said in that same expressionless voice:

"We spent a few weeks there one summer—many, many years ago. We didn't care for it—found it too relaxing."

"Yes," said Gwenda. "That's just what we find. Giles and I feel we'd prefer more bracing air."

Erskine came back with the cigarettes. He offered the box to Gwenda.

"You'll find it bracing enough round here," he said. There was a certain grimness in his voice.

Gwenda looked up at him as he lighted her cigarette for her.

"Do you remember Dillmouth at all well?" she asked artlessly.

His lips twitched in what she guessed to be a sudden spasm of pain. In a noncommittal voice he answered:

"Quite fairly well, I think. We stayed—let me see—at the Royal George—no, Royal Clarence Hotel."

"Oh yes, that's the nice old-fashioned one. Our house is quite near there. Hillside it's called, but it used to be called St.—St.—Mary's, was it, Giles?"

"St. Catherine's," said Giles.

This time there was no mistaking the reaction. Erskine turned sharply away, Mrs. Erskine's cup clattered on her saucer.

"Perhaps," she said abruptly, "you would like to see the garden."

"Oh yes, please."

They went out through the French windows. It was a well-kept, well-stocked garden, with a long border and flagged walks. The care of it was principally Major Erskine's, so Gwenda gathered. Talking to her about roses, about herbaceous plants, Erskine's dark, sad face lit up. Gardening was clearly his enthusiasm.

When they finally took their leave and were driving away in the car, Giles asked hesitantly:

"Did you—did you drop it?"

Gwenda nodded.

"By the second clump of delphiniums." She looked down at her finger and twisted the wedding ring on it absently.

"And supposing you never find it again?"

"Well, it's not my real engagement ring. I wouldn't risk *that.*"

"I'm glad to hear it."

"I'm very, very sentimental about that ring. Do you remember what you said when you put it on my finger? A green emerald because I was an intriguing green-eyed little cat."

"I daresay," said Giles dispassionately, "that our peculiar form of endearments might sound odd to someone of, say, Miss Marple's generation."

"I wonder what she's doing now, the dear old thing. Sitting in the sun on the front?"

"Up to something—if I know her! Poking here, or prying there, or asking a few questions. I hope she doesn't ask too many one of these days."

"It's quite a natural thing to do—for an old lady, I mean. It's not as noticeable as though we did it."

Giles's face sobered again.

"That's why I don't like—" He broke off. "It's you having to do it that I mind. I can't bear the feeling that I sit at home and send you out to do the dirty work."

Gwenda ran a finger down his worried cheek.

"I know, darling, I know. But you must admit, it's tricky. It's impertinent to catechize a man about his past love affairs—but it's the kind of impertinence a woman can just get away with—if she's clever. And I mean to be clever."

"I know you're clever. But if Erskine is the man we are looking for—"

Gwenda said meditatively:

"I don't think he is."

"You mean we're barking up the wrong tree?"

"Not entirely. I think he was in love with Helen all right. But he's *nice*, Giles; awfully nice. Not the strangling kind at all."

"You haven't an awful lot of experience of the strangling kind, have you, Gwenda?"

"No. But I've got my woman's instinct."

"I daresay that's what a strangler's victims often say. No, Gwenda, joking apart, do be careful, won't you?"

"Of course. I feel so sorry for the poor man—that dragon of a wife. I bet he's had a miserable life."

"She's an odd woman. . . . Rather alarming somehow."

"Yes, quite sinister. Did you see how she watched me all the time?"

"I hope the plan will go off all right."

III

The plan was put into execution the following morning.

Giles, feeling, as he put it, rather like a shady detective in a divorce suit, took up his position at a point of vantage overlooking the front gate of Anstell Manor. About half-past eleven he reported to Gwenda that all had gone well. Mrs. Erskine had left in a small Austin car, clearly bound for the market town three miles away. The coast was clear.

Gwenda drove up to the front door and rang the bell. She asked for Mrs. Erskine and was told she was out. She then asked for Major Erskine. Major Erskine was in the garden. He straightened up from operations on a flower bed as Gwenda approached.

"I'm so sorry to bother you," said Gwenda. "But I think I must have dropped a ring somewhere out here yesterday. I know I had it when we came out from tea. It's rather loose, but I couldn't bear to lose it because it's my engagement ring."

The hunt was soon under way. Gwenda retraced her steps of yesterday, tried to recollect where she had stood and what flowers she had touched. Presently the ring came to light near a large clump of delphiniums. Gwenda was profuse in her relief.

"And now can I get you a drink, Mrs. Reed? Beer? A glass of sherry? Or would you prefer coffee, or something like that?"

"I don't want anything—no, really. Just a cigarette—thanks."

She sat down on a bench and Erskine sat down beside her.

They smoked for a few minutes in silence. Gwenda's heart was beating rather fast. No two ways about it. She had got to take the plunge.

"I want to ask you something," she said. "Perhaps you'll think it terribly impertinent of me. But I want to know dreadfully—and you're probably the only person who could tell me. I believe you were once in love with my stepmother."

He turned an astonished face towards her.

"With your stepmother?"

"Yes. Helen Kennedy. Helen Halliday as she became afterwards."

"I see." The man beside her was very quiet. His eyes looked out across the sunlit lawn unseeingly. The cigarette between his fingers smouldered. Quiet as he was, Gwenda sensed a turmoil within that taut figure, the arm of which touched her own.

As though answering some question he had put to himself, Erskine said:

"Letters, I suppose."

Gwenda did not answer.

"I never wrote her many—two, perhaps three. She said she had destroyed them—but women never do destroy letters, do they? And so they came into *your* hands. And you want to know."

"I want to know more about her. I was—very fond of her. Although I was such a small child when—she went away."

"She went away?"

"Didn't you know?"

His eyes, candid and surprised, met hers.

"I've no news of her," he said, "since—since that summer in Dillmouth."

"Then you don't know where she is now?"

"How should I? It's years ago—years. All finished and done with—forgotten."

"Forgotten?"

He smiled rather bitterly.

"No, perhaps not forgotten. . . . You're very perceptive, Mrs. Reed. But tell me about her. She's not—dead, is she?"

A small cold wind sprang up suddenly, chilled their necks and passed.

"I don't know if she is dead or not," said Gwenda. "I don't know anything about her. I thought perhaps *you* might know?"

She went on as he shook his head:

"You see, she went away from Dillmouth that summer. Quite suddenly one evening. Without telling anyone. And she never came back."

"And you thought I might have heard from her?"

"Yes."

He shook his head.

"No. Never a word. But surely her brother—doctor chap—lives in Dillmouth. He must know. Or is he dead too?"

"No, he's alive. But he doesn't know either. You see—they all thought she went away—with somebody."

He turned his head to look at her. Deep sorrowful eyes.

"They thought she went away with *me?*"

"Well, it was a possibility."

"Was it a possibility? I don't think so. It was never that. Or were we fools—conscientious fools who passed up our chance of happiness?"

Gwenda did not speak. Again Erskine turned his head and looked at her.

"Perhaps you'd better hear about it. There isn't really very much to hear. But I wouldn't like you to misjudge Helen. We met on a boat going out to India. One of the children had been ill, and my wife was following on the next boat. Helen was going out to marry a man in the Woods and Forests or something of that kind. She didn't love him. He was just an old friend, nice and kind, and she wanted to get away from home, where she wasn't happy. We fell in love."

He paused.

"Always a bald kind of statement. But it wasn't—I want to make that quite clear—just the usual shipboard love affair. It was serious. We were both—well—shattered by it. And there wasn't anything to be done. I couldn't let Janet and the children down. Helen saw it the same way as I did. If it had been only Janet—but there were the boys. It was all hopeless. We agreed to say good-bye and try and forget."

He laughed, a short mirthless laugh.

"Forget? I never forgot—not for one moment. Life was just a living hell. I couldn't stop thinking about Helen. . . .

"Well, she didn't marry the chap she had been going out to marry. At the last moment, she just couldn't face it. She went home to England and on the way home she met this other man—your father, I suppose. She wrote to me a couple of months later telling me what she had done. He was very unhappy over the loss of his wife, she said, and there was a child. She thought that she could make him happy and that it was the best thing to do. She wrote from Dillmouth. About eight months later my father died and I came into this place. I sent in my papers and came back to England. We wanted a few weeks' holiday until we could get into this house. My wife suggested Dillmouth. Some friend had mentioned it as a pretty place and quiet. She didn't know, of course, about Helen— Can you imagine the temptation? To see her again. To see what this man she had married was like."

There was a short silence, then Erskine said:

"We came and stayed at the Royal Clarence. It was a mistake. Seeing Helen again was hell. . . . She seemed happy enough, on the whole—I don't know. She avoided being alone with me. . . .

I didn't know whether she cared still, or whether she didn't. . . . Perhaps she'd got over it. My wife, I think, suspected something. . . . She's—she's a very jealous woman—always has been."

He added brusquely:

"That's all there is to it. We left Dillmouth—"

"On August seventeenth," said Gwenda.

"Was that the date? Probably. I can't remember exactly."

"It was a Saturday," said Gwenda.

"Yes, you're right. I remember Janet said it might be a crowded day to travel north—but I don't think it was. . . ."

"Please try and remember, Major Erskine. When was the last time you saw my stepmother—Helen?"

He smiled a gentle tired smile.

"I don't need to try very hard. I saw her the evening before we left. On the beach. I'd strolled down there after dinner—and she was there. There was no one else about. I walked up with her to her house. We went through the garden—"

"What time?"

"I don't know . . . Nine o'clock, I suppose."

"And you said good-bye?"

"And we said good-bye." Again he laughed. "Oh, not the kind of good-bye you're thinking of. It was very brusque and curt. Helen said: 'Please go away now. Go quickly. I'd rather not—' She stopped then—and I—I just went."

"Back to the hotel?"

"Yes, yes, eventually. I walked a long way first—right out into the country."

Gwenda said:

"It's difficult with dates—after so many years. But I think that that was the night that she went away—and didn't come back."

"I see. And as I and my wife left the next day, people gossiped and said she'd gone away with me. Charming minds people have."

"Anyway," said Gwenda bluntly, "she didn't go away with you?"

"Good Lord, no. There was never any question of such a thing."

"Then why do you think," asked Gwenda, "that she went away?"

Erskine frowned. His manner changed, became interested.

"I see," he said. "That is a bit of a problem. She didn't—er—leave any explanation?"

Gwenda considered. Then she voiced her own belief.

"I don't think she left any word at all. Do you think she went away with someone else?"

"No, of course she didn't."

"You seem rather sure about that."

"I am sure."

"Then why did she go?"

"If she went off—suddenly—like that—I can only see one possible reason. She was running *away* from me."

"From you?"

"Yes. She was afraid, perhaps, that I'd try to see her again—that I'd pester her. She must have seen that I was still—crazy about her. . . . Yes, that must have been it."

"It doesn't explain," said Gwenda, "why she never came back. Tell me, did Helen say anything to you about my father? That she was worried about him? Or—or afraid of him? Anything like that?"

"Afraid of him? Why? Oh, I see, you thought he might have been jealous. Was he a jealous man?"

"I don't know. He died when I was a child."

"Oh, I see. No—looking back—he always seemed normal and pleasant. He was fond of Helen, proud of her. I don't think more. No, I was the one who was jealous of *him*."

"They seemed to you reasonably happy together?"

"Yes, they did. I was glad—and yet, at the same time, it hurt, to see it. . . . No, Helen never discussed him with me. As I tell you, we were hardly ever alone, never confidential together. But now that you have mentioned it, I do remember thinking that Helen was worried. . . ."

"Worried?"

"Yes. I thought perhaps it was because of my wife—" He broke off. "But it was more than that."

He looked again sharply at Gwenda.

"Was she afraid of her husband? Was he jealous of other men where she was concerned?"

"You seem to think not."

"Jealousy is a very queer thing. It can hide itself sometimes so that you'd never suspect it." He gave a short quick shiver. "But it can be frightening—very frightening. . . ."

"Another thing I would like to know—" Gwenda broke off.

A car had come up the drive. Major Erskine said:

"Ah, my wife has come back from shopping."

In a moment, as it were, he became a different person. His tone was easy yet formal, his face expressionless. A slight tremor betrayed that he was nervous.

Mrs. Erskine came striding round the corner of the house.

Her husband went towards her.

"Mrs. Reed dropped one of her rings in the garden yesterday," he said.

Mrs. Erskine said abruptly:

"Indeed?"

"Good morning," said Gwenda. "Yes, luckily I have found it."

"That's very fortunate."

"Oh, it is. I should have hated to lose it. Well, I must be going."

Mrs. Erskine said nothing. Major Erskine said:

"I'll see you to your car."

He started to follow Gwenda along the terrace. His wife's voice came sharply.

"Richard. If Mrs. Reed will excuse you, there is a very important call—"

Gwenda said hastily:

"Oh, that's quite all right. Please don't bother."

She ran quickly along the terrace and round the side of the house to the drive.

Then she stopped. Mrs. Erskine had drawn up her car in such a way that Gwenda doubted whether she could get her own car past and down the drive. She hesitated, then slowly retraced her steps to the terrace.

Just short of the French windows she stopped dead. Mrs. Erskine's voice, deep and resonant, came distinctly to her ears.

"I don't care what you say. You arranged it—arranged it yesterday. You fixed it up with that girl to come here while I was in Daith. You're always the same—any pretty girl. I won't stand it, I tell you. I won't stand it."

Erskine's voice cut in—quiet, almost despairing.

"Sometimes, Janet, I really think you're insane."

"I'm not the one who's insane. It's *you!* You can't leave women alone."

"You know that's not true, Janet."

"It *is* true! Even long ago—in the place where this girl comes from—Dillmouth. Do you dare tell me that you weren't in love with that yellow-haired Halliday woman?"

"Can you never forget anything? Why must you go on harping on these things. You simply work yourself up and—"

"It's you! You break my heart. . . . I won't stand it, I tell you! I won't stand it! Planning assignations! Laughing at me behind my back! You don't care for me—you've never cared for me. I'll kill myself! I'll throw myself over a cliff— I wish I were dead—"

"Janet—Janet—for God's sake. . . ."

The deep voice had broken. The sound of passionate sobbing floated out into the summer air.

On tiptoe Gwenda crept away and round into the drive again. She cogitated for a moment, then rang the front door bell.

"I wonder," she said, "if there is anyone who—er—could move this car. I don't think I can get out."

The servant went into the house. Presently a man came round from what had been the stableyard. He touched his cap to Gwenda, got into the Austin and drove it into the yard. Gwenda got into her car and drove rapidly back to the hotel, where Giles was waiting for her.

"What a time you've been," he greeted her. "Get anything?"

"Yes. I know all about it now. It's really rather pathetic. He was terribly in love with Helen."

She narrated the events of the morning.

"I really think," she ended, "that Mrs. Erskine is a bit insane. She sounded quite mad. I see now what he meant by jealousy. It must be awful to feel like that. Anyway, we know now that Erskine wasn't the man who went away with Helen, and that he knows nothing about her death. She was alive that evening when he left her."

"Yes," said Giles. "At least—that's what he says."

Gwenda looked indignant.

"That," repeated Giles firmly, "is what he *says*."

18

Bindweed

Miss Marple bent down on the terrace outside the French window and dealt with some insidious bindweed. It was only a minor victory, since beneath the surface the bindweed remained in possession as always. But at least the delphiniums knew a temporary deliverance.

Mrs. Cocker appeared in the drawing-room window.

"Excuse me, madam, but Dr. Kennedy has called. He is anxious to know how long Mr. and Mrs. Reed will be away, and I told him I couldn't take it upon myself to say exactly, but that you might know. Shall I ask him to come out here?"

"Oh. Oh, yes, please, Mrs. Cocker."

Mrs. Cocker reappeared shortly afterwards with Dr. Kennedy. Rather flutteringly, Miss Marple introduced herself.

"—and I arranged with dear Gwenda that I would come round and do a little weeding while she was away. I think, you know, that my young friends are being imposed upon by their jobbing gardener, Foster. He comes twice a week, drinks a great many cups of tea, does a lot of talking, and not—so far as I can see, very much work."

"Yes," said Dr. Kennedy rather absently. "Yes. They're all alike —all alike."

Miss Marple looked at him appraisingly. He was an older man than she had thought from the Reeds' description of him. Prematurely old, she guessed. He looked, too, both worried and unhappy. He stood there, his fingers caressing the long pugnacious line of his jaw.

"They've gone away," he said. "Do you know for how long?"

"Oh, not for long. They have gone to visit some friends in the North of England. Young people seem to me so restless, always dashing about here and there."

"Yes," said Dr. Kennedy. "Yes—that's true enough."

He paused and then said rather diffidently:

"Young Giles Reed wrote and asked me for some papers—or—letters, if I could find them—"

He hesitated, and Miss Marple said quietly:

"Your sister's letters?"

He shot her a quick, shrewd glance.

"So—you're in their confidence, are you? A relation?"

"Only a friend," said Miss Marple. "I have advised them to the best of my capacity. But people seldom take advice . . . A pity, perhaps, but there it is. . . ."

"What was your advice?" he asked curiously.

"To let sleeping murder lie," said Miss Marple firmly.

Dr. Kennedy sat down heavily on an uncomfortable rustic seat.

"That's not badly put," he said. "I'm fond of Gwennie. She was a nice small child. I should judge that she's grown up to be a nice young woman. I'm afraid that she's heading for trouble."

"There are so many kinds of trouble," said Miss Marple.

"Eh? Yes—yes—true enough."

He sighed. Then he said:

"Giles Reed wrote and asked me if I could let him have my sister's letters, written after she left here—and also some authentic specimen of her handwriting." He shot a keen glance at her. "You see what that means?"

Miss Marple nodded. "I think so."

"They're harking back to the idea that Kelvin Halliday, when he said he had strangled his wife, was speaking neither more nor less than the truth. They believe that the letters my sister Helen wrote after she went away weren't written by her at all—that they were forgeries. They believe that she never left this house alive."

Miss Marple said gently:

"And you are not, by now, so very sure yourself?"

"I was at the time." Kennedy still stared ahead of him. "It seemed absolutely clear. Pure hallucination on Kelvin's part. There was no body, a suitcase and clothes were taken—what else could I think?"

"And your sister had been—recently—rather—ahem"—Miss Marple coughed delicately—"interested in—in a certain gentleman?"

Dr. Kennedy looked at her. There was deep pain in his eyes.

"I loved my sister," he said, "but I have to admit that, with Helen, there was always some man in the offing. There are women who are made that way—they can't help it."

"It all seemed clear to you at the time," said Miss Marple. "But it does not seem so clear now. Why?"

"Because," said Kennedy with frankness, "it seems incredible to me that, if Helen is still alive, she has not communicated with me all these years. In the same way, if she is dead, it is equally strange that I have not been notified of the fact. Well—"

He got up. He took a packet from his pocket.

"Here is the best I can do. The first letter I received from Helen I must have destroyed. I can find no trace of it. But I did keep the second one—the one that gave the poste restante address. And here, for comparison, is the only bit of Helen's handwriting I've been able to find. It's a list of bulbs, and so forth, for planting. A copy that she had kept of some order. The handwriting of the order and the letter look alike to me, but then I'm no expert. I'll leave them here for Giles and Gwenda when they return. It's probably not worth forwarding."

"Oh no, I believe they expect to return tomorrow—or the next day."

The doctor nodded. He stood, looking along the terrace, his eyes still absent. He said suddenly:

"You know what's worrying me? If Kelvin Halliday did kill his wife, he must have concealed the body or got rid of it in some way—and that means (I don't know what else it can mean) that his story to me was a cleverly made-up tale—that he'd already hidden a suitcase full of clothes to give colour to the idea that Helen had gone away—that he'd even arranged for letters to arrive from abroad. . . . It means, in fact, that it was a cold-blooded, premeditated murder. Little Gwennie was a nice child. It would be bad enough for her to have a father who's a paranoiac, but it's ten times worse to have a father who's a deliberate murderer."

He swung round to the open window. Miss Marple arrested his departure by a swift question.

"Who was your sister afraid of, Dr. Kennedy?"

He turned back to her and stared.

"Afraid of? No one, as far as I know."

"I only wondered. . . . Pray excuse me if I am asking indiscreet questions—but there was a young man, wasn't there—I mean, some entanglement—when she was very young? Somebody called *Afflick*, I believe."

"Oh, that? Silly business most girls go through. An undesirable young fellow, shifty—and of course not her class, not her class at all. He got into trouble here afterwards."

"I just wondered if he could have been—revengeful."

Dr. Kennedy smiled rather sceptically.

"Oh, I don't think it went deep. Anyway, as I say, he got into trouble here, and left the place for good."

"What sort of trouble?"

"Oh, nothing criminal. Just indiscretions. Blabbed about his employer's affairs."

"And his employer was Mr. Walter Fane?"

Dr. Kennedy looked a little surprised.

"Yes—yes—now you say so, I remember, he did work in Fane and Watchman's. Not articled. Just an ordinary clerk."

Just an ordinary clerk? . . . Miss Marple wondered, as she stooped again to the bindweed after Dr. Kennedy had gone. . . .

19

Mr. Kimble Speaks

"I DUNNO, I'm sure," said Mrs. Kimble.

Her husband, driven into speech by what was neither more nor less than an outrage, became vocal.

He shoved his cup forward.

"What you thinking of, Lily?" he demanded. "*No sugar!*"

Mrs. Kimble hastily remedied the outrage, and then proceeded to elaborate on her own theme.

"Thinking about this advert, I am," she said. "Lily Abbott it says, plain as plain. And 'formerly house-parlourmaid at St. Catherine's Dillmouth.' That's me, all right."

"Ar," agreed Mr. Kimble.

"After all these years—you must agree it's odd, Jim."

"Ar," said Mr. Kimble.

"Well, what am I going to do, Jim?"

"Leave it be."

"Suppose there's money in it?"

There was a gurgling sound as Mr. Kimble drained his teacup to fortify himself for the mental effort of embarking on a long speech. He pushed his cup along and prefaced his remarks with a laconic "More." Then he got under way.

"You went on a lot at one time about what 'appened at St. Catherine's. I didn't take much account of it—reckoned as it was mostly foolishness—women's chatter. Maybe it wasn't. Maybe something did 'appen. If so, it's police business and you don't want to be mixed up in it. All over and done with, ain't it? You leave well alone, my girl."

"All very well to say that. It may be money as has been left me in a will. Maybe Mrs. Halliday's alive all the time and now she's dead and left me something in 'er will."

"Left you something in 'er will? What for? Ar!" said Mr. Kimble, reverting to his favourite monosyllable to express scorn.

"Even if it's police. . . . You know, Jim, there's a big reward sometimes for anyone as can give information to catch a murderer."

"And what could you give? All you know you made up yourself in your head!"

"That's what you say. But I've been thinking—"

"Ar," said Mr. Kimble disgustedly.

"Well, I have. Ever since I saw that first piece in the paper. Maybe I got things a bit wrong. That Layonee, she was a bit stupid like all foreigners, couldn't understand proper what you said to her—and her English was something awful. If she didn't mean what I thought she meant . . . I've been trying to remember the name of that man. . . . Now if it was him she saw. . . . Remember that picture I told you about? 'Secret Lover.' Ever so exciting. They tracked him down in the end through his car. Fifty thousand dollars he paid the garage man to forget he filled up with petrol that night. Dunno what that is in pounds. . . . And the other one was there, too, and the husband crazy with jealousy. All mad about her, they were. And in the end—"

Mr. Kimble pushed back his chair with a grating sound. He rose to his feet with slow and ponderous authority. Preparatory to leaving the kitchen, he delivered an ultimatum—the ultimatum of a man who, though usually inarticulate, had a certain shrewdness.

"You leave the whole thing alone, my girl," he said. "Or else, likely as not, you'll be sorry."

He went into the scullery, put on his boots (Lily was particular about her kitchen floor) and went out.

Lily sat on at the table, her sharp, foolish little brain working things out. Of course she couldn't exactly go against what her husband said, but all the same. . . . Jim was so hidebound, so stick-in-the-mud. She wished there was somebody else she could ask—someone who would know all about rewards and the police and what it all meant. Pity to turn up a chance of good money.

That wireless set . . . the home perm . . . that cherry-colour coat in Russell's (ever so smart) . . . even, maybe, a whole Jacobean suite for the sitting room. . . .

Eager, greedy, shortsighted, she went on dreaming. . . . What exactly *had* Layonee said all those years ago?

Then an idea came to her. She got up and fetched the bottle of ink, the pen, and a pad of writing paper.

"Know what I'll do," she said to herself. "I'll write to the doctor, Mrs. Halliday's brother. He'll tell me what I ought to do—if he's alive still, that is. Anyway, it's on my conscience I never told him about Layonee—or about that car."

There was silence for some time apart from the laborious scratching of Lily's pen. It was very seldom that she wrote a letter and she found the composition of it a considerable effort.

However, it was done at last and she put it into an envelope and sealed it up.

But she felt less satisfied than she had expected. Ten to one the doctor was dead or had gone away from Dillmouth.

Was there anyone else?

What was the name, now, of that fellow—

If she could only remember *that*. . . .

20

The Girl Helen

GILES AND GWENDA had just finished breakfast on the morning after their return from Northumberland when Miss Marple was announced. She came in rather apologetically.

"I'm afraid this is a very early call. Not a thing I am in the habit of doing. But there was something I wanted to explain."

"We're delighted to see you," said Giles, pulling out a chair for her. "Do have a cup of coffee."

"Oh no, no, thank you—nothing at all. I have breakfasted *most* adequately. Now let me explain. I came in whilst you were away, as you kindly said I might, to do a little weeding—"

"Angelic of you," said Gwenda.

"And it really did strike me that two days a week is not quite enough for this garden. In any case, I think Foster is taking advantage of you. Too much tea and too much talk. I found out that he couldn't manage another day himself, so I took it upon myself to engage another man just for one day a week—Wednesdays—today, in fact."

Giles looked at her curiously. He was a little surprised. It might be kindly meant, but Miss Marple's action savoured, very faintly, of interference. And interference was unlike her.

He said slowly:

"Foster's far too old, I know, for really hard work."

"I'm afraid, Mr. Reed, that Manning is even older. Seventy-five, he tells me. But you see, I thought employing him, just for a few odd days, might be quite an advantageous move, because he used, many years ago, to be employed at Dr. Kennedy's. The name of the young man Helen got engaged to was Afflick, by the way."

"Miss Marple," said Giles, "I maligned you in thought. You are a genius. You know I've got those specimens of Helen's handwriting from Kennedy?"

"I know. I was here when he brought them."

"I'm posting them off today. I got the address of a good handwriting expert last week."

"Let's go into the garden and see Manning," said Gwenda.

Manning was a bent, crabbed-looking old man with a rheumy and slightly cunning eye. The pace at which he was raking a path accelerated noticeably as his employers drew near.

"Morning, sir. Morning, m'am. The lady said as how you could do with a little extra help of a Wednesday. I'll be pleased. Shameful neglected, this place looks."

"I'm afraid the garden's been allowed to run down for some years."

"It has that. Remember it, I do, in Mrs. Findeyson's time. A picture it were then. Very fond of her garden she was, Mrs. Findeyson."

Giles leaned easily against a roller. Gwenda snipped off some rose heads. Miss Marple, retreating a little upstage, bent to the bindweed. Old Manning leant on his rake. All was set for a leisurely morning discussion of old times and gardening in the good old days.

"I suppose you know most of the gardens round here," said Giles encouragingly.

"Ar, I know this place moderate well, I do. And the fancies people went in for. Mrs. Yule, up at Niagra, she had a yew hedge used to be clipped like a squirrel. Silly, I thought it. Peacocks is one thing and squirrels is another. Then Colonel Lampard, he was a great man for begonias—lovely beds of begonias he used to have. Bedding out now, that's going out of fashion. I wouldn't like to tell you how often I've had to fill up beds in the front lawns and turf 'em over in the last six years. Seems people ain't got no eye for geraniums and a nice bit of lobelia edging no more."

"You worked at Dr. Kennedy's, didn't you?"

"Ar. Long time ago, that were. Must have been nineteen twenty and on. He's moved now—given up. Young Dr. Brent's up at Crosby Lodge now. Funny ideas, he has—little white tablets, and so on. Vittapins he calls 'em."

"I suppose you remember Miss Helen Kennedy, the doctor's sister."

"Ar, I remember Miss Helen right enough. Pretty maid, she

was, with her long yellow hair. The doctor set a lot of store by her. Come back and lived in this very house here, she did, after she was married. Army gentleman from India."

"Yes," said Gwenda. "We know."

"Ar. I did 'ear—Saturday night it was—as you and your 'usband was some kind of relations. Pretty as a picter, Miss Helen was, when she first come back from school. Full of fun, too. Wanting to go everywhere—dances and tennis and all that. 'Ad to mark the tennis court, I 'ad—hadn't been used for nigh twenty years, I'd say. And the shrubs overgrowing it cruel. 'Ad to cut 'em back, I did. *And* get a lot of whitewash and mark out the lines. Lot of work it made—and in the end hardly played on. Funny thing I always thought that was."

"What was a funny thing?" asked Giles.

"Business with the tennis net. Someone come along one night—and cut it to ribbons. Just to ribbons it was. Spite, as you might say. That was what it was—nasty bit of spite."

"But who would do a thing like that?"

"That's what the doctor wanted to know. Proper put out about it he was—and I don't blame him. Just paid for it, he had. But none of us could tell who'd done it. We never did know. And he said he wasn't going to get another—quite right, too, for if it's spite one time, it would be spite again. But Miss Helen, she was rare put out. She didn't have no luck, Miss Helen didn't. First that net—and then her bad foot."

"A bad foot?" asked Gwenda.

"Yes—fell over a scraper or somesuch and cut it. Not much more than a graze, it seemed, but it wouldn't heal. Fair worried about it, the doctor was. He was dressing it and treating it, but it didn't get well. I remember him saying: 'I can't understand it—there must have been something spectic—or some word like that—on that scraper. And anyway,' he says, 'what was the scraper doing out in the middle of the drive?' Because that's where it was when Miss Helen fell over it, walking home on a dark night. The poor maid, there she was, missing going to dances and sitting about with her foot up. Seemed as though there were nothing but bad luck for her."

The moment had come, Giles thought. He asked casually:

"Do you remember somebody called Afflick?"

"Ar. You mean Jackie Afflick? As was in Fane and Watchman's office?"

"Yes. Wasn't he a friend of Miss Helen's?"

"That were just a bit of nonsense. Doctor put a stop to it and quite right too. He wasn't any class, Jackie Afflick. And he was the kind that's too sharp by half. Cut themselves in the end, that kind do. But he weren't here long. Got himself into hot water. Good riddance. Us don't want the likes of he in Dillmouth. Go and be smart somewhere else, that's what he were welcome to do."

Gwenda asked:

"Was he here when that tennis net was cut up?"

"Ar. I see what you're thinking. But he wouldn't do a senseless thing like that. He were smart, Jackie Afflick were. Whoever did that, it was just spite."

"Was there anybody who had a down on Miss Helen? Who would be likely to feel spiteful?"

Old Manning chuckled softly.

"Some of the young ladies might have felt spiteful all right. Not a patch on Miss Helen to look at, most of 'em weren't. No, I'd say that was done just in foolishness. Some tramp with a grudge."

"Was Helen very upset about Jackie Afflick?" asked Gwenda.

"Don't think as Miss Helen cared much about any of the young fellows. Just liked to enjoy herself, that's all. Very devoted some of them were—young Mr. Walter Fane for one. Used to follow her round like a dog."

"But she didn't care for him at all?"

"Not Miss Helen. Just laughed—that's all she did. Went abroad to foreign parts, he did. But he come back later. Top one in the firm he is now. Never married. I don't blame him. Women causes a lot of trouble in a man's life."

"Are you married?" asked Gwenda.

"Buried two, I have," said old Manning. "Ar, well, I can't complain. Smoke me pipe in peace where I likes now."

In the ensuing silence, he picked up his rake again.

Giles and Gwenda walked back up the path towards the house and Miss Marple, desisting from her attack on bindweed, joined them.

"Miss Marple," said Gwenda. "You don't look well. Is there anything—"

"It's nothing, my dear." The old lady paused for a moment before saying with a strange kind of insistence: "You know, I don't like that bit about the tennis net. Cutting it to ribbons. . . . Even then—"

She stopped. Giles looked at her curiously.

"I don't quite understand—" he began.

"Don't you? It seems so horribly plain to me. But perhaps it's better that you shouldn't understand. And anyway—perhaps I am wrong. Now do tell me how you got on in Northumberland."

They gave her an account of their activities, and Miss Marple listened attentively.

"It's really all very sad," said Gwenda. "Quite tragic, in fact."

"Yes, indeed. Poor thing—poor thing."

"That's what I felt. How that man must suffer—"

"He? Oh yes. Yes, of course."

"But you meant—"

"Well, yes—I was thinking of *her*—of the wife. Probably very deeply in love with him, and he married her because she was suitable, or because he was sorry for her, or for one of those quite kindly and sensible reasons that men often have, and which are actually so terribly unfair."

> "I know a hundred ways of love,
> And each one makes the loved one rue,"

quoted Giles softly.

Miss Marple turned to him.

"Yes, that is so true. Jealousy, you know, is usually not an affair of *causes*. It is much more—how shall I say?—fundamental than that. Based on the knowledge that one's love is not returned. . . . And so one goes on waiting, watching, expecting . . . that the loved one will turn to someone else. Which, again, invariably happens. So this Mrs. Erskine has made life a hell for her husband, and he, without being able to help it, has made life a hell for her. But I think she has suffered most. And yet, you know, I daresay he is really quite fond of her."

"He can't be," cried Gwenda.

"Oh, my dear, you are very young. He has never left his wife, and that means something, you know."

"Because of the children. Because it was his duty."

"The children, perhaps," said Miss Marple. "But I must confess that gentlemen do not seem to me to have a great regard for duty in so far as their wives are concerned—public service is another matter."

Giles laughed.

"What a wonderful cynic you are, Miss Marple."

"Oh, dear, Mr. Reed, I *do* hope not *that*. One always has *hope* for human nature."

"I still don't feel it can have been Walter Fane," said Gwenda thoughtfully. "And I'm sure it wasn't Major Erskine. In fact I *know* it wasn't."

"One's feelings are not always reliable guides," said Miss Marple. "The most unlikely people do things—quite a sensation there was in my own little village when the treasurer of the Christmas club was found to have put every penny of the funds on a horse. He disapproved of horse racing and indeed any kind of betting or gambling. His father had been a turf agent and had treated his mother very badly—so, intellectually speaking, he was quite sincere. But he chanced one day to be motoring near Newmarket and saw some horses training. And then it all came over him—Blood does tell."

"The antecedents of both Walter Fane and Richard Erskine seem above suspicion," said Giles gravely but with a slight amused twist to his mouth. "But then murder is by way of being an amateur crime."

"The important thing is," said Miss Marple, "that they were *there*. On the spot. Walter Fane was here in Dillmouth. Major Erskine, by his own account, must actually have been with Helen Halliday very shortly before her death—*and* he did not return to his hotel for some time that night."

"But he was quite frank about it. He—"

Gwenda broke off. Miss Marple was looking at her very hard.

"I only want to emphasize," said Miss Marple, "the importance of being *on the spot*." She looked from one to the other of them.

Then she said: "I think you will have no trouble in finding out J. J. Afflick's address. As proprietor of the Daffodil Coaches, it should be easy enough."

Giles nodded. "I'll get onto it. Probably in the telephone directory." He paused. "You think we should go and see him?"

Miss Marple waited for a moment or two, then she said:

"If you do—you must be very careful. Remember what that old gardener just said—Jackie Afflick is smart. . . . Please—*please* be careful. . . ."

21

J. J. Afflick

J. J. Afflick, Daffodil Coaches, Devon & Dorset Tours, etc., had two numbers listed in the telephone book. An office address in Exeter and a private address on the outskirts of that town.

An appointment was made for the following day.

Just as Giles and Gwenda were leaving in the car, Mrs. Cocker ran out and gesticulated. Giles put on the brake and stopped.

"It's Dr. Kennedy on the telephone, sir."

Giles got out and ran back. He picked up the receiver.

"Giles Reed here."

"Morning. I've just received rather an odd letter. From a woman called Lily Kimble. I've been racking my brains to remember who she is. Thought of a patient first—that put me off the scent. But I rather fancy she must be a girl who was in service once at your house. House-parlourmaid at the time we know of. I'm almost sure her name was Lily, though I don't recollect her last name."

"There *was* a Lily. Gwenda remembers her. She tied a bow on the cat."

"Gwennie must have a very remarkable memory."

"Oh, she has."

"Well, I'd like to have a word with you about this letter—not over the phone. Will you be in if I come over?"

"We're just on our way to Exeter. We could drop in on you, if you prefer, sir. It's all on our way."

"Good. That'll do splendidly."

"I don't like to talk too much about all this over the phone," explained the doctor when they arrived. "I always have an idea the local exchanges listen in. Here's the woman's letter."

He spread the letter on the table. It was written on cheap lined paper in an uneducated hand.

Dear sir [Lily Kimble had written]

Id be grateful if you could give me advise about the enclosed wot i cut out of paper. i been thinking and i talked it over with mr Kimble, but i don't know wots best to do about it. Do you think as it means money or a reword becos i could do with the money im sure but woodnt want the police or anything like that. i offen hav been thinking about that nite wen mrs Halliday went away and i don't think sir she ever did becos the clothes was wrong. i thort at first the master done it but now im not so sure becos of the car i saw out of the window. A posh car it was and i seen it before but i woodnt like to do anything without asking you furst if it was all rite and not police becos i never hav been mixed up with police and mr Kimble woodnt like it. I could come and see you sir if i may next thursday as its market day and mr Kimble will be out. id be very grateful if you could

yours respectfully
Lily Kimble.

"It was addressed to my old house in Dillmouth," said Kennedy, "and forwarded on to me here. The cutting is your advertisement."

"It's wonderful," said Gwenda. "This Lily—you see—she *doesn't* think it was my father who did it!"

She spoke with jubilation. Dr. Kennedy looked at her with tired kindly eyes.

"Good for you, Gwennie," he said gently. "I hope you're right. Now this is what I think we'd better do. I'll answer her letter and tell her to come here on Thursday. The train connection is quite good. By changing at Dillmouth Junction she can get here shortly after four-thirty. If you two will come over that afternoon, we can tackle her all together."

"Splendid," said Giles. He glanced at his watch. "Come on, Gwenda, we must hurry. We've got an appointment," he explained. "With Mr. Afflick of the Daffodil Coaches, and, so he told us, he's a busy man."

"Afflick?" Kennedy frowned. "Of course! Devon Tours in Daffodil Coaches, horrible great butter-coloured brutes. But the name seemed familiar in some other way."

"Helen," said Gwenda.

"My goodness—not that chap?"

"Yes."

"But he was a miserable little rat. So he's come up in the world?"

"Will you tell me something, sir," said Giles. "You broke up some funny business between him and Helen. Was that—simply—because of his—well, social position?"

Dr. Kennedy gave him a dry glance.

"I'm old-fashioned, young man. In the modern gospel, one man is as good as another. That holds morally, no doubt. But I'm a believer in the fact that there is a state of life into which you are born—and I believe you're happiest staying in it. Besides," he added, "I thought the fellow was a wrong 'un. As he proved to be."

"What did he do exactly?"

"That I can't remember now. It was a case, as far as I can recall, of his trying to cash in on some information obtained through his employment with Fane. Some confidential matter relating to one of their clients."

"Was he—sore about his dismissal?"

Kennedy gave him a sharp glance and said briefly:

"Yes."

"And there wasn't any other reason at all for your disliking his friendship with your sister? You didn't think he was—well—odd in any way?"

"Since you have brought the matter up, I will answer you frankly. It seemed to me, especially after his dismissal from his employment, that Jackie Afflick displayed certain signs of an unbalanced temperament. Incipient persecution mania, in fact. But that does not seem to have been borne out by his subsequent rise in life."

"Who dismissed him? Walter Fane?"

"I have no idea if Walter Fane was concerned. He was dismissed by the firm."

"And he complained that he had been victimized?"

Kennedy nodded.

"I see. . . . Well, we must drive like the wind. Till Thursday, sir."

II

The house was newly built. It was of snow-crete, heavily curved, with a big expanse of window. They were shown in through an opulent hall to a study, half of which was taken up by a big chromium-plated desk.

Gwenda murmured nervously to Giles, "Really, I don't know what we should have done without Miss Marple. We lean upon her at every turn. First her friends in Northumberland and now her vicar's wife's Boys' Club Annual Outing."

Giles raised an admonitory hand as the door opened and J. J. Afflick surged into the room.

He was a stout man of middle age, dressed in a rather violently checked suit. His eyes were dark and shrewd, his face rubicund and good-natured. He looked like the popular idea of a successful bookmaker.

"Mr. Reed? Good morning. Pleased to meet you."

Giles introduced Gwenda. She felt her hand taken in a rather overzealous grip.

"And what can I do for you, Mr. Reed?"

Afflick sat down behind his large desk. He offered cigarettes from an onyx box.

Giles entered upon the subject of the Boys' Club Outing. Old friends of his ran the show. He was anxious to arrange for a couple of days' touring in Devon.

Afflick replied promptly in a businesslike manner—quoting prices and making suggestions. But there was a faintly puzzled look on his face.

Finally he said:

"Well, that's all clear enough, Mr. Reed, and I'll send you a line to confirm it. But this is strictly office business. I understood from my clerk that you wanted a private appointment at my private address?"

"We did, Mr. Afflick. There were actually two matters on which I wanted to see you. We've disposed of one. The other is a purely private matter. My wife here is very anxious to get in touch with her stepmother, whom she has not seen for many years, and we wondered if you could possibly help us."

"Well, if you tell me the lady's name—I gather that I'm acquainted with her?"

"You were acquainted with her at one time. Her name is Helen Halliday and before her marriage she was Miss Helen Kennedy."

Afflick sat quite still. He screwed up his eyes and tilted his chair slowly backwards.

"Helen Halliday—I don't recall . . . Helen Kennedy . . ."

"Formerly of Dillmouth," said Giles.

The legs of Afflick's chair came down sharply.

"Got it," he said. "Of course." His round rubicund face beamed with pleasure. "Little Helen Kennedy! Yes, I remember her. But it's a long time ago. Must be twenty years."

"Eighteen."

"Is it really? Time flies, as the saying goes. But I'm afraid you're going to be disappointed, Mrs. Reed. I haven't seen anything of Helen since that time. Never heard of her, even."

"Oh, dear," said Gwenda. "That's very disappointing. We did so hope you could help."

"What's the trouble?" His eyes flickered quickly from one face to another. "Quarrel? Left home? Matter of money?"

Gwenda said:

"She went away—suddenly—from Dillmouth—eighteen years ago with—with someone."

Jackie Afflick said amusedly:

"And you thought she might have gone away with me? Now why?"

Gwenda spoke boldly:

"Because we heard that you—and she—had once—been—well, fond of each other."

"Me and Helen? Oh, but there was nothing in that. Just a boy and girl affair. Neither of us took it seriously." He added drily, "We weren't encouraged to do so."

"You must think us dreadfully impertinent," began Gwenda, but he interrupted her.

"What's the odds? I'm not sensitive. You want to find a certain person and you think I may be able to help. Ask me anything you please—I've nought to conceal." He looked at her thoughtfully. "So you're Halliday's daughter?"

"Yes. Did you know my father?"

He shook his head.

"I dropped in to see Helen once when I was over at Dillmouth on business. I'd heard she was married and living there. She was civil enough"—he paused—"but she didn't ask me to stay to dinner. No, I didn't meet your father."

Had there, Gwenda wondered, been a trace of rancour in that "She didn't ask me to stay to dinner"?

"Did she—if you remember—seem happy?"

Afflick shrugged his shoulders.

"Happy enough. But there, it's a long time ago. I'd have remembered if she'd looked unhappy."

He added with what seemed a perfectly natural curiosity:

"Do you mean to say you've never heard anything of her since Dillmouth eighteen years ago?"

"Nothing."

"No—letters?"

"There were two letters," said Giles. "But we have some reason to think that she didn't write them."

"You think she didn't write them?" Afflick seemed faintly amused. "Sounds like a mystery on the flicks."

"That's rather what it seems like to us."

"What about her brother, the doctor chap, doesn't he know where she is?"

"No."

"I see. Regular mystery, isn't it? Why not advertise?"

"We have."

Afflick said casually:

"Looks as though she's dead. You mightn't have heard."

Gwenda shivered.

"Cold, Mrs. Reed?"

"No. I was thinking of Helen dead. I don't like to think of her dead."

"You're right there. I don't like to think of it myself. Stunning looks she had."

Gwenda said impulsively:

"You knew her. You knew her well. I've only got a child's memory of her. What was she like? What did people feel about her? What did *you* feel?"

He looked at her for a moment or two.

"I'll be honest with you, Mrs. Reed. Believe it or not, as you like. I was sorry for the kid."

"Sorry?" She turned a puzzled stare on him.

"Just that. There she was—just home from school. Longing for a bit of fun like any girl might, and there was that stiff middle-aged brother of hers with his ideas about what a girl could do and couldn't do. No fun at all, that kid hadn't. Well, I took her about a bit—showed her a bit of life. I wasn't really keen on her and she wasn't really keen on me. She just liked the fun of being a daredevil. Then of course they found out we were meeting and he put a stop to it. Don't blame him really. Cut above me, she was. We weren't engaged or anything of that kind. I meant to marry sometime—but not till I was a good bit older. And I meant to get on and to find a wife who'd help me get on. Helen hadn't any money, and it wouldn't have been a suitable match in any way. We were just good friends with a bit of flirtation thrown in."

"But you must have been angry when the doctor—"

Gwenda paused and Afflick said:

"I was riled, I admit. You don't fancy being told you're not good enough. But there, it's no good being thin-skinned."

"And then," said Giles, "you lost your job."

Afflick's face was not quite so pleasant.

"Fired, I was. Out of Fane and Watchman's. And I've a very good idea who was responsible for that."

"Oh?" Giles made his tone interrogative, but Afflick shook his head.

"I'm not saying anything. I've my own ideas. I was framed—that's all—and I've a very fair idea of who did it. *And* why!" The colour suffused his cheeks. "Dirty work," he said. "Spying on a man—laying traps for him—lying about him. Oh, I've had my enemies all right. But I've never let them get me down. I've always given as good as I got. *And* I don't forget."

He stopped. Suddenly his manner changed back again. He was genial once more.

"So I can't help you, I'm afraid. A little bit of fun between me and Helen—that was all. It didn't go deep."

Gwenda stared at him. It was a clear enough story—but was it true? She wondered. Something jarred—it came to the surface of her mind what that something was.

"All the same," she said, "you looked her up when you came to Dillmouth later."

He laughed.

"You've got me there, Mrs. Reed. Yes, I did. Wanted to show her perhaps that I wasn't down and out just because a long-faced lawyer had pushed me out of his office. I had a nice business and I was driving a posh car and I'd done very well for myself."

"You came to see her more than once, didn't you?"

He hesitated a moment.

"Twice—perhaps three times. Just dropped in."

He nodded with sudden finality.

"Sorry I can't help you."

Giles got up.

"We must apologize for taking up so much of your time."

"That's all right. Quite a change to talk about old times."

The door opened and a woman looked in and apologized swiftly.

"Oh, I'm so sorry—I didn't know you had anyone—"

"Come in, my dear, come in. Meet my wife. This is Mr. and Mrs. Reed."

Mrs. Afflick shook hands. She was a tall, thin, depressed-looking woman, dressed in rather unexpectedly well-cut clothes.

"Been talking over old times, we have," said Mr. Afflick. "Old times before I met you, Dorothy."

He turned to them.

"Met my wife on a cruise," he said. "She doesn't come from this part of the world. Cousin of Lord Polterham's, she is."

He spoke with pride—the thin woman flushed.

"They're very nice, these cruises," said Giles.

"Very educational," said Afflick. "Now, I didn't have any education to speak of."

"I always tell my husband we must go on one of those Hellenic cruises," said Mrs. Afflick.

"No time. I'm a busy man."

"And we mustn't keep you," said Giles. "Good-bye and thank you. You'll let me know about the quotation for the outing?"

Afflick escorted them to the door. Gwenda glanced back over her shoulder. Mrs. Afflick was standing in the doorway of the study. Her face, fastened on her husband's back, was curiously and rather unpleasantly apprehensive.

Giles and Gwenda said good-bye again and went towards their car.

"Bother, I've left my scarf," said Gwenda.

"You're always leaving something," said Giles.

"Don't look martyred. I'll get it."

She ran back into the house. Through the open door of the study she heard Afflick say loudly:

"What do you want to come butting in for? Never any sense."

"I'm sorry, Jackie. I didn't know. Who are those people and why have they upset you so?"

"They haven't upset me. I—" He stopped as he saw Gwenda standing in the doorway.

"Oh, Mr. Afflick, did I leave a scarf?"

"Scarf? No, Mrs. Reed. It's not here."

"Stupid of me. It must be in the car."

She went out again.

Giles had turned the car. Drawn up by the curb was a large yellow limousine, resplendent with chromium.

"Some car," said Giles.

" 'A posh car,' " said Gwenda. "Do you remember, Giles? Edith Pagett when she was telling us what Lily said? Lily had put her money on Captain Erskine, not 'our mystery man in the flashy car.' Don't you see, the mystery man in the flashy car was Jackie Afflick?"

"Yes," said Giles. "And in her letter to the doctor Lily mentioned a 'posh car.' "

They looked at each other.

"He was there—'on the spot,' as Miss Marple would say—on

that night. Oh, Giles, I can hardly wait until Thursday to hear what Lily Kimble says."

"Suppose she gets cold feet and doesn't turn up after all?"

"Oh, she'll come. Giles, if that flashy car was there that night—"

"Think it was a yellow peril like this?"

"Admiring my bus?" Mr. Afflick's genial voice made them jump. He was leaning over the neatly clipped hedge behind them. "Little Buttercup, that's what I call her. I've always liked a nice bit of bodywork. Hits you in the eye, doesn't she?"

"She certainly does," said Giles.

"Fond of flowers, I am," said Mr. Afflick. "Daffodils, buttercups, calceolarias—they're all my fancy. Here's your scarf, Mrs. Reed. It had slipped down behind the table. Good-bye. Pleased to have met you."

"Do you think he heard us calling his car a yellow peril?" asked Gwenda as they drove away.

Giles looked slightly uneasy.

"Oh, I don't think so. He seemed quite amiable, didn't he?"

"Yes-es—but I don't think that means much. . . . Giles, that wife of his—she's frightened of him. I saw her face."

"What? That jovial pleasant chap?"

"Perhaps he isn't so jovial and pleasant underneath. . . . Giles, I don't think I like Mr. Afflick. . . . I wonder how long he'd been there behind us listening to what we were saying. . . . Just what did we say?"

"Nothing much," said Giles.

But he still looked uneasy.

22

Lily Keeps an Appointment

"WELL, I'm damned," exclaimed Giles.

He had just torn open a letter that had arrived by the after-lunch post and was staring in complete astonishment at its contents.

"What's the matter?"

"It's the report of the handwriting experts."

Gwenda said eagerly:

"And she *didn't* write that letter from abroad?"

"That's just it, Gwenda. *She did.*"

They stared at each other.

Gwenda said incredulously:

"Then those letters weren't a fake. They were genuine. Helen *did* go away from the house that night. And she *did* write from abroad. And she wasn't strangled at all?"

Giles said slowly:

"It seems so. But it really is very upsetting. I don't understand it. Just as everything seems to be pointing the other way."

"Perhaps the experts are wrong?"

"I suppose they might be. But they seem quite confident. Gwenda, I really don't understand a single thing about all this. Have we been making the most colossal idiots of ourselves?"

"All based on my silly behaviour at the theatre? I tell you what, Giles, let's call round on Miss Marple. We'll have time before we get to Dr. Kennedy's at four-thirty."

Miss Marple, however, reacted rather differently from the way they had expected. She said it was very nice indeed.

"But, darling Miss Marple," said Gwenda, "what do you mean by that?"

"I mean, my dear, that somebody hasn't been as clever as they might have been."

"But how—in what way?"

"Slipped up," said Miss Marple, nodding her head with satisfaction.

"But how?" asked Giles.

"Well, dear Mr. Reed, surely you can see how it narrows the field."

"Accepting the fact that Helen actually wrote the letters—do you mean that she might still have been murdered?"

"I mean that it seemed very important to someone that the letters should actually be in Helen's handwriting."

"I see . . . At least I think I see. There must be certain possible circumstances in which Helen could have been induced to write those particular letters. . . . That would narrow things down. But what circumstances exactly?"

"Oh, come now, Mr. Reed. You're not really thinking. It's perfectly simple, really."

Giles looked annoyed and mutinous.

"It's not obvious to me, I can assure you."

"If you'd just reflect a little—"

"Come on, Giles," said Gwenda. "We'll be late."

They left Miss Marple smiling to herself.

"That old woman annoys me sometimes," said Giles. "I don't know now what the hell she was driving at."

They reached Dr. Kennedy's house in good time.

The doctor himself opened the door to them.

"I've let my housekeeper go out for the afternoon," he explained. "It seemed to be better."

He led the way into the sitting room, where a tea tray with cups and saucers, bread and butter and cakes was ready.

"Cup of tea's a good move, isn't it?" he asked rather uncertainly of Gwenda. "Put this Mrs. Kimble at her ease and all that."

"You're absolutely right," said Gwenda.

"Now what about you two? Shall I introduce you straightaway? Or will it put her off?"

Gwenda said slowly:

"Country people are very suspicious. I believe it would be better if you received her alone."

"I think so too," said Giles.

Dr. Kennedy said:

"If you were to wait in the room next door, and if this communicating door were slightly ajar, you would be able to hear what went on. Under the circumstances of the case, I think that you would be justified."

"I suppose it's eavesdropping, but I really don't care," said Gwenda.

Dr. Kennedy smiled faintly and said:

"I don't think any ethical principle is involved. I do not propose, in any case, to give a promise of secrecy—though I am willing to give my advice if I am asked for it."

He glanced at his watch.

"The train is due at Woodleigh Road at four thirty-five. It should arrive in a few minutes now. Then it will take her about five minutes to walk up the hill."

He walked restlessly up and down the room. His face was lined and haggard.

"I don't understand," he said. "I don't understand in the least what it all means? If Helen never left that house, if her letters to me were forgeries." Gwenda moved sharply—but Giles shook his head at her. The doctor went on: "If Kelvin, poor fellow, didn't kill her, then what on earth did happen?"

"Somebody else killed her," said Gwenda.

"But, my dear child, if somebody else killed her, why on earth should Kelvin insist that he had done so?"

"Because he thought he had. He found her there on the bed and he thought he had done it. That could happen, couldn't it?"

Dr. Kennedy rubbed his nose irritably.

"How should I know? I'm not a psychiatrist. Shock? Nervous condition already? Yes, I suppose it's possible. But who would want to kill Helen?"

"We think one of three people," said Gwenda.

"Three people? What three people? Nobody could have any possible reason for killing Helen—unless they were completely off their heads. She'd no enemies. Everybody liked her."

He went to the desk drawer and fumbled through its contents.

"Came across this the other day—when I was looking for those letters."

He held out a faded snapshot. It showed a tall schoolgirl in a gym tunic, her hair tied back, her face radiant. Kennedy—a younger, happy-looking Kennedy—stood beside her holding a terrier puppy.

"I've been thinking a lot about her lately," he said indistinctly. "For many years I hadn't thought about her at all—almost managed to forget . . . Now I think about her all the time. That's *your* doing."

His words sounded almost accusing.

"I think it's *her* doing," said Gwenda.

He wheeled round on her sharply.

"What do you mean?"

"Just that. I can't explain. But it's not really us. It's Helen herself."

The faint melancholy scream of an engine came to their ears. Dr. Kennedy stepped out of the window and they followed him. A trail of smoke showed itself retreating slowly along the valley.

"There goes the train," said Kennedy.

"Coming into the station?"

"No, leaving it." He paused. "She'll be here any minute now."

But the minutes passed and Lily Kimble did not come.

II

Lily Kimble got out of the train at Dillmouth Junction and walked across the bridge to the siding where the little local train was waiting. There were few passengers—a half dozen at most. It was a slack time of day and in any case it was market day at Helchester.

Presently the train started—puffing its way importantly along a winding valley. There were three stops before the terminus at Lonsbury Bay: Newton Langford, Matchings Halt (for Woodleigh Camp), and Woodleigh Bolton.

Lily Kimble looked out of the window with eyes that did not see the lush countryside, but saw instead a Jacobean suite upholstered in jade green . . .

She was the only person to alight at the tiny station of Matchings Halt. She gave up her ticket and went out through the booking office. A little way along the road a signpost with "To Woodleigh Camp" indicated a footpath leading up a steep hill.

Lily Kimble took the footpath and walked briskly uphill. The path skirted the side of a wood; on the other side the hill rose steeply, covered with heather and gorse.

Someone stepped out from the trees and Lily Kimble jumped.

"My, you did give me a start," she exclaimed. "I wasn't expecting to meet you here."

"Gave you a surprise, did I? I've got another surprise for you."

It was very lonely in among the trees. There was no one to hear a cry or a struggle. Actually there was no cry and the struggle was very soon over.

A wood pigeon, disturbed, flew out of the wood. . . .

III

"What can have become of the woman?" demanded Dr. Kennedy irritably.

The hands of the clock pointed to ten minutes to five.

"Could she have lost her way coming from the station?"

"I gave her explicit directions. In any case it's quite simple. Turn to the left when she got out of the station and then take the first road to the right. As I say, it's only a few minutes' walk."

"Perhaps she's changed her mind," said Giles.

"It looks like it."

"Or missed the train," suggested Gwenda.

Kennedy said slowly:

"No, I think it's more likely that she decided not to come after all. Perhaps her husband stepped in. All these country people are quite incalculable."

He walked up and down the room.

Then he went to the telephone and asked for a number.

"Hullo? Is that the station? This is Dr. Kennedy speaking. I was expecting someone by the four thirty-five. Middle-aged country woman. Did anyone ask to be directed to me? Or—what do you say?"

The others were near enough to hear the soft lazy accent of Woodleigh Bolton's one porter.

"Don't think as there could be anyone for you, Doctor. Weren't no strangers on the four thirty-five. Mr. Narracotts from Meadows, and Johnnie Lawes, and old Benson's daughter. Weren't no other passengers at all."

"So she changed her mind," said Dr. Kennedy. "Well, I can offer *you* tea. The kettle's on. I'll go out and make it."

He returned with the teapot and they sat down.

"It's only a temporary check," he said more cheerfully. "We've got her address. We'll go over and see her, perhaps."

The telephone rang and the doctor got up to answer.

"Dr. Kennedy?"

"Speaking."

"This is Inspector Last, Longford Police Station. Were you expecting a woman called Lily Kimble—Mrs. Lily Kimble—to call upon you this afternoon?"

"I was. Why? Has there been an accident?"

"Not what you'd call an accident exactly. She's dead. We found a letter from you on the body. That's why I rang you up. Can you make it convenient to come along to Longford Police Station as soon as possible?"

"I'll come at once."

IV

"Now let's get this quite clear," Inspector Last was saying.

He looked from Kennedy to Giles and Gwenda, who had accompanied the doctor. Gwenda was very pale and held her hands tightly clasped together. "You were expecting this woman by the train that leaves Dillmouth Junction at four-o-five? And gets to Woodleigh Bolton at four thirty-five?"

Dr. Kennedy nodded.

Inspector Last looked down at the letter he had taken from the dead woman's body. It was quite clear.

Dear Mrs. Kimble, [Dr. Kennedy had written]

I shall be glad to advise you to the best of my power. As you will see from the heading of this letter, I no longer live in Dillmouth. If you will take the train leaving Coombeleigh at 3:30, change at Dillmouth Junction, and come by the Lonsbury Bay train to Woodleigh Bolton, my house is only a few minutes' walk. Turn to the left as you come out of the station, then take the first road on the right. My house is at the end of it on the right. The name is on the gate.

Yours truly,
James Kennedy.

"There was no question of her coming by an earlier train?"

"An earlier train?" Dr. Kennedy looked astonished.

"Because that's what she did. She left Coombeleigh, not at three-thirty but at one-thirty—caught the two-o-five from Dillmouth Junction and got out, not at Woodleigh Bolton, but at Matchings Halt, the station before it."

"But that's extraordinary!"

"Was she consulting you professionally, Doctor?"

"No. I retired from practice some years ago."

"That's what I thought. You knew her well?"

Kennedy shook his head.

"I hadn't seen her for nearly twenty years."

"But you—er—recognized her just now?"

Gwenda shivered, but dead bodies did not affect a doctor, and Kennedy replied thoughtfully:

"Under the circumstances it is hard to say if I recognized her or not. She was strangled, I presume?"

"She was strangled. The body was found in a copse a short way along the track leading from Matchings Halt to Woodleigh Camp. It was found by a hiker coming down from the Camp at about ten minutes to four. Our police surgeon puts the time of death at between two-fifteen and three o'clock. Presumably she was killed shortly after she left the station. No other passenger got out at Matchings Halt. She was the only person to get out of the train there.

"Now why did she get out at Matchings Halt? Did she mistake the station? I hardly think so. In any case she was two hours early for her appointment with you, and had not come by the train you suggested, although she had your letter with her.

"Now just what was her business with you, Doctor?"

Dr. Kennedy felt in his pocket and brought out Lily's letter.

"I brought this with me. The enclosed cutting is an insertion put in the local paper by Mr. and Mrs. Reed here."

Inspector Last read Lily Kimble's letter and the enclosure. Then he looked from Dr. Kennedy to Giles and Gwenda.

"Can I have the story behind all this? It goes back a long way, I gather?"

"Eighteen years," said Gwenda.

Piecemeal, with additions and parentheses, the story came out. Inspector Last was a good listener. He let the three people in front of him tell things in their own way. Kennedy was dry and factual, Gwenda was slightly incoherent, but her narrative had imaginative power. Giles gave, perhaps, the most valuable contribution. He was clear and to the point, with less reserve than Kennedy, and with more coherence than Gwenda. It took a long time.

Then Inspector Last sighed and summed up.

"Mrs. Halliday was Dr. Kennedy's sister and your stepmother, Mrs. Reed. She disappeared from the house you are at present living in eighteen years ago. Lily Kimble (whose maiden name was Abbott) was a servant (house-parlourmaid) in the house at the time. For some reason Lily Kimble inclines (after the passage of years) to the theory that there was foul play. At the time it was assumed that Mrs. Halliday had gone away with a man (identity unknown). Major Halliday died in a mental establishment fifteen years ago still under the delusion that he had strangled his wife—if it was a delusion—"

He paused.

"These are all interesting but somewhat unrelated facts. The crucial point seems to be, is Mrs. Halliday alive or dead? If dead, when did she die? And what did Lily Kimble know?

"It seems, on the face of it, that she must have known something rather important. So important that she was killed in order to prevent her talking about it."

Gwenda cried:

"But how could anyone possibly know she was going to talk about it—except us?"

Inspector Last turned his thoughtful eyes on her.

"It is a significant point, Mrs. Reed, that she took the two-o-five instead of the four-o-five train from Dillmouth Junction. There must be some reason for that. Also, she got out at the station before Woodleigh Bolton. Why? It seems possible to me that, *after* writing to the doctor, she wrote to someone else, suggesting a rendezvous at Woodleigh Camp, perhaps, and that she proposed after that rendezvous, if it was unsatisfactory, to go on to Dr. Kennedy and ask his advice. It is possible that she had suspicions of some definite person, and she may have written to that person hinting at her knowledge and suggesting a rendezvous."

"Blackmail," said Giles bluntly.

"I don't suppose she thought of it that way," said Inspector Last. "She was just greedy and hopeful—and a little muddled about what she could get out of it all. We'll see, maybe the husband can tell us more."

V

"Warned her, I did," said Mr. Kimble heavily. "'Don't have nought to do with it,' them were my words. Went behind my back, she did. Thought as she knew best. That were Lily all over. Too smart by half."

Questioning revealed that Mr. Kimble had little to contribute. Lily had been in service at St. Catherine's before he met her and started walking out with her. Fond of the pictures, she was, and told him that, likely as not, she'd been in a house where there'd been a murder.

"Didn't pay much account, I didn't. All imagination, I thought. Never content with plain fact, Lily wasn't. Long rigmarole she told me, about the master doing in the missus and maybe putting the body in the cellar—and something about a French girl what had looked out of the window and seen something or somebody. 'Don't you pay no attention to foreigners, my girl,' I said. 'One and all they're liars. Not like us.' And when she run on about it, I didn't listen because, mark you, she was working it all up out of nothing. Liked a bit of crime, Lily did. Used to take the *Sunday News* what was running a series about Famous Murderers. Full of it, she was, and if she liked to think she'd been in a house where there was a murder—well, thinking don't hurt nobody. But when she was on at me about answering this advertisement—'You leave it alone,' I says to her. 'It's no good stirring up trouble.' And if she'd done as I telled her, she'd be alive today."

He thought for a moment or two.

"Ar," he said. "She'd be alive right now. Too smart by half, that was Lily."

23

Which of Them?

GILES AND GWENDA had not gone with Inspector Last and Dr. Kennedy to interview Mr. Kimble. They arrived home about seven o'clock. Gwenda looked white and ill. Dr. Kennedy had said to Giles: "Give her some brandy and make her eat something, then get her to bed. She's had a bad shock."

"It's so awful, Giles," Gwenda kept saying. "So awful. That

silly woman, making an appointment with the murderer, and going along so confidently—to be killed. Like a sheep to the slaughter."

"Well, don't think about it, darling. After all, we did know there was someone—a killer."

"No, we didn't. Not a killer *now*. I mean, it was *then*—eighteen years ago. It wasn't, somehow, quite real. . . . It might all have been a mistake."

"Well, this proves that it wasn't a mistake. You were right all the time, Gwenda."

Giles was glad to find Miss Marple at Hillside. She and Mrs. Cocker between them fussed over Gwenda, who refused brandy because she said it always reminded her of channel steamers, but accepted some hot whisky and lemon, and then, coaxed by Mrs. Cocker, sat down and ate an omelette.

Giles would have talked determinedly of other things, but Miss Marple, with what Giles admitted to be superior tactics, discussed the crime in a gentle, aloof manner.

"Very dreadful, my dear," she said. "And of course a great shock, but interesting, one must admit. And of course I am so old that death doesn't shock me as much as it does you—only something lingering and painful like cancer really distresses me. The really vital thing is that this proves definitely and beyond any possible doubt that poor young Helen Halliday was killed. We've thought so all along and now we know."

"And according to you we ought to know where the body is," said Giles. "The cellar, I suppose."

"No, no, Mr. Reed. You remember Edith Pagett said she went down there on the morning after because she was disturbed by what Lily had said, and she found no signs of anything of the kind—and there would be signs, you know—if somebody was really looking for them."

"Then what happened to it? Taken away in a car and thrown over a cliff into the sea?"

"No. Come now, my dears, what struck you first of all when you came here—struck you, Gwenda, I should say? The fact that from the drawing-room window, you had no view down to the sea. Where you felt, very properly, that steps should lead down to the lawn—there was instead a plantation of shrubs. The steps, you found subsequently, had been there originally, but had at some time been transferred to the end of the terrace. Why were they moved?"

Gwenda stared at her with dawning comprehension.

"You mean that *that's* where—"

"There must have been a reason for making the change, and there doesn't really seem to be a sensible one. It is, frankly, a stupid place to have steps down to the lawn. But that end of the terrace is a very quiet place—it's not overlooked from the house except by one window—the window of the nursery, on the first floor. Don't you see, that if you want to bury a body, the earth will be disturbed and there must be a *reason* for it being disturbed. The reason was that it had been decided to move the steps from in front of the drawing room to the end of the terrace. I've learnt already from Dr. Kennedy that Helen Halliday and her husband were very keen on the garden, and did a lot of work in it. The daily gardener they employed used merely to carry out their orders, and if he arrived to find that this change was in progress and some of the flags had already been moved, he would only have thought that the Hallidays had started on the work when he wasn't there. The body, of course, could have been buried at either place, but we can be quite certain, I think, that it is actually buried at the end of the terrace and not in front of the drawing-room window."

"Why can we be sure?" asked Gwenda.

"Because of what poor Lily Kimble said in her letter—that she changed her mind about the body being in the cellar because of what Leonie saw when she looked out of the window. That makes it very clear, doesn't it? The Swiss girl looked out of the nursery window at some time during the night and saw the grave being dug. Perhaps she actually saw who it was digging it."

"And never said anything to the police?"

"My dear, there was no question at the time of a *crime* having occurred. Mrs. Halliday had run away with a lover—that was all that Leonie would grasp. She probably couldn't speak much English anyway. She did mention to Lily, perhaps not at the time, but later, a curious thing she had observed from her window that night, and that stimulated Lily's belief in a crime having occurred.

But I've no doubt that Edith Pagett told Lily off for talking nonsense, and the Swiss girl would accept her point of view and would certainly not wish to be mixed up with the police. Foreigners always seem to be particularly nervous about the police when they are in a strange country. So she went back to Switzerland and very likely never thought of it again."

Giles said:

"If she's alive now—if she can be traced—"

Miss Marple nodded her head. "Perhaps."

Giles demanded:

"How can we set about it?"

Miss Marple said:

"The police will be able to do that much better than you can."

"Inspector Last is coming over here tomorrow morning."

"Then I think I should tell him—about the steps."

"And about what I saw—or think I saw—in the hall?" asked Gwenda nervously.

"Yes, dear. You've been very wise to say nothing of that until now. Very wise. But I think the time has come."

Giles said slowly:

"She was strangled in the hall, and then the murderer carried her upstairs and put her on the bed. Kelvin Halliday came in, passed out with doped whisky, and in his turn was carried upstairs to the bedroom. He came to, and thought he had killed her. The murderer must have been watching somewhere near at hand. When Kelvin went off to Dr. Kennedy's, the murderer took away the body, probably hid it in the shrubbery at the end of the terrace, and waited until everybody had gone to bed and was presumably asleep before he dug the grave and buried the body. That means he must have been here, hanging about the house, pretty well all that night?"

Miss Marple nodded.

"He had to be—on the spot. I remember your saying that that was important. We've got to see which of our three suspects fits in best with the requirements. We'll take Erskine first. Now he definitely was on the spot. By his own admission he walked up here with Helen Halliday from the beach at round about nine o'clock. He said good-bye to her. But did he say good-bye to her? Let's say instead that he strangled her."

"But it was all over between them," cried Gwenda. "Long ago. He said himself that he was hardly ever alone with Helen."

"But don't you see, Gwenda, that the way we must look at it now, we can't depend on anything anyone *says*."

"Now I'm so glad to hear you say that," said Miss Marple. "Because I've been a little worried, you know, by the way you two have seemed willing to accept, as actual fact, all the things that people have told you. I'm afraid I have a sadly distrustful nature, but, especially in a matter of murder, I make it a rule to take nothing that is told to me as true, unless it is *checked*. For instance, it does seem quite certain that Lily Kimble mentioned the clothes packed and taken away in a suitcase were not the ones Helen Halliday would herself have taken, because not only did Edith Pagett tell us that Lily said so to her, but Lily herself mentioned the fact in her letter to Dr. Kennedy. So that is one *fact*. Dr. Kennedy told us that Kelvin Halliday believed that his wife was secretly drugging him, and Kelvin Halliday in his diary confirms that—so there is another fact—and a very curious fact it is, don't you think? However, we will not go into that now.

"But I would like to point out that a great many of the assumptions you have made have been based upon what has been told you—possibly told you very plausibly."

Giles stared hard at her.

Gwenda, her colour restored, sipped coffee, and leaned across the table.

Giles said:

"Let's check up now on what three people have said to us. Take Erskine first. He says—"

"You've got a down on him," said Gwenda. "It's a waste of time going on about him, because now he's definitely out of it. He couldn't have killed Lily Kimble."

Giles went on imperturbably:

"He says that he met Helen on the boat going out to India and they fell in love, but that he couldn't bring himself to leave his wife and children, and that they agreed they must say good-bye. Suppose it wasn't quite like that. Suppose he fell desperately in love with Helen, and that it was *she* who wouldn't run off with him. Supposing he threatened that if she married anyone else, he would kill her."

"Most improbable," said Gwenda.

"Things like that do happen. Remember what you overheard his wife say to him. You put it all down to jealousy, but it may have been true. Perhaps she *has* had a terrible time with him where women are concerned—he may be a little bit of a sex maniac."

"I don't believe it."

"No, because he's attractive to women. I think, myself, that there is something a little queer about Erskine. However, let's go on with my case against him. Helen breaks off her engagement to Fane and comes home and marries your father and settles down here. And then suddenly, Erskine turns up. He comes down ostensibly on a summer holiday with his wife. That's an odd thing to do, really. He admits he came here to see Helen again. Now let's take it that *Erskine* was the man in the drawing room with her that day when Lily overheard her say she was afraid of him. '*I'm afraid of you—I've always been afraid of you—I think you're mad.*'

"And, because she's afraid, she makes plans to go and live in Norfolk, but she's very secretive about it. No one is to know. No one is to know, that is, until the Erskines have left Dillmouth. So far that fits. Now we come to the fatal night. What the Hallidays were doing earlier that evening, we don't know—"

Miss Marple coughed.

"As a matter of fact, I saw Edith Pagett again. She remembers that there was early supper that night—seven o'clock—because Major Halliday was going to some meeting—golf club, she thinks it was, or some parish meeting. Mrs. Halliday went out after supper."

"Right. Helen meets Erskine, by appointment, perhaps, on the beach. He is leaving the following day. Perhaps he refuses to go. He urges Helen to go away with him. She comes back here and he comes with her. Finally, in a fit of frenzy he strangles her. The next bit is as we have already agreed. He's slightly mad, he wants Kelvin Halliday to believe it is *he* who has killed her. Later, Erskine buries the body. You remember, he told Gwenda that he didn't go back to the hotel until very late because he was walking about Dillmouth."

"One wonders," said Miss Marple, "what his wife was doing?"

"Probably frenzied with jealousy," said Gwenda. "And gave him hell when he did get in."

"That's my reconstruction," said Giles. "And it's possible."

"But he couldn't have killed Lily Kimble," said Gwenda, "because he lives in Northumberland. So thinking about him is just waste of time. Let's take Walter Fane."

"Right. Walter Fane is the repressed type. He seems gentle and mild and easily pushed around. But Miss Marple has brought us one valuable bit of testimony. Walter Fane was once in such a rage that he nearly killed his brother. Admittedly he was a child at the time, but it was startling because he had always seemed such a gentle forgiving nature. Anyway, Walter Fane falls in love with Helen Halliday. Not merely in love, he's crazy about her. She won't have him and he goes off to India. Later, she writes him that she will come out and marry him. She starts. Then comes the second blow. She arrives and promptly jilts him. She has 'met someone on the boat.' She goes home and marries Kelvin Halliday. Possibly Walter Fane thinks that Kelvin Halliday was the original cause of her turning him down. He broods, nurses a crazy jealous hate and comes home. He behaves in a most forgiving, friendly manner, is often at this house, has become apparently a tame cat around the house, the faithful Dobbin. But perhaps Helen realizes that this isn't true. She gets a glimpse of what is going on below the surface. Perhaps, long ago, she sensed something disturbing in quiet young Walter Fane. She says to him, 'I think I've always been afraid of you.' She makes plans, secretly, to go right away from Dillmouth and live in Norfolk. Why? Because she's afraid of Walter Fane.

"Now we come again to the fatal evening. Here, we're not on very sure ground. We don't know what Walter Fane was doing that night, and I don't see any probability of ever finding out. But he fulfills Miss Marple's requirement of being 'on the spot' to the extent of living in a house that is only two or three minutes' walk away. He may have said he was going to bed early with a headache, or shut himself into his study with work to do—something of that kind. He could have done all the things we've decided the murderer did do, and I think that he's the most likely of the three to have made mistakes in packing a suitcase. He wouldn't know enough about what women wear to do it properly."

"It was queer," said Gwenda. "In his office that day. I had an odd sort of feeling that he was like a house with its blinds pulled down . . . and I even had a fanciful idea that—that there was someone dead in the house."

She looked at Miss Marple.

"Does that seem very silly to you?" she asked.

"No, my dear. I think that perhaps you were right."

"And now," said Gwenda, "we come to Afflick. Afflick's Tours. Jackie Afflick who was always too smart by half. The first thing against him is that Dr. Kennedy believed he had incipient persecution mania. That is—he was never really normal. He's told us about himself and Helen—but we'll agree now that that was all a pack of lies. He didn't just think she was a cute kid—he was madly, passionately in love with her. But she wasn't in love with him. She was just amusing herself. She was man mad, as Miss Marple says."

"No, dear, *I* didn't say that. Nothing of the kind."

"Well, a nymphomaniac, if you prefer the term. Anyway, she had an affair with Jackie Afflick and then wanted to drop him. He didn't want to be dropped. Her brother got her out of her scrape, but Jackie Afflick never forgave or forgot. He lost his job—according to him through being framed by Walter Fane. That shows definite signs of persecution mania."

"Yes," agreed Giles. "But on the other hand, if it was true, it's another point against Fane—quite a valuable point."

Gwenda went on.

"Helen goes abroad, and he leaves Dillmouth. But he never forgets her, and when she returns to Dillmouth, married, he comes over and visits her. He said first of all, he came *once*, but later on, he admits that he came more than once. And, oh, Giles, don't you remember? Edith Pagett used a phrase about 'our mystery man in a flashy car.' You see, he came often enough to make the servants talk. But Helen took pains not to ask him to a meal—not to let him meet Kelvin. Perhaps she was afraid of him. Perhaps—"

Giles interrupted.

"This might cut both ways. Supposing Helen was in love with him—the first man she ever was in love with, and supposing she went on being in love with him. Perhaps they had an affair together and she didn't let anyone know about it. But perhaps he wanted her to go away with him, and by that time she was tired of him, and wouldn't go, and so—and so—he killed her. And all the rest of it. Lily said in her letter to Dr. Kennedy there was a posh car standing outside that night. It was Jackie Afflick's car. Jackie Afflick was 'on the spot,' too."

"It's an assumption," said Giles. "But it seems to me a reasonable one. But there are Helen's letters to be worked into our reconstruction. I've been puzzling my brains to think of the 'circumstances,' as Miss Marple put it, under which she could have been induced to write those letters. It seems to me that to explain them, we've got to admit that she actually *had* a lover, and that she was expecting to go away with him. We'll test our three possibles again. Erskine first. Say that he still wasn't prepared to leave his wife or break up his home, but that Helen had agreed to leave Kelvin Halliday and go somewhere where Erskine could come and be with her from time to time. The first thing would be to disarm Mrs. Erskine's suspicions, so Helen writes a couple of letters to reach her brother in due course which will look as though she has gone abroad with someone. That fits in very well with her being so mysterious about who the man in question is."

"But if she was going to leave her husband for him, why did he kill her?" asked Gwenda.

"Perhaps because she suddenly changed her mind. Decided that she did really care for her husband after all. He just saw red and strangled her. Then he took the clothes and suitcase and used the letters. That's a perfectly good explanation covering everything."

"The same might apply to Walter Fane. I should imagine that scandal might be absolutely disastrous to a country solicitor. Helen might have agreed to go somewhere nearby where Fane could visit her but pretend that she had gone abroad with someone else. Letters all prepared and then, as you suggested, she changed her mind. Walter went mad and killed her."

"What about Jackie Afflick?"

"It's more difficult to find a reason for the letters with him. I shouldn't imagine that scandal would affect him. Perhaps Helen was afraid, not of him, but of my father—and so thought it would be better to pretend she'd gone abroad—or perhaps Afflick's wife had the money at that time, and he wanted her money to invest in his business. Oh yes, there are lots of possibilities for the letters."

"Which one do you fancy, Miss Marple?" asked Gwenda. "I don't really think Walter Fane—but then—"

Mrs. Cocker had just come in to clear away the coffee cups.

"There now, madam," she said. "I quite forgot. All this about a poor woman being murdered and you and Mr. Reed mixed up in it, not at all the right thing for you, madam, just now. Mr. Fane was here this afternoon, asking for you. He waited quite half an hour. Seemed to think you were expecting him."

"How strange," said Gwenda. "What time?"

"It must have been about four o'clock or just after. And then, after that, there was another gentleman, came in a great big yellow car. He was positive you were expecting him. Wouldn't take no for an answer. Waited twenty minutes. I wondered if you'd had some idea of a tea party and forgotten it."

"No," said Gwenda. "How odd."

"Let's ring up Fane now," said Giles. "He won't have gone to bed."

He suited the action to the word.

"Hullo, is that Fane speaking? Giles Reed here. I hear you came round to see us this afternoon—what?—no—no, I'm sure of it—no, how very odd. Yes, I wonder, too."

He laid down the receiver.

"Here's an odd thing. He was rung up in his office this morning. A message left would he come round and see us this afternoon. It was very important."

Giles and Gwenda stared at each other. Then Gwenda said:

"Ring up Afflick."

Again Giles went to the telephone, found the number and rang through. It took a little longer, but presently he got the connection.

"Mr. Afflick? Giles Reed, I—"

Here he was obviously interrupted by a flow of speech from the other end.

At last he was able to say:

"But we didn't—no—I assure you—nothing of the kind. Yes—yes, I know you're a busy man. I wouldn't have dreamed of— Yes, but look here, who was it rang you—a man?—no, I tell you it wasn't me. No—no, I see. Well, I agree, it's quite extraordinary."

He replaced the receiver and came back to the table.

"Well, there it is," he said. "Somebody, a man who said he was me, rang up Afflick and asked him to come over here. It was urgent—big sum of money involved."

They looked at each other.

"It could have been either of them," said Gwenda. "Don't you see, Giles? Either of them could have killed Lily and come on here as an alibi."

"Hardly an alibi, dear," put in Miss Marple.

"I don't mean quite an alibi, but an excuse for being away from their office. What I mean is, one of them is speaking the truth and one is lying. One of them rang up the other and asked him to come here—to throw suspicion on him—but we don't know which. It's a clear issue now between the two of them. Fane or Afflick. I say—Jackie Afflick."

"I think Walter Fane," said Giles.

They both looked at Miss Marple.

She shook her head.

"There's another possibility," she said.

"Of course, Erskine."

Giles fairly ran across to the telephone.

"What are you going to do?" asked Gwenda.

"Put through a trunk call to Northumberland."

"Oh, Giles—you can't really think—"

"We've got to know. If he's there—he can't have killed Lily Kimble this afternoon. No private aeroplanes or silly stuff like that."

They waited in silence until the telephone bell rang.

Giles picked up the receiver.

"You were asking for a personal call to Major Erskine. Go ahead, please. Major Erskine is waiting."

Clearing his throat nervously, Giles said:

"Er—Erskine? Giles Reed here—Reed, yes."

He cast a sudden agonized glance at Gwenda which said as plainly as possible: "What the hell do I say now?"

Gwenda got up and took the receiver from him.

"Major Erskine? This is Mrs. Reed here. We've heard of—of a house. Linscott Brake. Is—is it—do you know anything about it? It's somewhere near you, I believe."

Erskine's voice said:

"Linscott Brake? No, I don't think I've ever heard of it. What's the postal town?"

"It's terribly blurred," said Gwenda. "You know those awful typescripts agents send out. But it says fifteen miles from Daith, so we thought—"

"I'm sorry. I haven't heard of it. Who lives there?"

"Oh, it's empty. But never mind, actually we've—we've practically settled on a house. I'm so sorry to have bothered you. I expect you were busy."

"No, not at all. At least only busy domestically. My wife's away. And our cook had to go off to her mother, so I've been dealing with domestic routine. I'm afraid I'm not much of a hand at it. Better in the garden."

"I'd always rather do gardening than housework. I hope your wife isn't ill?"

"Oh no, she was called away to a sister. She'll be back tomorrow."

"Well, good night, and so sorry to have bothered you."

She put down the receiver.

"Erskine is out of it," she said triumphantly. "His wife's away and he's doing all the chores. So that leaves it between the two others. Doesn't it, Miss Marple?"

Miss Marple was looking grave.

"I don't think, my dears," she said, "that you have given quite enough thought to the matter. Oh, dear—I am really very worried. If only I knew exactly what to do. . . ."

24

The Monkey's Paws

GWENDA LEANED her elbows on the table and cupped her chin in them while her eyes roamed dispassionately over the remains of a hasty lunch. Presently she must deal with them, carry them out to the scullery, wash up, put things away, see what there would be, later, for supper.

But there was no wild hurry. She felt she needed a little time to take things in. Everything had been happening too fast.

The events of the morning, when she reviewed them, seemed to be chaotic and impossible. Everything had happened too quickly and too improbably.

Inspector Last had appeared early—at half-past nine. With him had come Detective Inspector Primer from headquarters and the Chief Constable of the county. The latter had not stayed long. It was Inspector Primer who was now in charge of the case of Lily Kimble deceased and all the ramifications arising therefrom.

It was Inspector Primer, a man with a deceptively mild manner and a gentle, apologetic voice, who had asked her if it would inconvenience her very much if his men did some digging in the garden.

From the tone of his voice, it might have been a case of giving his men some healthful exercise, rather than of seeking for a dead body which had been buried for eighteen years.

Giles had spoken up then. He had said:

"I think, perhaps, we could help you with a suggestion or two."

And he told the Inspector about the shifting of the steps leading down to the lawn, and took the Inspector out onto the terrace.

The Inspector had looked up at the barred window on the first floor at the corner of the house and had said:

"That would be the nursery, I presume."

And Giles said that it would.

Then the Inspector and Giles had come back into the house, and two men with spades had gone out into the garden, and Giles, before the Inspector could get down to questions, had said:

"I think, Inspector, you had better hear something that my wife has so far not mentioned to anyone except myself—and—er—one other person."

The gentle, rather compelling gaze of Inspector Primer came to rest on Gwenda. It was faintly speculative. He was asking himself, Gwenda thought: "Is this a woman who can be depended upon, or is she the kind who imagines things?"

So strongly did she feel this, that she started in a defensive way:

"I may have imagined it. Perhaps I did. But it seems awfully real."

Inspector Primer said softly and soothingly:

"Well, Mrs. Reed, let's hear about it."

And Gwenda had explained. How the house had seemed familiar to her when she first saw it. How she had subsequently learned that she had, in fact, lived there as a child. How she had remembered the nursery wallpaper, and the connecting door, and the feeling she had had that there ought to be steps down to the lawn.

Inspector Primer nodded. He did not say that Gwenda's childish recollections were not particularly interesting, but Gwenda wondered whether he were thinking it.

Then she nerved herself to the final statement. How she had suddenly remembered, when sitting at a theatre, looking through the banisters at Hillside and seeing a dead woman in the hall.

"With a blue face, strangled, and golden hair—and it was Helen— But it was so stupid, I didn't know at all who Helen *was*."

"We think that—" Giles began, but Inspector Primer, with unexpected authority, held up an arresting hand.

"Please let Mrs. Reed tell me in her own words."

And Gwenda had stumbled on, her face flushed, with Inspector Primer gently helping her out, using a dexterity that Gwenda did not appreciate as the highly technical performance it was.

"Webster?" he said thoughtfully. "H'm, *Duchess of Malfi*. Monkey's paws?"

"But that was probably a nightmare," said Giles.

"Please, Mr. Reed."

"It may all have been a nightmare," said Gwenda.

"No, I don't think it was," said Inspector Primer. "It would be very hard to explain Lily Kimble's death, unless we assume that there *was* a woman murdered in this house."

That seemed so reasonable and almost comforting that Gwenda hurried on.

"And it wasn't my father who murdered her. It wasn't really. Even Dr. Penrose says he wasn't the right type, and that he couldn't have murdered anybody. And Dr. Kennedy was quite sure he hadn't done it, but only thought he had. So you see it was someone who wanted it to *seem* as though my father had done it, and we think we know who—at least it's one of two people—"

"Gwenda," said Giles. "We can't really—"

"I wonder, Mr. Reed," said the Inspector, "if you would mind going out into the garden and seeing how my men are getting on. Tell them I sent you."

He closed the French windows after Giles and latched them and came back to Gwenda.

"Now just tell me all your ideas, Mrs. Reed. Never mind if they are rather incoherent."

And Gwenda had poured out all hers and Giles's speculations and reasonings, and the steps they had taken to find out all they could about the three men who might have figured in Helen Halliday's life, and the final conclusions they had come to—and how both Walter Fane and J. J. Afflick had been rung up, as though by Giles, and had been summoned to Hillside the preceding afternoon.

"But you do see, don't you, Inspector—that one of them might be lying?"

And in a gentle, rather tired voice, the Inspector said:

"That's one of the principal difficulties in my kind of work. So many people may be lying. And so many people usually are . . . Though not always for the reasons that you'd think. And some people don't even know they're lying."

"Do you think I'm like that?" Gwenda asked apprehensively.

And the Inspector smiled and said:

"I think you're a very truthful witness, Mrs. Reed."

"And you think I'm right about who murdered her?"

The Inspector sighed and said:

"It's not a question of thinking—not with us. It's a question of checking up. Where everybody was, what account everybody gives of their movements. We know accurately enough, to within ten minutes or so, when Lily Kimble was killed. Between two-twenty and two forty-five. Anyone could have killed her and then come on here yesterday afternoon. I don't see, myself, any reason for those telephone calls. It doesn't give either of the people you mention an alibi for the time of the murder."

"But you will find out, won't you, what they were doing at the time? Between two-twenty and two forty-five. You will ask them."

Inspector Primer smiled.

"We shall ask all the questions necessary, Mrs. Reed, you may be sure of that. All in good time. There's no good in rushing things. You've got to see your way ahead."

Gwenda had a sudden vision of patience and quiet unsensational work. Unhurried, remorseless . . .

She said:

"I see . . . yes. Because you're professional. And Giles and I are just amateurs. We might make a lucky hit—but we wouldn't really know how to follow it up."

"Something of the kind, Mrs. Reed."

The Inspector smiled again. He got up and unfastened the French windows. Then, just as he was about to step through them, he stopped. Rather, Gwenda thought, like a pointing dog.

"Excuse me, Mrs. Reed. That lady wouldn't be a Miss Jane Marple, would she?"

Gwenda had come to stand beside him. At the bottom of the garden Miss Marple was still waging a losing war with bindweed.

"Yes, that's Miss Marple. She's awfully kind in helping us with the garden."

"Miss Marple," said the Inspector. "*I* see."

Gwenda looked at him inquiringly and said:

"She's rather a dear."

He replied:

"She's a very celebrated lady, is Miss Marple. Got the Chief Constables of at least three counties in her pocket. She's not got my Chief yet, but I daresay that will come. So Miss Marple's got her finger in this pie."

"She's made an awful lot of helpful suggestions," said Gwenda.

"I bet she has," said the Inspector. "Was it her suggestion where to look for the deceased Mrs. Halliday?"

"She said that Giles and I ought to know quite well where to look," said Gwenda. "And it did seem stupid of us not to have thought of it before."

The Inspector gave a soft little laugh, and went down to stand by Miss Marple. He said:

"I don't think we've been introduced, Miss Marple. But you were pointed out to me once by Colonel Melrose."

Miss Marple stood up, flushed and grasping a handful of clinging green.

"Oh yes. Dear Colonel Melrose. He has always been *most* kind. Ever since—"

"Ever since a churchwarden was shot in the vicar's study. Quite a while ago. But you've had other successes since then. A little poison pen trouble down near Lymstock."

"You seem to know quite a lot about me, Inspector—"

"Primer, my name is. And you've been busy here, I expect."

"Well, I try to do what I can in the garden. Sadly neglected. This bindweed, for instance, such nasty stuff. Its roots," said Miss Marple, looking very earnestly at the Inspector, "go down underground a long way. A very long way—they run along underneath the soil."

"I think you're right about that," said the Inspector. "A long way down. A long way back . . . this murder, I mean. Eighteen years."

"And perhaps before that," said Miss Marple. "Running underground . . . And terribly harmful, Inspector, squeezing the life out of the pretty growing flowers . . ."

One of the police constables came along the path. He was perspiring and had a smudge of earth on his forehead.

"We've come to—something, sir. Looks as though it's her all right."

II

And it was then, Gwenda reflected, that the nightmarish quality of the day had begun. Giles coming in, his face rather pale, saying: "It's—she's there all right, Gwenda."

Then one of the constables had telephoned and the police surgeon, a short bustling man, had arrived.

And it was then that Mrs. Cocker, the calm and imperturbable Mrs. Cocker, had gone out into the garden—not led, as might have been expected by ghoulish curiosity, but solely in the quest of culinary herbs for the dish she was preparing for lunch. And Mrs. Cocker, whose reaction to the news of a murder on the preceding day had been shocked censure and an anxiety for the effect upon Gwenda's health (for Mrs. Cocker had made up her mind that the nursery upstairs was to be tenanted after the due number of months), had walked straight in upon the gruesome discovery, and had been immediately "taken queer" to an alarming extent.

"Too horrible, madam. Bones is a thing I never could abide. Not skeleton bones, as one might say. And here in the garden, just by the mint and all. And my heart's beating at such a rate—palpitations—I can hardly get my breath. And if I might make so bold, just a thimbleful of brandy . . . ."

Alarmed by Mrs. Cocker's gasps and her ashy colour, Gwenda had rushed to the sideboard, poured out some brandy and brought it to Mrs. Cocker to sip.

And Mrs. Cocker had said:

"That's just what I needed, madam—" when, quite suddenly, her voice had failed, and she had looked so alarming that Gwenda had screamed for Giles, and Giles had yelled to the police surgeon.

"And it's fortunate I was on the spot," the latter said afterwards. "It was touch and go anyway. Without a doctor, that woman would have died then and there."

And then Inspector Primer had taken the brandy decanter, and then he and the doctor had gone into a huddle over it, and Inspector Primer had asked Gwenda when she and Giles had last had any brandy out of it.

Gwenda said she thought not for some days. They'd been away —up North, and the last few times they'd had a drink, they'd had gin. "But I nearly had some brandy yesterday," said Gwenda. "Only it makes me think of channel steamers, so Giles opened a new bottle of whisky."

"That was very lucky for you, Mrs. Reed. If you'd drunk brandy yesterday, I doubt if you would be alive today."

"Giles nearly drank some—but in the end he had whisky with me."

Gwenda shivered.

Even now, alone in the house, with the police gone and Giles gone with them after a hasty lunch scratched up out of tins (since Mrs. Cocker had been removed to hospital), Gwenda could hardly believe in the morning turmoil of events.

One thing stood out clearly—the presence in the house yesterday of Jackie Afflick and Walter Fane. Either of them could have tampered with the brandy, and what was the purpose of the telephone calls unless it was to afford one or other of them the opportunity to poison the brandy decanter? Gwenda and Giles had been getting too near the truth. Or had a third person come in from outside, through the open dining-room window perhaps, while she and Giles had been sitting in Dr. Kennedy's house waiting for Lily Kimble to keep her appointment? A third person who had engineered the telephone calls to steer suspicion on the other two?

But a third person, Gwenda thought, didn't make sense. For a third person, surely, would have telephoned to only *one* of the two men. A third person would have wanted one suspect, not two. And anyway, who could the third person be? Erskine had definitely been in Northumberland. No, either Walter Fane had telephoned to Afflick and had pretended to be telephoned to himself. Or else Afflick had telephoned Fane, and had made the same pretence of receiving a summons. One of those two, and the police, who were cleverer and had more resources than she and Giles had, would find out which. And in the meantime both of those men would be watched. They wouldn't be able to—to try again.

Again Gwenda shivered. It took a little getting used to—the knowledge that someone had tried to kill you. "Dangerous," Miss Marple had said long ago. But she and Giles had not really taken the idea of danger seriously. Even after Lily Kimble had been killed, it still hadn't occurred to her that anyone would try and kill her and Giles. Just because she and Giles were getting too near the truth of what had happened eighteen years ago. Working out what must have happened then—and who had made it happen.

Walter Fane and Jackie Afflick . . .

"Which?"

Gwenda closed her eyes, seeing them afresh in the light of her new knowledge.

Quiet Walter Fane, sitting in his office—the pale spider in the centre of its web. So quiet, so harmless-looking. A house with its blinds down. Someone dead in the house. Someone dead eighteen years ago—but still there. How sinister the quiet Walter Fane seemed now. Walter Fane, who had once flung himself murderously upon his brother. Walter Fane, whom Helen had scornfully refused to marry, once here at home, and once again in India. A double rebuff. A double ignominy. Walter Fane, so quiet, so unemotional, who could express himself, perhaps, only in sudden murderous violence—as, possibly, quiet Lizzie Borden had once done. . . .

Gwenda opened her eyes. She had convinced herself, hadn't she, that Walter Fane was the man.

One might, perhaps, just consider Afflick. With his eyes open, not shut.

His loud check suit, his domineering manner—just the opposite to Walter Fane—nothing repressed or quiet about Afflick. But possibly he had put that manner on because of an inferiority complex. It worked that way, experts said. If you weren't sure of yourself, you had to boast and assert yourself and be overbearing. Turned down by Helen because he wasn't good enough for her. The sore festering, not forgotten. Determination to get on in the world. Persecution. Everyone against him. Discharged from his employment by a faked charge made up by an "enemy." Surely that did show that Afflick wasn't normal. And what a feeling of power a man like that would get out of killing. That good-natured jovial face of his, it was a cruel face really. He was a cruel man—and his thin pale wife knew it and was afraid of him. Lily Kimble had threatened him and Lily Kimble had died. Gwenda and Giles had interfered—then Gwenda and Giles must die, too, and he would involve Walter Fane, who had sacked him long ago. That fitted in very nicely.

Gwenda shook herself, came out of her imaginings, and returned to practicality. Giles would be home and want his tea. She must clear away and wash up lunch.

She fetched a tray and took the things out to the kitchen. Everything in the kitchen was exquisitely neat. Mrs. Cocker was really a treasure.

By the side of the sink was a pair of surgical rubber gloves. Mrs. Cocker always wore a pair for washing up. Her niece, who worked in a hospital, got them at a reduced price.

Gwenda fitted them on over her hands and began to wash up the dishes. She might as well keep her hands nice.

She washed the plates and put them in the rack, washed and dried the other things, and put everything neatly away.

Then, still lost in thought, she went upstairs. She might as well, she thought, wash out those stockings and a jumper or two. She'd keep the gloves on.

These things were in the forefront of her mind. But somewhere, underneath them, something was nagging at her.

Walter Fane or Jackie Afflick, she had said. One or the other of them. And she had made out quite a good case against either of them. Perhaps that was what really worried her. Because, strictly speaking, it would be much more satisfactory if you could only make out a good case against *one* of them. One ought to be sure, by now, *which*. And Gwenda wasn't sure.

If only there was someone else . . . But there couldn't be anyone else. Because Richard Erskine was out of it. Richard Erskine had been in Northumberland when Lily Kimble was killed and when the brandy in the decanter had been tampered with. Yes, Richard Erskine was right out of it.

She was glad of that, because she liked Richard Erskine. Richard Erskine was attractive—very attractive. How sad for him to be married to that megalith of a woman with her suspicious eyes and deep bass voice. Just like a man's voice . . .

Like a man's voice . . .

The idea flashed through her mind with a queer misgiving. . . .

A man's voice . . . Could it have been Mrs. Erskine, not her husband, who had replied to Giles on the telephone last night?

No—no, surely not. No, of course not. She and Giles would have known. And anyway, to begin with, Mrs. Erskine could have had no idea of who was ringing up. No, of course it was Erskine speaking, and his wife, as he said, was away.

His wife was away . . .

Surely—no, that was impossible . . . Could it have been *Mrs.* Erskine? Mrs. Erskine, driven insane by jealousy? Mrs. Erskine, to whom Lily Kimble had written? Was it a *woman* Leonie had seen in the garden that night when she looked out of the window?

There was a sudden bang in the hall below. Somebody had come in through the front door.

Gwenda came out from the bathroom onto the landing and looked over the banisters. She was relieved to see it was Dr. Kennedy. She called down:

"I'm here."

Her hands were held out in front of her—wet, glistening, a queer pinkish grey—they reminded her of something. . . .

Kennedy looked up, shading his eyes.

"Is that you, Gwennie? I can't see your face. . . . My eyes are dazzled—"

And then Gwenda screamed. . . .

Looking at those smooth monkey's paws and hearing that voice in the hall—

"It was you . . ." she gasped. "You killed her . . . Killed Helen . . . I—know now. It was you . . . all along. . . . You . . ."

He came up the stairs towards her—slowly—looking up at her.

"Why couldn't you leave me alone?" he said. "Why did you have to meddle? Why did you have to bring—her—back? Just when I'd begun to forget—to forget . . . You brought her back again—Helen—my Helen. Bringing it all up again. I had to kill Lily—now I'll have to kill you. Like I killed Helen . . . Yes, like I killed Helen . . ."

He was close upon her now—his hands out towards her—reaching, she knew, for her throat. That kind quizzical face—that nice ordinary, elderly face—the same still, but for the eyes—the eyes were not sane. . . .

Gwenda retreated before him slowly, the scream frozen in her throat. She had screamed once. She could not scream again. And if she did scream, no one would hear.

Because there was no one in the house—not Giles, and not Mrs. Cocker, not even Miss Marple in the garden. Nobody. And the house next door was too far away to hear if she screamed. And anyway, she couldn't scream. . . . Because she was too frightened to scream. Frightened of those horrible reaching hands . . .

She could back away and he would follow her until she stood there with her back to the nursery door and then—and then—those hands would fasten round her throat. . . .

A pitiful little stifled whimper came from between her lips . . .

And then, suddenly, Dr. Kennedy stopped and reeled back as a jet of soapy water struck him between the eyes. He gasped and blinked and his hands went to his face.

"So fortunate," said Miss Marple's voice, rather breathless, for she had run violently up the back stairs, "that I was just syringing the greenfly off your roses. . . ."

25

Postscript at Torquay

"But, of course, dear Gwenda, I should never have dreamed of going away and leaving you alone in the house," said Miss Marple. "I knew there was a very dangerous person at large, and I was keeping an unobtrusive watch from the garden."

"Did you know it was—him—all along?" asked Gwenda.

They were all three—Miss Marple, Gwenda and Giles—sitting on the terrace of the Imperial Hotel at Torquay.

"A change of scene," Miss Marple had said and Giles had agreed, would be the best thing for Gwenda. So Inspector Primer had concurred and they had driven to Torquay forthwith.

Miss Marple said in answer to Gwenda's question:

"Well, he did seem indicated, my dear. Although unfortunately there was nothing in the way of evidence to go upon. Just indications, nothing more."

Looking at her curiously, Giles said:

"But I can't see any indications even?"

"Oh, dear Giles, think. He was *on the spot*, to begin with."

"On the spot?"

"But certainly. When Kelvin Halliday came to him that night he *had just come back from the hospital*. And the hospital, at that time, as several people told us, was actually next door to Hillside, or St. Catherine's, as it was then called. So that, as you see, puts him in *the right place at the right time*. And then there were a hundred and one little significant facts. Helen Halliday told Richard Erskine she had gone out to marry Walter Fane because *she wasn't happy at home.* Not happy, that is, living with her brother. Yet her brother was by all accounts devoted to her. So why wasn't she happy? Mr. Afflick told you that he 'was sorry for the poor kid.' I think that he was absolutely truthful when he said that. He was sorry for her. Why did she have to go and meet young Afflick in that clandestine way? Admittedly she was not wildly in love with him. Was it because she couldn't meet young men in the ordinary normal way? Her brother was 'strict' and 'old-fashioned.' It is vaguely reminiscent, is it not, of Mr. Barrett of Wimpole Street?"

Gwenda shivered.

"He was mad," she said. "Mad."

"Yes," said Miss Marple. "He wasn't normal. He adored his half-sister, and that affection became possessive and unwholesome. That kind of thing happens oftener than you'd think. Fathers who don't want their daughters to marry—or even to meet young men. Like Mr. Barrett. I thought of that when I heard about the tennis net."

"The tennis net?"

"Yes, that seemed to me very significant. Think of that girl, young Helen, coming home from school, and eager for all a young girl wants out of life, anxious to meet young men—to flirt with them—"

"A little sex crazy."

"No," said Miss Marple with emphasis. "*That* is one of the wickedest things about this crime. Dr. Kennedy didn't only kill her physically. If you think back carefully, you'll see that the only evidence for Helen Kennedy's having been man mad or practically—what is the word you used, dear?—oh yes, a nymphomaniac, came actually from *Dr. Kennedy* himself. I think, myself, that she was a perfectly normal young girl who wanted to have fun and a good time and flirt a little and finally settle down with the man of her choice—no more than that. And see what steps her brother took. First he was strict and old-fashioned about allowing her liberty. Then, when she wanted to give tennis parties—a most normal and harmless desire—he pretended to agree and then one night secretly cut the tennis net to ribbons—a very significant and sadistic action. Then, since she could still go out to play tennis or to dances, he took advantage of a grazed foot which he treated, to infect it so that it wouldn't heal. Oh yes, I think he did that . . . in fact, I'm sure of it.

"Mind you, I don't think Helen realized any of all this. She knew her brother had a deep affection for her and I don't think she knew *why* she felt uneasy and unhappy at home. But she did feel like that and at last she decided to go out to India and marry young Fane simply in order to get away. To get away from *what?* She didn't know. She was too young and guileless to know. So she went off to India and on the way she met Richard Erskine and fell in love with him. There again, she behaved not like a sex-crazy girl, but like a decent and honourable girl. She didn't urge him to leave his wife. She urged him not to do so. But when she saw Walter Fane, she knew that she couldn't marry him, and because she didn't know what else to do, she wired her brother for money to go home.

"On the way home she met your father—and another way of escape showed itself. This time it was one with good prospects of happiness.

"She didn't marry your father under false pretences, Gwenda. He was recovering from the death of a dearly loved wife. She was getting over an unhappy love affair. They could both help each other. I think it is significant that she and Kelvin Halliday were married in London and then went down to Dillmouth to break the news to Dr. Kennedy. She must have had some instinct that that would be a wiser thing to do than to go down and be married in Dillmouth, which ordinarily would have been the normal thing to do. I still think she didn't know what she was up against—but she was uneasy, and she felt safer in presenting her brother with the marriage as a *fait accompli*.

"Kelvin Halliday was very friendly to Kennedy and liked him. Kennedy seems to have gone out of his way to appear pleased about the marriage. The couple took a furnished house there.

"And now we come to that very significant fact—the suggestion that Kelvin was being drugged by his wife. There are only two possible explanations of that—because there are only two people who could have had the opportunity of doing such a thing. Either Helen Halliday *was* drugging her husband, and if so, why? Or else the drugs were being administered by Dr. Kennedy. Kennedy was

Halliday's physician, as is clear by Halliday's consulting him. He had confidence in Kennedy's medical knowledge—and the suggestion that his wife was drugging him was very cleverly suggested to him by Kennedy."

"But could any drug make a man have the hallucination that he was strangling his wife?" asked Giles. "I mean there isn't any drug, is there, that has that particular effect?"

"My dear Giles, you've fallen into the trap again—the trap of believing *what is said to you.* There is only Dr. Kennedy's word for it that Halliday ever had *that* hallucination. He himself never says so in his diary. He had hallucinations, yes, but he does not mention their nature. But I daresay Kennedy talked to him about men who had strangled their wives after passing through a phase such as Kelvin Halliday was experiencing."

"Dr. Kennedy was really wicked," said Gwenda.

"I think," said Miss Marple, "that he'd definitely passed the border line between sanity and madness by that time. And Helen, poor girl, began to realize it. It was to her brother she must have been speaking that day when she was overheard by Lily. 'I think I've always been afraid of you.' That was one of the things she said. And that always was very significant. And so she determined to leave Dillmouth. She persuaded her husband to buy a house in Norfolk, she persuaded him not to tell anyone about it. That in itself, you know, was a very curious point. The secrecy about it was very illuminating. She was clearly very afraid of *someone* knowing about it—but that did not fit in with the Walter Fane theory or the Jackie Afflick theory—and certainly not with Richard Erskine's being concerned. No, it pointed to somewhere much nearer home.

"And in the end, Kelvin Halliday, whom doubtless the secrecy irked and who felt it to be pointless, told his brother-in-law.

"And in doing so, sealed his own fate and that of his wife. For Kennedy was not going to let Helen go and live happily with her husband. I think perhaps his idea was simply to break down Halliday's health with drugs. But at the revelation that his victim and Helen were going to escape him, he became completely unhinged. From the hospital he went through into the garden of St. Catherine's and he took with him a pair of surgical gloves. He caught Helen in the hall, and he strangled her. Nobody saw him, there was no one there to see him, or so he thought, and so, racked with love and frenzy, he quoted those tragic lines that were so apposite."

Miss Marple sighed and clucked her tongue.

"I was stupid—very stupid. We were all stupid. We should have seen at once. Those lines from *The Duchess of Malfi* were really the clue to the whole thing. They are said, are they not, by a *brother* who had just contrived his sister's death to avenge her marriage to the man she loved. Yes, we were stupid—"

"And then?" asked Giles.

"And then he went through with the whole devilish plan. The body carried upstairs. The clothes packed in a suitcase. A note written and thrown in the wastepaper basket to convince Halliday later."

"But I should have thought," said Gwenda, "that it would have been better from his point of view for my father actually to have been convicted of the murder."

Miss Marple shook her head.

"Oh no, he couldn't risk that. He had a lot of shrewd Scottish common sense, you know. He had a wholesome respect for the police. The police take a lot of convincing before they believe a man guilty of murder. The police might have asked a lot of awkward questions and made a lot of awkward inquiries as to times and places. No, his plan was simpler and, I think, more devilish. He only had Halliday to convince. First, that he had killed his wife. Secondly that he was mad. He persuaded Halliday to go into a mental home, but I don't think he really wanted to convince him that it was all a delusion. Your father accepted that theory, Gwennie, mainly, I should imagine, for your sake. He continued to believe that he had killed Helen. He died believing that."

"Wicked," said Gwenda. "Wicked—wicked—wicked."

"Yes," said Miss Marple. "There isn't really any other word. And I think, Gwenda, that that is why your childish impression of what you saw remained so strong. It was real evil that was in the air that night."

"But the letters," said Giles. "Helen's letters? They *were* in her handwriting, so they couldn't be forgeries."

"Of course they were forgeries! But that is where he overreached himself. He was so anxious, you see, to stop you and Giles making investigations. He could probably imitate Helen's handwriting quite nicely—but it wouldn't fool an expert. So the sample of Helen's handwriting he sent you with the letter wasn't her handwriting either. He wrote it himself. So naturally it tallied."

"Goodness," said Giles. "I never thought of that."

"No," said Miss Marple. "You believed what he said. It really is very dangerous to believe people. *I* never have for years."

"And the brandy?"

"He did that the day he came to Hillside with Helen's letter and talked to me in the garden. He was waiting in the house while Mrs. Cocker came out and told me he was there. It would only take a minute."

"Good Lord," said Giles. "And he urged me to take Gwenda home and give her brandy after we were at the police station when Lily Kimble was killed. How did he arrange to meet her earlier?"

"That was very simple. The original letter he sent her asked her to meet him at Woodleigh Camp and come to Matchings Halt by the two-o-five train from Dillmouth Junction. He came out of the copse of trees, probably, and accosted her as she was going up the lane—and strangled her. Then he simply substituted the letter you all saw for the letter she had with her (and which he had asked her to bring because of the directions in it) and went home to prepare for you and play out the little comedy of waiting for Lily."

"And Lily really was threatening him? Her letter didn't sound as though she was. Her letter sounded as though she suspected Afflick."

"Perhaps she did. But Leonie, the Swiss girl, had talked to Lily, and Leonie was the one danger to Kennedy. Because she looked out of the nursery window and saw him digging in the garden. In the morning he talked to her, told her bluntly that Major Halliday had killed his wife—that Major Halliday was insane, and that he, Kennedy, was hushing up the matter for the child's sake. If, however, Leonie felt she ought to go to the police, she must do so, but it would be very unpleasant for her—and so on.

"Leonie took immediate fright at the mention of the police. She adored you and had implicit faith in what monsieur le docteur thought best. Kennedy paid her a handsome sum of money and hustled her back to Switzerland. But before she went, she hinted something to Lily as to your father's having killed his wife and that she had seen the body buried. That fitted in with Lily's ideas at the time. She took it for granted it was Kelvin Halliday that Leonie had seen digging the grave."

"But Kennedy didn't know that, of course," said Giles.

"Of course not. When he got Lily's letter, the words in it that frightened him were that Leonie had told Lily what she had seen *out of the window* and the mention of the car outside."

"The car? Jackie Afflick's car?"

"Another misunderstanding. Lily remembered, or thought she remembered, a car like Jackie Afflick's being outside in the road. Already her imagination had got to work on the mystery man who came over to see Mrs. Halliday. With the hospital next door, no doubt a good many cars did park along this road. But you must remember that the *doctor's* car was actually standing outside the hospital that night—he probably leaped to the conclusion that she meant *his* car. The adjective posh was meaningless to him."

"I see," said Giles. "Yes, to a guilty conscience that letter of Lily's might look like blackmail. But how do you know all about Leonie?"

Her lips pursed close together, Miss Marple said:

"He went—right over the edge, you know. As soon as the men Inspector Primer had left rushed in and seized him. He went over the whole crime again and again—everything he'd done. Leonie died, it seems, very shortly after her return to Switzerland. Overdose of some sleeping tablets. . . . Oh no, he wasn't taking any chances."

"Like trying to poison me with the brandy."

"You were very dangerous to him, you and Giles. Fortunately you never told him about your memory of seeing Helen dead in the hall. He never knew there had been an eyewitness."

"Those telephone calls to Fane and Afflick," said Giles. "Did he put those through?"

"Yes. If there was an inquiry as to who could have tampered with the brandy, either of them would make an admirable suspect, and if Jackie Afflick drove over in his car alone, it might tie him in with Lily Kimble's murder. Fane would most likely have an alibi."

"And he seemed fond of me," said Gwenda. "Little Gwennie."

"He had to play his part," said Miss Marple. "Imagine what it meant to him. After eighteen years, you and Giles come along, asking questions, burrowing into the past, disturbing a murder that had seemed dead but was only sleeping. . . . Murder in retrospect. . . . A horribly dangerous thing to do, my dears. I have been sadly worried."

"Poor Mrs. Cocker," said Gwenda. "She had a terribly near escape. I'm glad she's going to be all right. Do you think she'll ever come back to us, Giles? After all this?"

"She will if there's a nursery," said Giles gravely, and Gwenda blushed, and Miss Marple smiled a little and looked out across Torbay.

"How very odd it was that it should happen the way it did," mused Gwenda. "My having those rubber gloves on, and looking at them, and then his coming into the hall and saying those words that sounded so like the others. 'Face' . . . and then: 'Eyes dazzled'—"

She shuddered.

"*Cover her face; mine eyes dazzle: she died young* . . . that might have been me . . . if Miss Marple hadn't been there."

She paused and said softly:

"Poor Helen . . . poor lovely Helen . . . who died young. . . . You know, Giles, she isn't there any more—in the house—in the hall. . . . I could feel that yesterday before we left. . . . There's just the house. And the house is fond of us. We can go back if we like. . . ."

The Murder at the Vicarage

To
ROSALIND

CHAPTER ONE

It is difficult to know quite where to begin this story, but I have fixed my choice on a certain Wednesday at luncheon at the Vicarage. The conversation, though in the main irrelevant to the matter in hand, yet contained one or two suggestive incidents which influenced later developments.

I had just finished carving some boiled beef (remarkably tough by the way), and on resuming my seat I remarked, in a spirit most unbecoming to my cloth, that anyone who murdered Colonel Protheroe would be doing the world at large a service.

My young nephew, Dennis, said instantly, "That'll be remembered against you when the old boy is found bathed in blood. Mary will give evidence, won't you, Mary? And describe how you brandished the carving knife in a vindictive manner."

Mary, who is in service at the Vicarage as a stepping stone to better things and higher wages, merely said, in a loud, businesslike voice, "Greens," and thrust a cracked dish at him in a truculent manner.

My wife said in a sympathetic voice, "Has he been *very* trying?"

I did not reply at once, for Mary, setting the greens on the table with a bang, proceeded to thrust a dish of singularly moist and unpleasant dumplings under my nose. I said, "No, thank you," and she deposited the dish with a clatter on the table and left the room.

"It is a pity that I am such a shocking housekeeper," said my wife with a tinge of genuine regret in her voice.

I was inclined to agree with her. My wife's name is Griselda—a highly suitable name for a parson's wife. But there the suitability ends. She is not in the least meek.

I have always been of the opinion that a clergyman should be unmarried. Why I should have urged Griselda to marry me at the end of twenty-four hours' acquaintance is a mystery to me. Marriage, I have always held, is a serious affair, to be entered into only after long deliberation and forethought, and suitability of tastes and inclinations is the most important consideration.

Griselda is nearly twenty years younger than myself. She is most distractingly pretty and quite incapable of taking anything seriously. She is incompetent in every way and extremely trying to live with. She treats the parish as a kind of huge joke arranged for her amusement. I have endeavored to form her mind and failed. I am more than ever convinced that celibacy is desirable for the clergy. I have frequently hinted as much to Griselda, but she has only laughed.

"My dear," I said. "If you would only exercise a little care—"

"I do sometimes," said Griselda. "But on the whole I think things go worse when I'm trying. I'm evidently *not* a housekeeper by nature. I find it better to leave things to Mary and just make up my mind to be uncomfortable and have nasty things to eat."

"And what about your husband, my dear?" I said reproachfully and, proceeding to follow the example of the devil in quoting Scripture for his own ends, I added, " 'She looketh to the ways of her household.' "

"Think how lucky you are not to be torn to pieces by lions," said Griselda quickly interrupting. "Or burned at the stake. Bad food and lots of dust and dead wasps is really nothing to make a fuss about. Tell me more about Colonel Protheroe. At any rate the early Christians were lucky enough not to have churchwardens."

"Pompous old brute," said Dennis. "No wonder his first wife ran away from him."

"I don't see what else she could do," said my wife.

"Griselda," I said sharply. "I will not have you speaking in that way."

"Darling," said my wife affectionately. "Tell me about him. What was the trouble? Was it Mr. Hawes's becking and nodding and crossing himself every other minute?"

Hawes is our new curate. He has been with us just over three weeks. He has High Church views and fasts on Fridays. Colonel Protheroe is a great opposer of ritual in any form.

"Not this time. He did touch on it in passing. No, the whole trouble arose out of Mrs. Price Ridley's wretched pound note."

Mrs. Price Ridley is a devout member of my congregation. Attending early service on the anniversary of her son's death, she put a pound note into the offertory bag. Later, reading the amount of the collection posted up, she was pained to observe that one ten-shilling note was the highest item mentioned.

She complained to me about it, and I pointed out, very reasonably, that she must have made a mistake.

"We're none of us so young as we were," I said, trying to turn it off tactfully. "And we must pay the penalty of advancing years."

Strangely enough my words only seemed to incense her further. She said that things had a very odd look and that she was surprised I didn't think so, also. And she flounced away and, I gather, took her troubles to Colonel Protheroe. Protheroe is the kind of man who enjoys making a fuss on every conceivable occasion. He made a fuss. It is a pity he made it on a Wednesday. I teach in the church day school on Wednesday mornings, a proceeding that causes me acute nervousness and leaves me unsettled for the rest of the day.

"Well, I suppose he must have some fun," said my wife, with the air of trying to sum up the position impartially. "Nobody flutters round him and calls him the dear Vicar, and embroiders awful slippers for him, and gives him bedsocks for Christmas. Both his wife and his daughter are fed to the teeth with him. I suppose it makes him happy to feel important somewhere."

"He needn't be offensive about it," I said with some heat. "I don't think he quite realized the implications of what he was saying. He wants to go over all the church accounts—in case of defalcations—that was the word he used. Defalcations! Does he suspect me of embezzling the church funds?"

"Nobody would suspect you of anything, darling," said Griselda. "You're so transparently above suspicion that really it would be a marvelous opportunity. I wish you'd embezzle the S.P.G. funds. I hate missionaries—I always have."

I would have reproved her for that sentiment, but Mary entered at that moment with a partially cooked rice pudding. I made a mild protest, but Griselda said that the Japanese always ate half-cooked rice and had marvelous brains in consequence.

"I daresay," she said, "that if you had a rice pudding like this every day till Sunday, you'd preach the most marvelous sermon."

"Heaven forbid," I said with a shudder.

"Protheroe's coming over tomorrow evening and we're going over the accounts together," I went on. "I must finish preparing my talk for the C.E.M.S. today. Looking up a reference I became so engrossed in Canon Shirley's 'Reality' that I haven't got on as well as I should. What are you doing this afternoon, Griselda?"

"My duty," said Griselda. "My duty as the Vicaress. Tea and scandal at four-thirty."

"Who is coming?"

Griselda ticked them off on her fingers with a glow of virtue on her face.

"Mrs. Price Ridley, Miss Wetherby, Miss Hartnell, and that terrible Miss Marple."

"I rather like Miss Marple," I said. "She has, at least, a sense of humor."

"She's the worst cat in the village," said Griselda. "And she always knows every single thing that happens—and draws the worst inferences from it."

Griselda, as I have said, is much younger than I am. At my time of life, one knows that the worst is usually true.

"Well, don't expect *me* in for tea, Griselda," said Dennis.

"Beast!" said Griselda.

"Yes, but look here, the Protheroes really *did* ask me for tennis today."

"Beast!" said Griselda again.

Dennis beat a prudent retreat, and Griselda and I went together into my study.

"I wonder what we shall have for tea," said Griselda seating herself on my writing table. "Doctor Stone and Miss Cram, I suppose, and perhaps Mrs. Lestrange. By the way, I called on her yesterday, but she was out. Yes, I'm sure we shall have Mrs. Lestrange for tea. It's so mysterious, isn't it, her arriving like this and taking a house down here, and hardly ever going outside it? Makes one think of detective stories. You know—'*Who was she, the mysterious woman with the pale, beautiful face? What was her past history? Nobody knew. There was something faintly sinister about her.*' I believe Doctor Haydock knows something about her."

"You read too many detective stories, Griselda," I observed mildly.

"What about you?" she retorted. "I was looking everywhere for 'The Stain on the Stairs' the other day when you were in here writing a sermon. And at last I came in to ask you if you'd seen it anywhere, and what did I find?"

I had the grace to blush.

"I picked it up at random. A chance sentence caught my eye and—"

"I know those chance sentences," said Griselda. She quoted impressively, "'*And then a very curious thing happened—Griselda rose, crossed the room, and kissed her elderly husband affectionately.*'"

She suited the action to the word.

"Is that a very curious thing?" I inquired.

"Of course it is," said Griselda. "Do you realize, Len, that I might have married a cabinet minister, a baronet, a rich company promoter, three subalterns, and a ne'er-do-well with attractive manners, and that instead I chose you? Didn't it astonish you very much?"

"At the time it did," I replied. "I have often wondered why you did it."

Griselda sighed.

"It made me feel so powerful," she murmured. "The others thought me simply wonderful, and, of course, it would have been very nice for *them* to have *me*. But I'm everything you most dislike and disapprove of, and yet you couldn't withstand me! My vanity couldn't hold out against that. It's so much nicer to be a secret and delightful sin to anybody than to be a feather in his cap. I make you frightfully uncomfortable and stir you up the wrong way the whole time, and yet you adore me madly. You do adore me madly, don't you?"

"Naturally, I am very fond of you, my dear."

"Oh! Len, you adore me. Do you remember that day when I stayed up in town and sent you a wire you never got because the postmistress's sister was having twins and she forgot to send it round? The state you got into, and you telephoned Scotland Yard and made the most frightful fuss."

There are things one hates being reminded of. I had really been strangely foolish on the occasion in question. I said, "If you don't mind, dear, I want to get on with the C.E.M.S."

Griselda gave a sigh of intense irritation, ruffled my hair up on end, smoothed it down again, said, "You don't deserve me. You really don't. I'll have an affair with the artist. I will—really and truly. And then think of the scandal in the parish."

"There's a good deal already," I said mildly.

Griselda laughed, blew me a kiss, and departed through the window.

CHAPTER TWO

Griselda is a very irritating woman. On leaving the luncheon table, I had felt myself to be in a good mood for preparing a really forceful address for the Church of England Men's Society. Now I felt restless and disturbed.

Just when I was really settling down to it, Lettice Protheroe drifted in.

I use the word *drifted* advisedly. I have read novels in which young people are described as bursting with energy—*joie de vivre*, the magnificent vitality of youth. Personally, all the young people I come across have the air of amiable wraiths.

Lettice was particularly wraithlike this afternoon. She is a pretty girl, very tall and fair and completely vague. She drifted through the French window, absently pulled off the yellow beret she was wearing, and murmured vaguely with a kind of faraway surprise. "Oh! It's you."

There is a path from Old Hall through the woods which comes out by our garden gate, so that most people coming from there come in at that gate and up to the study window instead of going a long way round by the road and coming to the front door. I was not surprised at Lettice coming in this way, but I did a little resent her attitude.

If you come to a Vicarage, you ought to be prepared to find a Vicar.

She came in and collapsed in a crumpled heap in one of my big armchairs. She plucked aimlessly at her hair, staring at the ceiling.

"Is Dennis anywhere about?"

"I haven't seen him since lunch. I understood he was going to play tennis at your place."

"Oh!" said Lettice. "I hope he isn't. He won't find anybody there."

"He said you'd asked him."

"I believe I did. Only that was Friday. And today's Tuesday."

"It's Wednesday," I said.

"Oh! How dreadful," said Lettice. "That means that I've forgotten to go to lunch with some people for the third time."

Fortunately it didn't seem to worry her much.

"Is Griselda anywhere about?"

"I expect you'll find her in the studio in the garden—sitting to Lawrence Redding."

"There's been quite a shemozzle about him," said Lettice. "With Father, you know. Father's dreadful."

"What was the she—whatever it was, about?" I inquired.

"About his painting me. Father found out about it. Why shouldn't I be painted in my bathing suit? If I go on a beach in it, why shouldn't I be painted in it?"

Lettice paused and then went on.

"It's really absurd—Father forbidding a young man the house. Of course, Lawrence and I simply shriek about it. I shall come and be done here in your studio."

"No, my dear," I said. "Not if your father forbids it."

"Oh, dear," said Lettice, sighing. "How tiresome everyone is. I feel shattered. Definitely. If only I had some money I'd go away, but without it I can't. If only Father would be decent and die, I should be all right."

"You must not say things like that, Lettice."

"Well, if he doesn't want me to want him to die, he shouldn't be so horrible over money. I don't wonder Mother left him. Do you know for years I believed she was dead. What sort of a young man did she run away with? Was he nice?"

"It was before your father came to live here."

"I wonder what's become of her? I expect Anne will have an affair with someone soon. Anne hates me—she's quite decent to me, but she hates me. She's getting old and she doesn't like it. That's the age you break out, you know."

I wondered if Lettice was going to spend the entire afternoon in my study.

"You haven't seen my Gramophone records, have you?" she asked.

"No."

"How tiresome. I know I've left them somewhere. And I've lost the dog. And my wrist watch is somewhere, only it doesn't much matter because it won't go. Oh, dear, I am so sleepy. I can't think why, because I didn't get up till eleven. But life's very shattering, don't you think? Oh, dear, I must go. I'm going to see Doctor Stone's barrow at three o'clock."

I glanced at the clock and remarked that it was now five and twenty to four.

"Oh, is it? How dreadful if they've waited or if they've gone without me. I suppose I'd better go down and do something about it."

She got up and drifted out again murmuring over her shoulder, "You'll tell Dennis, won't you?"

I said yes mechanically, only realizing too late that I had no idea what it was I was to tell Dennis. But I reflected that in all probability it did not matter. I fell to cogitating on the subject of Dr. Stone, a well-known archaeologist who had recently come to stay at the Blue Boar, while he superintended the excavation of a barrow situated on Colonel Protheroe's property. There had already been several disputes between him and the Colonel. I was amused at his appointment to take Lettice to see the operations.

It occurred to me that Lettice Protheroe was something of a minx. I wondered how she would get on with the archaeologist's secretary, Miss Cram. Miss Cram is a healthy young woman of twenty-five, noisy in manner, with a high color, fine animal spirits, and a mouth that always seems to have more than its full share of teeth.

Village opinion is divided as to whether she is no better than she should be or else a young woman of iron virtue who purposes to become Mrs. Stone at an early opportunity. She is in every way a great contrast to Lettice.

I could imagine that the state of things at Old Hall might not be too happy. Colonel Protheroe had married again some five years previously. The second Mrs. Protheroe was a remarkably handsome woman in a rather unusual style. I had always guessed that the relations between her and her stepdaughter were not too happy.

I had one more interruption. This time it was my curate, Hawes. He wanted to know the details of my interview with Protheroe. I told him that the Colonel had deplored his "Romish tendencies," but that the real purpose of his visit had been on quite another matter. At the same time I entered a protest of my own and told him plainly that he must conform to my ruling. On the whole, he took my remarks very well.

I felt rather remorseful, when he had gone, for not liking him better. These irrational likes and dislikes that one takes to people are, I am sure, very unchristian.

With a sigh I realized that the hands of the clock on my writing table pointed to a quarter to five, a sign that it was really half past four, and I made my way to the drawing-room.

Four of my parishioners were assembled there with teacups. Griselda sat behind the tea table trying to look natural in her environment, but only succeeding in looking more out of place than usual.

I shook hands all round and sat down between Miss Marple and Miss Wetherby.

Miss Marple is a white-haired old lady with a gentle, appealing manner—Miss Wetherby is a mixture of vinegar and gush. Of the two Miss Marple is much the more dangerous.

"We were just talking," said Griselda in a honey-sweet voice, "about Doctor Stone and Miss Cram."

A ribald rhyme concocted by Dennis shot through my head. *Miss Cram doesn't give a damn.* I had a sudden yearning to say it out loud and observe the effect, but fortunately I refrained.

Miss Wetherby said tersely, "No nice girl would do it," and shut her thin lips disapprovingly.

"Do what?" I inquired.

"Be a secretary to an unmarried man," said Miss Wetherby in a horrified tone.

"Oh, my dear," said Miss Marple. "I think married ones are the worst. Remember poor Mollie Carter."

"Married men living apart from their wives are, of course, notorious," said Miss Wetherby.

"And even some of the ones living with their wives," murmured Miss Marple. "I remember—"

I interrupted these unsavory reminiscences.

"But surely," I said, "in these days a girl can take a post in just the same way as a man does."

"To come away to the country? And stay at the same hotel?" said Mrs. Price Ridley in a severe voice.

Miss Wetherby murmured to Miss Marple in a low voice, "And all the bedrooms on the same floor."

They exchanged glances.

Miss Hartnell, who is weather-beaten and jolly and much dreaded by the poor, observed in a loud, hearty voice, "The poor man will be caught before he knows where he is. He's as innocent as a babe unborn, you can see that."

Curious what turns of phrase we employ. None of the ladies present would have dreamed of alluding to an actual baby till it was safely in the cradle, visible to all.

"Disgusting, I call it," continued Miss Hartnell with her usual tactlessness. "The man must be at least twenty-five years older than she is."

Three female voices rose at once making disconnected remarks about the Choir Boys' Outing, the regrettable incident at the last Mothers' Meeting, and the drafts in the church. Miss Marple twinkled at Griselda.

"Don't you think," said my wife, "that Miss Cram may just like having an interesting job, and that she considers Doctor Stone just as an employer?"

There was a silence. Evidently none of the four ladies agreed. Miss Marple broke the silence by patting Griselda on the arm.

"My dear," she said, "you are very young. The young have such innocent minds."

Griselda said indignantly that she hadn't got at all an innocent mind.

"Naturally," said Miss Marple, unheeding of the protest, "you think the best of everyone."

"Do you really think she wants to marry that bald-headed, dull man?"

"I understand he is quite well off," said Miss Marple. "Rather a violent temper, I'm afraid. He had quite a serious quarrel with Colonel Protheroe the other day."

Everyone leaned forward interestedly.

"Colonel Protheroe accused him of being an ignoramus."

"How like Colonel Protheroe, and how absurd," said Mrs. Price Ridley.

"Very like Colonel Protheroe, but I don't know about it being absurd," said Miss Marple. "You remember the woman who came down here and said she represented Welfare, and after taking subscriptions she was never heard of again, and proved to have nothing whatever to do with Welfare. One is so inclined to be trusting and take people at their own valuation."

I should never have dreamed of describing Miss Marple as trusting.

"There's been some fuss about that young artist, Mr. Redding, hasn't there?" asked Miss Wetherby.

Miss Marple nodded.

"Colonel Protheroe turned him out of the house. It appears he was painting Lettice in her bathing suit."

Suitable sensation!

"I always *thought* there was something between them," said Mrs. Price Ridley. "That young fellow is always mouching off up there. Pity the girl hasn't got a mother. A stepmother is never the same thing."

"I daresay Mrs. Protheroe does her best," said Miss Hartnell.

"Girls are so sly," deplored Mrs. Price Ridley.

"Quite a romance, isn't it?" said the softer-hearted Miss Wetherby. "He's a very good-looking young fellow."

"But loose," said Miss Hartnell. "Bound to be. An artist! Paris! Models! The Altogether!"

"Painting her in her bathing suit," said Mrs. Price Ridley. "Not quite nice."

"He's painting me, too," said Griselda.

"But not in your bathing suit, dear," said Miss Marple.

"It might be worse," said Griselda solemnly.

"Naughty girl," said Miss Hartnell, taking the joke broadmindedly. Everybody else looked slightly shocked.

"Did dear Lettice tell you of the trouble?" asked Miss Marple of me.

"Tell me?"

"Yes. I saw her pass through the garden and go round to the study window."

Miss Marple always sees everything. Gardening is as good as a smoke screen, and the habit of observing birds through powerful glasses can always be turned to account.

"She mentioned it, yes," I admitted.

"Mr. Hawes looked worried," said Miss Marple. "I hope he hasn't been working too hard."

"Oh!" cried Miss Wetherby excitedly. "I quite forgot. I knew I had some news for you. I saw Doctor Haydock coming out of Mrs. Lestrange's cottage."

Everyone looked at each other.

"Perhaps she's ill," suggested Mrs. Price Ridley.

"It must have been very sudden, if so," said Miss Hartnell. "For I saw her walking round her garden at three o'clock this afternoon, and she seemed in perfect health."

"She and Doctor Haydock must be old acquaintances," said Mrs. Price Ridley. "He's been very quiet about it."

"It's curious," said Miss Wetherby, "that he's never *mentioned* it."

"As a matter of fact—" said Griselda in a low, mysterious voice, and stopped.

Everyone leaned forward excitedly.

"I happen to *know*," said Griselda impressively. "Her husband was a missionary. Terrible story. *He was eaten*, you know. Actually eaten. And she was forced to become the chief's head wife. Doctor Haydock was with an expedition and rescued her."

For a moment excitement was rife, then Miss Marple said reproachfully, but with a smile, "Naughty girl!"

She tapped Griselda reprovingly on the arm.

"Very unwise thing to do, my dear. If you make up these things, people are quite likely to believe them. And sometimes that leads to complications."

A distinct frost had come over the assembly. Two of the ladies rose to take their departure.

"I wonder if there *is* anything between young Lawrence Redding and Lettice Protheroe," said Miss Wetherby. "It certainly looks like it. What do you think, Miss Marple?"

Miss Marple seemed thoughtful.

"I shouldn't have said so myself. Not *Lettice. Quite* another person, I should have said."

"But Colonel Protheroe must have thought—"

"He has always struck me as rather a stupid man," said Miss Marple. "The kind of man who gets the wrong idea into his head and is obstinate about it. Do you remember Joe Bucknell who used to keep the Blue Boar? Such a to-do about his daughter carrying on with young Bailey. And all the time it was that minx of a wife of his."

She was looking full at Griselda as she spoke, and I suddenly felt a wild surge of anger.

"Don't you think, Miss Marple," I said, "that we're all inclined to let our tongues run away with us too much? Charity thinketh no evil, you know. Inestimable harm may be done by the foolish wagging of tongues in ill-natured gossip."

"Dear Vicar," said Miss Marple, "you are so unworldly. I'm afraid that, observing human nature for as long as I have done, one gets not to expect very much from it. I daresay idle tittle-tattle is very wrong and unkind, but it is so often true, isn't it?"

That last Parthian shot went home.

CHAPTER THREE

"NASTY OLD CAT," said Griselda as soon as the door was closed.

She made a face in the direction of the departing visitors and then looked at me and laughed.

"Len, do you really suspect me of having an affair with Lawrence Redding?"

"My dear, of course not."

"But you thought Miss Marple was hinting at it. And you rose to my defense simply beautifully. Like—like an angry tiger."

A momentary uneasiness assailed me. A clergyman of the Church of England ought never to put himself in the position of being described as an angry tiger. However, I trusted that Griselda exaggerated.

"I felt the occasion could not pass without a protest," I said. "But, Griselda, I wish you would be a little more careful in what you say."

"Do you mean the cannibal story?" she asked. "Or the suggestion that Lawrence was painting me in the nude? If they only knew that he was painting me in a thick cloak with a very high fur collar—the sort of thing that you could go quite purely to see the Pope in—not a bit of sinful flesh showing anywhere! In fact, it's all marvelously pure. Lawrence never even attempts to make love to me. I can't think why."

"Surely, knowing that you're a married woman—"

"Don't pretend to come out of the Ark, Len. You know very well that an attractive young woman with an elderly husband is a kind of gift from heaven to a young man. There must be some other reason— It's not that I'm unattractive—I'm not."

"Surely you don't want him to make love to you?"

"N-N-o," said Griselda with more hesitation than I thought becoming.

"If he's in love with Lettice Protheroe—"

"Miss Marple didn't seem to think he was."

"Miss Marple may be mistaken."

"She never is. That kind of old cat is always right." She paused a minute and then said, with a quick, sidelong glance at me, "You do believe me, don't you? I mean, that there's nothing between Lawrence and me."

"My dear Griselda," I said, surprised. "Of course."

My wife came across and kissed me.

"I wish you weren't so terribly easy to deceive, Len. You'd believe me whatever I said."

"I should hope so. But, my dear, I do beg of you to guard your tongue and be careful what you say. These women are singularly deficient in humor, remember, and take everything seriously."

"What they need," said Griselda, "is a little immorality in their lives. Then they wouldn't be so busy looking for it in other people's."

On this she left the room, and, glancing at my watch, I hurried out to pay some visits that ought to have been made earlier in the day.

The Wednesday evening service was sparsely attended as usual, but when I came out through the church, after disrobing in the vestry, it was empty save for a woman who stood staring up at one of our windows. We have some rather fine old stained glass, and, indeed, the church itself is well worth looking at. She turned at my footsteps, and I saw that it was Mrs. Lestrange.

We both hesitated a moment and then I said, "I hope you like our little church."

"I've been admiring the screen," she said.

Her voice was pleasant, low yet very distinct with a clear-cut enunciation. She added, "I'm so sorry to have missed your wife yesterday."

We talked a few minutes longer about the church. She was evidently a cultured woman who knew something of church history and architecture. We left the building together and walked down the road, since one way to the Vicarage led past her house. As we arrived at the gate, she said pleasantly, "Come in, won't you? And tell me what you think of what I have done."

I accepted the invitation. Little Gates had formerly belonged to an Anglo-Indian colonel, and I could not help feeling relieved by the disappearance of the brass tables and the Burmese idols. It was furnished now very simply but in exquisite taste. There was a sense of harmony and rest about it.

Yet I wondered more and more what had brought such a woman as Mrs. Lestrange to St. Mary Mead. She was so very clearly a woman of the world that it seemed a strange taste to bury herself in a country village.

In the clear light of her drawing-room I had an opportunity of observing her closely for the first time.

She was a very tall woman. Her hair was gold with a tinge of red in it. Her eyebrows and eyelashes were dark, whether by art or by nature I could not decide. If she was, as I thought, made up, it was done very artistically. There was something sphinxlike about her face when it was in repose, and she had the most curious eyes I have ever seen—they were almost golden in shade.

Her clothes were perfect, and she had all the ease of manner of a well-bred woman, and yet there was something about her that was incongruous and baffling. You felt that she was a mystery. The word Griselda had used occurred to me—*sinister*. Absurd, of course, and yet—was it so absurd? The thought sprang unbidden into my mind: *This woman would stick at nothing.*

Our talk was on most normal lines—pictures, books, old churches. Yet somehow I got very strongly the impression that there was something else—something of quite a different nature that Mrs. Lestrange wanted to say to me.

I caught her eyes on me once or twice, looking at me with a curious hesitancy, as though she were unable to make up her mind. She kept the talk, I noticed, strictly to impersonal subjects. She made no mention of a husband or of friends or relations.

But all the time there was that strange, urgent appeal in her glance. It seemed to say, "Shall I tell you? I want to. Can't you help me?"

Yet in the end it died away—or perhaps it had all been my fancy. I had the feeling that I was being dismissed. I rose and took my leave. As I went out of the room, I glanced back and saw her staring after me with a puzzled, doubtful expression. On an impulse I came back.

"If there is anything I can do—"

She said doubtfully, "It's very kind of you—"

We were both silent. Then she said, "I wish I knew. It's very difficult. No, I don't think anyone can help me. But thank you for offering to do so."

That seemed final, so I went. But as I did so, I wondered. We are not used to mysteries in St. Mary Mead.

So much is this the case that as I emerged from the gate I was pounced upon. Miss Hartnell is very good at pouncing in a heavy and cumbrous way.

"*I* saw you!" she exclaimed with ponderous humor. "And I *was* so excited. Now you can tell us all about it."

"About what?"

"The mysterious lady! Is she a widow or has she a husband somewhere?"

"I really couldn't say. She didn't tell me."

"How very peculiar. One would think she would be certain to mention something casually. It almost looks, doesn't it, as though she had a reason for not speaking?"

"I really don't see that."

"Ah! But as dear Miss Marple says, you are so unworldly, dear Vicar. Tell me, has she known Doctor Haydock long?"

"She didn't mention him, so I don't know."

"Really? But what did you talk about, then?"

"Pictures, music, books," I said truthfully.

Miss Hartnell, whose only topics of conversation are the purely personal, looked suspicious and unbelieving. Taking advantage of a momentary hesitation on her part as to how to proceed next, I bade her good night and walked rapidly away.

I called in at a house farther down the village and returned to the Vicarage by the garden gate, passing, as I did so, the danger point of Miss Marple's garden. However, I did not see how it was humanly possible for the news of my visit to Mrs. Lestrange to have yet reached her ears, so I felt reasonably safe.

As I latched the gate, it occurred to me that I would just step down to the shed in the garden which young Lawrence Redding was using as a studio, and see for myself how Griselda's portrait was progressing.

I append a rough sketch here which will be useful in the light of after happenings, only sketching in such details as are necessary.

I had no idea there was anyone in the studio. There had been no voices from within to warn me, and I suppose that my own footsteps made no noise upon the grass.

I opened the door and then stopped awkwardly on the threshold. For there were two people in the studio, and the man's arms were round the woman and he was kissing her passionately.

The two people were the artist, Lawrence Redding, and Mrs. Protheroe.

I backed out precipitately and beat a retreat to my study. There I sat down in a chair, took out my pipe, and thought things over. The discovery had come as a great shock to me. Especially since my conversation with Lettice that afternoon, I had felt fairly certain that there was some kind of understanding growing up between her and the young man. Moreover, I was convinced that she herself thought so. I felt positive that she had no idea of the artist's feelings for her stepmother.

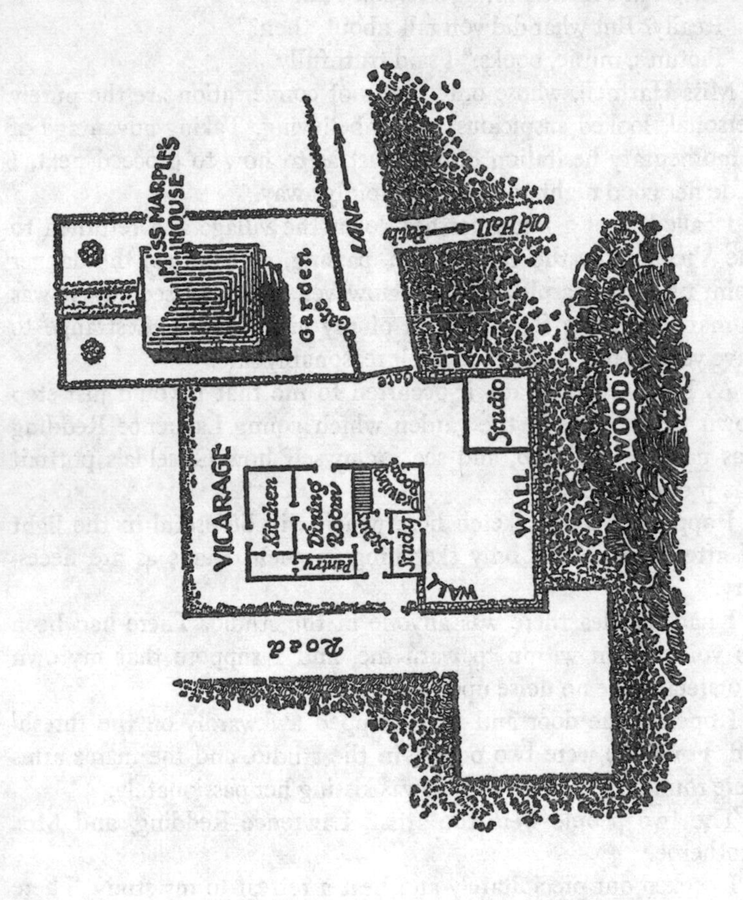
MISS MARPLE'S HOUSE
Garden
Gate
LANE
Path
Old Hall
Gate
Studio
WOODS
WALL
VICARAGE
Kitchen
Dining Room
Pantry
Stairs
Study
Drawing Room
WALL
WALL
Road
Path

A nasty tangle. I paid a grudging tribute to Miss Marple. She had not been deceived, but had evidently suspected the true state of things with a fair amount of accuracy. I had entirely misread her meaning glance at Griselda.

I had never dreamed of considering Mrs. Protheroe in the matter. There has always been rather a suggestion of Caesar's wife about Mrs. Protheroe—a quiet, self-contained woman whom one would not suspect of any great depths of feeling.

I had got to this point in my meditations when a tap on my study window roused me. I got up and went to it. Mrs. Protheroe was standing outside. I opened the window, and she came in, not waiting for an invitation on my part. She crossed the room in a breathless sort of way and dropped down on the sofa.

I had the feeling that I had never really seen her before. The quiet, self-contained woman that I knew had vanished. In her place was a quick-breathing, desperate creature. For the first time I realized that Anne Protheroe was beautiful.

She was a brown-haired woman with a pale face and very deep set gray eyes. She was flushed now, and her breast heaved. It was as though a statue had suddenly come to life. I blinked my eyes at the transformation.

"I thought it best to come," she said. "You—you saw just now?"

I bowed my head.

She said very quietly. "We love each other."

And even in the middle of her evident distress and agitation she could not keep a little smile from her lips. The smile of a woman who sees something very beautiful and wonderful.

I still said nothing, and she added presently, "I suppose to you that seems very wrong?"

"Can you expect me to say anything else, Mrs. Protheroe?"

"No—no; I suppose not."

I went on, trying to make my voice as gentle as possible. "You are a married woman—"

She interrupted me.

"Oh! I know—I know. Do you think I haven't gone over all that again and again? I'm not a bad woman, really—I'm not. And things aren't—aren't—as you might think they are."

I said gravely, "I'm glad of that."

She asked rather timorously, "Are you going to tell my husband?"

I said rather dryly, "There seems to be a general idea that a clergyman is incapable of behaving like a gentleman. That is not true."

She threw me a grateful glance.

"I'm so unhappy. Oh! I'm so dreadfully unhappy. I can't go on. I simply can't go on. And I don't know what to do." Her voice rose with a slightly hysterical note in it. "You don't know what my life is like. I've been miserable with Lucius from the beginning. No woman could be happy with him. I wish he were dead. It's awful, but I do. I'm desperate. I tell you, I'm desperate."

She started and looked over at the window.

"What was that? I thought I heard someone. Perhaps it's Lawrence."

I went over to the window, which I had not closed, as I had thought. I stepped out and looked down the garden, but there was no one in sight. Yet I was almost convinced that I, too, had heard someone. Or perhaps it was her certainty that had convinced me.

When I re-entered the room she was leaning forward, drooping her head down. She looked the picture of despair. She said again, "I don't know what to do. I don't know what to do."

I came and sat down beside her. I said the things I thought it was my duty to say, and tried to say them with the necessary conviction, uneasily conscious all the time that that same morning I had given voice to the sentiment that a world without Colonel Protheroe in it would be improved.

Above all, I begged her to do nothing rash. To leave her home and her husband was a very serious step.

I don't suppose I convinced her. I have lived long enough in the world to know that arguing with anyone in love is next door to useless, but I do think my words brought to her some measure of comfort.

When she rose to go, she thanked me and promised to think over what I had said.

Nevertheless, when she had gone, I felt very uneasy. I felt that hitherto I had misjudged Anne Protheroe's character. She impressed me now as a very desperate woman, the kind of woman who would stick at nothing, once her emotions were aroused. And she was desperately, wildly, madly in love with Lawrence Redding, a man several years younger than herself.

I didn't like it.

CHAPTER FOUR

I HAD ENTIRELY FORGOTTEN that we had asked Lawrence Redding to dinner that night. When Griselda burst in and scolded me, pointing out that it lacked two minutes to dinnertime, I was quite taken aback.

"I hope everything will be all right," Griselda called up the stairs after me. "I've thought over what you said at lunch and I've really thought of some quite good things to eat."

I may say, in passing, that our evening meal amply bore out Griselda's assertion that things went much worse when she tried than when she didn't. The menu was ambitious in conception, and Mary seemed to have taken a perverse pleasure in seeing how best she could alternate undercooking and overcooking. Some oysters which Griselda had ordered, and which would seem to be beyond the reach of incompetence, we were unfortunately not able to sample, as we had nothing in the house to open them with—an omission which was discovered only when the moment for eating them arrived.

I had rather doubted whether Lawrence Redding would put in an appearance. He might very easily have sent an excuse. However, he arrived punctually enough, and the four of us went in to dinner.

Lawrence Redding has an undeniably attractive personality. He is, I suppose, about thirty years of age. He has dark hair, but his eyes are of a brilliant, almost startling blue. He is the kind of man who does everything well. He is good at games, an excellent shot, a good amateur actor, and can tell a first-rate story. He is capable of making any party go. He has, I think, Irish blood in his veins. He is not at all one's idea of the typical artist. Yet I believe he is a clever painter in the modern style. I know very little of painting myself.

It was only natural that on this particular evening he should appear a shade *distrait*. On the whole, he carried off things very well. I don't think Griselda or Dennis noticed anything wrong. Probably I should not have noticed anything myself if I had not known beforehand.

Griselda and Dennis were particularly gay—full of jokes about Dr. Stone and Miss Cram—the Local Scandal! It suddenly came home to me with something of a pang that Dennis is nearer Griselda's age than I am. He calls me Uncle Len but her Griselda. It gave me, somehow, a lonely feeling.

I must, I think, have been upset by Mrs. Protheroe. I'm not usually given to such unprofitable reflections.

Griselda and Dennis went rather far now and then, but I hadn't the heart to check them. I have always thought it a pity that the mere presence of a clergyman should have a damping effect.

Lawrence took a gay part in the conversation. Nevertheless I was aware of his eyes continually straying to where I sat, and I was not surprised when after dinner he maneuvered to get me into the study.

As soon as we were alone, his manner changed. His face became grave and anxious. He looked almost haggard.

"You've surprised our secret, sir," he said. "What are you going to do about it?"

I could speak far more plainly to Redding than I could to Mrs. Protheroe, and I did so. He took it very well.

"Of course," he said when I had finished. "You're bound to say all this. You're a parson. I don't mean that in any way offensively. As a matter of fact, I think you're probably right. But this isn't the usual sort of thing between Anne and me."

I told him that people had been saying that particular phrase since the dawn of time, and a queer little smile creased his lips.

"You mean everyone thinks their case is unique? Perhaps so. But one thing you must believe."

He assured me that so far—"there was nothing wrong in it." Anne, he said, was one of the truest and most loyal women that ever lived. What was going to happen he didn't know.

"If this were only a book," he said gloomily, "the old man would die—and a good riddance to everybody."

I reproved him.

"Oh! I didn't mean I was going to stick him in the back with a knife, though I'd offer my best thanks to anyone else who did so. There's not a soul in the world who's got a good word to say for him. I rather wonder the first Mrs. Protheroe didn't do him in. I met her once, years ago, and she looked quite capable of it. One of those calm, dangerous women. He goes blustering along, stirring up trouble everywhere, mean as the devil, and with a particularly nasty temper. You don't know what Anne has had to stand from him. If I had a penny in the world I'd take her away without any more ado."

Then I spoke to him very earnestly. I begged him to leave St. Mary Mead. By remaining there he could only bring greater unhappiness on Anne Protheroe than was already her lot. People would talk; the matter would get to Colonel Protheroe's ears—and things would be made infinitely worse for her.

Lawrence protested.

"Nobody knows a thing about it except you, padre."

"My dear young man, you underestimate the detective instinct of village life. In St. Mary Mead everyone knows your most intimate affairs. There is no detective in England equal to a spinster lady of uncertain age with plenty of time on her hands."

He said easily that that was all right. Everyone thought it was Lettice.

"Has it occurred to you," I asked, "that possibly Lettice might think so herself?"

He seemed quite surprised by the idea. Lettice, he said, didn't care a hang about him. He was sure of that.

"She's a queer sort of girl," he said. "Always seems in a kind of dream, and yet underneath I believe she's really rather practical. I believe all that vague stuff is a pose. Lettice knows jolly well what she's doing. And there's a funny vindictive streak in her. The queer thing is that she hates Anne. Simply loathes her. And yet Anne's been a perfect angel to her always."

I did not, of course, take his word for this last. To infatuated young men, their inamorata always behaves like an angel. Still, to the best of my observation, Anne had always behaved to her stepdaughter with kindness and fairness. I had been surprised myself that afternoon at the bitterness of Lettice's tone.

We had to leave the conversation there, because Griselda and Dennis burst in upon us and said I was not to make Lawrence behave like an old fogy.

"Oh, dear," said Griselda, throwing herself into an armchair. "How I would like a thrill of some kind. A murder—or even a burglary."

"I don't suppose there's anyone much worth burgling," said Lawrence, trying to enter into her mood. "Unless we stole Miss Hartnell's false teeth."

"They do click horribly," said Griselda. "But you're wrong about there being no one worth while. There's some marvelous old silver at Old Hall. Trencher salts and a Charles the Second *tazza*—all kinds of things like that. Worth thousands of pounds, I believe."

"The old man would probably shoot you with an army revolver," said Dennis. "Just the sort of thing he'd enjoy doing."

"Oh! We'd get in first and hold him up," said Griselda. "Who's got a revolver?"

"I've got a Mauser pistol," said Lawrence.

"Have you? How exciting! Why do you have it?"

"Souvenir of the war," said Lawrence briefly.

"Old Protheroe was showing the silver to Stone today," volunteered Dennis. Old Stone was pretending to be no end interested in it."

"I thought they'd quarreled about the barrow," said Griselda.

"Oh, they've made that up," said Dennis. "I can't think what people want to grub about in barrows for, anyway."

"That man Stone puzzles me," said Lawrence. "I think he must be very absent-minded. You'd swear sometimes he knew nothing about his own subject."

"That's love," said Dennis. "Sweet Gladys Cram, you are no sham. Your teeth are white and fill me with delight. Come, fly with me, my bride to be. And at the Blue Boar, on the bedroom floor—"

"That's enough, Dennis," I said.

"Well," said Lawrence Redding, "I must be off. Thank you very much, Mrs. Clement, for a very pleasant evening."

Griselda and Dennis saw him off. Dennis returned to the study alone. Something had happened to ruffle the boy. He wandered about the room aimlessly, frowning and kicking the furniture.

Our furniture is so shabby already that it can hardly be damaged further, but I felt impelled to utter a mild protest.

"Sorry," said Dennis.

He was silent for a moment and then burst out, "What an absolutely rotten thing gossip is!"

I was a little surprised. Dennis does not usually take that attitude.

"What's the matter?" I asked.

"I don't know whether I ought to tell you."

I was more and more surprised.

"It's such an absolutely rotten thing," Dennis said again. "Going round and saying things. Not even saying them. Hinting them. No, I'm damned—sorry—if I'll tell you! It's too absolutely rotten."

I looked at him curiously but I did not press him further. I wondered very much, though. It is very unlike Dennis to take anything to heart.

Griselda came in at that moment.

"Miss Wetherby's just rung up," she said. "Mrs. Lestrange went out at a quarter past eight and hasn't come in yet. Nobody knows where she's gone."

"Why should they know?"

"But it isn't to Doctor Haydock's. Miss Wetherby does know that, because she telephoned to Miss Hartnell who lives next door to him and who would have been sure to see her."

"It is a mystery to me," I said, "how anyone ever gets any nourishment in this place. They must eat their meals standing up by the window so as to be sure of not missing anything."

"And that's not all," said Griselda bubbling with pleasure. "They've found out about the Blue Boar. Doctor Stone and Miss Cram have got rooms next door to each other *but*—" she waved an impressive forefinger—"*no communicating door!*"

"That," I said, "must be very disappointing to everybody."

At which Griselda laughed.

Thursday started badly. Two of the ladies of my parish elected to quarrel about the church decorations. I was called in to adjudicate between two middle-aged ladies, each of whom was literally trembling with rage. If it had not been so painful, it would have been quite an interesting physical phenomenon.

Then I had to reprove two of our choir boys for persistent sweet sucking during the hours of divine service, and I had an uneasy feeling that I was not doing the job as wholeheartedly as I should have done.

Then our organist, who is distinctly "touchy," had taken offense and had to be smoothed down.

And four of my poorer parishioners declared open rebellion against Miss Hartnell who came to me bursting with rage about it.

I was just going home when I met Colonel Protheroe. He was in high good humor having sentenced three poachers, in his capacity as magistrate.

"Firmness," he shouted in his stentorian voice. He is slightly deaf and raises his voice accordingly as deaf people often do. "That's what's needed nowadays—firmness! Make an example. That rogue Archer came out yesterday and is vowing vengeance against me, I hear. Impudent scoundrel. Threatened men live long, as the saying goes. I'll show him what his vengeance is worth, next time I catch him taking my pheasants. Lax! We're too lax nowadays! I believe in showing a man up for what he is. You're always being asked to consider a man's wife and children. Damned nonsense. Fiddlesticks. Why should a man escape the consequences of his acts just because he whines about his wife and children? It's all the same to me—no matter what a man is—doctor, lawyer, clergyman, poacher, drunken wastrel—if you catch him on the wrong side of the law, let the law punish him. You agree with me, I'm sure."

"You forget," I said. "My calling obliges me to respect one quality above all others—the quality of mercy."

"Well, I'm a just man. No one can deny that." I did not speak and he said sharply, "Why don't you answer? A penny for your thoughts, man."

I hesitated, then I decided to speak.

"I was thinking," I said, "that, when my time comes, I should be sorry if the only plea I had to offer was that of justice. Because it might mean that only justice would be meted out to me."

"Pah! What we need is a little militant Christianity. I've always done my duty, I hope. Well, no more of that. I'll be along this evening as I said. We'll make it a quarter past six instead of six, if you don't mind. I've got to see a man in the village."

"That will suit me quite well."

He flourished his stick and strode away. Turning, I ran into Hawes. I thought he looked distinctly ill this morning. I had meant to upbraid him mildly for various matters in his province which had been muddled or shelved, but seeing his white, strained face, I felt that the man was ill.

I said as much and he denied it, but not very vehemently. Finally he confessed that he was not feeling too fit, and appeared ready to accept my advice of going home to bed.

I had a hurried lunch and went out to do some visits. Griselda had gone to London by the cheap Thursday train.

I came in about a quarter to four with the intention of sketching the outline of my Sunday sermon, but Mary told me that Mr. Redding was waiting for me in the study.

I found him pacing up and down with a worried face. He looked white and haggard.

He turned abruptly at my entrance.

"Look here, sir. I've been thinking over what you said yesterday. I've had a sleepless night thinking about it. You're right. I've got to cut and run."

"My dear boy," I said.

"You were right in what you said about Anne. I'll only bring trouble on her by staying here. She's—she's too good for anything else. I see I've got to go. I've made things hard enough for her as it is, heaven help me."

"I think you have made the only decision possible," I said. "I know that it is a hard one, but, believe me, it will be for the best in the end."

I could see that he thought that that was the kind of thing easily said by someone who didn't know what he was talking about.

"You'll look after Anne? She needs a friend."

"You can rest assured that I will do everything in my power."

"Thank you, sir." He wrung my hand. "You're a good sort, padre. I shall see her to say good-by this evening, and I shall probably pack up and go tomorrow. No good prolonging the agony.

Thanks for letting me have the shed to paint in. I'm sorry not to have finished Mrs. Clement's portrait."

"Don't worry about that, my dear boy. Good-by, and God bless you."

When he had gone I tried to settle down to my sermon, but with very poor success. I kept thinking of Lawrence and Anne Protheroe.

I had rather an unpalatable cup of tea, cold and black, and at half past five the telephone rang. I was informed that Mr. Abbott of Lower Farm was dying and would I please come at once.

I rang up Old Hall immediately, for Lower Farm was nearly two miles away and I could not possibly get back by six-fifteen. I have never succeeded in learning to ride a bicycle.

I was told, however, that Colonel Protheroe had just started out in the car, so I departed, leaving word with Mary that I had been called away but would try to be back by six-thirty or soon after.

CHAPTER FIVE

IT WAS NEARER SEVEN than half past six when I approached the Vicarage gate on my return. Before I reached it, it swung open and Lawrence Redding came out. He stopped dead on seeing me and I was immediately struck by his appearance. He looked like a man who was on the point of going mad. His eyes stared in a peculiar manner; he was deathly white, and he was shaking and twitching all over.

I wondered for a moment whether he could have been drinking, but repudiated the idea immediately.

"Hullo," I said, "have you been to see me again? Sorry I was out. Come back now. I've got to see Protheroe about some accounts—but I daresay we shan't be long."

"Protheroe," he said. He began to laugh. "Protheroe? You're going to see Protheroe? Oh! You'll see Protheroe all right. Oh, my God—yes."

I stared. Instinctively I stretched out a hand toward him. He drew sharply aside.

"No," he almost cried out. "I've got to get away—to think. I've got to think. I must think."

He broke into a run and vanished rapidly down the road toward the village leaving me staring after him, my first idea of drunkenness recurring.

Finally I shook my head and went on to the Vicarage. The front door is always left open, but nevertheless I rang the bell. Mary came wiping her hands on her apron.

"So you're back at last," she observed.

"Is Colonel Protheroe here?" I asked.

"In the study. Been here since a quarter past six."

"And Mr. Redding's been here?"

"Come a few minutes ago. Asked for you. I told him you'd be back any minute and that Colonel Protheroe was waiting in the study, and he said he'd wait, too, and went there. He's there now."

"No, he isn't," I said. "I've just met him going down the road."

"Well, I didn't hear him leave. He can't have stayed more than a couple of minutes. The mistress isn't back from town yet."

I nodded absent-mindedly. Mary beat a retreat to the kitchen quarters and I went down the passage and opened the study door.

After the dusk of the passage, the evening sunshine that was pouring into the room made my eyes blink. I took a step or two across the floor and then stopped dead.

For a moment I could hardly take in the meaning of the scene before me.

Colonel Protheroe was lying sprawled across my writing table in a horrible, unnatural position. There was a pool of some dark fluid on the desk by his head, and it was slowly dripping onto the floor with a horrible drip, drip, drip.

I pulled myself together and went across to him. His skin was cold to the touch. The hand that I raised fell back lifeless. The man was dead—shot through the head.

I went to the door and called Mary. When she came I ordered her to run as fast as she could and fetch Dr. Haydock, who lives just at the corner of the road. I told her there had been an accident.

Then I went back and closed the door to await the doctor's coming.

Fortunately Mary found him at home. Haydock is a good fellow, a big, fine, strapping fellow, with an honest, rugged face.

His eyebrows went up when I pointed silently across the room. But like a true doctor he showed no signs of emotion. He bent over the dead man, examining him rapidly. Then he straightened himself and looked across at me.

"Well?" I asked.

"He's dead right enough—been dead half an hour, I should say."

"Suicide?"

"Out of the question, man. Look at the position of the wound. Besides, if he shot himself, where's the weapon?"

True enough, there was no sign of any such thing.

"We'd better not mess around with anything," said Haydock. "I'd better ring up the police."

He picked up the receiver and spoke into it. He gave the facts as curtly as possible and then replaced the telephone and came across to where I was sitting.

"This is a rotten business. How did you come to find him?"

I explained.

"A rotten business," he repeated.

"Is—is it murder?" I asked rather faintly.

"Looks like it. Mean to say, what else can it be? Extraordinary business. Wonder who had a down on the poor old fellow? Of course I know he wasn't popular, but one isn't often murdered for that reason—worse luck."

"There's one rather curious thing," I said. "I was telephoned for this afternoon to go to a dying parishioner. When I got there everyone was very surprised to see me. The sick man was very much better than he had been for some days, and his wife flatly denied telephoning for me at all."

Haydock drew his brows together.

"That's suggestive—very. You were being got out of the way. Where's your wife?"

"Gone up to London for the day."

"And the maid?"

"In the kitchen—right at the other side of the house."

"Where she wouldn't be likely to hear anything that went on in here. It's a nasty business. Who knew that Protheroe was coming here this evening?"

"He referred to the fact this morning in the village street, at the top of his voice as usual."

"Meaning that the whole village knew it! Which they always do in any case. Know of anyone who had a grudge against him?"

The thought of Lawrence Redding's white face and staring eyes came to my mind. I was spared answering by a noise of shuffling feet in the passage outside.

"The police," said my friend, and rose to his feet.

Our police force was represented by Constable Hurst, looking very important but slightly worried.

"Good evening, gentlemen," he greeted us. "The Inspector will be here any minute. In the meantime I'll follow out his instructions. I understand Colonel Protheroe's been found shot—in the Vicarage."

He paused and directed a look of cold suspicion at me which I tried to meet with a suitable bearing of conscious innocence.

He moved over to the writing table and announced, "Nothing to be touched till the Inspector comes."

For the convenience of my readers, I append a sketch plan of the room.

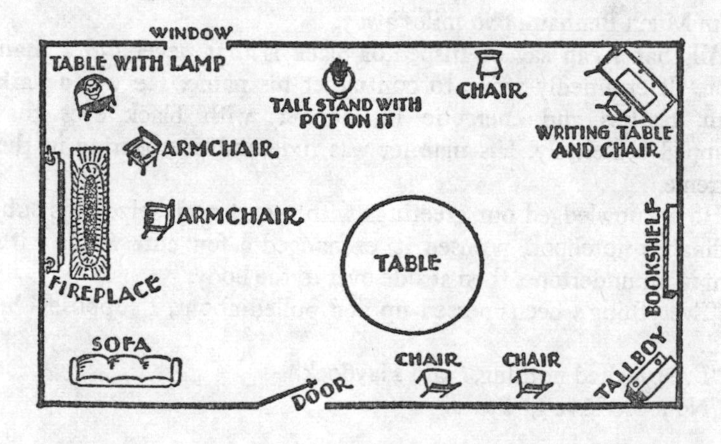

He got out his notebook, moistened his pencil, and looked expectantly at both of us.

I repeated my story of discovering the body. When he had got it all down, which took some time, he turned to the doctor.

"In your opinion, Doctor Haydock, what was the cause of death?"

"Shot through the head at close quarters."

"And the weapon?"

"I can't say with certainty until we get the bullet out. But I should say in all probability the bullet was fired from a pistol of small caliber—say a Mauser twenty-five."

I started, remembering our conversation of the night before and Lawrence Redding's admission. The police constable brought his cold fishlike eye round on me.

"Did you speak, sir?"

I shook my head. Whatever suspicions I might have, they were no more than suspicions, and as such to be kept to myself.

"When, in your opinion, did the tragedy occur?"

The doctor hesitated for a minute before he answered. Then he said, "The man has been dead just over half an hour, I should say. Certainly not longer."

Hurst turned to me.

"Did the girl hear anything?"

"As far as I know she heard nothing," I said. "But you had better ask her."

But at this moment Inspector Slack arrived, having come by car from Much Benham, two miles away.

All that I can say of Inspector Slack is that never did a man more determinedly strive to contradict his name. He was a dark man, restless and energetic in manner, with black eyes that snapped ceaselessly. His manner was rude and overbearing in the extreme.

He acknowledged our greetings with a curt nod, seized his subordinate's notebook, perused it, exchanged a few curt words with him in an undertone, then strode over to the body.

"Everything's been messed up and pulled about, I suppose," he said.

"I've touched nothing," said Haydock.

"No more have I," I said.

The Inspector busied himself for some time peering at the things on the table and examining the pool of blood.

"Ah!" he said in a tone of triumph. "Here's what we want. Clock overturned when he fell forward. That'll give us the time of the crime. Twenty-two minutes past six. What time did you say death occurred, doctor?"

"I said about half an hour, but—"

The Inspector consulted his watch.

"Five minutes past seven. I got word about ten minutes ago, at five minutes to seven. Discovery of the body was at about a quarter to seven. I understand you were fetched immediately. Say you examined it at ten minutes to— Why, that brings it to the identical second almost!"

"I don't guarantee the time absolutely," said Haydock. "That is an approximate estimate."

"Good enough, sir, good enough."

I had been trying to get a word in.

"About that clock—"

"If you'll excuse me, sir, I'll ask you any questions I want to know. Time's short. What I want is absolute silence."

"Yes, but I'd like to tell you—"

"Absolute silence," said the Inspector, glaring at me ferociously.

I gave him what he asked for.

He was still peering about the writing table.

"What was he sitting here for?" he grunted. "Did he want to write a note? Hullo—what's this?"

He held up a piece of notepaper triumphantly. So pleased was he with his find that he permitted us to come to his side and examine it with him.

It was a piece of Vicarage notepaper, and it was headed at the top 6:20.

Dear Clement: (it began) *Sorry I cannot wait any longer, but I must* . . . Here the writing tailed off in a scrawl.

"Plain as a pikestaff," said Inspector Slack triumphantly. "He sits down here to write this; an enemy comes softly in through the window and shoots him as he writes. What more do you want?"

"I'd just like to say—" I began.

"Out of the way, if you please, sir. I want to see if there are footprints."

He went down on his hands and knees, moving toward the open window.

"I think you ought to know—" I said obstinately.

The Inspector rose. He spoke without heat, but firmly.

"We'll go into all that later. I'd be obliged if you gentlemen will clear out of here. Right out, if you please."

We permitted ourselves to be shooed out like children.

Hours seemed to have passed—yet it was only a quarter past seven.

"Well," said Haydock. "That's that. When that conceited ass wants me, you can send him over to the surgery. So long."

"The mistress is back," said Mary, making a brief appearance from the kitchen. Her eyes were round and agog with excitement. "Come in about five minutes ago."

I found Griselda in the drawing-room. She looked frightened but excited.

I told her everything and she listened attentively.

"The letter is headed six-twenty," I ended. "And the clock fell over and has stopped at six twenty-two."

"Yes," said Griselda. "But that clock, didn't you tell him that it was always kept a quarter of an hour fast?"

"No," I said. "I didn't. He wouldn't let me. I tried my best."

Griselda was frowning in a puzzled manner.

"But, Len," she said. "That makes the whole thing perfectly extraordinary. Because when that clock said twenty past six it was really five minutes past, and at five minutes past I don't suppose Colonel Protheroe had even arrived at the house."

CHAPTER SIX

We puzzled over the business of the clock for some time, but we could make nothing of it. Griselda said I ought to make another effort and tell Inspector Slack about it, but on that point I was feeling what I can only describe as mulish.

Inspector Slack had been abominably and most unnecessarily

rude. I was looking forward to a moment when I could produce my valuable contribution and effect his discomfiture. I would then say in a tone of mild reproach, "If you had only listened to me, Inspector Slack—"

I expected that he would at least speak to me before he left the house, but to our surprise we learned from Mary that he had departed, having locked up the study door and issued orders that no one was to attempt to enter the room.

Griselda suggested going up to Old Hall.

"It will be so awful for Anne Protheroe—with the police and everything," she said. "Perhaps I might be able to do something for her."

I cordially approved of this plan, and Griselda set off with instructions that she was to telephone to me if she thought that I could be of any use or comfort to either of the ladies.

I now proceeded to ring up the Sunday School teachers who were coming at 7:45 for their weekly preparation class. I thought that under the circumstances it would be better to put them off.

Dennis was the next person to arrive on the scene, having just returned from a tennis party. The fact that murder had taken place at the Vicarage seemed to afford him acute satisfaction.

"Fancy being right on the spot in a murder case," he exclaimed. "I've always wanted to be right in the midst of one. Why have the police locked up the study? Wouldn't one of the other door keys fit it?"

I refused to allow anything of the sort to be attempted. Dennis gave in with a bad grace. After extracting every possible detail from me he went out into the garden to look for footprints, remarking cheerfully that it was lucky it was only old Protheroe, whom everyone disliked.

His cheerful callousness rather grated on me, but I reflected that I was perhaps being hard on the boy. At Dennis's age a detective story is one of the best things in life, and to find a real detective story, complete with corpse, waiting on one's own front doorstep, so to speak, is bound to send a healthy-minded boy into the seventh heaven of enjoyment. Death means very little to a boy of sixteen.

Griselda came back in about an hour's time. She had seen Anne

Protheroe, having arrived just after the Inspector had broken the news to her.

On hearing that Mrs. Protheroe had last seen her husband in the village about a quarter to six, and that she had no light of any kind to throw upon the matter, he had taken his departure, explaining that he would return on the morrow for a fuller interview.

"He was quite decent in his way," said Griselda grudgingly.

"How did Mrs. Protheroe take it?" I asked.

"Well—she was very quiet—but then she always is."

"Yes," I said. "I can't imagine Anne Protheroe going into hysterics."

"Of course it was a great shock. You could see that. She thanked me for coming and said she was very grateful, but that there was nothing I could do."

"What about Lettice?"

"She was out playing tennis somewhere. She hadn't got home yet."

There was a pause and then Griselda said, "You know, Len, she was really very queer—very queer indeed."

"The shock," I suggested.

"Yes—I suppose so. And yet—" Griselda furrowed her brows perplexedly. "It wasn't like that somehow. She didn't seem so much bowled over as—well—terrified."

"Terrified?"

"Yes—not showing it, you know. At least not meaning to show it. But a queer, watchful look in her eyes. I wonder if she has a sort of idea who did kill him? She asked again and again if anyone were suspected."

"Did she?" I said thoughtfully.

"Yes. Of course, Anne's got marvelous self-control, but one could see that she was terribly upset. More so than I would have thought, for after all it wasn't as though she were so devoted to him. I should have said she rather disliked him, if anything."

"Death alters one's feelings sometimes," I said.

"Yes, I suppose so."

Dennis came in and was full of excitement over a footprint he had found in one of the flower beds. He was sure that the police had overlooked it, and that it would turn out to be the turning point of the mystery.

I spent a troubled night. Dennis was up and about and out of the house long before breakfast, to "study the latest developments," as he said.

Nevertheless it was not he but Mary who brought us the morning's sensational bit of news.

We had just sat down to breakfast when she burst into the room, her cheeks red and her eyes shining, and addressed us with her customary lack of ceremony.

"Would you believe it? The baker's just told me. They've arrested young Mr. Redding."

"Arrested Lawrence?" cried Griselda incredulously. "Impossible. It must be some stupid mistake."

"No mistake about it, mum," said Mary with a kind of gloating exultation. "Mr. Redding, he went there himself and gave himself up. Last night last thing. Went right in, threw down the pistol on the table, and, 'I did it,' he says. Just like that."

She looked at us both, nodded her head vigorously, and withdrew, satisfied with the effect she had produced. Griselda and I stared at each other.

"Oh! It isn't true," said Griselda. "It *can't* be true."

She noticed my silence and said, "Len, *you* don't think it's true?"

I found it hard to answer her. I sat silent, thoughts whirling through my head.

"He must be mad," said Griselda. "Absolutely mad. Or do you think they were looking at the pistol together and it suddenly went off?"

"That doesn't sound at all a likely thing to happen."

"But it must have been an accident of some kind. Because there's not a shadow of a motive. What earthly reason could Lawrence have for killing Colonel Protheroe?"

I could have answered that question very decidedly, but I wished to spare Anne Protheroe as far as possible. There might still be a chance of keeping her name out of it.

"Remember, they had had a quarrel," I said.

"About Lettice and her bathing suit. Yes, but that's absurd.

And even if he and Lettice were engaged secretly, well, that's not a reason for killing her father."

"We don't know what the true facts of the case may be, Griselda."

"You *do* believe it, Len! Oh! how can you? I tell you, I'm *sure* Lawrence never touched a hair of his head."

"Remember, I met him just outside the gate. He looked like a madman."

"Yes, but—oh, it's impossible."

"There's the clock, too," I said. "This explains the clock. Lawrence must have put it back to six twenty-two with the idea of making an alibi for himself. Look how Inspector Slack fell into the trap."

"You're wrong, Len. Lawrence knew about that clock being fast. 'Keeping the Vicar up to time!' he used to say. Lawrence would never have made the mistake of putting it back to six twenty-two. He'd have put the hands somewhere possible—like a quarter to seven."

"He mayn't have known what time Protheroe got here. Or he may have simply forgotten about the clock being fast."

Griselda disagreed.

"No, if you were committing a murder, you'd be awfully careful about things like that."

"You don't know, my dear," I said mildly. "You've never done one."

Before Griselda could reply, a shadow fell across the breakfast table, and a very gentle voice said, "I hope I am not intruding. You must forgive me. But in the sad circumstances—the very sad circumstances—"

It was our neighbor, Miss Marple. Accepting our polite disclaimers, she stepped in through the window and I drew up a chair for her. She looked faintly flushed and quite excited.

"Very terrible, is it not? Poor Colonel Protheroe. Not a very pleasant man, perhaps, and not exactly popular, but it's none the less sad for that. And actually shot in the Vicarage study, I understand?"

I said that that had indeed been the case.

"But the dear Vicar was not here at the time?" Miss Marple questioned Griselda.

I explained where I had been.

"Mr. Dennis is not with you this morning?" said Miss Marple glancing round.

"Dennis," said Griselda, "fancies himself as an amateur detective. He is very excited about a footprint he found in one of the flower beds and I fancy has gone off to tell the police about it."

"Dear, dear," said Miss Marple. "Such a to-do, is it not? And Mr. Dennis thinks he knows who committed the crime. Well, I suppose we all think we know."

"You mean it is obvious?" said Griselda.

"No, dear, I didn't mean that at all. I daresay everyone thinks it is somebody different. That is why it is so important to have *proofs*. I, for instance, am quite *convinced* I know who did it. But I must admit I haven't one shadow of proof. One must, I know, be very careful of what one says at a time like this—criminal libel, don't they call it? I had made up my mind to be *most* careful with Inspector Slack. He sent word he would come and see me this morning, but now he has just phoned up to say it won't be necessary after all."

"I suppose since the arrest it isn't necessary," I said.

"The arrest?" Miss Marple leaned forward, her cheeks pink with excitement. "I didn't know there had been an arrest."

It is so seldom that Miss Marple is worse informed than we are that I had taken it for granted that she would know the latest developments.

"It seems we have been talking at cross purposes," I said. "Yes, there has been an arrest—Lawrence Redding."

"Lawrence Redding?" Miss Marple seemed very surprised. "Now I should not have thought—"

Griselda interrupted vehemently.

"I can't believe it even now. No, not though he has actually confessed."

"Confessed?" said Miss Marple. "You say he has confessed? Oh, dear, I see I have been sadly at sea—yes, sadly at sea."

"I can't help feeling it must have been some kind of an accident," said Griselda. "Don't you think so, Len? I mean his coming forward to give himself up looks like that."

Miss Marple leaned forward eagerly.

"He gave himself up, you say?"

"Yes."

"Oh!" said Miss Marple, with a deep sigh. "I am so glad—so very glad."

I looked at her in some surprise.

"It shows a true state of remorse, I suppose," I said.

"Remorse?" Miss Marple looked very surprised. "Oh, but surely, dear, dear Vicar, you don't think that he is guilty?"

It was my turn to stare.

"But since he has confessed—"

"Yes, but that just proves it, doesn't it? I mean that he had nothing to do with it."

"No," I said. "I may be dense, but I can't see that it does. If you have not committed a murder, I cannot see the object of pretending you have."

"Oh, of course, there's a reason," said Miss Marple. "Naturally. There's always a reason, isn't there? And young men are so hotheaded and often prone to believe the worst."

She turned to Griselda.

"Don't you agree with me, my dear?"

"I—I don't know," said Griselda. "It's difficult to know what to think. I can't see any reason for Lawrence behaving like a perfect idiot."

"If you had seen his face last night—" I began.

"Tell me," said Miss Marple.

I described my home-coming while she listened attentively.

When I had finished she said, "I know that I am very often rather foolish and don't take in things as I should, but I really do not see your point. It seems to me that if a young man had made up his mind to the great wickedness of taking a fellow creature's life, he would not appear distraught about it afterward. It would be a premeditated and cold-blooded action and, though the murderer might be a little flurried and possibly might make some small mistake, I do not think it likely he would fall into a state of agitation such as you describe. It is difficult to put oneself in such a position, but I cannot imagine getting into a state like that myself."

"We don't know the circumstances," I argued. "If there was a quarrel, the shot may have been fired in a sudden gust of passion, and Lawrence might afterward have been appalled at what he had done. Indeed, I prefer to think that that is what did actually occur."

"I know, dear Mr. Clement, that there are many ways we prefer to look at things. But one must actually take facts as they are, must one not? And it does not seem to me that the facts bear the interpretation you put upon them. Your maid distinctly stated that Mr. Redding was only in the house a couple of minutes, not long enough, surely, for a quarrel such as you describe. And then again, I understand the Colonel was shot through the back of the head while he was writing a letter—at least that is what my maid told me."

"Quite true," said Griselda. "He seems to have been writing a note to say he couldn't wait any longer. The note was dated six-twenty, and the clock on the table was overturned and had stopped at six twenty-two and that's just what has been puzzling Len and myself so frightfully."

She explained our custom of keeping the clock a quarter of an hour fast.

"Very curious," said Miss Marple. "Very curious indeed. But the note seems to me even more curious still. I mean—"

She stopped and looked round. Lettice Protheroe was standing outside the window. She came in, nodding to us and murmuring, "Morning."

She dropped into a chair and said, with rather more animation than usual, "They've arrested Lawrence, I hear."

"Yes," said Griselda. "It's been a great shock to us."

"I never really thought anyone would murder Father," said Lettice. She was obviously taking a pride in letting no hint of distress or emotion escape her. "Lots of people wanted to, I'm sure. There are times when I'd have liked to do it myself."

"Won't you have something to eat or drink, Lettice?" asked Griselda.

"No, thank you. I just drifted round to see if you'd got my beret here—a queer little yellow one. I think I left it in the study the other day."

"If you did, it's there still," said Griselda. "Mary never tidies anything."

"I'll go and see," said Lettice rising. "Sorry to be such a bother, but I seem to have lost everything else in the hat line."

"I'm afraid you can't get it now," I said. "Inspector Slack has locked the room up."

"Oh, what a bore. Can't we get in through the window?"

"I'm afraid not. It is latched in the inside. Surely, Lettice, a yellow beret won't be much good to you at present?"

"You mean mourning and all that? I shan't bother about mourning. I think it's an awfully archaic idea. It's a nuisance about Lawrence—yes, it's a nuisance."

She got up and stood frowning abstractedly.

"I suppose it's all on account of me and my bathing suit. So silly, the whole thing."

Griselda opened her mouth to say something, but for some unexplained reason shut it again.

A curious smile came to Lettice's lips.

"I think," she said softly, "I'll go home and tell Anne about Lawrence being arrested."

She went out of the window again. Griselda turned to Miss Marple.

"Why did you step on my foot?"

The old lady was smiling.

"I thought you were going to say something, my dear. And it is often so much better to let things develop on their own lines. I don't think, you know, that that child is half so vague as she pretends to be. She's got a very definite idea in her head, and she's acting upon it."

Mary gave a loud knock on the dining-room door and entered hard upon it.

"What is it?" said Griselda. "And Mary, you must remember not to knock on doors. I've told you about it before."

"Thought you might be busy," said Mary. "Colonel Melchett's here. Wants to see the master."

Colonel Melchett is Chief Constable of the County. I rose at once.

"I thought you wouldn't like my leaving him in the hall, so I put him in the drawing-room," went on Mary. "Shall I clear?"

"Not yet," said Griselda. "I'll ring."

She turned to Miss Marple, and I left the room.

CHAPTER SEVEN

Colonel Melchett is a dapper little man with a habit of snorting suddenly and unexpectedly. He has red hair and rather keen, bright-blue eyes.

"Good morning, Vicar," he said. "Nasty business, eh? Poor old Protheroe. Not that I liked him. I didn't. Nobody did for that matter. Nasty bit of work for you, too. Hope it hasn't upset your missus."

I said Griselda had taken it very well.

"That's lucky. Rotten thing to happen in one's house. I must say I'm surprised at young Redding—doing it the way he did. No sort of consideration for anyone's feelings."

A wild desire to laugh came over me, but Colonel Melchett evidently saw nothing odd in the idea of a murderer being considerate, so I held my peace.

"I must say I was rather taken aback when I heard the fellow had marched in and given himself up," continued Colonel Melchett, dropping onto a chair.

"How did it happen, exactly?"

"Last night. About ten o'clock. Fellow rolls in, throws down a pistol, and says, 'Here I am. I did it.' Just like that."

"What account does he give of the business?"

"Precious little. He was warned, of course, about making a statement. But he merely laughed. Said he came here to see you—found Protheroe here. They had words and he shot him. Won't say what the quarrel was about. Look here, Clement—just between you and me—do you know anything about it? I've heard rumors—about his being forbidden the house and all that. What was it—did he seduce the daughter or what? We don't want to bring the girl into it more than we can help, for everybody's sake. Was that the trouble?"

"No," I said. "You can take it from me that it was something quite different, but I can't say more at the present juncture."

He nodded and rose.

"I'm glad to know. There's a lot of talk. Too many women in this part of the world. Well, I must get along. I've got to see Haydock. He was called out to some case or other, but he ought to be back by now. I don't mind telling you I'm sorry about Redding. He always struck me as a decent young chap. Perhaps they'll think out some kind of defense for him. Aftereffects of war, shell-shock, or something. Especially if no very adequate motive turns up. I must be off. Like to come along?"

I said I would like to very much, and we went out together.

Haydock's house is next door to mine. His servant said the doctor had just come in, and showed us into the dining-room, where Haydock was sitting down to a steaming plate of eggs and bacon.

He greeted us with an amiable nod.

"Sorry I had to go out. Confinement case. I've been up most of the night over your business. I've got the bullet for you."

He shoved a little box along the table. Melchett examined it.

"Twenty-five?"

Haydock nodded.

"I'll keep the technical details for the inquest," he said. "All you want to know is that death was practically instantaneous. Silly young fool, what did he want to do it for? Amazing, by the way, that nobody heard the shot."

"Yes," said Melchett, "that surprises me."

"The kitchen window gives on the other side of the house," I said. "With the study door, the pantry door, and the kitchen door all shut, I doubt if you would hear anything, and there was no one but the maid in the house."

"H'm," said Melchett. "It's odd, all the same. I wonder the old lady—what's her name—Marple didn't hear it. The study window was open."

"Perhaps she did," said Haydock.

"I don't think she did," said I. "She was over at the Vicarage just now and she didn't mention anything of the kind, which I'm certain she would have done if there had been anything to tell."

"May have heard it and paid no attention to it—thought it was a car backfiring."

It struck me that Haydock was looking much more jovial and

good-humored this morning. He seemed like a man who was decorously trying to subdue unusually good spirits.

"Or what about a silencer?" he added. "That's quite likely. Nobody would hear anything then."

Melchett shook his head.

"Slack didn't find anything of the kind, and he asked Redding, and Redding didn't seem to know what he was talking about at first, and then denied point-blank using anything of the kind. And I suppose one can take his word for it."

"Yes, indeed, poor devil."

"Damned young fool," said Colonel Melchett. "Sorry, Clement. But he really is! Somehow one can't get used to thinking of him as a murderer."

"Any motive?" asked Haydock, taking a final draft of coffee and pushing back his chair.

"He says they quarreled, and he lost his temper and shot him."

"Hoping for manslaughter, eh?" The doctor shook his head. "That story doesn't hold water. He stole up behind him as he was writing and shot him through the head. Precious little 'quarrel' about that."

"Anyway, there wouldn't have been time for a quarrel," I said, remembering Miss Marple's words. "To creep up, shoot him, alter the clock hands back to six twenty-two, and leave again would have taken him all his time. I shall never forget his face when I met him outside the gate, or the way he said, 'You want to see Protheroe— Oh! You'll see him, all right!' That in itself ought to have made me suspicious of what had just taken place a few minutes before."

Haydock stared at me.

"What do you mean—what had just taken place? When do you think Redding shot him?"

"A few minutes before I got to the house."

The doctor shook his head.

"Impossible. Plumb impossible. He'd been dead much longer than that."

"But, my dear man," cried Colonel Melchett. "You said yourself that half an hour was only an approximate estimate."

"Half an hour, thirty-five minutes, twenty-five minutes, twenty minutes—possibly, but less, no. Why, the body would have been warm when I got to it."

We stared at each other. Haydock's face had changed. It had gone suddenly gray and old. I wondered at the change in him.

"But look here, Haydock." The Colonel found his voice. "If Redding admits shooting him at a quarter to seven—"

Haydock sprang to his feet.

"I tell you it's impossible," he roared. "If Redding says he killed Protheroe at a quarter to seven, then Redding lies. Hang it all, I tell you I'm a doctor, and I know. The blood had begun to congeal."

"If Redding is lying—" began Melchett. He stopped, shook his head.

"We'd better go down to the police station and see him," he said.

CHAPTER EIGHT

WE WERE RATHER SILENT on our way down to the police station. Haydock drew behind a little and murmured to me.

"You know I don't like the look of this. I don't like it. There's something here we don't understand."

He looked thoroughly worried and upset.

Inspector Slack was at the police station, and presently we found ourselves face to face with Lawrence Redding.

He looked pale and strained but quite composed—marvelously so, I thought, considering the circumstances. Melchett snorted and hummed, obviously nervous.

"Look here, Redding," he said. "I understand you made a statement to Inspector Slack here. You state you went to the Vicarage at approximately a quarter to seven, found Protheroe there, quarreled with him, shot him, and came away. I'm not reading it over to you, but that's the gist of it."

"Yes."

"I'm going to ask you a few questions. You've already been told that you needn't answer them unless you choose. Your solicitor—"

Lawrence interrupted. "I've nothing to hide. I killed Protheroe."

"Ah! Well—" Melchett snorted. "How did you happen to have a pistol with you?"

Lawrence hesitated. "It was in my pocket."

"You took it with you to the Vicarage?"

"Yes."

"Why?"

"I always take it."

He had hesitated again before answering, and I was absolutely sure that he was not speaking the truth.

"Why did you put the clock back?"

"The clock?"

He seemed puzzled.

"Yes, the hands pointed to six twenty-two."

A look of fear sprang up in his face. "Oh, that—yes. I—I altered it."

Haydock spoke suddenly. "Where did you shoot Colonel Protheroe?"

"In the study at the Vicarage."

"I mean in what part of the body?"

"Oh! I—through the head I think. Yes, through the head."

"Aren't you sure?"

"Since you know, I can't see why it is necessary to ask me."

It was a feeble kind of bluster. There was some commotion outside. A constable without a helmet brought in a note.

"For the Vicar. It says very urgent on it."

I tore it open and read.

Please—please—come to me. I don't know what to do. It is all too awful. I want to tell someone. Please come immediately, and bring anyone you like with you. Anne Protheroe.

I gave Melchett a meaning glance. He took the hint. We all went out together. Glancing over my shoulder I had a glimpse of Lawrence Redding's face. His eyes were riveted on the paper in my hand, and I have hardly ever seen such a terrible look of anguish and despair in any human being's face.

I remembered Anne Protheroe sitting on my sofa and saying,

"I'm a desperate woman"; and my heart grew heavy within me. I saw now the possible reason for Lawrence Redding's heroic self-accusation.

Melchett was speaking to Slack.

"Have you got any line on Redding's movements earlier in the day? There's some reason to think he shot Protheroe earlier than he says. Get on to it, will you?"

He turned to me, and without a word I handed him Anne Protheroe's letter. He read it and pursed up his lips in astonishment. Then he looked at me inquiringly.

"Is this what you were hinting at this morning?"

"Yes. I was not sure then if it was my duty to speak. I am quite sure now." And I told him of what I had seen that night in the studio.

The Colonel had a few words with the Inspector, and then we set off for Old Hall. Dr. Haydock came with us.

A very correct butler opened the door, with just the right amount of gloom in his bearing.

"Good morning," said Melchett. "Will you ask Mrs. Protheroe's maid to tell her we are here and would like to see her; and then return here and answer a few questions."

The butler hurried away, and presently returned with the news that he had dispatched the message.

"Now, let's hear something about yesterday," said Colonel Melchett. "Your master was in to lunch?"

"Yes, sir."

"And in his usual spirits?"

"As far as I could see; yes, sir."

"What happened after that?"

"After luncheon Mrs. Protheroe went to lie down, and the Colonel went to his study. Miss Lettice went out to a tennis party in the two-seater. Colonel and Mrs. Protheroe had tea at four-thirty, in the drawing-room. The car was ordered for five-thirty to take them to the village. Immediately after they had left, Mr. Clement rang up." He bowed to me. "I told him they had started."

"H'm," said Colonel Melchett. "When was Mr. Redding last here?"

"On Tuesday afternoon, sir."

"I understand that there was a disagreement between them?"

"I believe so, sir. The Colonel gave me orders that Mr. Redding was not to be admitted in future."

"Did you overhear the quarrel at all?" asked Colonel Melchett bluntly.

"Colonel Protheroe, sir, had a very loud voice, especially when it was raised in anger. I was unable to help overhearing a few words here and there."

"Enough to tell you the cause of the dispute?"

"I understood, sir, that it had to do with a portrait Mr. Redding had been painting—a portrait of Miss Lettice."

Melchett grunted. "Did you see Mr. Redding when he left?"

"Yes, sir; I let him out."

"Did he seem angry?"

"No, sir; if I may say so, he seemed rather amused."

"Ah! He didn't come to the house yesterday?"

"No, sir."

"Anyone else come?"

"Not yesterday, sir."

"Well, the day before?"

"Mr. Dennis Clement came in the afternoon. And Doctor Stone was here for some time. And there was a lady in the evening."

"A lady?" Melchett was surprised. "Who was she?"

The butler couldn't remember her name. It was a lady he had not seen before. Yes, she had given her name, and when he told her that the family was at dinner, she had said that she would wait. So he had shown her into the little morning room.

She had asked for Colonel Protheroe, not Mrs. Protheroe. He had told the Colonel, and the Colonel had gone to the morning room directly dinner was over.

How long had the lady stayed? He thought about half an hour. The Colonel himself had let her out. Ah, yes, he remembered her name now. The lady had been a Mrs. Lestrange.

This was a surprise.

"Curious," said Melchett. "Really very curious."

But we pursued the matter no further, for at that moment a message came that Mrs. Protheroe would see us.

Anne was in bed. Her face was pale and her eyes very bright.

There was a look on her face that puzzled me—a kind of grim determination.

She spoke to me.

"Thank you for coming so promptly," she said. "I see you've understood what I meant by bringing anyone you liked with you."

She paused.

"It's best to get it over quickly, isn't it?" she said. She gave a queer, half-pathetic little smile. "I suppose you're the person I ought to say it to, Colonel Melchett. You see, it was I who killed my husband."

Colonel Melchett said gently, "My dear Mrs. Protheroe—"

"Oh, it's quite true. I suppose I've said it rather bluntly, but I never can go into hysterics over anything. I've hated him for a long time, and yesterday I shot him."

She lay back on the pillows and closed her eyes.

"That's all. I suppose you'll arrest me and take me away. I'll get up and dress as soon as I can. At the moment I am feeling rather sick."

"Are you aware, Mrs. Protheroe, that Mr. Lawrence Redding has already accused himself of committing the crime?"

Anne opened her eyes and nodded brightly.

"I know. Silly boy. He's very much in love with me, you know. It was frightfully noble of him—but very silly."

"He knew that it was you who had committed the crime?"

"Yes."

"How did he know?"

She hesitated.

"Did you tell him?"

Still she hesitated. Then at last she seemed to make up her mind.

"Yes—I told him."

She twitched her shoulders with a movement of irritation.

"Can't you go away now? I've told you. I don't want to talk about it any more."

"Where did you get the pistol, Mrs. Protheroe?"

"The pistol? Oh! It was my husband's. I got it out of the drawer of his dressing table."

"I see. And you took it with you to the Vicarage?"

"Yes. I knew he would be there—"

"What time was this?"

"It must have been after six—quarter—twenty past—something like that."

"You took the pistol meaning to shoot your husband?"

"No—I—I meant it for myself."

"I see. But you went to the Vicarage?"

"Yes. I went along to the window. There were no voices. I looked in. I saw my husband. Something came over me—and I fired."

"And then?"

"Then? Oh, then I went away."

"And told Mr. Redding what you had done?"

Again I noticed the hesitation in her voice before she said, "Yes."

"Did anybody see you entering or leaving the Vicarage?"

"No—at least, yes. Old Miss Marple. I talked to her a few minutes. She was in her garden."

She moved restlessly on the pillows.

"Isn't that enough? I've told you. Why do you want to go on bothering me?"

Dr. Haydock moved to her side and felt her pulse.

He beckoned to Melchett.

"I'll stay with her," he said in a whisper, "while you make the necessary arrangements. She oughtn't to be left. Might do herself a mischief."

Melchett nodded.

We left the room and descended the stairs. I saw a thin, cadaverous-looking man come out of the adjoining room and, on impulse, I remounted the stairs.

"Are you Colonel Protheroe's valet?"

The man looked surprised. "Yes, sir."

"Do you know whether your late master kept a pistol anywhere?"

"Not that I know of, sir."

"Not in one of the drawers of his dressing table? Think, man."

The valet shook his head decisively.

"I'm quite sure he didn't, sir. I'd have seen it if so. Bound to."

I hurried down the stairs after the others.

Mrs. Protheroe had lied about the pistol.

Why?

CHAPTER NINE

After leaving a message at the police station, the Chief Constable announced his intention of paying a visit to Miss Marple.

"You'd better come with me, Vicar," he said. "I don't want to give a member of your flock hysterics. So lend the weight of your soothing presence."

I smiled. For all her fragile appearance, Miss Marple is capable of holding her own with any policeman or chief constable in existence.

"What's she like?" asked the Colonel as we rang the bell. "Anything she says to be depended upon or otherwise?"

I considered the matter.

"I think she is quite dependable," I said cautiously. "That is, in so far as she is talking of what she has actually seen. Beyond that, of course, when you get on to what she thinks—well, that is another matter. She has a powerful imagination, and systematically thinks the worst of everyone."

"The typical elderly spinster, in fact," said Melchett with a laugh. "Well, I ought to know the breed by now. Gad, the tea parties down here!"

We were admitted by a very diminutive maid and shown into a small drawing-room.

"A bit crowded," said Colonel Melchett, looking round. "But plenty of good stuff. A lady's room, eh, Clement?"

I agreed, and at that moment the door opened and Miss Marple made her appearance.

"Very sorry to bother you, Miss Marple," said the Colonel when I had introduced him, putting on his bluff, military manner, which he had an idea was attractive to elderly ladies. "Got to do my duty, you know."

"Of course, of course," said Miss Marple. "I quite understand. Won't you sit down? And might I offer you a little glass of cherry brandy? My own making. A receipt of my grandmother's."

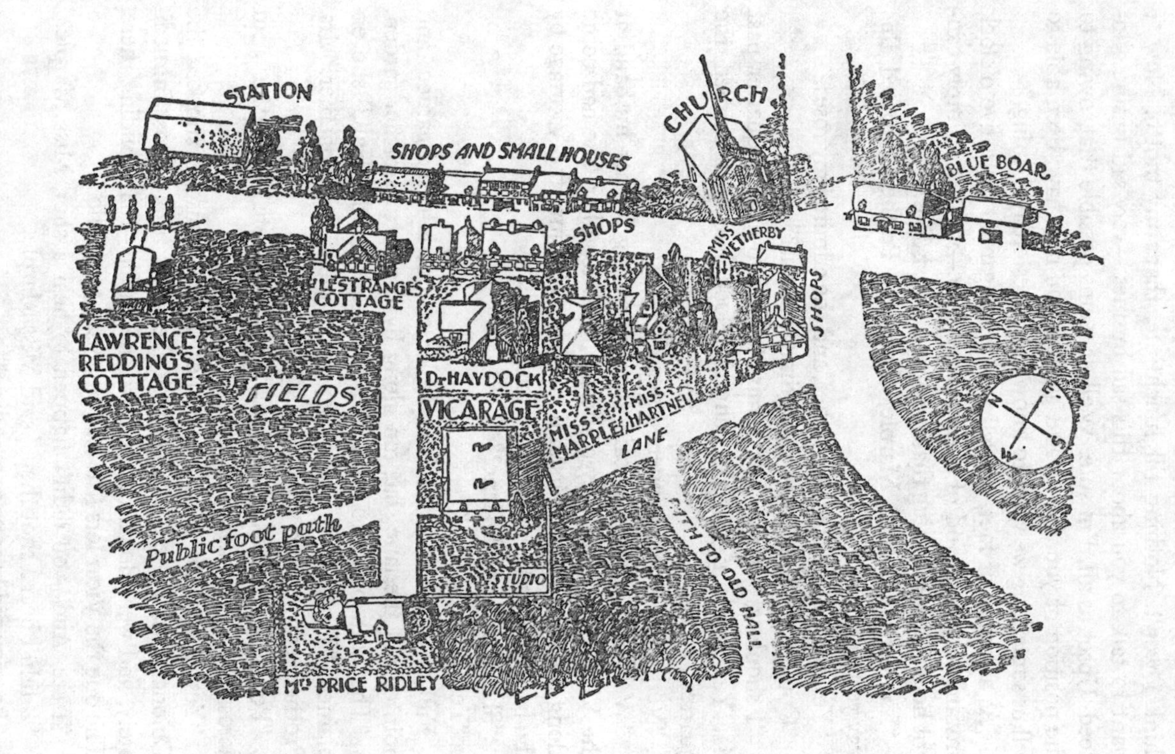
STATION
SHOPS AND SMALL HOUSES
CHURCH
BLUE BOAR
SHOPS
MISS WETHERBY
SHOPS
L'ESTRANGE'S COTTAGE
LAWRENCE REDDING'S COTTAGE
FIELDS
Dr HAYDOCK
VICARAGE
MISS MARPLE
MISS HARTNELL
LANE
PATH TO OLD HALL
Public foot path
STUDIO
Mrs PRICE RIDLEY
N
E
S
W

"Thank you very much, Miss Marple. Very kind of you. But I think I won't. Nothing till lunchtime, that's my motto. Now, I want to talk to you about this sad business—very sad business indeed. Upset us all, I'm sure. Well, it seems possible that, owing to the position of your house and garden, you may have been able to tell us something we want to know about yesterday evening."

"As a matter of fact, I *was* in my little garden from five o'clock onward yesterday, and of course from there—well, one simply cannot help seeing anything that is going on next door."

"I understand, Miss Marple, that Mrs. Protheroe passed this way yesterday evening."

"Yes, she did. I called out to her, and she admired my roses."

"Could you tell us about what time that was?"

"I should say it was just a minute or two after a quarter past six. Yes, that's right. The church clock had just chimed the quarter."

"Very good. What happened next?"

"Well, Mrs. Protheroe said she was calling for her husband at the Vicarage, so that they could go home together. She had come along the lane, you understand, and she went into the Vicarage by the back gate and across the garden."

"She came from the lane?"

"Yes, I'll show you."

Full of eagerness, Miss Marple led us out into the garden, and pointed out the lane that ran along by the bottom of her garden.

"The path opposite with the stile leads to the Hall," she explained. "That was the way they were going home together. Mrs. Protheroe came from the village."

"Perfectly, perfectly," said Colonel Melchett. "And she went across to the Vicarage, you say?"

"Yes. I saw her turn the corner of the house. I suppose the Colonel wasn't there yet, because she came back almost immediately, and went down the lawn to the studio—that building there. The one the Vicar lets Mr. Redding use as a studio."

"I see. And—you didn't happen to hear a shot, Miss Marple?"

"I didn't hear a shot then," said Miss Marple.

"But you did hear one sometime?"

"Yes, I think there was a shot somewhere in the woods. But

quite five or ten minutes afterward—and, as I say, out in the woods. At least, I think so. It couldn't have been—surely it couldn't have been—"

She stopped, pale with excitement.

"Yes, yes, we'll come to all that presently," said Colonel Melchett. "Please go on with your story. Mrs. Protheroe went down to the studio?"

"Yes, she went inside and waited. Presently Mr. Redding came along the lane from the village. He came to the Vicarage gate, looked all round—"

"And saw you, Miss Marple."

"As a matter of fact, he didn't see me," said Miss Marple flushing slightly. "Because, you see, just at that minute I was bending right over—trying to get up one of those nasty dandelions, you know. So difficult. And then he went through the gate and down to the studio."

"He didn't go near the house?"

"Oh, no, he went straight to the studio. Mrs. Protheroe came to the door to meet him, and then they both went inside."

Here Miss Marple contributed a singularly eloquent pause.

"Perhaps she was sitting to him," I suggested.

"Perhaps," said Miss Marple.

"And they came out—when?"

"About ten minutes later."

"That was roughly?"

"The church clock had chimed the half-hour. They strolled out through the garden gate and along the lane, and just at that minute Doctor Stone came down the path leading to the Hall and climbed over the stile and joined them. They all walked toward the village together. At the end of the lane I think, but I can't be quite sure, they were joined by Miss Cram. I think it must have been Miss Cram, because her skirts were so short."

"You must have very good eyesight, Miss Marple, if you can observe as far as that."

"I was observing a bird," said Miss Marple. "A golden-crested wren, I think he was. A sweet little fellow. I had my glasses out, and that's how I happened to see Miss Cram (if it was Miss Cram, and I think so) join them."

"Ah! Well, that may be so," said Colonel Melchett. "Now, since you seem very good at observing, did you happen to notice, Miss Marple, what sort of expression Mrs. Protheroe and Mr. Redding had as they passed along the lane?"

"They were smiling and talking," said Miss Marple. "They seemed very happy to be together, if you know what I mean."

"They didn't seem upset or disturbed in any way?"

"Oh, no. Just the opposite."

"Deuced odd," said the Colonel. "There's something deuced odd about the whole thing."

Miss Marple suddenly took our breath away by remarking in a placid voice, "Has Mrs. Protheroe been saying that she committed the crime now?"

"Upon my soul," said the Colonel. "How did you come to guess that, Miss Marple?"

"Well, I rather thought it might happen," said Miss Marple. "I think dear Lettice thought so, too. She's really a very sharp girl. Not always very scrupulous, I'm afraid. So Anne Protheroe says she killed her husband. Well, well. I don't think it's true. No, I'm almost sure it isn't true. Not with a woman like Anne Protheroe. Although one never can be quite sure about anyone, can one? At least that's what I've found. When does she say she shot him?"

"At twenty minutes past six. Just after speaking to you."

Miss Marple shook her head slowly and pityingly. The pity was, I think, for two full grown men being so foolish as to believe such a story. At least that is what we felt like.

"What did she shoot him with?"

"A pistol."

"Where did she find it?"

"She brought it with her."

"Well, that she didn't do," said Miss Marple with unexpected decision. "I can swear to that. She'd no such thing with her."

"You mightn't have seen it."

"Of course I should have seen it."

"If it had been in her handbag."

"She wasn't carrying a handbag."

"Well, it might have been concealed—er—upon her person."

Miss Marple directed a glance of sorrow and scorn upon him.

"My dear Colonel Melchett. You know what young women are nowadays. Not ashamed to show exactly how the creator made them. She hadn't so much as a handkerchief in the top of her stocking."

Melchett was obstinate.

"You must admit that it all fits in," he said. "The time, the overturned clock pointing to six twenty-two—"

Miss Marple turned on me.

"Do you mean you haven't told him about that clock yet?"

"What about the clock, Clement?"

I told him. He showed a good deal of annoyance.

"Why on earth didn't you tell Slack this last night?"

"Because," I said, "he wouldn't let me."

"Nonsense, you ought to have insisted."

"Probably," I said, "Inspector Slack behaves quite differently to you than he does to me. I had no earthly chance of insisting."

"It's an extraordinary business altogether," said Melchett. "If a third person comes along and claims to have done this murder, I shall go into a lunatic asylum."

"If I might be allowed to suggest—" murmured Miss Marple.

"Well?"

"If you were to tell Mr. Redding what Mrs. Protheroe has done, and then explain that you don't really believe it is her; and then if you were to go to Mrs. Protheroe and tell her that Mr. Redding is all right—why then, they might each of them tell you the truth. And the truth *is* helpful, though I daresay they don't know very much themselves, poor things."

"It's all very well, but they are the only two people who had a motive for making away with Protheroe."

"Oh, I wouldn't say that, Colonel Melchett," said Miss Marple.

"Why, can you think of anyone else?"

"Oh, yes, indeed. Why," she counted on her fingers, "one, two, three, four, five, six—yes, and a possible seven. I can think of at least seven people who might be very glad to have Colonel Protheroe out of the way."

The Colonel looked at her feebly.

"Seven people? In St. Mary Mead?"

Miss Marple nodded brightly.

"Mind you, I name no names," she said. "That wouldn't be

right. But I'm afraid there's a lot of wickedness in the world. A nice, honorable, upright soldier like you doesn't know about these things, Colonel Melchett."

I thought the Chief Constable was going to have apoplexy.

CHAPTER TEN

HIS REMARKS on the subject of Miss Marple as we left the house were far from complimentary.

"I really believe that wizened-up old maid thinks she knows everything there is to know. And hardly been out of this village all her life. Preposterous. What can she know of life?"

I said mildly that, though doubtless Miss Marple knew next to nothing of life with a capital L, she knew practically everything that went on in St. Mary Mead.

Melchett admitted that grudgingly. She was a valuable witness—particularly valuable from Mrs. Protheroe's point of view.

"I suppose there's no doubt about what she says, eh?"

"If Miss Marple says she had no pistol with her, you can take it for granted that it is so," I said. "If there was the least possibility of such a thing, Miss Marple would have been on to it like a knife."

"That's true enough. We'd better go and have a look at the studio."

The so-called studio was a mere rough shed with a skylight. There were no windows, and the door was the only means of entrance or egress. Satisfied on this score, Melchett announced his intention of visiting the Vicarage with the Inspector.

I nodded.

"I'm going to the police station now."

As I entered through the front door, a murmur of voices caught my ear. I opened the drawing-room door.

On the sofa beside Griselda, conversing animatedly, sat Miss Gladys Cram. Her legs, which were encased in particularly shiny pink stockings, were crossed.

"Hullo, Len," said Griselda.

"Good morning, Mr. Clement," said Miss Cram. "Isn't the news about the Colonel reely too awful? Poor old gentleman."

"Miss Cram," said my wife, "very kindly came in to offer to help us with the Guides. We asked for helpers last Sunday, you remember."

I did remember and I was convinced, and so, I knew from her tone, was Griselda, that the idea of enrolling herself among them would never have occurred to Miss Cram but for the exciting incident which had taken place at the Vicarage.

"I was only just saying to Mrs. Clement," went on Miss Cram, "you could have struck me all of a heap when I heard the news. A murder? I said. In this quiet, one-horse village—for quiet it is, you must admit—not so much as a picture house. And then when I heard it was Colonel Protheroe—why, I simply couldn't believe it. He didn't seem the kind, somehow, to get murdered."

I don't know what Miss Cram considers are the necessary qualifications for being murdered. It has never struck me that the murdered belong to a special class, but doubtless she had some idea in her golden shingled head.

"And so," said Griselda, "Miss Cram came round to find out all about it."

I feared this plain speaking might offend the lady, but she merely flung her head back and laughed uproariously, showing every tooth she possessed.

"That's too bad. You're a sharp one, aren't you, Mrs. Clement? But it's only natural, isn't it, to want to hear the ins and outs of a case like this? And I'm sure I'm willing enough to help with the Guides in any way you like. Exciting, that's what it is. I've been stagnating for a bit of fun. I have; reely I have. Not that my job isn't a very good one, well paid, and Doctor Stone quite the gentleman in every way. But a girl wants a bit of life out of office hours, and, except for you, Mrs. Clement, who is there in the place to talk to, except a lot of old cats?"

"There's Lettice Protheroe," I said.

Gladys Cram tossed her head.

"She's too high and mighty for the likes of me. Fancies herself the County, and wouldn't demean herself by noticing a girl who had to work for her living. Not but what I *did* hear her talking of earning her living herself. And who'd employ her, I should like to know? Why, she'd be fired in less than a week. Unless she went as one of those mannequins, all dressed up and sidling about. She could do that, I expect."

"She'd make a very good mannequin," said Griselda. "She's got such a lovely figure." There's nothing of the cat about Griselda. "When was she talking of earning her own living?"

Miss Cram seemed momentarily discomfited, but recovered herself with her usual archness.

"That would be telling, wouldn't it?" she said. "But she did say so. Things not very happy at home, I fancy. Catch me living at home with a stepmother. I wouldn't sit down under it for a minute."

"Ah! But you're so high-spirited and independent," said Griselda gravely, and I looked at her with suspicion.

Miss Cram was clearly pleased.

"That's right. That's me all over. Can be led, not driven. A palmist told me that not so very long ago. No, I'm not one to sit down and be bullied. And I've made it clear all along to Doctor Stone that I must have my regular times off. These scientific gentlemen, they think a girl's a kind of machine—half the time they just don't notice her or remember she's there."

"Do you find Doctor Stone pleasant to work with? It must be an interesting job if you are interested in archaeology."

"Of course, I don't know much about it," confessed the girl. "It still seems to me that digging up people that are dead and have been dead for hundreds of years isn't—well, it seems a bit nosy, doesn't it? And there's Doctor Stone so wrapped up in it all that half the time he'd forget his meals if it wasn't for me."

"Is he at the barrow this morning?" asked Griselda.

Miss Cram shook her head.

"A bit under the weather this morning," she explained. "Not up to doing any work. That means a holiday for little Gladys."

"I'm sorry," I said.

"Oh, it's nothing much. There's not going to be a second death. But do tell me, Mr. Clement, I hear you've been with the police all the morning. What do they think?"

"Well," I said slowly. "There is still a little—uncertainty."

"Ah!" cried Miss Cram. "Then they don't think it is Mr.

Lawrence Redding after all. So handsome, isn't he? Just like a movie star. And such a nice smile when he says good morning to you. I really couldn't believe my ears when I heard the police had arrested him. Still one always hears they're very stupid—the country police."

"You can hardly blame them in this instance," I said. "Mr. Redding came in and gave himself up."

"What?" the girl was clearly dumfounded. "Well—of all the poor fish! If I'd committed the murder, I wouldn't go straight off and give myself up. I should have thought Lawrence Redding would have had more sense. To give in like that! What did he kill Protheroe for? Did he say? Was it just a quarrel?"

"It's not absolutely certain that he did kill him," I said.

"But surely—if he says he has—why, really, Mr. Clement, he ought to know."

"He ought to, certainly," I agreed. "But the police are not satisfied with his story."

"But why should he say he'd done it if he hasn't?"

That was a point on which I had no intention of enlightening Miss Cram. Instead I said rather vaguely, "I believe that in all prominent murder cases, the police receive numerous letters from people accusing themselves of the crime."

Miss Cram's reception of this piece of information was: "They must be chumps!" in a tone of wonder and scorn.

She added, "I'd never do a thing like that."

"I'm sure you wouldn't," I said.

"Well," she said with a sigh. "I suppose I must be trotting along." She rose. "Mr. Redding accusing himself of the murder will be a bit of news for Doctor Stone."

"Is he interested?" asked Griselda.

Miss Cram furrowed her brows perplexedly.

"He's a queer one. You never can tell with him. All wrapped up in the past. He'd a hundred times rather look at a nasty old bronze knife out of one of those humps of ground than he would see the knife Crippen cut up his wife with, supposing he had a chance to."

"Well," I said. "I must confess I agree with him."

Miss Cram's eyes expressed incomprehension and slight contempt. Then, with reiterated good-bys, she took her departure.

"Not such a bad sort, really," said Griselda as the door closed behind her. "Terribly common, of course, but one of those big, bouncing, good-humored girls that you can't dislike. I wonder what really brought her here?"

"Curiosity."

"Yes, I suppose so. Now, Len, tell me all about it. I'm simply dying to hear."

I sat down and recited faithfully all the happenings of the morning, Griselda interpolating the narrative with little exclamations of surprise and interest.

"So it was Anne Lawrence was after all along! Not Lettice. How blind we've all been. That must have been what old Miss Marple was hinting at yesterday. Don't you think so?"

"Yes," I said, averting my eyes.

Mary entered.

"There's a couple of men here—come from a newspaper, so they say. Do you want to see them?"

"No," I said. "Certainly not. Refer them to Inspector Slack at the police station."

Mary nodded and turned away.

"And when you've got rid of them," I said, "come back here. There's something I want to ask you."

Mary nodded again.

It was some few minutes before she returned.

"Had a job getting rid of them," she said. "Persistent. You never saw anything like it. Wouldn't take no for an answer."

"I expect we shall be a good deal troubled with them," I said. "Now, Mary, what I want to ask you is this—are you quite certain you didn't hear the shot yesterday evening?"

"The shot what killed him? No, of course I didn't. If I had of done, I should have gone in to see what had happened."

"Yes, but—" I was remembering Miss Marple's statement that she had heard a shot in the woods. I changed the form of my question. "Did you hear any other shot—one down in the woods, for instance?"

"Oh, that!" The girl paused. "Yes, now I come to think of it, I believe I did. Not a lot of shots, just one. Queer sort of bang it was."

"Exactly," I said. "Now what time was that?"

"Time?"

"Yes, time."

"I couldn't say, I'm sure. Well after teatime. I do know that."

"Can't you get a little nearer than that?"

"No, I can't. I've got my work to do, haven't I? I can't go on looking at clocks the whole time—and it wouldn't be much good anyway—the alarm loses a good three quarters every day, and what with putting it on, and one thing and another, I'm never exactly sure what time it is."

This perhaps explains why our meals are never punctual. They are sometimes too late and sometimes bewilderingly early.

"Was it long before Mr. Redding came?"

"No, it wasn't long. Ten minutes—a quarter of an hour—not longer than that."

I nodded my head, satisfied.

"Is that all?" said Mary. "Because what I mean to say is, I've got the joint in the oven and the pudding boiling over as likely as not."

"That's all right. You can go."

She left the room, and I turned to Griselda.

"Is it quite out of the question to induce Mary to say 'sir' or 'ma'am'?"

"I have told her. She doesn't remember. She's just a raw girl, remember."

"I am perfectly aware of that," I said. "But raw things do not necessarily remain raw forever. I feel a tinge of cooking might be induced in Mary."

"Well, I don't agree with you," said Griselda. "You know how little we can afford to pay a servant. If once we got her smartened up at all, she'd leave. Naturally. And get higher wages. But as long as Mary can't cook and has these awful manners—well, we're safe; nobody else would have her."

I perceived that my wife's methods of housekeeping were not so entirely haphazard as I had imagined. A certain amount of reasoning underlay them. Whether it was worth while having a maid at the price of her not being able to cook, and having a habit of throwing dishes and remarks at one with the same disconcerting abruptness was a debatable matter.

"And anyway," continued Griselda, "you must make allowances for her manners being worse than usual just now. You can't expect her to feel exactly sympathetic about Colonel Protheroe's death when he jailed her young man."

"Did he jail her young man?"

"Yes, for poaching. You know, that man Archer. Mary has been walking out with him for two years."

"I didn't know that."

"Darling Len, you never know anything."

"It's queer," I said, "that everyone says the shot came from the woods."

"I don't think it's queer at all," said Griselda. "You see, one so often does hear shots in the woods. So, naturally, when you do hear a shot, you just assume as a matter of course that it *is* in the woods. It probably just sounds a bit louder than usual. Of course, if you were in the next room, you'd realize that it was in the house, but from Mary's kitchen, with the window right the other side of the house, I don't believe you'd ever think of such a thing."

The door opened again.

"Colonel Melchett's back," said Mary. "And that police inspector with him, and they say they'd be glad if you'd join them. They're in the study."

CHAPTER ELEVEN

I SAW AT A GLANCE that Colonel Melchett and Inspector Slack had not been seeing eye to eye about the case. Melchett looked flushed and annoyed, and the Inspector looked sulky.

"I'm sorry to say," said Melchett, "that Inspector Slack doesn't agree with me in considering young Redding innocent."

"If he didn't do it, what does he go and say he did it for?" asked Slack skeptically.

"Mrs. Protheroe acted in an exactly similar fashion, remember, Slack."

"That's different. She's a woman, and women act in that silly way. I'm not saying she did it, for a moment. She heard he was accused, and she trumped up a story. I'm used to that sort of game. You wouldn't believe the fool things I've known women do. But Redding's different. He's got his head screwed on all right. And if he admits he did it, well, I say he did do it. It's his pistol—you can't get away from that. And, thanks to this business of Mrs. Protheroe, we know the motive. That was the weak point before, but now we know it—why, the whole thing's plain sailing."

"You think he can have shot him earlier? At six-thirty, say?"

"He can't have done that."

"You've checked up his movements?"

The Inspector nodded.

"He was in the village near the Blue Boar at ten past six. From there he came along the back lane where you say the old lady next door saw him—she doesn't miss much, I should say—and kept his appointment with Mrs. Protheroe in the studio in the garden. They left there together just after six-thirty and went along the lane to the village, being joined by Doctor Stone. He corroborates that, all right—I've seen him. They all stood talking just by the post office for a few minutes; then Mrs. Protheroe went into Miss Hartnell's to borrow a gardening magazine. That's all right, too. I've seen Miss Hartnell. Mrs. Protheroe remained there talking to her till just on seven o'clock, when she exclaimed at the lateness of the hour and said she must get home."

"What was her manner?"

"Very easy and pleasant, Miss Hartnell said. She seemed in good spirits—Miss Hartnell is quite sure there was nothing on her mind."

"Well, go on."

"Redding, he went with Doctor Stone to the Blue Boar, and they had a drink together. He left there at twenty minutes to seven, went rapidly along the village street and down the road to the Vicarage. Lots of prople saw him."

"Not down the back lane this time?" commented the Colonel.

"No—he came to the front, asked for the Vicar, heard Colonel Protheroe was there, went in—and shot him—just as he said he did! That's the truth of it and we needn't look further."

Melchett shook his head.

"There's the doctor's evidence. You can't get away from that. Protheroe was shot not later than six-thirty."

"Oh, doctors!" Inspector Slack looked contemptuous. "If you're going to believe doctors. Take out all your teeth—that's what they do nowadays—and then say they're very sorry, but all the time it was appendicitis. Doctors!"

"This isn't a question of diagnosis. Doctor Haydock was absolutely positive on the point. You can't go against the medical evidence, Slack."

"And there's my evidence for what it is worth," I said, suddenly recalling a forgotten incident. "I touched the body and it was cold. That I can swear to."

"You see, Slack?" said Melchett.

Inspector Slack gave in with a good grace.

"Well, of course, if that's so. But there it was—a beautiful case. Mr. Redding only too anxious to be hanged, so to speak."

"That, in itself strikes me as a little unnatural," observed Colonel Melchett.

"Well, there's no accounting for tastes," said the Inspector. "There's a lot of gentlemen went a bit balmy after the war. Now I suppose it means starting again at the beginning." He turned on me. "Why you went out of your way to mislead me about the clock, sir, I can't think. Obstructing the ends of justice, that's what that was."

I was stung.

"I tried to tell you on three separate occasions," I said. "And each time you shut me up and refused to listen."

"That's just a way of speaking, sir. You could have told me perfectly well if you had had a mind to. The clock and the note seemed to tally perfectly. Now, according to you, the clock was all wrong. I never knew such a case. What's the sense of keeping a clock a quarter of an hour fast anyway?"

"It is supposed," I said, "to induce punctuality."

The Inspector snorted.

"I don't think we need go farther into that now, Inspector," said Colonel Melchett tactfully. "What we want now is the true story from both Mrs. Protheroe and young Redding. I telephoned to Haydock and asked him to bring Mrs. Protheroe over here with him. They ought to be here in about a quarter of an hour. I think it would be as well to have Redding here first."

"I'll get on to the station," said Inspector Slack, and took up the telephone. He spoke down it. "And now," he said, replacing the receiver, "we'll get to work on this room."

He looked at me in a meaning fashion.

"Perhaps," I said, "you'd like me out of the way."

The Inspector immediately opened the door for me. Melchett called out, "Come back when young Redding arrives, will you, Vicar? You're a friend of his, and you may have sufficient influence to persuade him to speak the truth."

I found my wife and Miss Marple with their heads together.

"We've been discussing all sorts of possibilities," said Griselda. "I wish you'd solve the case, Miss Marple, like you did the way Miss Wetherby's gill of picked shrimps disappeared. And all because it reminded you of something quite different about a sack of coals."

"You're laughing, my dear," said Miss Marple. "But, after all, that is a very sound way of arriving at the truth. It's really what people call intuition and make such a fuss about. Intuition is like reading a word without having to spell it out. A child can't do that, because it has had so little experience. But a grown-up person knows the word because he's seen it often before. You catch my meaning, Vicar?"

"Yes," I said slowly. "I think I do. You mean that if a thing reminds you of something else—well, it's probably the same kind of thing."

"Exactly."

"And what precisely does the murder of Colonel Protheroe remind you of?"

Miss Marple sighed.

"That is just the difficulty. So many parallels come to the mind. For instance, there was Major Hargraves, a churchwarden and a man highly respected in every way. And all the time he was keeping a separate second establishment—a former housemaid, just think of it! And five children—actually five children—a terrible shock to his wife and daughter."

I tried hard to visualize Colonel Protheroe in the role of secret sinner, and failed.

"And then there was that laundry business," went on Miss Marple. "Miss Hartnell's opal pin—left most imprudently in a frilled blouse and sent to the laundry. And the woman who took it didn't want it in the least, and wasn't by any means a thief. She simply hid it in another woman's house and told the police she'd seen this other woman take it. Spite, you know, sheer spite. It's an astonishing motive—spite. A man in it, of course. There always is."

This time I failed to see any parallel, however remote. Miss Marple went on in a dreamy voice.

"And then there was poor Elwell's daughter—such a pretty, ethereal girl—tried to stifle her little brother. And there was the money for the Choir Boys' Outing (before your time, Vicar) actually taken by the organist. His wife was sadly in debt. Yes, this case makes one think of so many things—too many. It's very hard to arrive at the truth."

"I wish you would tell me," I said. "Who were the seven suspects?"

"The seven suspects?"

"You said you could think of seven people who would—well, be glad of Colonel Protheroe's death."

"Did I? Yes, I remember I did."

"Was that true?"

"Oh, certainly it was true. But I mustn't mention names. You can think of them quite easily yourself, I am sure."

"Indeed I can't. There is Lettice Protheroe, I suppose, since she probably comes into money on her father's death. But it is absurd to think of her in such a connection, and outside her I can think of nobody."

"And you, my dear?" said Miss Marple, turning to Griselda.

Rather to my surprise Griselda colored up. Something very like tears started into her eyes. She clenched both her small hands.

"Oh!" she cried indignantly. "People are hateful—hateful. The things they say! The beastly things they say!"

I looked at her curiously. It is very unlike Griselda to be so upset. She noticed my glance and tried to smile.

"Don't look at me as though I were an interesting specimen you didn't understand, Len. Don't let's get heated and wander from the point. I don't believe that it was Lawrence or Anne, and

Lettice is out of the question. There must be some clue or other that would help us."

"There is the note, of course," said Miss Marple. "You will remember my saying this morning that that struck me as exceedingly peculiar."

"It seems to fix the time of his death with remarkable accuracy," I said. "And yet, is that possible? Mrs. Protheroe would only have just left the study. She would hardly have had time to reach the studio. The only way in which I can account for it is that he consulted his own watch and that his watch was slow. That seems to me a feasible solution."

"I have another idea," said Griselda. "Suppose, Len, that the clock had already been put back—no, that comes to the same thing—how stupid of me!"

"It hadn't been altered when I left," I said. "I remember comparing it with my watch. Still, as you say, that has no bearing on the present matter."

"What do you think, Miss Marple?" asked Griselda.

The old lady shook her head.

"My dear, I confess I wasn't thinking about it from that point of view at all. What strikes me as so curious, and has done from the first, is the subject matter of that letter."

"I don't see that," I said. "Colonel Protheroe merely wrote that he couldn't wait any longer—"

"*At twenty minutes past six?*" said Miss Marple. "Your maid, Mary, had already told him that you wouldn't be in till half past six at the earliest, and he had appeared to be quite willing to wait until then. And yet, at twenty past six, he sits down and says he can't wait any longer."

I stared at the old lady, feeling an increased respect for her mental powers. Her keen wits had seen what we had failed to perceive. It *was* an odd thing—a very odd thing.

"If only," I said, "the letter hadn't been dated—"

Miss Marple nodded her head.

"Exactly," she said. "If it *hadn't* been dated!"

I cast my mind back, trying to recall that sheet of notepaper and the blurred scrawl, and at the top that neatly printed 6:20. Surely these figures were on a different scale to the rest of the letter.

I gave a gasp.

"Supposing," I said, "it wasn't dated. Supposing that round about six-thirty Colonel Protheroe got impatient and sat down to say he couldn't wait any longer. And as he was sitting there writing, someone came in through the window—"

"Or through the door," suggested Griselda.

"He'd hear the door and look up."

"Colonel Protheroe was rather deaf, you remember," said Miss Marple.

"Yes, that's true. He wouldn't hear it. Whichever way the murderer came, he stole up behind the Colonel and shot him. Then he saw the note and the clock and the idea came to him. He put six-twenty at the top of the letter and he altered the clock to six-twenty-two. It was a clever idea. It gave him, or so he would think, a perfect alibi."

"And what we want to find," said Griselda, "is someone who has a cast-iron alibi for six-twenty, but no alibi at all for—well, that isn't so easy. One can't fix the time."

"We can fix it within very narrow limits," I said. "Haydock places six-thirty as the outside limit of time. I suppose one could perhaps shift it to six thirty-five, from the reasoning we have just been following out; it seems clear that Protheroe would not have got impatient before six-thirty. I think we can say we do know pretty well."

"Then that shot I heard—yes, I suppose it is quite possible. And I thought nothing about it—nothing at all. Most vexing. And yet, now I try to recollect, it does seem to me that it was different from the usual sort of shot one hears. Yes, there was a difference."

"Louder?" I suggested.

No, Miss Marple didn't think it had been louder. In fact, she found it hard to say in what way it had been different, but she still insisted that it was.

I thought she was probably persuading herself of the fact rather than actually remembering it, but she had just contributed such a valuable new outlook to the problem that I felt highly respectful toward her.

She rose, murmuring that she must really get back—it had been so tempting just to run over and discuss the case with dear Griselda. I escorted her to the boundary wall and the back gate, and returned to find Griselda wrapped in thought.

"Still puzzling over that note?" I asked.

"No."

She gave a sudden shiver and shook her shoulders impatiently.

"Len, I've been thinking. How badly someone must have hated Anne Protheroe."

"Hated her?"

"Yes. Don't you see? There's no real evidence against Lawrence —all the evidence against him is what you might call accidental. He just happens to take it into his head to come here. If he hadn't—well, no one would have thought of connecting him with the crime. But Anne is different. Suppose someone knew that she was here at exactly six-twenty—the clock and the time on the letter—everything pointing to her. I don't think it was only because of an alibi it was moved to that exact time—I think there was more in it than that—a direct attempt to fasten the business on her. If it hadn't been for Miss Marple saying she hadn't got the pistol with her, and noticing that she was only a moment before going down to the studio— Yes, if it hadn't been for that—" She shivered again. "Len—I feel that someone hated Anne Protheroe very much. I—I don't like it."

CHAPTER TWELVE

I WAS SUMMONED to the study when Lawrence Redding arrived. He looked haggard and, I thought, suspicious. Colonel Melchett greeted him with something approaching cordiality.

"We want to ask you a few questions—here, on the spot," he said.

Lawrence sneered slightly.

"Isn't that a French idea? Reconstruction of the crime?"

"My dear boy," said Colonel Melchett. "Don't take that tone with us. Are you aware that someone else has also confessed to committing the crime which you pretend to have committed?"

The effect of these words on Lawrence was painful and immediate.

"S-S-omeone else?" he stammered. "Who—who?"

"Mrs. Protheroe," said Colonel Melchett, watching him.

"Absurd. She never did it. She couldn't have. It's impossible."

Melchett interrupted him.

"Strangely enough, we did not believe her story. Neither, I may say, do we believe yours. Doctor Haydock says positively that the murder could not have been committed at the time you say it was."

"Doctor Haydock says that?"

"Yes; so, you see, you are cleared whether you like it or not. And now we want you to help us, to tell us exactly what occurred."

Lawrence still hesitated.

"You're not deceiving me about—about Mrs. Protheroe? You really don't suspect her?"

"On my word of honor," said Colonel Melchett.

Lawrence drew a deep breath.

"I've been a fool," he said. "An absolute fool. How I could have thought for one minute that she did it—"

"Suppose you tell us all about it?" suggested the Chief Constable.

"There's not much to tell. I—I met Mrs. Protheroe that afternoon—"

He paused.

"We know all about that," said Melchett. "You may think that your feeling for Mrs. Protheroe and hers for you was a dead secret, but in reality it was known and commented upon. In any case everything is bound to come out now."

"Very well, then. I expect you are right. I had promised the Vicar here"—he glanced at me—"to—to go right away. I met Mrs. Protheroe that evening in the studio at a quarter past six. I told her of what I had decided. She, too, agreed, that it was the only thing to do. We—we said good-by to each other.

"We left the studio, and almost at once Doctor Stone joined us. Anne managed to seem marvelously natural. I couldn't do it. I went off with Stone to the Blue Boar and had a drink. Then I thought I'd go home, but, when I got to the corner of this road,

I changed my mind and decided to come along and see the Vicar. I felt I wanted someone to talk to about the matter.

"At the door, the maid told me the Vicar was out but would be in shortly, but that Colonel Protheroe was in the study waiting for him. Well, I didn't like to go away again—looked as though I were shirking meeting him. So I said I'd wait, too, and I went into the study."

He stopped.

"Well?" said Colonel Melchett.

"Protheroe was sitting at the writing table—just as you found him. I went up to him. I saw that he was dead. Then I looked down and saw the pistol lying on the floor beside him. I picked it up—*and at once saw that it was my pistol!*

"That gave me a turn. My pistol! And then, straightway I leaped to one conclusion. Anne must have bagged my pistol sometime or other—meaning it for herself if she couldn't bear things any longer. Perhaps she had had it with her today. After we parted in the village she must have come back here and—and—Oh! I suppose I was mad to think of it. But that's what I thought. I slipped the pistol in my pocket and came away. Just outside the Vicarage gate, I met the Vicar. He said something nice and normal about seeing Protheroe—and suddenly I had a wild desire to laugh. His manner was so ordinary and everyday, and there was I all strung up. I remember shouting out something absurd and seeing his face change. I was nearly off my head, I believe. I went walking—walking— At last I couldn't bear it any longer. If Anne had done this ghastly thing, I was at least morally responsible. I went and gave myself up."

There was a silence when he had finished. Then the Colonel said in a businesslike voice, "I would like to ask just one or two questions. First, did you touch or move the body in any way?"

"No, I didn't touch it at all. One could see he was dead without touching him."

"Did you notice a note lying on the blotter half concealed by his body?"

"No."

"Did you interfere in any way with the clock?"

"I never touched the clock. I seem to remember a clock lying overturned on the table, but I never touched it."

"Now as to this pistol of yours, when did you last see it?"

Lawrence Redding reflected.

"It's hard to say exactly."

"Where do you keep it?"

"Oh, in a litter of odds and ends in the sitting-room in my cottage. On one of the shelves of the bookcase."

"You left it lying about carelessly?"

"Yes. I really didn't think about it. It was just there."

"So that anyone who came to your cottage could have seen it?"

"Yes."

"And you don't remember when you last saw it?"

Lawrence drew his brows together in a frown of recollection.

"I'm almost sure it was there the day before yesterday. I remember pushing it aside to get an old pipe. I think it was the day before yesterday—but it may have been the day before that."

"Who has been to your cottage lately?"

"Oh! Crowds of people. Someone is always drifting in and out. I had a sort of tea party the day before yesterday. Lettice Protheroe, Dennis, and all their crowd. And then one or other of the old pussies comes in now and again."

"Do you lock the cottage up when you go out?"

"No, why on earth should I? I've nothing to steal. And no one does lock his house up round here."

"Who looks after your wants there?"

"An old Mrs. Archer comes in every morning to 'do for me,' as it's called."

"Do you think she would remember when the pistol was there last?"

"I don't know. She might. But I don't fancy conscientious dusting is her strong point."

"It comes to this—that almost anyone might have taken that pistol?"

"It seems so—yes."

The door opened, and Dr. Haydock came in with Anne Protheroe.

She started at seeing Lawrence. He, on his part, made a tentative step toward her.

"Forgive me, Anne," he said. "It was abominable of me to think what I did."

"I—" She faltered, then looked appealingly at Colonel Melchett. "It is true, what Doctor Haydock told me?"

"That Mr. Redding is cleared of suspicion? Yes. And now what about this story of yours, Mrs. Protheroe? Eh, what about it?"

She smiled rather shamefacedly.

"I suppose you think it dreadful of me?"

"Well, shall we say—very foolish? But that's all over. What I want now, Mrs. Protheroe, is the truth—the absolute truth."

She nodded gravely.

"I will tell you. I suppose you know about—about everything."

"Yes."

"I was to meet Lawrence—Mr. Redding—that evening at the studio. At a quarter past six. My husband and I drove into the village together. I had some shopping to do. As we parted he mentioned casually that he was going to see the Vicar. I couldn't get word to Lawrence, and I was rather uneasy. I— Well, it was awkward meeting him in the Vicarage garden while my husband was at the Vicarage."

Her cheeks burned as she said this. It was not a pleasant moment for her.

"I reflected that perhaps my husband would not stay very long. To find this out, I came along the back lane and into the garden. I hoped no one would see me, but, of course, old Miss Marple had to be in her garden! She stopped me and we said a few words, and I explained I was going to call for my husband. I felt I had to say something. I don't know whether she believed me or not. She looked rather—funny.

"When I left her, I went straight across to the Vicarage and round the corner of the house to the study window. I crept up to it very softly expecting to hear the sound of voices. But to my surprise there were none. I just glanced in, saw the room was empty, and hurried across the lawn and down to the studio where Lawrence joined me almost at once."

"You say the room was empty, Mrs. Protheroe?"

"Yes; my husband was not there."

"Extraordinary."

"You mean, ma'am, that you didn't see him?" said the Inspector.

"No, I didn't see him."

Inspector Slack whispered to the Chief Constable, who nodded his head.

"Do you mind, Mrs. Protheroe, just showing us exactly what you did?"

"Not at all."

She rose; Inspector Slack pushed open the window for her, and she stepped out on the terrace and round the house to the left.

Inspector Slack beckoned me imperiously to go and sit at the writing table.

Somehow I didn't much like doing it. It gave me an uncomfortable feeling. But, of course, I complied.

Presently I heard footsteps outside; they paused for a minute, then retreated. Inspector Slack indicated to me that I could return to the other side of the room. Mrs. Protheroe re-entered through the window.

"Is that exactly how it was?" asked Colonel Melchett.

"I think exactly."

"Then can you tell us, Mrs. Protheroe, just exactly where the Vicar was in the room when you looked in?" asked Inspector Slack.

"The Vicar? I— No, I'm afraid I can't. I didn't see him."

Inspector Slack nodded.

"That's how you didn't see your husband. He was round the corner at the writing desk."

"Oh!" She paused. Suddenly her eyes grew round with horror. "It wasn't there that—that—"

"Yes, Mrs. Protheroe. It was while he was sitting there."

"Oh!" She shivered.

He went on with his questions.

"Did you know, Mrs. Protheroe, that Mr. Redding had a pistol?"

"Yes. He told me so once."

"Did you ever have that pistol in your possession?"

She shook her head.

"No."

"Did you know where he kept it?"

"I'm not sure. I think—yes, I think I've seen it on a shelf in his cottage. Didn't you keep it there, Lawrence?"

"When was the last time you were at the cottage, Mrs. Protheroe?"

"Oh, about three weeks ago. My husband and I had tea there with him."

"And you have not been there since?"

"No. I never went there. You see, it would probably cause a lot of talk in the village."

"Doubtless," said Colonel Melchett dryly. "Where were you in the habit of seeing Mr. Redding, if I may ask?"

She blushed. "He used to come up to the Hall. He was painting Lettice. We—we often met in the woods afterward."

The Chief Constable nodded.

"Isn't that enough?" Her voice was suddenly broken. "It's so awful—having to tell you all these things. And—and there wasn't anything wrong about it. There wasn't—indeed, there wasn't. We were just friends. We—we couldn't help caring for each other."

She looked pleadingly at Dr. Haydock, and that soft-hearted man stepped forward.

"I really think, Melchett," he said, "that Mrs. Protheroe has had enough. She's had a great shock—in more ways than one."

The Chief Constable nodded.

"There is really nothing more I want to ask you, Mrs. Protheroe," he said. "Thank you for answering my questions so frankly."

"Then—then I may go?"

He bowed his head in assent, but I noticed him make an almost imperceptible sign to Slack, which that worthy answered with a nod of understanding. Anne Protheroe was not yet completely cleared of suspicion. The evidence of the note was too strong.

"Is your wife in?" asked Haydock. "I think Mrs. Protheroe would like to see her."

"Yes," I said, "Griselda is in. You'll find her in the drawing-room."

She and Haydock left the room together, and Lawrence Redding with them.

Colonel Melchett had pursed up his lips and was playing with a paper knife. Slack was looking at the note. It was then that I mentioned Miss Marple's theory.

Slack looked closely at it.

"My word," he said. "I believe the old lady's right. Look here, sir, don't you see? These figures are written in different ink. That date was written with a fountain pen or I'll eat my boots!"

We were all rather excited.

"You've examined the note for fingerprints, of course," said the Chief Constable.

"What do you think, Colonel? No fingerprints on the note at all. Fingerprints on the pistol those of Mr. Lawrence Redding. May have been some others once, before he went fooling round with it and carrying it around in his pocket, but there's nothing clear enough to get hold of now."

"At first the case looked very black against Mrs. Protheroe," said the Colonel thoughtfully. "Much blacker than against young Redding. There was that old woman Marple's evidence that she didn't have the pistol with her, but these elderly ladies are often mistaken."

I was silent, but I did not agree with him. I was quite sure that Anne Protheroe had had no pistol with her, since Miss Marple had said so. Miss Marple is not the type of elderly lady who makes mistakes. She has got an uncanny knack of being always right.

"What did get me was that nobody heard the shot. If it was fired then—somebody *must* have heard it—wherever they thought it came from. Slack, you'd better have a word with the maid."

Inspector Slack moved with alacrity toward the door.

"I shouldn't ask her if she heard a shot in the house," I said. "Because if you do, she'll deny it. Call it a shot in the woods. That's the only kind of shot she'll admit to hearing."

"I know how to manage them," said Inspector Slack, and disappeared.

"Miss Marple says she heard a shot later," said Colonel Melchett thoughtfully. "We must see if she can fix the time at all precisely. Of course it may be a stray shot that had nothing to do with the case."

"It may be, of course," I agreed.

The Colonel took a turn or two up and down the room.

"Do you know, Clement," he said suddenly, "I've a feeling that this is going to turn out a much more intricate and difficult business than any of us think. Dash it all, there's something behind it." He snorted. "Something we don't know about. We're only beginning, Clement. Mark my words, we're only beginning. All these things, the clock, the note, the pistol—they don't make sense as they stand."

I shook my head. They certainly didn't.

"But I'm going to get to the bottom of it. No calling in of Scotland Yard. Slack's a smart man. He's a very smart man. He's a kind of ferret. He'll nose his way through to the truth. He's done several very good things already and this case will be his chef-d'oeuvre. Some men would call in Scotland Yard. I shan't. We'll get to the bottom of this here in Downshire."

"I hope so, I'm sure," I said.

I tried to make my voice enthusiastic, but I had already taken such a dislike to Inspector Slack that the prospect of his success failed to appeal to me. A successful Slack would, I thought, be even more odious than a baffled one.

"Who has the house next door?" asked the Colonel suddenly.

"You mean at the end of the road? Mrs. Price Ridley."

"We'll go along to her after Slack has finished with your maid. She might just possibly have heard something. She isn't deaf or anything, is she?"

"I should say her hearing was remarkably keen. I'm going by the amount of scandal she has started by 'just happening to overhear accidentally.'"

"That's the kind of woman we want. Oh! Here's Slack."

The Inspector had the air of one emerging from a severe tussle. He looked hot.

"Phew!" he said. "That's a tartar you've got, sir."

"Mary is essentially a girl of strong character," I replied.

"Doesn't like the police," he said. "I cautioned her—did what I could to put the fear of the Law into her, but no good. She stood right up to me."

"Spirited," I said, feeling more kindly toward Mary.

"But I pinned her down, all right. She heard one shot—and one shot only. And it was a good long time after Colonel Protheroe came. I couldn't get her to name a time, but we fixed it at last by means of the fish. The fish was late, and she blew the boy up when he came, and he said it was barely half past six anyway, and it was just after that she heard the shot. Of course, that's not accurate, so to speak, but it gives us an idea."

"H'm," said Melchett.

"I don't think Mrs. Protheroe's in this after all," said Slack, with a note of regret in his voice. "She wouldn't have had time, to begin with, and then women never like fiddling about with firearms. Arsenic's more in their line. No, I don't think she did it. It's a pity!"

He sighed.

Melchett explained that he was going round to Mrs. Price Ridley's, and Slack approved.

"May I come with you?" I asked. "I'm getting interested."

I was given permission and we set forth. A loud "Hi" greeted us as we emerged from the Vicarage gate, and my nephew, Dennis, came running up the road from the village to join us.

"Look here," he said to the Inspector. "What about that footprint I told you about?"

"Gardener's," said Inspector Slack laconically.

"You don't think it might be someone else wearing the gardener's boots?"

"No, I don't," said Inspector Slack in a discouraging way.

It would take more than that to discourage Dennis, however.

He held out a couple of burned matches.

"I found these by the Vicarage gate."

"Thank you," said Slack and put them in his pocket.

Matters appeared now to have reached a deadlock.

"You're not arresting Uncle Len, are you?" inquired Dennis facetiously.

"Why should I?" inquired Slack.

"There's a lot of evidence against him," declared Dennis. "You ask Mary. Only the day before the murder he was wishing Colonel Protheroe out of the world. Weren't you, Uncle Len?"

"Er—" I began.

Inspector Slack turned a slow, suspicious stare upon me, and I felt hot all over. Dennis is exceedingly tiresome. He ought to realize that a policeman seldom has a sense of humor.

"Don't be absurd, Dennis," I said irritably.

The innocent child opened his eyes in a stare of surprise.

"I say, it's only a joke," he said. "Uncle Len just said that anyone who murdered Colonel Protheroe would be doing the world a service."

"Ah!" said Inspector Slack. "That explains something the maid said."

Servants very seldom have any sense of humor either. I cursed Dennis heartily in my mind for bringing the matter up. That and the clock together will make the Inspector suspicious of me for life.

"Come on, Clement," said Colonel Melchett.

"Where are you going? Can I come, too?" asked Dennis.

"No, you can't," I snapped.

We left him looking after us with a hurt expression. We went up to the neat front door of Mrs. Price Ridley's house, and the Inspector knocked and rang in what I can only describe as an official manner.

A pretty parlor maid answered the bell.

"Mrs. Price Ridley in?" inquired Melchett.

"No, sir." The maid paused and added, "She's just gone down to the police station."

This was a totally unexpected development. As we retraced our steps, Melchett caught me by the arm and murmured, "If she's gone to confess to the crime, too, I really shall go off my head."

CHAPTER THIRTEEN

I HARDLY THOUGHT it likely that Mrs. Price Ridley had anything so dramatic in view, but I did wonder what had taken her to the police station. Had she really got evidence of importance, or that she thought of importance, to offer? At any rate we should soon know.

We found Mrs. Price Ridley talking at a high rate of speed to a somewhat bewildered looking police constable. That she was extremely indignant I knew from the way the bow in her hat was trembling. Mrs. Price Ridley wears what I believe are known as Hats for Matrons—they make a specialty of them in our adjacent town of Much Benham. They perch easily on a superstructure of hair and are somewhat overweighted with large bows of ribbon. Griselda is always threatening to get a Matron's hat.

Mrs. Price Ridley paused in her flow of words upon our entrance.

"Mrs. Price Ridley?" inquired Colonel Melchett, lifting his hat.

"Let me introduce Colonel Melchett to you, Mrs. Price Ridley," I said. "Colonel Melchett is our Chief Constable."

Mrs. Price Ridley looked at me coldly, but produced the semblance of a gracious smile for the Colonel.

"We've just been round to your house, Mrs. Price Ridley," explained the Colonel, "and heard you had come down here."

Mrs. Price Ridley thawed altogether.

"Ah!" she said. "I'm glad *some* notice is being taken of the occurrence. Disgraceful, I call it. Simply disgraceful."

There is no doubt that murder is disgraceful, but it is not the word I should use to describe it myself. It surprised Melchett, too, I could see.

"Have you any light to throw upon the matter?" he asked.

"That's your business. It's the business of the police. What do we pay rates and taxes for, I should like to know?"

One wonders how many times that query is uttered in a year!

"We're doing our best, Mrs. Price Ridley," said the Chief Constable.

"But the man here hadn't even heard of it till I told him about it!" cried the lady.

We all looked at the constable.

"Lady been rung up on the telephone," he said. "Annoyed. Matter of obscene language, I understand."

"Oh! I see." The Colonel's brow cleared. "We've been talking at cross purposes. You came down here to make a complaint, did you?"

Melchett is a wise man. He knows that, when it is a question of an irate middle-aged lady, there is only one thing to be done—to listen to her. When she has said all that she wants to say, there is a chance that she will listen to you.

Mrs. Price Ridley surged into speech.

"Such disgraceful occurrences ought to be prevented. They ought not to occur. To be rung up in one's own house and insulted—yes, insulted. I'm not accustomed to such things happening. Ever since the war there has been a loosening of moral fiber. Nobody minds what they say, and as to the clothes they wear—"

"Quite," said Colonel Melchett hastily. "What happened exactly?"

Mrs. Price Ridley took breath and started again.

"I was rung up—"

"When?"

"Yesterday afternoon—evening to be exact. About half past six. I went to the telephone, suspecting nothing. Immediately I was foully attacked, threatened—"

"What actually was said?"

Mrs. Price Ridley got slightly pink.

"That I decline to state."

"Obscene language," murmured the constable in a ruminative bass.

"Was bad language used?" asked Colonel Melchett.

"It depends on what you call bad language."

"Could you understand it?" I asked.

"Of course I could understand it."

"Then it couldn't have been bad language," I said.

Mrs. Price Ridley looked at me suspiciously.

"A refined lady," I explained, "is naturally unacquainted with bad language."

"It wasn't that kind of thing," said Mrs. Price Ridley. "At first, I must admit, I was quite taken in. I thought it was a genuine message. Then the—er—person became abusive."

"Abusive?"

"Most abusive. I was quite alarmed."

"Used threatening language, eh?"

"Yes. I am not accustomed to being threatened."

"What did they threaten you with? Bodily damage?"

"Not exactly."

"I'm afraid, Mrs. Price Ridley, you must be more explicit. In what way were you threatened?"

This Mrs. Price Ridley seemed singularly reluctant to answer.

"I can't remember exactly. It was all so upsetting. But right at the end—when I was really *very* upset, this—this—*wretch* laughed."

"Was it a man's voice or a woman's?"

"It was a degenerate voice," said Mrs. Price Ridley with dignity. "I can only describe it as a kind of perverted voice. Now gruff, now squeaky. Really a very *peculiar* voice."

"Probably a practical joke," said the Colonel soothingly.

"A most wicked thing to do, if so. I might have had a heart attack."

"We'll look into it," said the Colonel. "Eh, Inspector? Trace the telephone call. You can't tell me more definitely exactly what was said, Mrs. Price Ridley?"

A struggle began in Mrs. Price Ridley's ample black bosom. The desire for reticence fought against a desire for vengeance. Vengeance triumphed.

"This, of course, will go no farther," she began.

"Of course not."

"This creature began by saying—I can hardly bring myself to repeat it—"

"Yes, yes," said Melchett encouragingly.

" 'You are a wicked, scandal-mongering old woman!' Me, Colonel Melchett—a scandal-mongering old woman. 'But this time you've gone too far. Scotland Yard are after you for libel.' "

"Naturally, you were alarmed," said Melchett, biting his mustache to conceal a smile.

" 'Unless you hold your tongue in future, it will be the worse for you—in more ways than one.' I can't describe to you the menacing way *that* was said. I gasped, 'Who are you?' faintly—like that, and the voice answered, 'The Avenger.' I gave a little shriek; it sounded so awful, and then—the person laughed. Laughed! Distinctly. And that was all. I heard him hang up the receiver. Of course I asked the exchange what number had been ringing me up, by they said they didn't know. You know what exchanges are. Thoroughly rude and unsympathetic."

"Quite," I said.

"I felt quite faint," continued Mrs. Price Ridley. "All on edge and so nervous that when I heard a shot in the woods I do declare I jumped almost out of my skin. That will show you."

"A shot in the woods," said Inspector Slack alertly.

"In my excited state, it simply sounded to me like a cannon going off. 'Oh!' I said, and sank down on the sofa in a state of prostration. Clara had to bring me a glass of damson gin."

"Shocking," said Melchett. "Shocking. All very trying for you. And the shot sounded very loud, you say? As though it were near at hand?"

"That was simply the state of my nerves."

"Of course. Of course. And what time was all this? To help us in tracing the telephone call, you know."

"About half past six."

"You can't give it us more exactly than that?"

"Well, you see, the little clock on my mantelpiece had just chimed the half-hour, and I said, 'Surely that clock is fast.' It does gain, that clock. And I compared it with the watch I was wearing and that only said ten minutes past, but then I put it to my ear and found it had stopped. So I thought, 'Well, if that clock *is* fast, I shall hear the church tower in a moment or two.' And then, of course, the telephone bell rang, and I forgot all about it."

She paused breathless.

"Well, that's near enough," said Colonel Melchett. "We'll have it looked into for you, Mrs. Price Ridley."

"Just think of it as a silly joke, and don't worry, Mrs. Price Ridley," I said.

She looked at me coldly. Evidently the incident of the pound note still rankled.

"Very strange things have been happening in this village lately," she said, addressing herself to Melchett. "Very strange things indeed. Colonel Protheroe was going to look into them, and what happend to him, poor man? Perhaps I shall be the next."

And on that she took her departure, shaking her head with a kind of ominous melancholy. Melchett muttered under his breath, "No such luck." Then his face grew grave, and he looked inquiringly at Inspector Slack.

That worthy nodded his head slowly.

"This about settles it, sir. That's three people who heard the shot. We've got to find out now who fired it. This business of Mr. Redding's has delayed us. But we've got several starting points. Thinking Mr. Redding was guilty, I didn't bother to look into them. But that's all changed now. And now one of the first things to do is to look up that telephone call."

"Mrs. Price Ridley's?"

The Inspector grinned.

"No—though I suppose we'd better make a note of that or else we shall have the old girl bothering in here again. No, I meant that fake call that got the Vicar out of the way."

"Yes," said Melchett. "That's important."

"And the next thing is to find out what everyone was doing that evening between six and seven. Everyone at Old Hall, I mean, and pretty well everyone in the village as well."

I gave a sigh.

"What wonderful energy you have, Inspector Slack."

"I believe in hard work. We'll begin by just noting down your own movements, Mr. Clement."

"Willingly. The telephone call came through about half past five."

"A man's voice, or a woman's?"

"A woman's. At least it sounded like a woman's. But of course I took it for granted it was Mrs. Abbott speaking."

"You didn't recognize it as being Mrs. Abbott's?"

"No, I can't say I did. I didn't notice the voice particularly, or think about it."

"And you started right away? Walked? Haven't you got a bicycle?"

"No."

"I see. So it took you—how long?"

"It's very nearly two miles, whichever way you go."

"Through Old Hall woods is the shortest way, isn't it?"

"Actually, yes. But it's not particularly good going. I went and came back by the footpath across the fields."

"The one that comes out opposite the Vicarage gate?"

"Yes."

"And Mrs. Clement?"

"My wife was in London. She arrived back by the six-fifty train."

"Right. The maid I've seen. That finishes with the Vicarage. I'll be off to Old Hall next. And then I want an interview with Mrs. Lestrange. Queer, her going to see Protheroe the night before he was killed. A lot of queer things about this case."

I agreed.

Glancing at the clock, I realized that it was nearly lunchtime. I invited Melchett to partake of pot luck with us, but he excused himself on the plea of having to go to the Blue Boar. The Blue Boar gives you a first-rate meal of the joint-and-two-vegetable type. I thought his choice was a wise one. After her interview with the police, Mary would probably be feeling more temperamental than usual.

CHAPTER FOURTEEN

ON MY WAY HOME, I ran into Miss Hartnell, and she detained me at least ten minutes, declaiming in her deep-bass voice against the improvidence and ungratefulness of the lower classes. The crux of the matter seemed to be that The Poor did not want Miss Hartnell in their houses. My sympathies were entirely on their side. I am debarred by my social standing from expressing my prejudices in the forceful manner they do. I soothed her as best I could and made my escape.

Haydock overtook me in his car at the corner of the Vicarage road.

"I've just taken Mrs. Protheroe home," he called.

He waited for me at the gate of his house.

"Come in a minute," he said.

I complied.

"This is an extraordinary business," he said as he threw his hat on a chair and opened the door into his surgery.

He sank down on a shabby leather chair, and stared across the room. He looked harried and perplexed.

I told him that we had succeeded in fixing the time of the shot. He listened with an almost abstracted air.

"That lets Anne Protheroe out," he said. "Well, well, I'm glad it's neither of those two. I like 'em both."

I believed him, and yet it occurred to me to wonder why, since, as he said, he liked them both, the freedom from complicity seemed to have had the result of plunging him in gloom. This morning he had looked like a man with a weight lifted from his mind; now he looked thoroughly rattled and upset.

And yet I was convinced that he meant what he said. He was fond of both Anne Protheroe and Lawrence Redding. Why, then, this gloomy absorption?

He roused himself with an effort.

"I meant to tell you about Hawes. All this business has driven him out of my mind."

"Is he really ill?"

"There's nothing radically wrong with him. You know, of course, that he's had *encephalitis lethargica*—sleeping sickness, as it's commonly called?"

"No," I said, very much surprised. "I didn't know anything of the kind. He never told me anything about it. When did he have it?"

"About a year ago. He recovered all right—as far as one ever recovers. It's a strange disease—has a queer moral effect. The whole character may change after it."

He was silent for a moment or two and then said, "We think with horror now of the days when we burned witches. I believe the day will come when we will shudder to think that we ever hanged criminals."

"You don't believe in capital punishment?"

"It's not so much that." He paused. "You know," he said slowly, "I'd rather have my job than yours."

"Why?"

"Because your job deals very largely with what we call right and wrong—and I'm not at all sure that there's any such thing. Suppose it's all a question of glandular secretion. Too much of one gland, too little of another—and you get your murderer, your thief, your habitual criminal. Clement, I believe the time will come when we'll be horrified to think of the long centuries in which we've indulged in what you may call moral reprobation, to think how we've punished people for disease—which they can't help, poor devils. You don't hang a man for having tuberculosis."

"He isn't dangerous to the community."

"In a sense he is. He infects other people. Or take a man who fancies he's the Emperor of China. You don't say 'how wicked of him.' I take your point about the community. The community must be protected. Shut up these people where they can't do any harm—even put them peacefully out of the way—yes, I'd go as far as that. But don't call it punishment. Don't bring shame on them and their innocent families."

I looked at him curiously.

"I've never heard you speak like this before."

"I don't usually air my theories abroad. Today I'm riding my hobby. You're an intelligent man, Clement, which is more than some parsons are. You won't admit, I daresay, that there's no such thing as what is technically termed 'sin,' but you're broad-minded enough to consider the possibility of such a thing."

"It strikes at the root of all our accepted ideas," I said.

"Yes, we're a narrow-minded, self-righteous lot, only too keen to judge matters we know nothing about. I honestly believe crime is a case for the doctor, not the policeman and not the parson. In the future, perhaps, there won't be any such thing."

"You'll have cured it?"

"We'll have cured it. Rather a wonderful thought. Have you ever studied the statistics of crime? No—very few people have. I have, though. You'd be amazed at the amount there is of adolescent crime—glands again, you see. Young Neil, the Oxfordshire murderer, killed five little girls before he was suspected. Nice lad—never given any trouble of any kind. Lily Rose, the little Cornish girl, killed her uncle because he docked her of sweets. Hit him when he was asleep with a coal hammer. Went home and a fortnight later killed her elder sister who had annoyed her about some trifling matter. Neither of them hanged, of course. Sent to a home. May be all right later—may not. Doubt if the girl will. The only thing she cares about is seeing the pigs killed. Do you know when suicide is commonest? Fifteen to sixteen years of age. From self-murder to murder of someone else isn't a very long step. But it's not a moral lack—it's a physical one."

"What you say is terrible!"

"No—it's only new to you. New truths have to be faced. One's ideas adjusted. But sometimes—it makes life difficult."

He sat there frowning, yet with a strange look of weariness.

"Haydock," I said, "if you suspected—if you knew—that a certain person was a murderer, would you give that person up to the law or would you be tempted to shield him?"

I was quite unprepared for the effect of my question. He turned on me angrily and suspiciously.

"What makes you say that, Clement? What's in your mind? Out with it, man."

"Why, nothing particular," I said rather taken aback. "Only—well, murder is in our minds just now. If by any chance you happened to discover the truth—I wondered how you would feel about it, that was all."

His anger died down. He stared once more straight ahead of him, like a man trying to read the answer to a riddle that perplexes him, yet which exists only in his own brain.

"If I suspected—if I knew—I should do my duty, Clement. At least, I hope so."

"The question is—which way would you consider your duty lay?"

He looked at me with inscrutable eyes.

"That question comes to every man sometime in his life, I suppose, Clement. And every man has to decide it in his own way."

"You don't know?"

"No, I don't know."

I felt the best thing was to change the subject.

"That nephew of mine is enjoying this case thoroughly," I said. "Spends his entire time looking for footprints and cigarette ash."

Haydock smiled. "What age is he?"

"Just sixteen. You don't take tragedies seriously at that age. It's all Sherlock Holmes and Arsène Lupin to you."

Haydock said thoughtfully, "He's a fine-looking boy. What are you going to do with him?"

"I can't afford a University education, I'm afraid. The boy himself wants to go into the Merchant Service. He failed for the Navy."

"Well—it's a hard life—but he might do worse. Yes, he might do worse."

"I must be going," I exclaimed, catching sight of the clock. "I'm nearly half an hour late for lunch."

My family was just sitting down when I arrived. They demanded a full account of the morning's activities, which I gave them, feeling, as I did so, that most of it was in the nature of an anticlimax.

Dennis, however, was highly entertained by the history of Mrs. Price Ridley's telephone call, and went into fits of laughter as I enlarged upon the nervous shock her system had sustained and the necessity for reviving her with damson gin.

"Serve the old cat right," he exclaimed. "She's got the worst tongue in the place. I wish I'd thought of ringing her up and giving her a fright. I say, Uncle Len, what about giving her a second dose?"

I hastily begged him to do nothing of the sort. Nothing is more dangerous than the well-meant efforts of the younger generation to assist you and show their sympathy.

Dennis's mood changed suddenly. He frowned and put on his man-of-the-world air.

"I've been with Lettice most of the morning," he said. "You know, Griselda, she's really *very* worried. She doesn't want to show it, but she is. Very worried indeed."

"I should hope so," said Griselda with a toss of her head.

Griselda is not too fond of Lettice Protheroe.

"I don't think you're ever quite fair to Lettice."

"Don't you?" said Griselda.

"Lots of people don't wear mourning."

Griselda was silent and so was I. Dennis continued.

"She doesn't talk to most people, but she *does* talk to me. She's awfully worried about the whole thing, and she thinks something ought to be done about it."

"She will find," I said, "that Inspector Slack shares her opinion. He is going up to Old Hall this afternoon, and will probably make the life of everybody there quite unbearable to them in his efforts to get at the truth."

"What do you think *is* the truth, Len?" asked my wife suddenly.

"It's hard to say, my dear. I can't say that at the moment I've any idea at all."

"Did you say that Inspector Slack was going to trace that telephone call—the one that took you to the Abbotts'?"

"Yes."

"But can he do it? Isn't it a very difficult thing to do?"

"I should not imagine so. The exchange will have a record of the calls."

"Oh!" My wife relapsed into thought.

"Uncle Len," said my nephew. "Why were you so ratty with

me this morning for joking about your wishing Colonel Protheroe to be murdered?"

"Because," I said, "there is a time for everything. Inspector Slack has no sense of humor. He took your words quite seriously, will probably cross-examine Mary, and will get out a warrant for my arrest."

"Doesn't he know when a fellow's ragging?"

"No," I said. "He does not. He has attained to his present position through hard work and zealous attention to duty. That has left him no time for the minor recreations of life."

"Do you like him, Uncle Len?"

"No," I said. "I do not. From the first moment I saw him I disliked him intensely. But I have no doubt that he is a highly successful man in his profession."

"You think he'll find out who shot old Protheroe?"

"If he doesn't," I said, "it will not be for the want of trying."

Mary appeared and said, "Mr. Hawes wants to see you. I've put him in the drawing-room, and here's a note. Waiting for an answer. Verbal will do."

I tore open the note and read it.

Dear Mr. Clement: I should be so very grateful if you could come and see me this afternoon as early as possible. I am in great trouble and would like your advice. Sincerely yours,

Estelle Lestrange.

"Say I will come round in about half an hour," I said to Mary. Then I went into the drawing-room to see Hawes.

CHAPTER FIFTEEN

HAWES'S APPEARANCE distressed me very much. His hands were shaking and his face kept twitching nervously. In my opinion he should have been in bed, and I told him so. He insisted that he was perfectly well.

"I assure you, sir, I never felt better. Never in my life."

This was so obviously wide of the truth that I hardly knew how to answer. I have a certain admiration for a man who will not give in to illness, but Hawes was carrying the thing rather too far.

"I called to tell you how sorry I was—that such a thing should happen in the Vicarage."

"Yes," I said. "It's not very pleasant."

"It's terrible—quite terrible. It seems they haven't arrested Mr. Redding after all."

"No. That was a mistake. He made—er—rather a foolish statement."

"And the police are now quite convinced that he is innocent?"

"Perfectly."

"Why is that, may I ask? Is it— I mean, do they suspect anyone else?"

I should never have suspected that Hawes would take such a keen interest in the details of a murder case. Perhaps it is because it happened in the Vicarage. He appeared as eager as a reporter.

"I don't know that I am completely in Inspector Slack's confidence. So far as I know he does not suspect anyone in particular. He is at present engaged in making inquiries."

"Yes. Yes—of course. But who can one imagine doing such a dreadful thing?"

I shook my head.

"Colonel Protheroe was not a popular man, I know that. But murder! For murder—one would need a very strong motive."

"So I should imagine," I said.

"Who could have such a motive? Have the police any idea?"

"I couldn't say."

"He might have made enemies, you know. The more I think about it, the more I am convinced that he was the kind of man to have enemies. He had a reputation on the Bench for being very severe."

"I suppose he had."

"Why, don't you remember, sir? He was telling you yesterday morning about having been threatened by that man, Archer."

"Now I come to think of it, so he did," I said. "Of course I remember. You were quite near us at the time."

"Yes, I overheard what he was saying. Almost impossible to help it with Colonel Protheroe. He had such a very loud voice, hadn't he? I remember being impressed by your own words, that when his time came, he might have justice meted out to him instead of mercy."

"Did I say that?" I asked frowning. My remembrance of my own words was slightly different.

"You said it very impressively, sir. I was struck by your words. Justice is a terrible thing. And to think the poor man was struck down shortly afterward. It's almost as though you had a premonition."

"I had nothing of the sort," I said shortly. I rather dislike Hawes's tendency to mysticism. There is a touch of the visionary about him.

"Have you told the police about this man Archer, sir?"

"I know nothing about him."

"I mean, have you repeated to them what Colonel Protheroe said—about Archer having threatened him?"

"No," I said slowly. "I have not."

"But you are going to do so?"

I was silent. I dislike hounding a man down who has already got the forces of law and order against him. I held no brief for Archer. He is an inveterate poacher—one of those cheerful ne'er-do-wells that are to be found in any parish. Whatever he may have said in the heat of anger when he was sentenced I had no definite knowledge that he felt the same when he came out of prison.

"You heard the conversation," I said at last. "If you feel it your duty to go to the police with it, you must do so."

"It would come better from you, sir."

"Perhaps—but to tell the truth—well, I've no fancy for doing it. I might be helping to put the rope round the neck of an innocent man."

"But if he shot Colonel Protheroe—"

"Oh, if! There's no evidence of any kind that he did."

"His threats."

"Strictly speaking, the threats were not his but Colonel Protheroe's. Colonel Protheroe was theatening to show Archer what vengeance was worth next time he caught him."

"I don't understand your attitude, sir."

"Don't you?" I said wearily. "You're a young man. You're zealous in the cause of right. When you get to my age, you'll find that you like to give people the benefit of the doubt."

"It's not— I mean—" He paused and I looked at him in surprise. "You haven't any—any ideas of your own—as to the identity of the murderer, I mean?"

"Good heavens, no."

Hawes persisted. "Or as to the—the motive?"

"No. Have you?"

"I? No, indeed. I just wondered. If Colonel Protheroe had—had confided in you in any way—mentioned anything—"

"His confidences, such as they were, were heard by the whole village street yesterday morning," I said dryly.

"Yes. Yes—of course. And you don't think—about Archer?"

"The police will know all about Archer soon enough," I said. "If I'd heard him threaten Colonel Protheroe myself, that would be a different matter. But you may be sure that if he actually has threatened him, half the people in the village will have heard him, and the news will get to the police all right. You, of course, must do as you like about the matter."

But Hawes seemed curiously unwilling to do anything himself.

The man's whole attitude was nervous and queer. I recalled what Haydock had said about his illness. There, I supposed, lay the explanation.

He took his leave unwillingly, as though he had more to say and didn't know how to say it.

Before he left, I arranged with him to take the service for the Mothers' Union followed by the meeting of District Visitors. I had several projects of my own for the afternoon.

Dismissing Hawes and his troubles from my mind, I started off for Mrs. Lestrange's.

On the table in the hall lay the *Guardian* and the *Church Times* unopened.

As I walked I remembered that Mrs. Lestrange had had an interview with Colonel Protheroe the night before his death. It was possible that something had transpired in that interview which would throw light upon the problem of his murder.

I was shown straight into the little drawing-room, and Mrs. Lestrange rose to meet me. I was struck anew by the marvelous atmosphere that this woman could create. She wore a dress of some dead-black material that showed off the extraordinary fairness of her skin. There was something curiously dead about her face. Only the eyes were burningly alive. There was a watchful look in them today. Otherwise she showed no signs of animation.

"It was very good of you to come, Mr. Clement," she said as she shook hands. "I wanted to speak to you the other day. Then I decided not to do so. I was wrong."

"As I told you then, I shall be glad to do anything that can help you."

"Yes, you said that. And you said it as though you meant it. Very few people, Mr. Clement, in this world have ever sincerely wished to help me."

"I can hardly believe that, Mrs. Lestrange."

"It is true. Most people—most men, at any rate, are out for their own hand." There was a bitterness in her voice. I did not answer and she went on. "Sit down, won't you?"

I obeyed, and she took a chair facing me. She hesitated a moment and then began to speak very slowly and thoughtfully, seeming to weigh each word as she uttered it.

"I am in a very peculiar position, Mr. Clement, and I want to ask your advice. That is, I want to ask your advice as to what I should do next. What is past is past and cannot be undone. You understand?"

Before I could reply, the maid who had admitted me opened the door and said, with a scared face, "Oh! Please, ma'am, there's a police inspector here, and he says he must speak to you, please."

There was a pause. Mrs. Lestrange's face did not change. Only her eyes very slowly closed and opened again. She seemed to swallow once or twice, then she said in exactly the same clear, calm voice, "Show him in, Hilda."

I was about to rise, but she motioned me back again with an imperious hand.

"If you do not mind—I should be much obliged if you would stay."

I resumed my seat.

"Certainly, if you wish it," I murmured, as Slack entered with a brisk regulation tread.

"Good afternoon, madam," he began.

"Good afternoon, Inspector."

At this moment he caught sight of me and scowled. There is no doubt about it; Slack does not like me.

"You have no objection to the Vicar's presence, I hope?"

I suppose that Slack could not very well say he had.

"No-o," he said grudgingly. "Though, perhaps, it might be better—"

Mrs. Lestrange paid no attention to the hint.

"What can I do for you, Inspector?" she asked.

"It's this way, madam. Murder of Colonel Protheroe. I'm in charge of the case and making inquiries."

Mrs. Lestrange nodded.

"Just as a matter of form, I'm asking everyone just where they were yesterday evening between the hours of six and seven. Just as a matter of form, you understand."

Mrs. Lestrange did not seem in the least discomposed.

"You want to know where I was yesterday evening between six and seven?"

"If you please, madam."

"Let me see." She reflected a moment. "I was here. In this house."

"Oh!" I saw the Inspector's eyes flash. "And your maid—you have only one maid, I think—can confirm that statement?"

"No, it was Hilda's afternoon out."

"I see."

"So unfortunately you will have to take my word for it," said Mrs. Lestrange pleasantly.

"You seriously declare that you were at home all the afternoon?"

"You said between six and seven, Inspector. I was out for a walk early in the afternoon. I returned some time before five o'clock."

"Then if a lady—Miss Hartnell, for instance—were to declare that she came here about six o'clock, rang the bell but could make no one hear, and was compelled to go away again, you'd say she was mistaken, eh?"

"Oh, no." Mrs. Lestrange shook her head.

"But—"

"If your maid is in she can say not at home. If one is alone and does not happen to want to see callers—well, the only thing to do is to let them ring."

Inspector Slack looked slightly baffled.

"Elderly women bore me dreadfully," said Mrs. Lestrange. "And Miss Hartnell is particularly boring. She must have rung at least half a dozen times before she went away."

She smiled sweetly at Inspector Slack.

The Inspector shifted his ground.

"Then if anyone were to say they'd seen you out and about then—"

"Oh! but they didn't, did they?" She was quick to sense his weak point. "No one saw me out, because I was in, you see."

"Quite so, madam."

The Inspector hitched his chair a little nearer.

"Now, I understand, Mrs. Lestrange, that you paid a visit to Colonel Protheroe at Old Hall the night before his death."

Mrs. Lestrange said calmly, "That is so."

"Can you indicate to me the nature of that interview?"

"It concerned a private matter, Inspector."

"I'm afraid I must ask you to tell me the nature of that private matter."

"I shall not tell you anything of the kind. I will only assure you that nothing which was said at that interview could possibly have any bearing upon the crime."

"I don't think you are the best judge of that."

"At any rate, you will have to take my word for it, Inspector."

"In fact, I have to take your word about everything."

"It does seem rather like it," she agreed, still with the same smiling calm.

Inspector Slack grew very red.

"This is a serious matter, Mrs. Lestrange. I want the truth—" He banged his fist down on a table. "And I mean to get it."

Mrs. Lestrange said nothing at all.

"Don't you see, madam, that you're putting yourself in a very fishy position?"

Still Mrs. Lestrange said nothing.

"You'll be required to give evidence at the inquest."

"Yes."

Just the monosyllable. Unemphatic, uninterested. The Inspector altered his tactics.

"You were acquainted with Colonel Protheroe?"

"Yes, I was acquainted with him."

"Well acquainted?"

There was a pause before she said, "I had not seen him for several years."

"You were acquainted with Mrs. Protheroe?"

"No."

"You'll excuse me, but it was a very unusual time to make a call."

"Not from my point of view."

"What do you mean by that?"

She said clearly and distinctly, "I wanted to see Colonel Protheroe alone. I did not want to see Mrs. Protheroe or Miss Protheroe. I considered this the best way of accomplishing my object."

"Why didn't you want to see Mrs. or Miss Protheroe?"

"That, Inspector, is my business."

"Then you refuse to say more?"

"Absolutely."

Inspector Slack rose.

"You'll be putting yourself in a nasty position, madam, if you're not careful. All this looks bad—it looks very bad."

She laughed. I could have told Inspector Slack that this was not the kind of woman who is easily frightened.

"Well," he said, extricating himself with dignity, "don't say I haven't warned you, that's all. Good afternoon, madam, and mind you, we're going to get at the truth."

He departed. Mrs. Lestrange rose and held out her hand.

"I am going to send you away— Yes, it is better so. You see, it is too late for advice now. I have chosen my part." She repeated, in a rather forlorn voice, "I have chosen my part."

CHAPTER SIXTEEN

As I WENT OUT, I ran into Haydock on the doorstep. He glanced sharply after Slack, who was just passing through the gate, and demanded, "Has he been questioning her?"

"Yes."

"He's been civil, I hope?"

Civility, to my mind, is an art which Inspector Slack has never learned, but I presumed that according to his own lights, civil he had been, and anyway I didn't want to upset Haydock any further. He was looking worried and upset as it was. So I said he had been quite civil.

Haydock nodded and passed on into the house, and I went on down the village street where I soon caught up with the Inspector. I fancy that he was walking slowly on purpose. Much as he dislikes me, he is not the man to let dislike stand in the way of acquiring any useful information.

"Do you know anything about the lady?" he asked me pointblank.

I said I knew nothing whatever.

"She's never said anything about why she came here to live?"

"No."

"Yet you go and see her?"

"It is one of my duties to call on my parishioners," I replied, evading to remark that I had been sent for.

"H'm, I suppose it is." He was silent for a minute or two and then, unable to resist discussing his recent failure, he went on. "Fishy business, it looks to me."

"You think so?"

"If you ask me, I say blackmail. Seems funny, when you think of what Colonel Protheroe was always supposed to be. But there, you never can tell. He wouldn't be the first churchwarden who'd led a double life."

Faint remembrances of Miss Marple's remarks on the same subject floated through my mind.

"You really think that's likely?"

"Well, it fits the facts, sir. Why did a smart, well-dressed lady come down to this quiet little hole? Why did she go and see him at that funny time of day? Why did she avoid seeing Mrs. and Miss Protheroe? Yes, it all hangs together. Awkward for her to admit—blackmail's a punishable offense. But we'll get the truth out of her. For all we know it may have a very important bearing on the case. If Colonel Protheroe had some guilty secret in his life—

something disgraceful—well, you can see for yourself what a field it opens up."

I suppose it did.

"I've been trying to get the butler to talk. He might have overheard some of the conversation between Colonel Protheroe and Lestrange. Butlers do sometimes. But he swears he hasn't the least idea of what the conversation was about. By the way, he got the sack through it. The Colonel went for him, being angry at his having let her in. The butler retorted by giving notice. Says he didn't like the place anyway, and had been thinking of leaving for some time."

"Really."

"So that gives us another person who had a grudge against the Colonel."

"You don't seriously suspect the man—what's his name by the way?"

"His name's Reeves, and I don't say I do suspect him. What I say is, you never know. I don't like that soapy, oily manner of his."

I wonder what Reeves would say of Inspector Slack's manner.

"I'm going to question the chauffeur now."

"Perhaps, then," I said, "you'll give me a lift in your car. I want a short interview with Mrs. Protheroe."

"What about?"

"The funeral arrangements."

"Oh!" Inspector Slack was slightly taken aback. "The inquest's tomorrow, Saturday."

"Just so. The funeral will probably be arranged for Tuesday."

Inspector Slack seemed to be a little ashamed of himself for his brusqueness. He held out an olive branch in the shape of an invitation to be present at the interview with the chauffeur, Manning.

Manning was a nice lad, not more than twenty-five or six years of age. He was inclined to be awed by the Inspector.

"Now, then, my lad," said Slack. "I want a little information from you."

"Yes, sir," stammered the chauffeur. "Certainly, sir."

If he had committed the murder himself he could not have been more alarmed.

"You took your master to the village yesterday?"

"Yes, sir."

"What time was that?"

"Five-thirty."

"Mrs. Protheroe went, too?"

"Yes, sir."

"You went straight to the village?"

"Yes, sir."

"You didn't stop anywhere on the way?"

"No, sir."

"What did you do when you got there?"

"The Colonel got out and told me he wouldn't want the car again. He'd walk home. Mrs. Protheroe had some shopping to do. The parcels were put in the car. Then she said that was all and I drove home."

"Leaving her in the village?"

"Yes, sir."

"What time was that?"

"A quarter past six, sir. A quarter past exactly."

"Where did you leave her?"

"By the church, sir."

"Had the Colonel mentioned at all where he was going?"

"He said something about having to see the vet—something to do with one of the horses."

"I see. And you drove straight back here?"

"Yes, sir."

"There are two entrances to Old Hall, by the South Lodge and by the North Lodge. I take it that going to the village you would go by the South Lodge?"

"Yes, sir, always."

"And you came back the same way?"

"Yes, sir."

"H'm. I think that's all. Ah! Here's Miss Protheroe."

Lettice drifted toward us.

"I want the Fiat, Manning," she said. "Start her for me, will you?"

"Very good, miss."

He went toward a two-seater and lifted the bonnet.

"Just a minute, Miss Protheroe," said Slack. "It's necessary that I should have a record of everybody's movements yesterday afternoon. No offense meant."

Lettice stared at him.

"I never know the time of anything," she said.

"I understand you went out soon after lunch yesterday."

She nodded.

"Where to, please?"

"To play tennis."

"Who with?"

"The Hartley Napiers."

"At Much Benham?"

"Yes."

"And you returned?"

"I don't know. I tell you I never know these things."

"You returned," I said, "about seven-thirty."

"That's right," said Lettice. "In the middle of the shemozzle. Anne having fits and Griselda supporting her."

"Thank you, miss," said the Inspector. "That's all I want to know."

"How queer," said Lettice. "It seems so uninteresting."

She moved toward the Fiat.

The Inspector touched his forehead in a surreptitious manner.

"A bit wanting?" he suggested.

"Not in the least," I said. "But she likes to be thought so."

"Well, I'm off to question the maids now."

One cannot really like Slack, but one can admire his energy.

We parted company and I inquired of Reeves if I could see Mrs. Protheroe.

"She is lying down, sir, at the moment."

"Then I'd better not disturb her."

"Perhaps if you would wait, sir, I know that Mrs. Protheroe is anxious to see you. She was saying as much at luncheon."

He showed me into the drawing-room, switching on the electric lights, since the blinds were down.

"A very sad business all this," I said.

"Yes, sir."

His voice was cold and respectful.

I looked at him. What feelings were at work under that impassive demeanor? Were there things that he knew and could have told us? There is nothing so inhuman as the mask of the good servant.

"Is there anything more, sir?"

Was there just a hint of anxiety to be gone behind that correct expression?

"There's nothing more," I said.

I had a very short time to wait before Anne Protheroe came to me. We discussed and settled a few arrangements and then: "What a wonderfully kind man Doctor Haydock is," she exclaimed.

"Haydock is the best fellow I know."

"He has been amazingly kind to me. But he looks very sad, doesn't he?"

It had never occurred to me to think of Haydock as sad. I turned the idea over in my mind.

"I don't think I've ever noticed it," I said at last.

"I never have, until today."

"One's own troubles sharpen one's eyes sometimes," I said.

"That's very true."

She paused and then said, "Mr. Clement, there's one thing I absolutely *cannot* make out. If my husband was shot immediately after I left him, how was it that I didn't hear the shot?"

"They have reason to believe that the shot was fired later."

"But the six-twenty on the note."

"Was possibly added by a different hand—the murderer's."

Her cheek paled.

"How horrible!"

"It didn't strike you that the date was not in his handwriting?"

"None of it looked like his handwriting."

There was some truth in this observation. It was a somewhat illegible scrawl, not so precise as Protheroe's writing usually was.

"You are sure they don't still suspect Lawrence?"

"I think he is definitely cleared."

"But Mr. Clement, who can it be? Lucius was not popular, I know, but I don't think he had any real enemies. Not—not that kind of enemy."

I shook my head. "It's a mystery."

I thought wonderingly of Miss Marple's seven suspects. Who could they be?

After I took leave of Anne, I proceeded to put a certain plan of mine into action.

I returned from Old Hall by way of the private path. When I reached the stile, I retraced my steps and, choosing a place where I fancied the undergrowth showed signs of being disturbed, I turned aside from the path and forced my way through the bushes. The wood was a thick one, with a good deal of tangled undergrowth. My progress was not very fast, and I suddenly became aware that someone else was moving among the bushes not very far from me. As I paused irresolutely, Lawrence Redding came into sight. He was carrying a large stone.

I suppose I must have looked surprised, for he suddenly burst out laughing.

"No," he said, "it's not a clue; it's a peace offering."

"A peace offering?"

"Well, a basis for negotiations, shall we say? I want an excuse for calling on your neighbor, Miss Marple, and I have been told that there is nothing she likes so much as a nice bit of rock or stone for the Japanese gardens she makes."

"Quite true," I said. "But what do you want with the old lady?"

"Just this. If there was anything to be seen yesterday evening Miss Marple saw it. I don't mean anything necessarily connected with the crime—that she would think connected with the crime. I mean some *outré* or bizarre incident, some simple little happening that might give us a clue to the truth. Something that she wouldn't think worth while mentioning to the police."

"It's possible, I suppose."

"It's worth trying, anyhow. Clement, I'm going to get to the bottom of this business. For Anne's sake, if nobody else's. And I haven't any too much confidence in Slack—he's a zealous fellow, but zeal can't really take the place of brains."

"I see," I said, "that you are that favorite character of fiction, the amateur detective. I don't know that they really hold their own with the professional in real life."

He looked at me shrewdly and suddenly laughed.

"What are you doing in the woods, padre?"

I had the grace to blush.

"Just the same as I am doing, I dare swear. We've got the same idea, haven't we? *How did the murderer come to the study?* First way, along the lane and through the gate; second way, by the front door; third way—is there a third way? My idea was to see if there were any signs of the bushes being disturbed or broken anywhere near the wall of the Vicarage garden."

"That was just my idea," I admitted.

"I haven't really got down to the job, though," continued Lawrence, "because it occurred to me that I'd like to see Miss Marple first, to make quite sure that no one did pass along the lane yesterday evening while we were in the studio."

I shook my head. "She was quite positive that nobody did."

"Yes, nobody whom she would call anybody—sounds mad, but you see what I mean. But there might have been someone like a postman or a milkman or a butcher's boy—someone whose presence would be so natural that you wouldn't think of mentioning it."

"You've been reading G. K. Chesterton," I said, and Lawrence did not deny it.

"But don't you think there's just possibly something in the idea?"

"Well, I suppose there might be," I admitted.

Without further ado we made our way to Miss Marple's. She was working in the garden, and called out to us as we climbed over the stile.

"You see," murmured Lawrence, "she sees everybody."

She received us very graciously, and was much pleased with Lawrence's immense rock, which he presented with all due solemnity.

"It's very thoughtful of you, Mr. Redding. Very thoughtful indeed."

Emboldened by this, Lawrence embarked on his questions. Miss Marple listened attentively.

"Yes, I see what you mean, and I quite agree; it is the sort of thing no one mentions or bothers to mention. But I can assure you that there was nothing of the kind. Nothing whatever."

"You are sure, Miss Marple?"

"Quite sure."

"Did you see anyone go by the path into the wood that afternoon?" I asked. "Or come from it?"

"Oh, yes, quite a number of people. Doctor Stone and Miss Cram went that way. It's the nearest way to the barrow for them. That was a little after two o'clock. And Doctor Stone returned that way—as you know, Mr. Redding, since he joined you and Mrs. Protheroe."

"By the way," I said, "that shot—the one you heard, Miss Marple. Mr. Redding and Mrs. Protheroe must have heard it, too."

I looked inquiringly at Lawrence.

"Yes," he said frowning. "I believe I did hear some shots. Weren't there one or two shots?"

"I only heard one," said Miss Marple.

"It's only the vaguest impression in my mind," said Lawrence. "Curse it all, I wish I could remember. If only I'd known. You see I was so completely taken up with—with—"

He paused, embarrassed. I gave a tactful cough. Miss Marple, with a touch of prudishness, changed the subject.

"Inspector Slack has been trying to get me to say whether I heard the shot after Mr. Redding and Mrs. Protheroe had left the studio or before. I've had to confess that I really could not say definitely, but I have the impression—which is growing stronger the more I think about it—that it was after."

"Then that lets the celebrated Doctor Stone out anyway," said Lawrence with a laugh. "Not that there has ever been the slightest reason why he should be suspected of shooting poor old Protheroe."

"Ah!" said Miss Marple. "But I always find it prudent to suspect everybody just a little. What I say is, you really never *know*, do you?"

This was typical of Miss Marple. I asked Lawrence if he agreed with her about the shot.

"I really can't say. You see, it was such an ordinary sound. I should be inclined to think it had been fired when we were in the studio. The sound would have been deadened and—and one would have noticed it less there."

For other reasons than the sound being deadened! I thought to myself.

"I must ask Anne," said Lawrence. "She may remember. By the

way, there seems to me to be one curious fact that needs explanation. Mrs. Lestrange, the Mystery Lady of St. Mary Mead, paid a visit to old Protheroe after dinner on Wednesday night. And nobody seems to have any idea what it was all about. Old Protheroe said nothing to either his wife or Lettice."

"Perhaps the Vicar knows," said Miss Marple.

Now how did the woman know that I had been to visit Mrs. Lestrange that afternoon? The way she always knows things is uncanny.

I shook my head and said I could throw no light upon the matter.

"What does Inspector Slack think?" asked Miss Marple.

"He's done his best to bully the butler—but apparently the butler wasn't curious enough to listen at the door. So there it is—no one knows."

"I expect someone overheard something, though, don't you?" said Miss Marple. "I mean, somebody always *does*. I think that is where Mr. Redding might find out something."

"But Mrs. Protheroe knows nothing."

"I didn't mean Anne Protheroe," said Miss Marple. "I meant the women servants. They do so hate telling anything to the police. But a nice-looking young man—you'll excuse me, Mr. Redding—and one who has been unjustly suspected— Oh! I'm sure they'd tell him at once."

"I'll go and have a try this evening," said Lawrence with vigor. "Thanks for the hint, Miss Marple. I'll go after—well, after a little job the Vicar and I are going to do."

It occurred to me that we had better be getting on with it. I said good-by to Miss Marple and we entered the woods once more.

First we went up the path till we came to a new spot, where it certainly looked as though someone had left the path on the right-hand side. Lawrence explained that he had already followed this particular trail and found it led nowhere, but he added that we might as well try again. He might have been wrong.

It was, however, as he had said. After about ten or twelve yards, any sign of broken and trampled leaves petered out. It was from this spot that Lawrence had broken back toward the path to meet me earlier in the afternoon.

We emerged on the path again and walked a little farther along it. Again we came to a place where the bushes seemed disturbed. The signs were very slight but, I thought, unmistakable. This time the trail was more promising. By a devious course, it wound steadily nearer to the Vicarage. Presently we arrived at where the bushes grew thickly up to the wall. The wall is a high one and ornamented with fragments of broken bottles on the top. If anyone had placed a ladder against it, we ought to find traces of their passage.

We were working our way slowly along the wall when a sound came to our ears of a breaking twig. I pressed forward, forcing my way through a thick tangle of shrubs—and came face to face with Inspector Slack.

"So it's you," he said. "And Mr. Redding. Now what do you think you two gentlemen are doing?"

Slightly crestfallen, we explained.

"Quite so," said the Inspector. "Not being the fools we're usually thought to be, I had the same idea myself. I've been here over an hour. Would you like to know something?"

"Yes," I said meekly.

"Whoever murdered Colonel Protheroe didn't come this way to do it! There's not a sign either on this side of the wall nor the other. Whoever murdered Colonel Protheroe came through the front door. There's no other way he could have come."

"Impossible," I cried.

"Why impossible? Your door stands open. Anyone's only got to walk in. They can't be seen from the kitchen. They know you're safely out of the way; they know Mrs. Clement's in London; they know Mr. Dennis is at a tennis party. Simple as A.B.C. And they don't need to go or come through the village. Just opposite the Vicarage gate is a public footpath and, from it, you can turn into these same woods and come out whichever way you choose. Unless Mrs. Price Ridley were to come out of her front gate at that particular minute, it's all clear sailing. A great deal more so than climbing over walls. The side windows of the upper story of Mrs. Price Ridley's house do overlook most of that wall. No, depend upon it, that's the way he came."

It really seemed as though he must be right.

CHAPTER SEVENTEEN

Inspector Slack came round to see me the following morning. He is, I think, thawing toward me. In time, he may forget the incident of the clock.

"Well, sir," he greeted me. "I've traced that telephone call that you received."

"Indeed?" I said eagerly.

"It's rather odd. It was put through from the North Lodge of Old Hall. Now that lodge is empty; the lodgekeepers have been pensioned off, and the new lodgekeepers aren't in yet. The place was empty and convenient—a window at the back was open. No fingerprints on the instrument itself—it had been wiped clean. That's suggestive."

"How do you mean?"

"I mean that it shows that call was put through deliberately to get you out of the way. Therefore the murder was carefully planned in advance. If it had been just a harmless practical joke, the fingerprints wouldn't have been wiped off so carefully."

"No, I see that."

"It also shows that the murderer was well acquainted with Old Hall and its surroundings. It wasn't Mrs. Protheroe who put that call through. I've accounted for every moment of her time that afternoon. There are half a dozen servants who can swear that she was at home up till five-thirty. Then the car came round and drove Colonel Protheroe and her to the village. The Colonel went to see Quinton, the vet, about one of the horses. Mrs. Protheroe did some ordering at the grocer's and at the fish shop, and from there came straight down the back lane where Miss Marple saw her. All the shops agree she carried no handbag with her. The old lady was right."

"She usually is," I said mildly.

"And Miss Protheroe was over at Much Benham at five-thirty."

"Quite so," I said. "My nephew was there, too."

"That disposes of her. The maids seem all right—a bit hysterical and upset, but what can you expect? Of course, I've got my eye on the butler—what with giving notice and all. But I don't think he knows anything about it."

"Your inquiries seem to have had rather a negative result, Inspector."

"They do and they do not, sir. There's one very queer thing has turned up—quite unexpectedly, I may say."

"Yes?"

"You remember the fuss that Mrs. Price Ridley, who lives next door to you, was kicking up yesterday morning? About being rung up on the telephone?"

"Yes?" I said.

"Well, we traced the call just to calm her—and where on this earth do you think it was put through from?"

"A call office?" I hazarded.

"No, Mr. Clement. That call was put through from Mr. Lawrence Redding's cottage."

"What?" I exclaimed, surprised.

"Yes. A bit odd, isn't it? Mr. Redding had nothing to do with it. At that time, six thirty-five, he was on his way to the Blue Boar with Doctor Stone, in full view of the village. But there it is. Suggestive, eh? Someone walked into that empty cottage and used the telephone. Who was it? That's two queer telephone calls in one day. Makes you think there's some connection between them. I'll eat my hat if they weren't both put through by the same person."

"But with what object?"

"Well, that's what we've got to find out. There seems no particular point in the second one, but there must be a point somewhere. And you see the significance? Mr. Redding's house used to telephone from. Mr. Redding's pistol. All throwing suspicion on Mr. Redding."

"It would be more to the point to have put through the *first* call from his house," I objected.

"Ah! But I've been thinking that out. What did Mr. Redding do most afternoons? He went up to Old Hall and painted Miss Protheroe. And from his cottage, he'd go on his motor bicycle, passing through the North Gate. Now you see the point of the call being put through from there. *The murderer is someone who didn't know about the quarrel, and that Mr. Redding wasn't going up to Old Hall any more.*"

I reflected a moment to let the Inspector's points sink into my brain. They seemed to me logical and unavoidable.

"Were there any fingerprints on the receiver in Mr. Redding's cottage?" I asked.

"There were not," said the Inspector bitterly. "That dratted old woman who goes and does for him had been and dusted them off yesterday morning." He reflected wrathfully for a few minutes. "She's a stupid old fool anyway. Can't remember when she saw the pistol last. It might have been there on the morning of the crime or it might not. She couldn't say, she's sure. They're all alike!

"Just as a matter of form, I went round and saw Doctor Stone," he went on. "I must say he was pleasant as could be about it. He and Miss Cram went up to that mound—or barrow—or whatever you call it, about half past two yesterday, and stayed there all the afternoon. Doctor Stone came back alone, and she came later. He says he didn't hear any shot, but admits he's absent-minded. But it all bears out what we think."

"Only," I said, "you haven't caught the murderer."

"H'm," said the Inspector. "It was a woman's voice you heard through the telephone. It was, in all probability, a woman's voice Mrs. Price Ridley heard. If only that shot hadn't come hard on the close of the telephone call—well, I'd know where to look."

"Where?"

"Ah! That's just what it's best not to say, sir."

Unblushingly, I suggested a glass of old port. I have some very fine old vintage port. Eleven o'clock in the morning is not the usual time for drinking port, but I did not think that mattered with Inspector Slack. It was, of course, cruel abuse of the vintage port, but one must not be squeamish about such things.

When Inspector Slack had polished off the second glass, he began to unbend and become genial. Such is the effect of that particular port.

"I don't suppose it matters with you, sir," he said. "You'll keep it to yourself? No letting it get round the parish."

I reassured him.

"Seeing as the whole thing happened in your house, it almost seems as though you had a right to know."

"Just what I feel myself," I said.

"Well, then, sir, what about the lady who called on Colonel Protheroe the night before the murder?"

"Mrs. Lestrange?" I cried, speaking rather loud in my astonishment.

The Inspector threw me a reproachful glance.

"Not so loud, sir. Mrs. Lestrange is the lady I've got my eye on. You remember what I told you—blackmail."

"Hardly a reason for murder. Wouldn't it be a case of killing the goose that laid the golden eggs? That is, assuming that your hypothesis is true, which I don't for a minute admit."

The Inspector winked at me in a common manner.

"Ah! She's the kind the gentlemen will always stand up for. Now look here, sir. Suppose she's successfully blackmailed the old gentleman in the past. After a lapse of years, she gets wind of him, comes down here and tries it on again. *But* in the meantime, things have changed. The law has taken up a very different stand. Every facility is given nowadays to people prosecuting for blackmail—names are not allowed to be reported in the press. Suppose Colonel Protheroe turns round and says he'll have the law on her. She's in a nasty position. They give a very severe sentence for blackmail. The boot's on the other leg. The only thing to do to save herself is to put him out good and quick."

I was silent. I had to admit that the case the Inspector had built up was plausible. Only one thing to my mind made it inadmissible—the personality of Mrs. Lestrange.

"I don't agree with you, Inspector," I said. "Mrs. Lestrange doesn't seem to me to be a potential blackmailer. She's—well, it's an old-fashioned word, but she's a—lady."

He threw me a pitying glance.

"Ah, well, sir," he said tolerantly. "You're a clergyman. You don't know half of what goes on. Lady indeed! You'd be surprised if you knew some of the things I know."

"I'm not referring to mere social position. Anyway I should imagine Mrs. Lestrange to be a *déclassée*. What I mean is a question of—personal refinement."

"You don't see her with the same eyes as I do, sir. I may be a man—but I'm a police officer, too. They can't get over me with their personal refinement. Why, that woman is the kind who could stick a knife into you without turning a hair."

Curiously enough, I could believe Mrs. Lestrange guilty of murder more easily than I could believe her capable of blackmail.

"But, of course, she can't have been telephoning to the old lady next door and shooting Colonel Protheroe at one and the same time," continued the Inspector.

The words were hardly out of his mouth when he slapped his leg ferociously.

"Got it," he exclaimed. "That's the point of the telephone call. Kind of *alibi.* Knew we'd connect it with the first one. I'm going to look into this. She may have bribed some village lad to do the phoning for her. *He'd* never think of connecting it with the murder."

The Inspector hurried off.

"Miss Marple wants to see you," said Griselda putting her head in. "She sent over a very incoherent note—all spidery and underlined. I couldn't read most of it. Apparently she can't leave home herself. Hurry up and go across and see her and find out what it is. I've got my old women coming in two minutes or I'd come myself. I do hate old women—they tell you about their bad legs, and sometimes insist on showing them to you. What luck that the inquest is this afternoon! You won't have to go and watch the Boys' Club cricket match."

I hurried off considerably exercised in my own mind as to the reason for this summons.

I found Miss Marple in what I believe is described as a fluster. She was very pink and slightly incoherent.

"My nephew," she explained. "My nephew, Raymond West, the author. He is coming down today. Such a to-do. I have to see to everything myself. You cannot trust a maid to air a bed properly, and we must, of course, have a meat meal tonight. Gentlemen require such a lot of meat, do they not? And drink. There certainly should be some drink in the house—and a siphon."

"If I can do anything—" I began.

"Oh, how very kind. But I did not mean that. There is plenty of time really. He brings his own pipe and tobacco, I am glad to say. Glad because it saves me from knowing which kind of cigarettes are right to buy. But rather sorry, too, because it takes so long for the smell to get out of the curtains. Of course, I open the window and shake them well very early every morning. Raymond gets up very late—I think writers often do. He writes very clever books, I believe, though people are not really nearly so unpleasant as he makes out. Clever young men know so little of life, don't you think?"

"Would you like to bring him to dinner at the Vicarage?" I asked, still unable to gather why I had been summoned.

"Oh! No, thank you," said Miss Marple. "It's very kind of you," she added.

"There was—er—something you wanted to see me about, I think," I suggested desperately.

"Oh, of course. In all the excitement it had gone right out of my head." She broke off and called to her maid. "Emily—Emily. Not those sheets. The frilled ones with the monogram, and don't put them too near the fire."

She closed the door and returned to me on tiptoe.

"It's just rather a curious thing that happened last night," she explained. "I thought you would like to hear about it, though at the moment it doesn't seem to make sense. I felt very wakeful last night—wondering about all this sad business. And I got up and looked out of my window. And what do you think I saw?"

I looked inquiring.

"Gladys Cram," said Miss Marple, with great emphasis. "As I live, going into the woods with a suitcase."

"A suitcase?"

"Isn't it extraordinary? What should she want with a suitcase in the woods at twelve o'clock at night?"

We both stared at each other.

"You see," said Miss Marple. "I daresay it has nothing to do with the murder. But it is a Peculiar Thing. And just at present we all feel we must take notice of Peculiar Things."

"Perfectly amazing," I said. "Was she going to—er—sleep in the barrow by any chance?"

"She didn't, at any rate," said Miss Marple. "Because quite a short time afterward she came back, and she hadn't got the suitcase with her."

We stared at each other again.

CHAPTER EIGHTEEN

THE INQUEST was held that afternoon, Saturday, at two o'clock at the Blue Boar. The local excitement was, I need hardly say, tremendous. There has been no murder in St. Mary Mead for at least fifteen years. And to have someone like Colonel Protheroe murdered actually in the Vicarage study is such a feast of sensation as rarely falls to the lot of a village population.

Various comments floated to my ears which I was probably not meant to hear.

"There's Vicar. Look pale, don't he? I wonder if he had a hand in it? 'Twas done at Vicarage, after all."

"How can you, Mary Adams? And him visiting Henry Abbott at the time."

"Ah! But they do say him and the Colonel had words. There's Mary Hill. Giving herself airs, she is, on account of being in service there. Hush, here's coroner."

The coroner was Dr. Roberts of our adjoining town of Much Benham. He cleared his throat, adjusted his eyeglasses, and looked important.

To recapitulate all the evidence would be merely tiresome. Lawrence Redding gave evidence of finding the body and identified the pistol as belonging to him. To the best of his belief he had seen it on the Tuesday, two days previously. It was kept on a shelf in his cottage, and the door of the cottage was habitually unlocked.

Mrs. Protheroe gave evidence that she had last seen her husband at about a quarter to six, when they separated in the village street. She agreed to call for him at the Vicarage later. She had gone to the Vicarage about a quarter past six, by way of the back lane and the garden gate. She had heard no voices in the study, and had imagined that the room was empty, but her husband might have been sitting at the writing table, in which case she would not have seen him. As far as she knew, he had been in his usual health and spirits. She knew of no enemy who might have had a grudge against him.

I gave evidence next, told of my appointment with Protheroe and my summons to the Abbotts'. I described how I had found the body and my summoning of Dr. Haydock.

"How many people, Mr. Clement, were aware that Colonel Protheroe was coming to see you that evening?"

"A good many, I should imagine. My wife knew and my nephew, and Colonel Protheroe himself alluded to the fact that morning when I met him in the village. I should think several people might have overheard him, as, being slightly deaf, he spoke in a loud voice."

"It was then, a matter of common knowledge? Anyone might know?"

I agreed.

Haydock followed. He was an important witness. He described carefully and technically the appearance of the body and the exact injuries. It was his opinion that deceased had been shot while actually in the act of writing. He placed the time of death at approximately 6:20 to 6:30—certainly not later than 6:35. That was the outside limit. He was positive and emphatic on that point. There was no question of suicide; the wound could not have been self-inflicted.

Inspector Slack's evidence was discreet and abridged. He described his summons, and the circumstances under which he had found the body. The unfinished letter was produced and the time on it—6:20—noted. Also the clock. It was tacitly assumed that the time of death was 6:22. The police were giving nothing away. Anne Protheroe told me afterward that she had been told to suggest a slightly earlier period of time than 6:20 for her visit.

Our maid, Mary, was the next witness and proved a somewhat truculent one. She hadn't heard anything and didn't want to hear anything. It wasn't as though gentlemen who came to see the Vicar usually got shot. They didn't. She'd got her own jobs to look after. Colonel Protheroe had arrived at a quarter past six exactly. No, she didn't look at the clock. She heard the church chime after she had shown him into the study. She didn't hear any shot. If there had been a shot she'd have heard it. Well, of course she knew there must have been a shot, since the gentleman was found shot—but there it was. She hadn't heard it.

The coroner did not press the point. I realized that he and Colonel Melchett were working in agreement.

Mrs. Lestrange had been subpoenaed to give evidence, but a medical certificate, signed by Dr. Haydock, was produced saying she was too ill to attend.

There was only one other witness, a somewhat doddering old woman, the one who, in Slack's phrase, "did for" Lawrence Redding.

Mrs. Archer was shown the pistol and recognized it as the one she had seen in Mr. Redding's sitting-room—"Over against the bookcase, he kept it, lying about." She had last seen it on the day of the murder. Yes—in answer to a further question—she was quite sure it was there at lunchtime on Thursday—quarter to one when she left.

I remembered what the Inspector had told me, and I was mildly surprised. However vague she might have been when he questioned her, she was quite positive about it now.

The coroner summed up in a negative manner but with a good deal of firmness. The verdict was given almost immediately.

Murder by person or persons unknown.

As I left the room I was aware of a small army of young men with bright, alert faces, and a kind of superficial resemblance to each other. Several of them were already known to me by sight, as having haunted the Vicarage the last few days. Seeking to escape, I plunged back into the Blue Boar, and was lucky enough to run straight into the archaeologist, Dr. Stone. I clutched at him without ceremony.

"Journalists," I said briefly and expressively. "If you could deliver me from their clutches?"

"Why, certainly, Mr. Clement. Come upstairs with me."

He led the way up the narrow staircase and into his sitting-room, where Miss Cram was sitting rattling the keys of a typewriter with a practiced touch. She greeted me with a broad smile of welcome, and seized the opportunity to stop work.

"Awful, isn't it?" she said. "Not knowing who did it, I mean. Not but that I'm disappointed in an inquest. Tame, that's what I call it. Nothing what you might call spicy from beginning to end."

"You were there, then, Miss Cram?"

"I was there, all right. Fancy your not seeing me. Didn't you see me? I feel a bit hurt about that. Yes, I do. A gentleman, even if he is a clergyman, ought to have eyes in his head."

"Were you present, also?" I asked Dr. Stone, in an effort to escape from this playful badinage. Young women like Miss Cram always make me feel awkward.

"No, I'm afraid I feel very little interest in such things. I am a man very wrapped up in his own hobby."

"It must be a very interesting hobby," I said.

"You know something of it, perhaps?"

I was obliged to confess that I knew next to nothing.

Dr. Stone was not the kind of man whom a confession of ignorance daunts. The result was exactly the same as though I had said that the excavation of barrows was my only relaxation. He surged and eddied into speech. Long barrows, round barrows, stone age, bronze age, paleolithic, neolithic, kistvaens, and cromlechs, it burst forth in a torrent. I had little to do save nod my head and look intelligent—and that last is perhaps overoptimistic. Dr. Stone boomed on. He is a little man. His head is round and bald; his face is round and rosy, and he beams at you through very strong glasses. I have never known a man so enthusiastic on so little encouragement. He went into every argument for and against his own pet theory—which by the way, I quite failed to grasp!

He detailed at great length his difference of opinion with Colonel Protheroe.

"An opinionated boor," he said with heat. "Yes, yes, I know he is dead, and one should speak no ill of the dead. But death does not alter facts. An opinionated boor describes him exactly. Because he had read a few books, he set himself up as an authority—against a man who has made a lifelong study of the subject. My whole life, Mr. Clement, has been given up to this work. My whole life—"

He was spluttering with excitement. Gladys Cram brought him back to earth with a terse sentence.

"You'll miss your train if you don't look out," she observed.

"Oh!" The little man stopped in midspeech and dragged a watch from his pocket. "Bless my soul. Quarter to? Impossible."

"Once you start talking you never remember the time. What you'd do without me to look after you, I reely don't know."

"Quite right, my dear, quite right." He patted her affectionately on the shoulder. "This is a wonderful girl, Mr. Clement. Never forgets anything. I consider myself extremely lucky to have found her."

"Oh, go on, Doctor Stone," said the lady. "You spoil me, you do."

I could not help feeling that I should be in a material position to add my support to the second school of thought—that which foresees lawful matrimony as the future of Dr. Stone and Miss Cram. I imagined that in her own way Miss Cram was rather a clever young woman.

"You'd better be getting along," said Miss Cram.

"Yes, yes, so I must."

He vanished into the room next door and returned carrying a suitcase.

"You are leaving?" I asked in some surprise.

"Just running up to town for a couple of days," he explained. "My old mother to see tomorrow, some business with my lawyers on Monday. On Tuesday I shall return. By the way, I suppose that Colonel Protheroe's death will make no difference to our arrangements. As regards the barrow, I mean. Mrs. Protheroe will have no objection to our continuing the work?"

"I should not think so."

As he spoke, I wondered who actually would be in authority at Old Hall. It was just possible that Protheroe might have left it to Lettice. I felt that it would be interesting to know the contents of Protheroe's will.

"Causes a lot of trouble in a family, a death does," remarked Miss Cram with a kind of gloomy relish. "You wouldn't believe what a nasty spirit there sometimes is."

"Well, I must really be going." Dr. Stone made ineffectual attempts to control the suitcase, a large rug, and an unwieldy umbrella. I came to his rescue. He protested.

"Don't trouble—don't trouble. I can manage perfectly. Doubtless there will be somebody downstairs."

But down below there was no trace of a boots or anyone else. I suspect that they were being regaled at the expense of the Press.

Time was getting on, so we set out together to the station, Dr. Stone carrying the suitcase, and I holding the rug and umbrella.

Dr. Stone ejaculated remarks in between panting breaths as we hurried along.

"Really too good of you—didn't mean—to trouble you. Hope we shan't miss—the train—Gladys is a good girl—really a wonderful girl—a very sweet nature—not too happy at home, I'm afraid—absolutely—the heart of a child—heart of a child, I do assure you—in spite of—difference in our ages—find a lot in common—"

I felt that several well-known parallels would have occurred to Miss Marple, had she been there.

We saw Lawrence Redding's cottage just as we turned off to the station. It stands in an isolated position with no other house near it. I observed two young men of smart appearance standing on the doorstep, and a couple more peering in at the windows. It was a busy day for the Press.

"Nice fellow, young Redding," I remarked to see what my companion would say.

He was so out of breath by this time that he found it difficult to say anything, but he puffed out a word which I did not at first quite catch.

"Dangerous," he gasped when I asked him to repeat his remark.

"Dangerous?"

"Most dangerous. Innocent girls—know no better—taken in by a fellow like that—always hanging round women. No good."

From which I deduced that the only young man in the village had not passed unnoticed by the fair Gladys.

"Goodness," ejaculated Dr. Stone. "The train!"

We were close to the station by this time and we broke into a fast sprint. A down train was standing in the station and the up London train was just coming in.

At the door of the booking office we collided with a rather exquisite young man, and I recognized Miss Marple's nephew just arriving. He is, I think, a young man who does not like to be collided with. He prides himself on his poise and general air of detachment, and there is no doubt that vulgar contact is detrimental to poise of any kind. He staggered back. I apologized hastily and we passed in. Dr. Stone climbed on the train and I handed up his baggage just as the train gave an unwilling jerk and started.

I waved to him and then turned away. Raymond West had departed, but our local chemist, who rejoices in the name of Cherubim, was just setting out for the village. I walked beside him.

"Close shave that," he observed. "Well, how did the inquest go, Mr. Clement?"

I gave him the verdict.

"Oh! So that's what happened. I rather thought they'd adjourn the inquest. Where's Doctor Stone off to?"

I repeated what he had told me.

"Lucky not to miss the train. Not that you ever know on this line. I tell you, Mr. Clement, it's a crying shame. Disgraceful, that's what I call it. Train I came down by was ten minutes late. And that on a Saturday, with no traffic to speak of. And on Wednesday—no, Thursday—yes, Thursday it was—I remember it was the day of the murder because I meant to write a strongly worded complaint to the company—and the murder put it out of my head—yes, last Thursday. I had been to a meeting of the pharmaceutical society. How late do you think the six-fifty was? *Half an hour*. Half an hour exactly! What do you think of that? Ten minutes I don't mind. But if the train doesn't get in till twenty past seven, well, you can't get home before half past. What I say is, why call it the six-fifty?"

"Quite so," I said and, wishing to escape from the monologue, I broke away with the excuse that I had something to say to Lawrence Redding whom I saw approaching us on the other side of the road.

CHAPTER NINETEEN

"VERY GLAD to have met you," said Lawrence. "Come to my place."

We turned in at the little rustic gate, went up the path, and he drew a key from his pocket and inserted it in the lock.

"You keep the door locked now," I observed.

"Yes." He laughed rather bitterly. "Case of stable door when the steed is gone, eh? It is rather like that. You know, padre," he held the door open and I passed inside, "there's something about all this business that I don't like. It's too much of—how shall I put it?—an inside job. Someone knew about that pistol of mine. That means that the murderer, whoever he was, must have actually been in this house—perhaps even had a drink with me."

"Not necessarily," I objected. "The whole village of St. Mary Mead probably knows exactly where you keep your toothbrush and what kind of tooth powder you use."

"But why should it interest them?"

"I don't know," I said, "but it does. If you change your shaving cream it will be a topic of conversation."

"They must be very hard up for news."

"They are. Nothing exciting ever happens here."

"Well, it has now—with a vengeance."

I agreed.

"And who tells them all these things, anyway? Shaving cream and things like that?"

"Probably old Mrs. Archer."

"That old crone? She's practically a half-wit, as far as I can make out."

"That's merely the camouflage of the poor," I explained. "They take refuge behind a mask of stupidity. You'll probably find that the old lady has all her wits about her. By the way, she seems very certain now that the pistol was in its proper place midday Thursday. What's made her so positive all of a sudden?"

"I haven't the least idea."

"Do you think she's right?"

"There again I haven't the least idea. I don't go round taking an inventory of my possessions every day."

I looked round the small living-room. Every shelf and table was littered with miscellaneous articles. Lawrence lived in the midst of an artistic disarray that would have driven me quite mad.

"It's a bit of a job finding things sometimes," he said, observing my glance. "On the other hand, everything is handy—not tucked away."

"Nothing is tucked away, certainly," I agreed. "It might perhaps have been better if the pistol had been."

"Do you know, I rather expected the coroner to say something of the sort. Coroners are such asses. I expected to be censured, or whatever they call it."

"By the way," I asked. "Was it loaded?"

Lawrence shook his head.

"I'm not quite so careless as that. It was unloaded, but there was a box of cartridges beside it."

"It was apparently loaded in all six chambers, and one shot had been fired."

Lawrence nodded.

"And whose hand fired it? It's all very well, sir, but unless the real murderer is discovered I shall be suspected of the crime to the day of my death."

"Don't say that, my boy."

"But I do say it."

He became silent, frowning to himself. He roused himself at last and said, "But let me tell you how I got on last night. You know, old Miss Marple knows a thing or two."

"She is, I believe, rather unpopular on that account."

Lawrence proceeded to recount his story.

He had, following Miss Marple's advice, gone up to Old Hall. There, with Anne's assistance, he had had an interview with the parlormaid.

Anne had said simply, "Mr. Redding wants to ask you a few questions, Rose."

Then she had left the room.

Lawrence had felt somewhat nervous. Rose, a pretty girl of twenty-five, gazed at him with a limpid gaze which he found rather disconcerting.

"It's—it's about Colonel Protheroe's death."

"Yes, sir?"

"I'm very anxious, you see, to get at the truth."

"Yes, sir."

"I feel that there may be—that someone might—that—that—there might be some incident—"

At this point Lawrence felt that he was not covering himself with glory, and heartily cursed Miss Marple and her suggestions.

"I wondered if you could help me?"

"Yes, sir?"

Rose's demeanor was still that of the perfect servant, polite, anxious to assist, and completely uninterested.

"Dash it all," said Lawrence. "Haven't you talked the thing over in the servants' hall?"

This method of attack flustered Rose slightly. Her perfect poise was shaken.

"In the servants' hall, sir?"

"Or the housekeeper's room, or the bootboy's dugout, or wherever you do talk? There must be *some* place."

Rose displayed a very faint disposition to giggle, and Lawrence felt encouraged.

"Look here, Rose, you're an awfully nice girl. I'm sure you must understand what I'm feeling like. I don't want to be hanged. I didn't murder your master, but a lot of people think I did. Can't you help me in any way?"

I can imagine at this point that Lawrence must have looked extremely appealing. His handsome head thrown back, his Irish blue eyes appealing. Rose softened and capitulated.

"Oh! Sir, I'm sure—if any of us could help in any way. None of us think you did it, sir. Indeed we don't."

"I know, my dear girl, but that's not going to help me with the police."

"The police!" Rose tossed her head. "I can tell you, sir, we don't think much of that Inspector. Slack, he calls himself. The police indeed."

"All the same, the police are very powerful. Now, Rose, you say you'll do your best to help me. I can't help feeling that there's a lot we haven't got at yet. The lady, for instance, who called to see Colonel Protheroe the night before he died."

"Mrs. Lestrange?"

"Yes, Mrs. Lestrange. I can't help feeling there's something rather odd about that visit of hers."

"Yes, indeed, sir; that's what we all said."

"You did?"

"Coming the way she did. And asking for the Colonel. And, of course, there's been a lot of talk—nobody knowing anything about her down here. And Mrs. Simmons, she's the housekeeper, sir, she gave it as her opinion that she was a regular bad lot. But after hearing what Gladdie said, well, I didn't know what to think."

"What did Gladdie say?"

"Oh, nothing, sir. It was just—we were talking, you know."

Lawrence looked at her. He had the feeling of something kept back.

"I wonder very much what her interview with Colonel Protheroe was about."

"Yes, sir."

"I believe you know, Rose?"

"Me? Oh, no, sir. Indeed I don't. How could I?"

"Look here, Rose. You said you'd help me. If you overheard anything, anything at all—it mightn't seem important, but anything— I'd be so awfully grateful to you. After all, anyone might—might chance—just *chance* to overhear something."

"But I didn't, sir, really I didn't."

"Then somebody else did," said Lawrence acutely.

"Well, sir—"

"Do tell me, Rose."

"I don't know what Gladdie would say, I'm sure."

"She'd want you to tell me. Who *is* Gladdie, by the way?"

"She's the kitchen maid, sir. And you see, she'd just stepped out to speak to a friend, and she was passing the window—the study window—and the master was there with the lady. And of course he did speak very loud, the master did, always. And naturally, feeling a little curious—I mean—"

"Awfully natural," said Lawrence. "I mean one would simply have to listen."

"But, of course, she didn't tell anyone—except me. And we both thought it very odd. But Gladdie couldn't say anything, you see, because if it was known she'd gone out to meet a—a friend—well, it would have meant a lot of unpleasantness with Mrs. Pratt; that's the cook, sir. But I'm sure she'd tell you anything, sir, willing."

"Well, can I go to the kitchen and speak to her?"

Rose was horrified by the suggestion.

"Oh! No, sir, that would never do. And Gladdie's a very nervous girl anyway."

At last the matter was settled, after a lot of discussion over difficult points. A clandestine meeting was arranged in the shrubbery.

Here, in due course, Lawrence was confronted by the nervous Gladdie, whom he described as more like a shivering rabbit than anything human. Ten minutes were spent in trying to put the girl at her ease, the shivering Gladys explaining that she couldn't ever—that she didn't ought, that she didn't think Rose would have given her away, that anyway she hadn't meant no harm, indeed she hadn't, and that she'd catch it badly if Mrs. Pratt ever came to hear of it.

Lawrence reassured, cajoled, persuaded—at last Gladys consented to speak.

"If you'll be sure it'll go no farther, sir."

"Of course it won't."

"And it won't be brought up against me in a court of law?"

"Never."

"And you won't tell the mistress?"

"Not on any account."

"If it were to get to Mrs. Pratt's ears—"

"It won't. Now tell me, Gladys."

"If you're sure it's all right?"

"Of course it is. You'll be glad some day you've saved me from being hanged."

Gladys gave a little shriek.

"Oh! Indeed, I wouldn't like that, sir. Well, it's very little I heard—and that entirely by accident, as you might say—"

"I quite understand."

"But the master, he was evidently very angry. 'After all these years'—that's what he was saying—'you dare to come here. It's an outrage—' I couldn't hear what the lady said—but after a bit he said, 'I utterly refuse—utterly.' I can't remember everything—seemed as though they were at it hammer and tongs, she wanting him to do something and he refusing. 'It's a disgrace that you should have come down here.' That's one thing he said. And 'You shall not see her—I forbid it.' And that made me prick up my ears. Looked as though the lady wanted to tell Mrs. Protheroe a thing or two, and he was afraid about it. And I thought to myself, 'Well, now, fancy the master. Him so particular. And maybe no beauty himself when all's said and done. Fancy!' I said. And 'Men are all alike,' I said to my friend later. Not that he'd agree. Argued, he did. But he did admit he was surprised at Colonel

Protheroe—him being a churchwarden and handing round the plate and reading the lessons on Sundays. 'But there,' I said, 'that's very often the worst.' For that's what I've heard my mother say, many a time."

Gladdie paused, out of breath, and Lawrence tried tactfully to get back to where the conversation had started.

"Did you hear anything else?"

"Well, it's difficult to remember exactly, sir. It was all much the same. He said once or twice, 'I don't believe it.' Just like that. 'Whatever Haydock says, I don't believe it.'"

"He said that, did he? 'Whatever Haydock says'?"

"Yes. And he said it was all a plot."

"You didn't hear the lady speak at all?"

"Only just at the end. She must have got up to go and come nearer the window. And I heard what she said. Made my blood run cold, it did. I'll never forget it. '*By this time tomorrow night, you may be dead,*' she said. Wicked the way she said it. As soon as I heard the news: 'There,' I said to Rose. 'There!'"

Lawrence wondered. Principally he wondered how much of Gladys's story was to be depended upon. True, in the main, he suspected that it had been embellished and polished since the murder. In especial he doubted the accuracy of the last remark. He thought it highly possible that it owed its being to the fact of the murder.

He thanked Gladys, rewarded her suitably, reassured her as to her misdoings being made known to Mrs. Pratt, and left Old Hall with a good deal to think over.

One thing was clear—Mrs. Lestrange's interview with Colonel Protheroe had certainly not been a peaceful one, and it was one which he was anxious to keep from the knowledge of his wife.

I thought of Miss Marple's churchwarden with his separate establishment. Was this a case resembling that?

I wondered more than ever where Haydock came in. He had saved Mrs. Lestrange from having to give evidence at the inquest. He had done his best to protect her from the police.

How far would he carry that protection?

Supposing he suspected her of crime—would he still try and shield her?

She was a curious woman—a woman of very strong magnetic charm. I myself hated the thought of connecting her with the crime in any way.

Something in me said, "It can't be her!"

Why?

And an imp in my brain replied, "Because she's a very beautiful and attractive woman. That's why."

There is, as Miss Marple would say, a lot of human nature in all of us.

CHAPTER TWENTY

WHEN I GOT BACK to the Vicarage I found that we were in the middle of a domestic crisis.

Griselda met me in the hall and, with tears in her eyes, dragged me into the drawing-room.

"She's going."

"Who's going?"

"Mary. She's given notice."

I really could not take the announcement in a tragic spirit.

"Well," I said, "we'll have to get another servant."

It seemed to me a perfectly reasonable thing to say. When one servant goes, you get another. I was at a loss to understand Griselda's look of reproach.

"Len—you are absolutely heartless. You don't *care*."

I didn't. In fact, I felt almost lighthearted at the prospect of no more burned puddings and undercooked vegetables.

"I'll have to look about for a girl and find one and train her," continued Griselda in a voice of acute self-pity.

"Is Mary trained?" I said.

"Of course she is."

"I suppose," I said, "that somebody has heard her address us as 'sir' or 'ma'am,' and has immediately wrested her from us as a paragon. All I can say is, they'll be disappointed."

"It isn't that," said Griselda. "Nobody else wants her. I don't see how they could. It's her feelings. They're upset because Lettice Protheroe said she didn't dust properly."

Griselda often comes out with surprising statements, but this seemed to me so surprising that I questioned it. It seemed to me the most unlikely thing in the world that Lettice Protheroe should go out of her way to interfere in our domestic affairs and reprove our maid for slovenly housework. It was completely un-Lettice like, and I said so.

"I don't see," I said, "what our dust has to do with Lettice Protheroe."

"Nothing at all," said my wife. "That's why it's so unreasonable. I wish you'd go and talk to Mary yourself. She's in the kitchen."

I had no wish to talk to Mary on the subject, but Griselda, who is very energetic and quick, fairly pushed me through the baize door into the kitchen before I had time to rebel.

Mary was peeling potatoes at the sink.

"Er—good afternoon," I said nervously.

Mary looked up and snorted, but made no other response.

"Mrs. Clement tells me that you wish to leave us," I said.

Mary condescended to reply to this.

"There's some things," she said darkly, "as no girl can be asked to put up with."

"Will you be more explicit, please?"

"Eh?"

"Will you tell me exactly what it is that has upset you?"

"Tell you that in two words, I can." Here, I may say she vastly underestimated. "People coming snooping round here when my back's turned. Poking round. And what business of hers, is it, how often the study is dusted or turned out? If you and the missus don't complain, it's nobody else's business. If I give satisfaction to you that's all that matters, I say."

Mary has never given satisfaction to me. I confess that I have a hankering after a room thoroughly dusted and tidied every morning. Mary's practice of flicking off the more obvious deposit on the surface of low tables is to my thinking grossly inadequate. However, I realized that at the moment it was no good to go into side issues.

"Had to go to that inquest, didn't I? Standing up before twelve men, a respectable girl like me! And who knows what questions you may be asked. I'll tell you this. I've never before been in a place where they had a murder in the house, and I never want to be again."

"I hope you won't," I said. "On the law of averages I should say it was very unlikely."

"I don't hold with the law. *He* was a magistrate. Many a poor fellow sent to jail for potting at a rabbit—and him with his pheasants and what not. And then, before he's so much as decently buried, that daughter of his comes round and says I don't do my work properly."

"Do you mean that Miss Protheroe has been here?"

"Found her here when I came back from the Blue Boar. In the study she was. And: 'Oh,' she says. 'I'm looking for my little yellow berry—a little yellow hat. I left it here the other day.' 'Well,' I said, 'I haven't seen no hat. It wasn't here when I done the room on Thursday morning,' I says. And: 'Oh!' she says, 'but I daresay you wouldn't see it. You don't spend much time doing a room, do you?' And with that she draws her finger along the mantelshelf and looks at it. As though I had time on a morning like this to take off all them ornaments and put them back, with the police only unlocking the room the night before. 'If the Vicar and his lady are satisfied that's all that matters, I think, miss,' I said. And she laughs and goes out of the window and says, 'Oh! But are you sure they are?' "

"I see," I said.

"And there it is! A girl has her feelings! I'm sure I'd work my fingers to the bone for you and the missus. And if she wants a new-fangled dish tried I'm always ready to try it."

"I'm sure you are," I said soothingly.

"But she must have heard something or she wouldn't have said what she did. And if I don't give satisfaction I'd rather go. Not that I take any notice of what Miss Protheroe says. She's not loved up at the Hall, I can tell you. Never a 'please' or a 'thank you,' and everything scattered right and left. I wouldn't set any store by Miss Lettice Protheroe myself, for all that Mr. Dennis is so set upon her. But she's the kind that can always twist a young gentleman round her little finger."

During all this, Mary had been extracting eyes from potatoes with such energy that they had been flying round the kitchen like hailstones. At this moment one hit me in the eye and caused a momentary pause in the conversation.

"Don't you think," I said, as I dabbed my eye with my handkerchief, "that you have been rather too inclined to take offense where none is meant? You know, Mary, your mistress will be very sorry to lose you."

"I've nothing against the mistress—or against you, sir, for that matter."

"Well, then, don't you think you're being rather silly?"

Mary sniffed.

"I was a bit upset like—after the inquest and all. And a girl has her feelings. But I wouldn't like to cause the mistress inconvenience."

"Then that's all right," I said.

I left the kitchen to find Griselda and Dennis waiting for me in the hall.

"Well?" exclaimed Griselda.

"She's staying," I said, and sighed.

"Len," said my wife. "You *have* been clever."

I felt rather inclined to disagree with her. I do not think I had been clever. It is my firm opinion that no servant could be a worse one than Mary. Any change, I consider, would have been a change for the better. But I like to please Griselda. I detailed the heads of Mary's grievance.

"How like Lettice," said Dennis. "She couldn't have left that yellow beret of hers here on Wednesday. She was wearing it for tennis on Thursday."

"That seems to me highly probable," I said.

"She never knows where she's left anything," said Dennis, with a kind of affectionate pride and admiration that I felt was entirely uncalled for. "She loses about a dozen things every day."

"A remarkably attractive trait," I observed.

Any sarcasm missed Dennis.

"She *is* attractive," he said, with a deep sigh. "People are always proposing to her—she told me so."

"They must be illicit proposals if they're made to her down here," I remarked. "We haven't got a bachelor in the place."

"There's Doctor Stone," said Griselda, her eyes dancing.

"He asked her to come and see the barrow the other day," I admitted.

"Of course he did," said Griselda. "She *is* attractive, Len. Even bald-headed archaeologists feel it."

"Lots of S.A.," said Dennis sapiently.

And yet Lawrence Redding is completely untouched by Lettice's charm. Griselda, however, explained that with the air of one who knew she was right.

"Lawrence has got lots of S.A. himself. That kind always likes the—how shall I put it—the Quaker type. Very restrained and diffident. The kind of women whom everybody calls cold. I think Anne is the only woman who could ever hold Lawrence. I don't think they'll ever tire of each other. All the same, I think he's been rather stupid in one way. He's rather made use of Lettice, you know. I don't think he ever dreamed she cared—he's awfully modest in some ways—but I have a feeling she does."

"She can't bear him," said Dennis positively. "She told me so."

I have never seen anything like the pitying silence with which Griselda received this remark.

I went into my study. There was, to my fancy, still a rather eerie feeling in the room. I knew that I must get over this. Once give in to that feeling, and I should probably never use the study again. I walked thoughtfully over to the writing table. Here Protheroe had sat, red-faced, hearty, self-righteous, and here, in a moment of time, he had been struck down. Here, where I was standing, an enemy had stood.

And so—no more Protheroe.

Here was the pen his fingers had held.

On the floor was a faint dark stain—the rug had been sent to the cleaner's, but the blood had soaked through.

I shivered.

"I can't use this room," I said aloud. "I can't use it."

Then my eye was caught by something—a mere speck of bright blue. I bent down. Between the floor and the desk I saw a small object. I picked it up.

I was standing staring at it in the palm of my hand when Griselda came in.

"I forgot to tell you, Len, Miss Marple wants us to go over tonight after dinner. To amuse the nephew. She's afraid of his being dull. I said we'd go."

"Very well, my dear."

"What are you looking at?"

"Nothing."

I closed my hand and, looking at my wife, observed, "If you don't amuse Master Raymond West, my dear, he must be very hard to please."

My wife said, "Don't be ridiculous, Len," and turned pink.

She went out again, and I unclosed my hand.

In the palm of my hand was a blue lapis lazuli earring, set in seed pearls.

It was rather an unusual jewel, and I knew very well where I had seen it last.

CHAPTER TWENTY-ONE

I CANNOT SAY that I have at any time a great admiration for Mr. Raymond West. He is, I know, supposed to be a brilliant novelist, and has made quite a name as a poet. His poems have no capital letters in them, which is, I believe, the essence of modernity. His books are about unpleasant people leading lives of surpassing dullness.

He has a tolerant affection for "Aunt Jane," whom he alludes to in her presence as a "survival." She listens to his talk with a flattering interest, and if there is sometimes an amused twinkle in her eye I am sure he never notices it.

He fastened on Griselda at once with flattering abruptness. They discussed modern plays, and from there went on to modern schemes of decoration. Griselda affects to laugh at Raymond West, but she is, I think, susceptible to his conversation.

During my (dull) conversation with Miss Marple, I heard at intervals the reiteration "buried as you are down here."

It began at last to irritate me. I said suddenly, "I suppose you consider us very much out of things down here?"

Raymond West waved his cigarette.

"I regard St. Mary Mead," he said authoritatively, "as a stagnant pool."

He looked at us, prepared for resentment at his statement; but somewhat, I think, to his chagrin, no one displayed annoyance.

"That is really not a very good simile, dear Raymond," said Miss Marple briskly. "Nothing, I believe, is so full of life under the microscope as a drop of water from a stagnant pool."

"Life—of a kind," admitted the novelist.

"It's all much the same kind, really, isn't it?" said Miss Marple.

"You compare yourself to a denizen of a stagnant pond, Aunt Jane?"

"My dear, you said something of the sort in your last book, I remember."

No clever young man likes having his works quoted against himself. Raymond West was no exception.

"That was entirely different," he snapped.

"Life is, after all, very much the same everywhere," said Miss Marple in her placid voice. "Getting born, you know, and growing up—and coming into contact with other people—getting jostled—and then marriage and more babies—"

"And finally death," said Raymond West. "And not death with a death certificate always. Death in life."

"Talking of death," said Griselda. "You know we've had a murder here?"

Raymond West waved murder away with his cigarette.

"Murder is so crude," he said. "I take no interest in it."

That statement did not take me in for a moment. They say all the world loves a lover—apply that saying to murder and you have an even more infallible truth. No one can fail to be interested in a murder. Simple people like Griselda and myself can admit the fact, but anyone like Raymond West has to pretend to be bored—at any rate for the first five minutes.

Miss Marple, however, gave her nephew away by remarking, "Raymond and I have been discussing nothing else all through dinner."

"I take a great interest in all the local news," said Raymond hastily. He smiled benignly and tolerantly at Miss Marple.

"Have you a theory, Mr. West?" asked Griselda.

"Logically," said Raymond West, again flourishing his cigarette, "only one person could have killed Protheroe."

"Yes?" said Griselda.

We hung upon his words with flattering attention.

"The Vicar," said Raymond, and pointed an accusing finger at me.

I gasped.

"Of course," he reassured me, "I know you didn't do it. Life is never what it should be. But think of the drama—the fitness—Churchwarden murdered in the Vicar's study by the Vicar. Delicious!"

"And the motive?" I inquired.

"Oh! That's interesting." He sat up—allowed his cigarette to go out. "Inferiority complex, I think. Possibly too many inhibitions. I should like to write the story of the affair. Amazingly complex. Week after week, year after year, he's seen the man—at vestry meetings—at choir boys' outings—handing round the bag in church—bringing it to the altar. Always he dislikes the man—always he chokes down his dislike. It's unchristianlike, he won't encourage it. And so it festers underneath, and one day—"

He made a graphic gesture.

Griselda turned to me. "Have you ever felt like that, Len?"

"Never," I said truthfully.

"Yet I hear you were wishing him out of the world not so long ago," remarked Miss Marple.

That miserable Dennis! But my fault, of course, for ever making the remark.

"I'm afraid I was," I said. "It was a stupid remark to make, but really I'd had a very trying morning with him."

"That's disappointing," said Raymond West. "Because, of course, if your subconscious were really planning to do him in, it would never have allowed you to make that remark."

He sighed.

"My theory falls to the ground. This is probably a very ordinary murder—a revengeful poacher or something of that sort."

"Miss Cram came to see me this afternoon," said Miss Marple. "I met her in the village and I asked her if she would like to see my garden."

"Is she fond of gardens?" asked Griselda.

"I don't think so," said Miss Marple with a faint twinkle. "But it makes a very useful excuse for talk, don't you think?"

"What did you make of her?" asked Griselda. "I don't believe she's really so bad."

"She volunteered a lot of information—really a lot of information," said Miss Marple. "About herself, you know, and her people. They all seem to be dead or in India. Very sad. By the way, she has gone to Old Hall for the week-end."

"What?"

"Yes, it seems Mrs. Protheroe asked her—or she suggested it to Mrs. Protheroe—I don't quite know which way about it was. To do some secretarial work for her—there are so many letters to cope with. It turned out rather fortunately. Doctor Stone being away, she has nothing to do. What an excitement this barrow has been."

"Stone?" said Raymond. "Is that the archaeologist fellow?"

"Yes, he is excavating a barrow. On the Protheroe property."

"He's a good man," said Raymond. "Wonderfully keen on his job. I met him at a dinner not long ago, and we had a most interesting talk. I must look him up."

"Unfortunately," I said, "he's just gone to London for the week-end. Why, you actually ran into him at the station this afternoon."

"I ran into you. You had a little fat man with you—with glasses on."

"Yes—Doctor Stone."

"But, my dear fellow—that wasn't Stone."

"Not Stone?"

"Not the archaeologist. I know him quite well. The man wasn't Stone—not the faintest resemblance."

We stared at each other. In particular I stared at Miss Marple.

"Extraordinary," I said.

"The suitcase," said Miss Marple.

"But why?" said Griselda.

"It reminds me of the time the man went round pretending to be the gas inspector," murmured Miss Marple. "Quite a little haul, he got."

"An impostor," said Raymond West. "Now this is really interesting."

"The question is, has it anything to do with murder?" said Griselda.

"Not necessarily," I said. "But—" I looked at Miss Marple.

"It is," she said, "a Peculiar Thing. Another Peculiar Thing."

"Yes," I said rising. "I rather feel the Inspector ought to be told about this at once."

CHAPTER TWENTY-TWO

INSPECTOR SLACK'S ORDERS, once I had got him on the telephone, were brief and emphatic. Nothing was to "get about." In particular, Miss Cram was not to be alarmed. In the meantime, a search was to be instituted for the suitcase in the neighborhood of the barrow.

Griselda and I returned home very excited over this new development. We could not say much with Dennis present, as we had faithfully promised Inspector Slack to breathe no word to anybody.

In any case, Dennis was full of his own troubles. He came into my study and began fingering things and shuffling his feet and looking thoroughly embarrassed.

"What is it, Dennis?" I said at last.

"Uncle Len. I don't want to go to sea."

I was astonished. The boy had been so very decided about his career up to now.

"But you were so keen on it."

"Yes, but I've changed my mind."

"What do you want to do?"

"I want to go into finance."

I was even more surprised.

"What do you mean—finance?"

"Just that. I want to go into the City."

"But my dear boy, I am sure you would not like the life. Even if I obtained a post for you in a bank—"

Dennis said that wasn't what he meant. He didn't want to go

into a bank. I asked him what exactly he did mean, and, of course, as I suspected, the boy didn't really know.

By "going into finance" he simply meant getting rich quickly, which, with the optimism of youth, he imagined was a certainty if one "went into the City." I disabused him of this notion as gently as I could.

"What's put it into your head?" I asked. "You were so satisfied with the idea of going to sea."

"I know, Uncle Len, but I've been thinking. I shall want to marry some day—and, I mean, you've got to be rich to marry a girl."

"Facts disprove your theory," I said.

"I know—but a real girl. I mean, a girl who's used to things."

It was very vague but I thought I knew what he meant.

"You know," I said gently, "all girls aren't like Lettice Protheroe."

He fired up at once.

"You're awfully unfair to her. You don't like her. Griselda doesn't either. She says she's tiresome."

From the feminine point of view, Griselda is quite right. Lettice *is* tiresome. I could quite realize, however, that a boy would resent the adjective.

"If only people made a few allowances. Why even the Hartley Napiers are going about grousing about her at a time like this! Just because she left their old tennis party a bit early. Why should she stay if she was bored? Jolly decent of her to go at all, I think."

"Quite a favor," I said, but Dennis suspected no malice. He was full of his own grievance on Lettice's behalf.

"She's awfully unselfish really. Just to show you, she made me stay. Naturally I wanted to go, too. But she wouldn't hear of it. Said it was too bad on the Napiers. So, just to please her, I stopped on a quarter of an hour."

The young have very curious views on unselfishness.

"And now I hear Susan Hartley Napier is going about everywhere saying Lettice has rotten manners."

"If I were you," I said, "I shouldn't worry."

"It's all very well, but—" He broke off. "I'd—I'd do anything for Lettice."

"Very few of us can do anything for anyone else," I said. "However much we wish it, we are powerless."

"I wish I were dead," said Dennis.

Poor lad. Calf love is a virulent disease. I forebore to say any of the obvious and probably irritating things which come so easily to one's lips. Instead I said good night, and went up to bed.

I took the eight-o'clock service the following morning, and when I returned found Griselda sitting at the breakfast table with an open note in her hand. It was from Anne Protheroe.

Dear Griselda, If you and the Vicar could come up and lunch here quietly today, I should be so very grateful. Something very strange has occurred and I should like Mr. Clement's advice.

Please don't mention this when you come, as I have said nothing to anyone. With love, Yours affectionately, Anne Protheroe.

"We must go, of course," said Griselda.

I agreed.

"I wonder what can have happened?"

I wondered, too.

"You know," I said to Griselda, "I don't feel we are really at the end of this case yet."

"You mean not till someone has really been arrested?"

"No," I said. "I didn't mean that. I mean that there are ramifications, undercurrents, that we know nothing about. There are a whole lot of things to clear up before we get the truth."

"You mean things that don't really matter, but that get in the way?"

"Yes, I think that expresses my meaning very well."

"I think we're all making a great fuss," said Dennis, helping himself to marmalade. "It's a jolly good thing old Protheroe is dead. Nobody liked him. Oh! I know the police have got to worry—it's their job. But I rather hope myself they'll never find out. I should hate to see Slack promoted, going about swelling with importance over his cleverness."

I am human enough to feel that I agreed over the matter of Slack's promotion. A man who goes about systematically rubbing people up the wrong way cannot hope to be popular.

"Doctor Haydock thinks rather like I do," went on Dennis. "He'd never give a murderer up to justice. He said so."

I think that that is the danger of Haydock's views. They may be sound in themselves—it is not for me to say—but they produce an impression on the young, careless mind which I am sure Haydock himself never meant to convey.

Griselda looked out of the window and remarked that there were reporters in the garden.

"I suppose they're photographing the study windows again," she said with a sigh.

We had suffered a good deal in this way. There was first the idle curiosity of the village—everyone had come to gape and stare. There were next the reporters armed with cameras, and the village again to watch the reporters. In the end we had to have a constable from Much Benham on duty outside the window.

"Well," I said, "the funeral is tomorrow morning. After that, surely, the excitement will die down."

I noticed a few reporters hanging about Old Hall when we arrived there. They accosted me with various queries, to which I gave the invariable answer (we had found it the best) that I had nothing to say.

We were shown by the butler into the drawing-room, the sole occupant of which turned out to be Miss Cram—apparently in a state of high enjoyment.

"This is a surprise, isn't it?" she said as she shook hands. "I never should have thought of such a thing, but Mrs. Protheroe is kind, isn't she? And, of course, it isn't what you might call nice for a young girl to be staying alone at a place like the Blue Boar, reporters about and all. And, of course, it's not as though I haven't been able to make myself useful—you really need a secretary at a time like this, and Miss Protheroe doesn't do anything to help, does she?"

I was amused to notice that the old animosity against Lettice persisted, but that the girl had apparently become a warm partisan of Anne's. At the same time I wondered if the story of her coming here was strictly accurate. In her account, the initiative had come from Anne, but I wondered if that were really so. The first mention of disliking to be at the Blue Boar alone might have easily come from the girl herself. While keeping an open mind on the subject, I did not fancy that Miss Cram was strictly truthful.

At that moment Anne Protheroe entered the room.

She was dressed very quietly in black. She carried in her hand a Sunday paper, which she held out to me with a rueful glance.

"I've never had any experience of this sort of thing. It's pretty ghastly, isn't it? I saw a reporter at the inquest. I just said that I was terribly upset and had nothing to say, and then he asked me if I wasn't very anxious to find my husband's murderer, and I said yes. And then whether I had any suspicions and I said no. And whether I didn't think the crime showed local knowledge, and I said it seemed to, certainly. And that was all. And now look at this!"

In the middle of the page was a photograph, evidently taken at least ten years ago—Heaven knows where they had dug it out. There were large headlines.

WIDOW DECLARES SHE WILL NEVER REST TILL SHE HAS HUNTED DOWN HUSBAND'S MURDERER.

Mrs. Protheroe, the widow of the murdered man, is certain that the murderer must be looked for locally. She has suspicions but no certainty. She declared herself prostrated with grief, but reiterated her determination to hunt down the murderer.

"It doesn't sound like me, does it?" said Anne.

"I daresay it might have been worse," I said handing back the paper.

"Impudent, aren't they?" said Miss Cram. "I'd like to see one of those fellows trying to get something out of me."

By the twinkle in Griselda's eye, I was convinced that she regarded this statement as being more literally true than Miss Cram intended it to appear.

Luncheon was announced, and we went in. Lettice did not come in till halfway through the meal, when she drifted into the empty place with a smile for Griselda and a nod for me. I watched her with some attention, for reasons of my own, but she seemed much the same vague creature as usual. Extremely pretty —that in fairness I had to admit. She was still not wearing mourning, but was dressed in a shade of pale green that brought out all the delicacy of her fair coloring.

After we had had coffee, Anne said quietly, "I want to have a little talk with the Vicar. I will take him up to my sitting-room."

At last I was to learn the reason of our summons. I rose and followed her up the stairs. She paused at the door of the room. As I was about to speak, she stretched out a hand to stop me. She remained listening, looking down toward the hall. "Good. They are going out into the garden. No—don't go in there. We can go straight up."

Much to my surprise she led the way along the corridor to the extremity of the wing. Here a narrow, ladderlike staircase rose to the floor above, and she mounted it, I following. We found ourselves in a dusty boarded passage. Anne opened a door and led me into a large, dim attic which was evidently used as a lumber room. There were trunks there, old broken furniture, a few stacked pictures, and the many countless odds and ends which a lumber room collects.

My surprise was so evident that she smiled faintly.

"First of all, I must explain. I am sleeping very lightly just now. Last night—or rather this morning about three o'clock—I was convinced that I heard someone moving about the house. I listened for some time, and at last got up and came out to see. Out on the landing I realized that the sounds came, not from down below, but from up above. I came along to the foot of these stairs. Again I thought I heard a sound. I called up, 'Is anybody there?' But there was no answer, and I heard nothing more, so I assumed that my nerves had been playing tricks on me and went back to bed.

"However, early this morning, I came up here—simply out of curiosity. And I found *this!*"

She stooped down and turned round a picture that was leaning against the wall with the back of the canvas toward us.

I gave a gasp of surprise. The picture was evidently a portrait in oils, but the face had been hacked and cut in such a savage way as to render it unrecognizable. Moreover the cuts were clearly quite fresh.

"What an extraordinary thing," I said.

"Isn't it? Tell me, can you think of any explanation?"

I shook my head.

"There's a kind of savagery about it," I said, "that I don't like. It looks as though it had been done in a fit of maniacal rage."

"Yes, that's what I thought."

"What is the portrait?"

"I haven't the least idea. I have never seen it before. All these things were in the attic when I married Lucius and came here to live. I have never been through them or bothered about them."

"Extraordinary," I commented.

I stooped down and examined the other pictures. They were very much what you would expect to find—some very mediocre landscapes, some oleographs, and a few cheaply framed reproductions.

There was nothing else helpful. A large, old-fashioned trunk, of the kind that used to be called an "ark," had the initials *E.P.* upon it. I raised the lid. It was empty. Nothing else in the attic was the least suggestive.

"It really is a most amazing occurrence," I said. "It's so—senseless."

"Yes," said Anne. "That frightens me a little."

There was nothing more to see. I accompanied her down to her sitting-room where she closed the door.

"Do you think I ought to do anything about it? Tell the police?"

I hesitated.

"It's hard to say on the face of it whether—"

"It has anything to do with the murder or not," finished Anne. "I know. That's what is so difficult. On the face of it, there seems no connection whatever."

"No," I said, "but it is another Peculiar Thing."

We both sat silent with puzzled brows.

"What are your plans, if I may ask?" I said presently.

She lifted her head.

"I'm going to live here for at least another six months!" She said it defiantly. "I don't want to. I hate the idea of living here. But I think it's the only thing to be done. Otherwise people will say that I ran away—that I had a guilty conscience."

"Surely not."

"Oh, yes, they will. Especially when—" She paused and then said, "When the six months are up—I am going to marry Lawrence." Her eyes met mine. "We're neither of us going to wait any longer."

"I supposed," I said, "that that would happen."

Suddenly she broke down, burying her head in her hands.

"You don't know how grateful I am to you—you don't know. We'd said good-by to each other—he was going away. I feel—I feel not so awful about Lucius's death. If we'd been planning to go away together, and he'd died then—it would be so awful now. But you made us both see how wrong it would be. That's why I'm grateful."

"I, too, am thankful," I said gravely.

"All the same, you know"—she sat up—"unless the real murderer is found, they'll always think it was Lawrence. Oh, yes, they will. And especially when he marries me."

"My dear, Doctor Haydock's evidence made it perfectly clear—"

"What do people care about evidence? They don't even know about it. And medical evidence never means anything to outsiders anyway. That's another reason why I'm staying on here. Mr. Clement, *I'm going to find out the truth.*"

Her eyes flashed as she spoke. She added, "That's why I asked that girl here."

"Miss Cram?"

"Yes."

"You did ask her, then. I mean, it was your idea?"

"Entirely. Oh! As a matter of fact, she whined a bit. At the inquest—she was there when I arrived. No, I asked her here deliberately."

"But surely," I cried, "you don't think that that silly young woman could have had anything to do with the crime?"

"It's awfully easy to appear silly, Mr. Clement. It's one of the easiest things in the world."

"Then you really think—"

"No, I don't. Honestly I don't. What I do think is that that girl knows something—or might know something. I wanted to study her at close quarters."

"And the very night she arrives, that picture is slashed," I said thoughtfully.

"You think she did it? But why? It seems so utterly absurd and impossible."

"It seems to me utterly impossible and absurd that your husband should have been murdered in my study," I said bitterly. "But he was."

"I know." She laid her hand on my arm. "It's dreadful for you. I do realize that, though I haven't said very much about it."

I took the blue lapis lazuli earring from my pocket and held it out to her.

"This is yours, I think?"

"Oh! Yes." She held out her hand for it with a pleased smile. "Where did you find it?"

But I did not put the jewel into her outstretched hand.

"Would you mind," I said, "if I kept it a little longer?"

"Why, certainly." She looked puzzled and a little inquiring. I did not satisfy her curiosity.

Instead I asked her how she was situated financially.

"It is an impertinent question," I said. "But I really do not mean it as such."

"I don't think it's impertinent at all. You and Griselda are the best friends I have here. And I like that funny old Miss Marple. Lucius was very well off, you know. He left things pretty equally divided between me and Lettice. Old Hall goes to me, but Lettice is to be allowed to choose enough furniture to furnish a small house, and she is left a separate sum for the purpose of buying one, so as to even things up."

"What are her plans, do you know?"

Anne made a comical grimace.

"She doesn't tell them to me. I imagine she will leave here as soon as possible. She doesn't like me—she never has. I daresay it's my fault, though I've really always tried to be decent. But I suppose any girl resents a young stepmother."

"Are you fond of her?" I asked bluntly.

She did not reply at once, which convinced me that Anne Protheroe is a very honest woman.

"I was at first," she said. "She was such a pretty little girl. I don't think I am now. I don't know why. Perhaps it's because she doesn't like me. I like being liked, you know."

"We all do," I said, and Anne Protheroe smiled.

I had one more task to perform. That was to get a word alone with Lettice Protheroe. I managed that easily enough, catching sight of her in the deserted drawing-room. Griselda and Gladys Cram were out in the garden.

I went in and shut the door.

"Lettice," I said, "I want to speak to you about something."

She looked up indifferently.

"Yes?"

I had thought beforehand what to say. I held out the lapis earring and said quietly, "Why did you drop that in my study?"

I saw her stiffen for a moment—it was almost instantaneous. Her recovery was so quick that I myself could hardly have sworn to the movement. Then she said carelessly, "I never dropped anything in your study. That's not mine. That's Anne's."

"I know that," I said.

"Well, why ask me, then? Anne must have dropped it."

"Mrs. Protheroe has only been in my study once since the murder, and then she was wearing black and so would not have been likely to have had on a blue earring."

"In that case," said Lettice, "I suppose she must have dropped it before." She added, "That's only logical."

"It's very logical," I said. "I suppose you don't happen to remember when your stepmother was wearing these earrings last?"

"Oh!" She looked at me with a puzzled, trustful gaze. "Is it very important?"

"It might be," I said.

"I'll try and think." She sat there knitting her brows. I have never seen Lettice Protheroe look more charming than she did at that moment. "Oh, yes," she said suddenly. "She had them on on Thursday. I remember now."

"Thursday," I said slowly, "was the day of the murder. Mrs. Protheroe came to the studio in the garden that day, but, if you remember, in her evidence, she only came as far as the study window, not inside the room."

"Where did you find this?"

"Rolled underneath the desk."

"Then it looks, doesn't it," said Lettice coolly, "as though she hadn't spoken the truth?"

"You mean that she came right in and stood by the desk?"

"Well, it looks like it, doesn't it?"

Her eyes met mine calmly.

"If you want to know," she said calmly, "I never have thought she was speaking the truth."

"And I *know you* are not, Lettice."

"What do you mean?"

She was startled.

"I mean," I said, "that the last time I saw this earring was on Friday morning when I came up here with Colonel Melchett. It was lying with its fellow on your stepmother's dressing table. I actually handled them both."

"Oh!" She wavered, then suddenly flung herself sideways over the arm of her chair and burst into tears. Her short, fair hair hung down almost touching the floor. It was a strange attitude—beautiful and unrestrained.

I let her sob for some moments in silence and then I said very gently, "Lettice, why did you do it?"

"What?"

She sprang up, flinging her hair wildly back. She looked wild—almost terrified.

"What do you mean?"

"What made you do it? Was it jealousy? Dislike of Anne?"

"Oh! Oh, yes." She pushed the hair back from her face and seemed suddenly to regain complete self-possession. "Yes, you can call it jealousy. I've always disliked Anne—ever since she came queening it here. I put the damned thing under the desk. I hoped it would get her into trouble. It would have done if you hadn't been such a nosy Parker, fingering things on dressing tables. Anyway, it isn't a clergyman's business to go about helping the police."

It was a spiteful childish outburst. I took no notice of it. Indeed at that moment, she seemed a very pathetic child indeed.

Her childish attempt at vengeance against Anne seemed hardly to be taken seriously. I told her so, and added that I should return the earring to her and say nothing of the circumstances in which I had found it. She seemed rather touched by that.

"That's nice of you," she said.

She paused a minute and then said, keeping her face averted and evidently choosing her words with care, "You know, Mr. Clement, I should—I should get Dennis away from here soon, if I were you. I—I think it would be better."

"Dennis?" I raised my eyebrows in slight surprise but with a trace of amusement, too.

"I think it would be better," she added, still in the same awkward manner. "I'm sorry about Dennis. I didn't think he— Anyway, I'm sorry."

We left it at that.

CHAPTER TWENTY-THREE

On the way back, I proposed to Griselda that we should make a detour and go round by the barrow. I was anxious to see if the police were at work and, if so, what they had found. Griselda, however, had things to do at home, so I was left to make the expedition on my own.

I found Constable Hurst in charge of operations.

"No sign so far, sir," he reported, "and yet it stands to reason that this is the only place for a cache."

His use of the word *cache* puzzled me for the moment, as he pronounced it *catch*, but his real meaning occurred to me almost at once.

"Whatimeantersay is, sir, where else could the young woman be going, starting into the wood by that path? It leads to Old Hall, and it leads here, and that's about all."

"I suppose," I said, "that Inspector Slack would disdain such a simple course as asking the young lady straight out."

"Anxious not to put the wind up her," said Hurst. "Anything she writes to Stone or he writes to her may throw light on things —once she knows we're on to her, she'd shut up like *that*."

Like *what* exactly was left in doubt, but I personally doubted Miss Gladys Cram ever being shut up in the way described. It was impossible to imagine her as other than overflowing with conversation.

"When a man's an h'impostor, you want to know *why* he's an h'impostor," said Constable Hurst didactically.

"Naturally," I said.

"And the answer is to be found in this here barrow—or else why was he forever messing about with it?"

"A *raison d'être* for prowling about," I suggested, but this bit of French was too much for the constable.

He revenged himself for not understanding it by saying coldly, "That's the h'amateur's point of view."

"Anyway you haven't found the suitcase," I said.

"We shall do, sir. Not a doubt of it."

"I'm not so sure," I said. "I've been thinking. Miss Marple said it was quite a short time before the girl reappeared emptyhanded. In that case, she wouldn't have had time to get up here and back."

"You can't take any notice of what old ladies say. When they've seen something curious, and are waiting all eager like, why time simply flies for them. And anyway, no lady knows anything about time."

I often wonder why the whole world is so prone to generalize. Generalizations are seldom or ever true, and are usually utterly inaccurate. I have a poor sense of time myself (hence the keeping of my clock fast), and Miss Marple, I should say, has a very acute one. Her clocks keep time to the minute, and she herself is rigidly punctual on every occasion.

However I had no intention of arguing with Constable Hurst on the point. I wished him good afternoon and good luck, and went on my way.

It was just as I was nearing home that the idea came to me. There was nothing to lead up to it. It just flashed into my brain as a possible solution.

You will remember that on my first search of the path, the day after the murder, I had found the bushes disturbed in a certain place. They proved, or so I thought at the time, to have been disturbed by Lawrence, bent on the same errand as myself.

But I remembered that afterward he and I together had come upon another faintly marked trail which proved to be that of the Inspector. On thinking it over, I distinctly remembered that the first trail, Lawrence's, had been much more noticeable than the second, as though more than one person had been passing that way. And I reflected that that was probably what had drawn Lawrence's attention to it in the first instance. Supposing that it had originally been made by either Dr. Stone or else Miss Cram?

I remembered, or else I imagined remembering, that there had been several withered leaves on broken twigs. If so, the trail could not have been made the afternoon of our search.

I was just approaching the spot in question. I recognized it easily enough, and once more forced my way through the bushes. This time I noticed fresh twigs broken. Someone *had* passed this way since Lawrence and myself.

I soon came to the place where I had encountered Lawrence. The faint trail, however, persisted farther, and I continued to follow it. Suddenly it widened out into a little clearing, which showed signs of recent upheaval. I saw a clearing, because the denseness of the undergrowth was thinned out there, but the branches of the trees met overhead and the whole place was not more than a few feet across.

On the other side, the undergrowth grew densely again and it seemed quite clear that no one had forced a way through it recently. Nevertheless, it seemed to have been disturbed in one place.

I went across and kneeled down, thrusting the bushes aside with both hands. A glint of a shiny brown surface rewarded me. Full of excitement I thrust my arm in and with a good deal of difficulty I extracted a small brown suitcase.

I uttered an ejaculation of triumph. I had been successful. Coldly snubbed by Constable Hurst, I had yet proved right in my reasoning. Here without doubt was the suitcase carried by Miss Cram. I tried the hasp, but it was locked.

As I rose to my feet, I noticed a small brownish crystal lying on the ground. Almost automatically, I picked it up and slipped it into my pocket.

Then, grasping my find by the handle, I retraced my steps to the path.

As I climbed over the stile into the lane, an agitated voice near at hand called out, "Oh! Mr. Clement. You've found it! How clever of you!"

Mentally registering the fact that, in the art of seeing without being seen, Miss Marple had no rival, I balanced my find on the palings between us.

"That's the one," said Miss Marple. "I'd know it anywhere."

This, I thought, was a slight exaggeration. There are thousands of cheap, shiny suitcases all exactly alike. No one could recognize one, particularly one seen from such a distance away by moonlight, but I realized that the whole business of the suitcase was Miss Marple's particular triumph and, as such, she was entitled to a little pardonable exaggeration.

"It's locked, I suppose, Mr. Clement?"

"Yes. I'm just going to take it down to the police station."

"You don't think it would be better to telephone?"

Of course unquestionably it would be better to telephone. To stride through the village, suitcase in hand, would be to court a probably undesirable publicity.

So I unlatched Miss Marple's garden gate and entered the house by the French window, and from the sanctity of the drawing-room, with the door shut, I telephoned my news.

The result was that Inspector Slack announced he would be up himself in a couple of jiffies.

When he arrived it was in his most cantankerous mood.

"So we've got it, have we?" he said. "You know, sir, you shouldn't keep things to yourself. If you've any reason to believe you know where the article in question was hidden, you ought to have reported it to the proper authorities."

"It was a pure accident," I said. "The idea just happened to occur to me."

"And that's a likely tale. Nearly three quarters of a mile of woodland, and you go right to the proper spot and lay your hand upon it."

I would have given Inspector Slack the steps in reasoning which led me to this particular spot, but he had achieved his usual result of putting my back up. I said nothing.

"Well!" said Inspector Slack, eyeing the suitcase with dislike and would-be indifference. "I suppose we might as well have a look at what's inside."

He had brought an assortment of keys and wire with him. The lock was a cheap affair. In a couple of seconds the case was open.

I don't know what we had expected to find—something sternly sensational, I imagine. But the first thing that met our eyes was a greasy plaid scarf. The Inspector lifted it out. Next came a faded dark-blue overcoat, very much the worse for wear. A checked cap followed.

"A shoddy lot," said the Inspector.

A pair of boots, very down at heel and battered, came next. At the bottom of the suitcase was a parcel done up in newspaper.

"Fancy shirt, I suppose," said the Inspector bitterly, as he tore it open.

A moment later he had caught his breath in surprise.

For inside the parcel were some demure little silver objects and a round platter of the same metal.

Miss Marple gave a shrill exclamation of recognition. "The trencher salts," she exclaimed. "Colonel Protheroe's trencher salts, and the Charles the Second *tazza*. Did you ever hear of such a thing!"

The Inspector had got very red.

"So that was the game," he muttered. "Robbery. But I can't make it out. There's been no mention of these things being missing."

"Perhaps they haven't discovered the loss," I suggested. "I presume these valuable things would not have been kept out in common use. Colonel Protheroe probably kept them locked away in a safe."

"I must investigate this," said the Inspector. "I'll go right up to Old Hall now. So that's why our Doctor Stone made himself scarce. What with the murder and one thing and another, he was afraid we'd get wind of his activities. As likely as not his belongings might have been searched. He got the girl to hide them in the wood with a suitable change of clothing. He meant to come back by a roundabout route and go off with them one night while she stayed here to disarm suspicion. Well, there's one thing to the good. This lets him out over the murder. He'd nothing to do with that. Quite a different game."

He repacked the suitcase and took his departure, refusing Miss Marple's offer of a glass of sherry.

"Well, that's one mystery cleared up," I said with a sigh. "What Slack says is quite true; there are no grounds for suspecting him of the murder. Everything's accounted for quite satisfactorily."

"It really would seem so," said Miss Marple. "Although one never can be quite certain, can one?"

"There's a complete lack of motive," I pointed out. "He'd got what he came for and was clearing out."

"Y—es."

She was clearly not quite satisfied, and I looked at her in some curiosity. She hastened to answer my inquiring gaze with a kind of apologetic eagerness.

"I've no doubt I am *quite* wrong. I'm so stupid about these things. But I just wondered—I mean this silver is very valuable, is it not?"

"A *tazza* sold the other day for over a thousand pounds, I believe."

"I mean—it's not the value of the metal."

"No, it's what one might call a connoisseur's value."

"That's what I mean. The sale of such things would take a little time to arrange, or, even if it was arranged, it couldn't be carried through without secrecy. I mean—if the robbery were reported and a hue and cry were raised, well, the things couldn't be marketed at all."

"I don't quite see what you mean," I said.

"I know I'm putting it badly." She became more flustered and apologetic. "But it seems to me that—that the things couldn't just have been abstracted, so to speak. The only satisfactory thing to do would be to replace these things with copies. Then, perhaps, the robbery wouldn't be discovered for some time."

"That's a very ingenious idea," I said.

"It would be the only way to do it, wouldn't it? And if so, of course, as you say, once the substitution had been accomplished, there wouldn't have been any reason for murdering Colonel Protheroe—quite the reverse."

"Exactly," I said. "That's what I said."

"Yes, but I just wondered—I don't know, of course—and Colonel Protheroe always talked a lot about doing things before he actually did do them, and, of course, sometimes never did them at all, but he did say—"

"Yes?"

"That he was going to have all his things valued—a man down

from London. For probate—no, that's when you're dead—for insurance. Someone told him that was the thing to do. He talked about it a great deal, and the importance of having it done. Of course, I don't know if he had made any actual arrangement, but if he had—"

"I see," I said slowly.

"Of course, the moment the expert saw the silver, he'd know, and then Colonel Protheroe would remember having shown the things to Doctor Stone—I wonder if it was done then—legerdemain, don't they call it? So clever—and then, well, the fat would be in the fire, to use an old-fashioned expression."

"I see your idea," I said. "I think we ought to find out for certain."

I went once more to the telephone. In a few minutes I was through to Old Hall and speaking to Anne Protheroe.

"No, it's nothing very important. Has the Inspector arrived yet? Oh! Well, he's on his way. Mrs. Protheroe, can you tell me if the contents of Old Hall were ever valued? What's that you say?"

Her answer came clear and prompt. I thanked her, replaced the receiver, and turned to Miss Marple.

"That's very definite. Colonel Protheroe had made arrangements for a man to come down from London on Monday—tomorrow—to make a full valuation. Owing to the Colonel's death, the matter has been put off."

"Then there *was* a motive," said Miss Marple softly.

"A motive, yes. But that's all. You forget. When the shot was fired, Doctor Stone had just joined the others, or was climbing over the stile in order to do so."

"Yes," said Miss Marple thoughtfully. "So that rules him out."

CHAPTER TWENTY-FOUR

I RETURNED to the Vicarage to find Hawes waiting for me in my study. He was pacing up and down nervously, and when I entered the room he started as though he had been shot.

"You must excuse me," he said, wiping his forehead. "My nerves are all to pieces lately."

"My dear fellow," I said, "you positively must get away for a change. We shall have you breaking down altogether, and that will never do."

"I can't desert my post. No, that is a thing I will never do."

"It's not a case of desertion. You are ill. I'm sure Haydock would agree with me."

"Haydock—Haydock. What kind of doctor is he? An ignorant country practitioner."

"I think you're unfair to him. He has always been considered a very able man in his profession."

"Oh, perhaps. Yes, I daresay. But I don't like him. However, that's not what I came to say. I came to ask you if you would be kind enough to preach tonight instead of me. I—I really do not feel equal to it."

"Why, certainly. I will take the service for you."

"No, no. I wish to take the service. I am perfectly fit. It is only the idea of getting up in the pulpit, of all those eyes staring at me—"

He shut his eyes and swallowed convulsively.

It was clear to me that there was something very wrong indeed the matter with Hawes. He seemed aware of my thoughts, for he opened his eyes and said quickly, "There is nothing really wrong with me. It is just these headaches—these awful racking headaches. I wonder if you could let me have a glass of water?"

"Certainly," I said.

I went and fetched it myself from the tap. Ringing bells is a profitless form of exercise in our house.

I brought the water to him and he thanked me. He took from his pocket a small cardboard box and, opening it, extracted a rice-paper capsule, which he swallowed with the aid of the water.

"A headache powder," he explained.

I suddenly wondered whether Hawes might have become addicted to drugs. It would explain a great many of his peculiarities.

"You don't take too many, I hope," I said.

"No—oh, no. Doctor Haydock warned me against that. But it is really wonderful. They bring instant relief."

Indeed he already seemed calmer and more composed.

He stood up.

"Then you will preach tonight? It's very good of you, sir."

"Not at all. And I insist on taking the service, too. Get along home and rest. No, I won't have any argument. Not another word."

He thanked me again. Then he said, his eyes sliding past me to the window, "You—you have been up at Old Hall today, haven't you, sir?"

"Yes."

"Excuse me—but were you sent for?"

I looked at him in surprise, and he flushed.

"I'm sorry, sir. I—I just thought some new development might have arisen, and that that was why Mrs. Protheroe had sent for you."

I had not the faintest intention of satisfying Hawes's curiosity.

"She wanted to discuss the funeral arrangements and one or two other small matters with me," I said.

"Oh! That was all. I see."

I did not speak. He fidgeted from foot to foot, and finally said, "Mr. Redding came to see me last night. I—I can't imagine why."

"Didn't he tell you?"

"He—he just said he thought he'd look me up. Said it was a bit lonely in the evenings. He's never done such a thing before."

"Well, he's supposed to be pleasant company," I said smiling.

"What does he want to come and see me for? I don't like it." His voice rose shrilly. "He spoke of dropping in again. What does it all mean? What idea do you think he has got into his head?"

"Why should you suppose he has any ulterior motive?" I asked.

"I don't like it," repeated Hawes obstinately. "I've never gone against *him* in any way. I never suggested that *he* was guilty—even when he accused himself, I said it seemed most incomprehensible. If I've had suspicions of anybody, it's been of Archer—never of him. Archer is a totally different proposition—a godless, irreligious ruffian. A drunken blackguard."

"Don't you think you're being a little harsh?" I said. "After all, we really know very little about the man."

"A poacher, in and out of prison, capable of anything."

"Do you really think he shot Colonel Protheroe?" I asked curiously.

Hawes has an inveterate dislike of answering yes or no. I have noticed it several times lately.

"Don't you think yourself, sir, that it's the only possible solution?"

"As far as we know," I said, "there's no evidence of any kind against him."

"His threats," said Hawes eagerly. "You forget about his threats."

"I am sick and tired of hearing about Archer's threats. As far as I can make out, there is no direct evidence that he ever made any."

"He was determined to be revenged on Colonel Protheroe. He primed himself with drink and then shot him."

"That's pure supposition."

"But you will admit that it's perfectly probable?"

"No, I don't."

"Possible, then?"

"Possible, yes."

Hawes glanced at me sideways.

"Why don't you think it's probable?"

"Because," I said, "a man like Archer wouldn't think of shooting a man with a pistol. It's the wrong weapon."

Hawes seemed taken aback by my argument. Evidently it wasn't the objection he had expected.

"Do you really think the objection is feasible?" he asked doubtingly.

"To my mind it is a complete stumbling block to Archer's having committed the crime," I said.

In face of my positive assertion, Hawes said no more. He thanked me again and left.

I had gone as far as the front door with him, and on the hall table I saw four notes. They had certain characteristics in common. The handwriting was almost unmistakably feminine; they all bore the words: *By hand, Urgent*, and the only difference I could see was that one was noticeably dirtier than the rest.

Their similarity gave me a curious feeling of seeing—not double but quadruple.

Mary came out of the kitchen and caught me staring at them.

"Come by hand since lunchtime," she volunteered. "All but one. I found that in the box."

I nodded, gathered them up, and took them into the study.

The first one ran thus:

Dear Mr. Clement, Something has come to my knowledge which I feel you ought to know. It concerns the death of poor Colonel Protheroe. I should much appreciate your advice on the matter—whether to go to the police or not. Since my dear husband's death, I have such a shrinking from every kind of publicity. Perhaps you could run in and see me for a few minutes this afternoon. Yours sincerely, Martha Price Ridley.

I opened the second.

Dear Mr. Clement, I am so troubled—so exercised *in my mind—to know what I ought to do. Something has come to my ears that I feel may be important. I have such a* horror *of being mixed up with the police in any way. I am so disturbed and distressed. Would it be asking too much of you, dear Vicar, to drop in for a few minutes and solve my doubts and perplexities for me in the wonderful way you always do? Forgive my troubling you. Yours very sincerely, Caroline Wetherby.*

The third, I felt, I could almost have recited beforehand.

Dear Mr. Clement, Something most important has come to my ears. I feel you should be the first to know about it. Will you call in and see me this afternoon sometime? I will wait in for you.

This militant epistle was signed: *Amanda Hartnell.*

I opened the fourth missive. It has been my good fortune to be troubled with very few anonymous letters. An anonymous letter is, I think, the meanest and cruelest weapon there is. This one was no exception. It purported to be written by an illiterate person, but several things inclined me to disbelieve that assumption.

Dear Vicar, i think you ought to know what is Going On. Your lady has been seen coming out of Mr. Redding's cottage in a surreptitious manner. You know wot i mean. The two are Carrying On together. i think you ought to know. A Friend.

I made a faint exclamation of disgust and, crumpling up the paper, tossed it into the open grate just as Griselda entered the room.

"What's that you're throwing down so contemptuously?" she asked.

"Filth," I said.

Taking a match from my pocket, I struck it and bent down. Griselda, however, was too quick for me. She had stooped down and caught up the crumpled ball of paper and smoothed it out before I could stop her.

She read it, gave a little exclamation of disgust, and tossed it back to me, turning away as she did so. I lighted it and watched it burn.

Griselda had moved away. She was standing by the window looking out into the garden.

"Len," she said without turning round.

"Yes, my dear?"

"I'd like to tell you something. Yes, don't stop me. I want to, please. When—when Lawrence Redding came here, I let you think that I had only known him slightly before. That wasn't true. I—I had known him rather well. In fact, before I met you, I had been rather in love with him. I think most people are with Lawrence. I was—well—absolutely silly about him at one time. I don't mean I wrote him compromising letters or anything idiotic like they do in books. But I was rather keen on him once."

"Why didn't you tell me?" I asked.

"Oh! Because! I don't know exactly except that—well, you're foolish in some ways. Just because you're so much older than I am, you think that I—well, that I'm likely to like other people. I thought you'd be tiresome, perhaps, about me and Lawrence being friends."

"You're very clever at concealing things," I said, remembering what she had told me in that room less than a week ago, and the ingenuous, natural way she had talked.

"Yes, I've always been able to hide things. In a way, I like doing it."

Her voice held a childlike ring of pleasure in it.

"But it's quite true what I said. I didn't know about Anne, and

I wondered why Lawrence was so different, not—well, really not noticing me. I'm not used to it."

There was a pause.

"You do understand, Len?" said Griselda anxiously.

"Yes," I said. "I understand."

But did I?

CHAPTER TWENTY-FIVE

I FOUND IT HARD to shake off the impression left by the anonymous letter. Pitch soils. However, I gathered up the other three letters, glanced at my watch, and started out.

I wondered very much what this might be that had "come to the knowledge" of three ladies simultaneously. I took it to be the same piece of news. In this, I was to realize that my psychology was at fault.

I cannot pretend that my calls took me past the police station. My feet gravitated there of their own accord. I was anxious to know whether Inspector Slack had returned from Old Hall.

I found that he had and, further, that Miss Cram had returned with him. The fair Gladys was seated in the police station carrying off matters with a high hand. She denied absolutely having taken the suitcase to the woods.

"Just because one of these gossiping old cats has nothing better to do than look out of her window all night, you go and pitch upon me. She's been mistaken once, remember, when she said she saw me at the end of the lane on the afternoon of the murder, and if she was mistaken then, in daylight, how can she possibly have recognized me by moonlight?

"Wicked, it is, the way these old ladies go on down here. Say anything, they will. And me asleep in my bed as innocent as can be. You ought to be ashamed of yourselves, the lot of you."

"And supposing the landlady of the Blue Boar identifies the suitcase as yours, Miss Cram?"

"If she says anything of the kind, she's wrong. There's no name on it. Nearly everybody's got a suitcase like that. As for poor Doctor Stone, accusing him of being a common burglar! And he with a lot of letters after his name."

"You refuse to give us any explanation, then, Miss Cram?"

"No refusing about it. You've made a mistake, that's all. You and your meddlesome Marples. I won't say a word more—not without my solicitor present. I'm going this minute—unless you're going to arrest me."

For answer, the Inspector rose and opened the door for her, and, with a toss of the head, Miss Cram walked out.

"That's the line she takes," said Slack, coming back to his chair. "Absolute denial. And, of course, the old lady *may* have been mistaken. No jury would believe you could recognize anyone from that distance on a moonlit night. And of course, as I say, the old lady may have made a mistake."

"She may," I said, "but I don't think she did. Miss Marple is usually right. That's what makes her unpopular."

The Inspector grinned.

"That's what Hurst says. Lord, these villages!"

"What about the silver, Inspector?"

"Seemed to be perfectly in order. Of course that meant one lot or the other must be a fake. There's a very good man in Much Benham, an authority on old silver. I've phoned over to him and sent a car to fetch him. We'll soon know which is which. Either the burglary was an accomplished fact, or else it was only planned. Doesn't make a frightful lot of difference either way—I mean as far as we're concerned. Robbery's a small business compared with murder. These two aren't concerned with the murder. We'll maybe get a line on him through the girl—that's why I let her go without any more fuss."

"I wondered," I said.

"A pity about Mr. Redding. It's not often you find a man who goes out of his way to oblige you."

"I suppose not," I said smiling slightly.

"Women cause a lot of trouble," moralized the Inspector.

He sighed and then went on, somewhat to my surprise. "Of course, there's Archer."

"Oh!" I said. "You've thought of him?"

"Why, naturally, sir, first thing. It didn't need any anonymous letters to put me on his track."

"Anonymous letters," I said sharply. "Did you get one, then?"

"That's nothing new, sir. We get a dozen a day, at least. Oh, yes, we were put wise to Archer. As though the police couldn't look out for themselves! Archer's been under suspicion from the first. The trouble of it is, he's got an alibi. Not that it amounts to anything, but it's awkward to get over."

"What do you mean by its not amounting to anything?" I asked.

"Well, it appears he was with a couple of pals all the afternoon. Not, as I say, that that counts much. Men like Archer and his pals would swear to anything. There's no believing a word they say. *We* know that. But the public doesn't, and the jury's taken from the public, more's the pity. They know nothing, and ten to one believe everything that's said in the witness box, no matter who it is that says it. And, of course, Archer himself will swear till he's black in the face that he didn't do it."

"Not so obliging as Mr. Redding," I said with a smile.

"Not he," said the Inspector, making the remark as a plain statement of fact.

"It is natural, I suppose, to cling to life," I mused.

"You'd be surprised if you knew the murderers that have got off through the soft-heartedness of the jury," said the Inspector gloomily.

"But do you really think that Archer did it?" I asked.

It has struck me as curious all along that Inspector Slack never seems to have any personal views of his own on the murder. The easiness or difficulty of getting a conviction are the only points that seem to appeal to him.

"I'd like to be a bit surer," he admitted. "A fingerprint, now, or a footprint, or seen in the vicinity about the time of the crime. Can't risk arresting him without something of that kind. He's been seen round Mr. Redding's house once or twice, but he'd say that was to speak to his mother. A decent body, she is. No, on the whole, I'm for the lady. If I could only get definite proof of blackmail—but you can't get definite proof of anything in this crime! It's theory, theory, theory. It's a sad pity that there's not a single spinster lady living along your road, Mr. Clement. I bet she'd have seen something if there had been."

His words reminded me of my calls, and I took leave of him. It was about the solitary instance when I had seen him in a genial mood.

My first call was on Miss Hartnell. She must have been watching for me from the window, for before I had time to ring she had opened the front door and, clasping my hand firmly in hers, had led me over the threshold.

"So good of you to come. In here. More private."

We entered a microscopic room, about the size of a hencoop. Miss Hartnell shut the door and, with an air of deep secrecy, waved me to a seat (there were only three). I perceived that she was enjoying herself.

"I'm never one to beat about the bush," she said in her jolly voice, the latter slightly toned down to meet the requirements of the situation. "You know how things go round in a village like this?"

"Unfortunately," I said, "I do."

"I agree with you. Nobody dislikes gossip more than I do. But there it is. I thought it my duty to tell the police inspector that I'd called on Mrs. Lestrange the afternoon of the murder and that she was out. I don't expect to be thanked for doing my duty; I just do it. Ingratitude is what you meet with first and last in this life. Why, only yesterday that impudent Mrs. Baker—"

"Yes, yes," I said hoping to avert the usual tirade. "Very sad, very sad. But you were saying."

"The lower classes don't know who are their best friends," said Miss Hartnell. "I always say a word in season when I'm visiting. Not that I'm ever thanked for it."

"You were telling the Inspector about your call upon Mrs. Lestrange," I prompted.

"Exactly—and, by the way, he didn't thank me. Said he'd ask for information when he wanted it—not those words exactly, but that was the spirit. There's a different class of men in the police force nowadays."

"Very probably," I said. "But you were going on to say something?"

"I decided that this time I wouldn't go near any wretched Inspector. After all, a clergyman is a gentleman—at least some are," she added.

I gathered that the qualification was not intended to include me.

"If I can help you in any way," I began.

"It's a matter of duty," said Miss Hartnell and closed her mouth with a snap. "I don't want to have to say these things. No one likes it less. But duty is duty."

I waited.

"I've been given to understand," went on Miss Hartnell, turning rather red, "that Mrs. Lestrange gives out that she was at home all the time—that she didn't answer the door because—well, because she didn't choose. Such airs and graces. I only called as a matter of duty, and to be treated like that!"

"She has been ill," I said mildly.

"Ill? Fiddlesticks. You're too unworldly, Mr. Clement. There's nothing the matter with that woman. Too ill to attend the inquest indeed! Medical certificate from Doctor Haydock! She can wind him round her little finger; everyone knows that. Well, where was I?"

I didn't quite know. It is difficult with Miss Hartnell to know where narrative ends and vituperation begins.

"Oh! About calling on her that afternoon. Well, it's fiddlesticks to say she was in the house. She wasn't. I know."

"How can you possibly know?"

Miss Hartnell's face turned a little redder. In someone less truculent, her demeanor might have been called embarrassed.

"I'd knocked and rung," she explained. "Twice. If not three times. And it occurred to me suddenly that the bell might be out of order."

She was, I was glad to note, unable to look me in the face when saying this. The same builder builds all our houses, and the bells he installs are always clearly audible when standing on the mat outside the front door. Both Miss Hartnell and I knew this perfectly well, but I suppose decencies have to be preserved.

"Yes?" I murmured.

"I didn't want to push my card through the letter box. That would seem so rude, and whatever I am, I am never rude."

She made this amazing statement without a tremor.

"So I thought I would just go round the house and—and tap on the windowpane," she continued unblushingly. "I went all round the house and looked in at all the windows, but there was no one in the house at all."

I understood her perfectly. Taking advantage of the fact that the house was empty, Miss Hartnell had given unbridled rein to her curiosity and had gone round the house, examining the garden and peering in at all the windows to see as much as she could of the interior. She had chosen to tell her story to me, believing that I should be a more sympathetic and lenient audience than the police. The clergy are supposed to give the benefit of the doubt to their parishioners.

I made no comment on the situation. I merely asked a question.

"What time was this, Miss Hartnell?"

"As far as I can remember," said Miss Hartnell, "it must have been close on six o'clock. I went straight home afterward, and I got in about ten past six, and Mrs. Protheroe came in somewhere round about the half-hour, leaving Doctor Stone and Mr. Redding outside, and we talked about bulbs. And all the time the poor Colonel lying murdered. It's a sad world."

"It is sometimes a rather unpleasant one," I said.

I rose.

"And that is all you have to tell me?"

"I just thought it might be important."

"It might," I agreed.

And refusing to be drawn further, much to Miss Hartnell's disappointment, I took my leave.

Miss Wetherby, whom I visited next, received me in a kind of flutter.

"Dear Vicar, how truly kind. You've had tea? Really, you won't? A cushion for your back? It is so kind of you to come round so promptly. Always willing to put yourself out for others."

There was a good deal of this before we came to the point, and even then it was approached with a good deal of circumlocution.

"You must understand that I heard this on the best authority."

In St. Mary Mead, the best authority is always somebody else's servant.

"You can't tell me who told you?"

"I promised, dear Mr. Clement. And I always think a promise should be a sacred thing."

She looked very solemn.

"Shall we say a little bird told me? That is safe, isn't it?"

I longed to say, "It's damned silly." I rather wish I had. I should have liked to observe the effect on Miss Wetherby.

"Well, this little bird told that she saw a certain lady who shall be nameless."

"Another kind of bird?" I inquired.

To my great surprise Miss Wetherby went off into paroxysms of laughter and tapped me playfully on the arm saying, "Oh! Vicar, you must not be so naughty."

When she had recovered, she went on.

"A certain lady, and where do you think this certain lady was going? She turned into the Vicarage road, but before she did so, she looked up and down the road in a most peculiar way—to see if anyone she knew were noticing her, I imagine."

"And the little bird?" I inquired.

"Paying a visit to the fishmonger's—in the room over the shop."

I now know where maids go on their days out. I know there is one place they never go if they can help—anywhere in the open air.

"And the time," continued Miss Wetherby, leaning forward mysteriously, "was just before six o'clock."

"On which day?"

Miss Wetherby gave a little scream.

"The day of the murder, of course, didn't I say so?"

"I inferred it," I replied. "And the name of the lady?"

"Begins with an L," said Miss Wetherby nodding her head several times.

Feeling that I had got to the end of the information Miss Wetherby had to impart, I rose to my feet.

"You won't let the police cross-question me, will you?" said Miss Wetherby pathetically, as she clasped my hand in both of hers. "I do shrink from publicity. And to stand up in court!"

"In special cases," I said, "they let witnesses sit down."

And I escaped.

There was still Mrs. Price Ridley to see. That lady put me in my place at once.

"I will not be mixed up in any police-court business," she said firmly, after shaking my hand coldly. "You understand that. On the other hand, having come across a circumstance which needs explaining, I think it should be brought to the notice of the authorities."

"Does it concern Mrs. Lestrange?" I asked.

"Why should it?" demanded Mrs. Price Ridley coldly.

She had me at a disadvantage there.

"It's a very simple matter," she continued. "My maid, Clara, was standing at the front gate; she went down there for a minute or two—*she* says to get a breath of fresh air. Most unlikely, I should say. Much more probable that she was looking out for the fishmonger's boy—if he calls himself a boy—impudent young jackanapes, thinks because he's seventeen he can joke with all the girls. Anyway, as I say, she was standing at the gate and she heard a sneeze."

"Yes," I said waiting for more.

"That's all. I tell you she heard a sneeze. And don't start telling me I'm not so young as I once was and may have made a mistake, because it was Clara who heard it and she's only nineteen."

"But," I said, "why shouldn't she have heard a sneeze?"

Mrs. Price Ridley looked at me in obvious pity for my poorness of intellect.

"She heard a sneeze on the day of the murder at a time when there was no one in your house. Doubtless the murderer was concealed in the bushes waiting his opportunity. What you have to look for is a man with a cold in his head."

"Or a sufferer from hay fever," I suggested. "But as a matter of fact, Mrs. Price Ridley, I think that mystery has a very easy solution. Our maid, Mary, has been suffering from a severe cold in the head. In fact, her sniffing has tried us very much lately. It must have been her sneeze your maid heard."

"It was a man's sneeze," said Mrs. Price Ridley firmly. "And you couldn't hear your maid sneeze in your kitchen from our gate."

"You couldn't hear anyone sneezing in the study from your gate," I said. "Or at least I very much doubt it."

"I said the man might have been concealed in the shrubbery," said Mrs. Price Ridley. "Doubtless when Clara had gone in, he effected an entrance by the front door."

"Well, of course, that's possible," I said.

I tried not to make my voice consciously soothing, but I must have failed, for Mrs. Price Ridley glared at me suddenly.

"I am accustomed not to be listened to, but I might mention also that to leave a tennis racket carelessly flung down on the grass without a press completely ruins it. And tennis rackets are very expensive nowadays."

There did not seem to be rhyme or reason in this flank attack. It bewildered me utterly.

"But perhaps you don't agree," said Mrs. Price Ridley.

"Oh! I do—certainly."

"I am glad. Well, that is all I have to say. I wash my hands of the whole affair."

She leaned back and closed her eyes like one weary of this world. I thanked her and said good-by.

On the doorstep, I ventured to ask Clara about her mistress's statement.

"It's quite true, sir, I heard a sneeze. And it wasn't an ordinary sneeze—not by any means."

Nothing about a crime is ever ordinary. The shot was not an ordinary kind of shot. The sneeze was not a usual kind of sneeze. It was, I presume, a special murderer's sneeze. I asked the girl what time this had been, but she was very vague—sometime between a quarter and half past six she thought. Anyway, "It was before the mistress had the telephone call and was took bad."

I asked her if she had heard a shot of any kind. And she said the shots had been something awful. After that, I placed very little credence in her statements.

I was just turning in at my own gate when I decided to pay a friend a visit.

Glancing at my watch, I saw that I had just time for it before taking Evensong. I went down the road to Haydock's house. He came out on the doorstep to meet me.

I noticed afresh how worried and haggard he looked. This business seemed to have aged him out of all knowledge.

"I'm glad to see you," he said. "What's the news?"

I told him the latest Stone development.

"A high-class thief," he commented. "Well, that explains a lot of things. He'd read up his subject, but he made slips from time to time to me. Protheroe must have caught him out once. You remember the row they had. What do you think about the girl? Is she in it, too?"

"Opinion as to that is undecided," I said. "For my own part, I think the girl is all right. She's such a prize idiot," I added.

"Oh! I wouldn't say that. She's rather shrewd, is Miss Gladys Cram. A remarkably healthy specimen. Not likely to trouble members of my profession."

I told him that I was worried about Hawes, and that I was anxious that he should get away for a real rest and change.

Something evasive came into his manner when I said this. His answer did not ring quite true.

"Yes," he said slowly. "I suppose that would be the best thing. Poor chap. Poor chap."

"I thought you didn't like him."

"I don't—not much. But I'm sorry for a lot of people I don't like." He added, after a minute or two, "I'm even sorry for Protheroe. Poor fellow—nobody ever liked him much. Too full of his own rectitude and too self-assertive. It's an unlovable mixture. He was always the same—even as a young man."

"I didn't know you knew him then?"

"Oh, yes. When he lived in Westmoreland, I had a practice not far away. That's a long time ago now. Nearly twenty years."

I sighed. Twenty years ago Griselda was five years old. Time is an odd thing.

"Is that all you came to say to me, Clement?"

I looked up with a start. Haydock was watching me with keen eyes.

"There's something else, isn't there?" he said.

I nodded.

I had been uncertain whether to speak or not when I came in, but now I decided to do so. I like Haydock as well as any man I know. He is a splendid fellow in every way. I felt that what I had to tell might be useful to him.

I recited my interviews with Miss Hartnell and Miss Wetherby. He was silent for a long time after I'd spoken.

"It's quite true, Clement," he said at last. "I've been trying to shield Mrs. Lestrange from any inconvenience that I could. As a matter of fact, she's an old friend. But that's not my only reason. That medical certificate of mine isn't the put-up job you all think it was."

He paused and then said gravely, "This is between you and me, Clement. Mrs. Lestrange is doomed."

"What?"

"She's a dying woman. I give her a month at longest. Do you wonder that I want to keep her from being badgered and questioned?"

He went on. "When she turned into this road that evening, it was here she came—to this house."

"You haven't said so before."

"I didn't want to create talk. Six to seven isn't my time for seeing patients, and everyone knows that. But you can take my word for it that she was here."

"She wasn't here when I came for you, though. I mean when we discovered the body."

"No," he seemed perturbed. "She'd left—to keep an appointment."

"In what direction was the appointment? In her own house?"

"I don't know, Clement. On my honor, I don't know."

I believed him, but—

"And supposing an innocent man is hanged?" I said.

He shook his head.

"No," he said. "No one will be hanged for the murder of Colonel Protheroe. You can take my word for that."

But that is just what I could not do. And yet the certainty in his voice was very great.

"No one will be hanged," he repeated.

"This man, Archer—"

He made an impatient movement.

"Hasn't got brains enough to wipe his fingerprints off the pistol."

"Perhaps not," I said dubiously.

Then I remembered something, and taking the little brownish crystal I had found in the wood from my pocket I held it out to him and asked him what it was.

"H'm." He hesitated. "Looks like picric acid. Where did you find it?"

"That," I replied, "is Sherlock Holmes's secret."

He smiled.

"What is picric acid?"

"Well, it's an explosive."

"Yes, I know that, but it's got another use, hasn't it?"

He nodded.

"It's used medically—in solution for burns. Wonderful stuff."

I held out my hand, and rather reluctantly he handed it back to me.

"It's of no consequence probably," I said. "But I found it in rather an unusual place."

"You won't tell me where?"

Rather childishly, I wouldn't. He had his secrets. Well, I would have mine. I was a little hurt that he had not confided in me more fully.

CHAPTER TWENTY-SIX

I WAS IN A STRANGE MOOD when I mounted the pulpit that night.

The church was unusually full. I cannot believe that it was the prospect of Hawes preaching which had attracted so many. Hawes's sermons are dull and dogmatic. And if the news had got round that I was preaching instead, that would not have attracted them either. For my sermons are dull and scholarly. Neither, I am afraid, can I attribute it to devotion.

Everybody had come, I concluded, to see who else was there, and possibly to exchange a little gossip in the church porch afterward.

Haydock was in church, which is unusual, and also Lawrence Redding. And, to my surprise, beside Lawrence I saw the white, strained face of Hawes. Anne Protheroe was there, but she usually attends Evensong on Sundays, though I had hardly thought she would today. I was far more surprised to see Lettice. Church-going was compulsory on Sunday morning—Colonel Protheroe was adamant on that point—but I had never seen Lettice at evening service before.

Gladys Cram was there, looking rather blatantly young and healthy against a background of wizened spinsters, and I fancied that a dim figure at the end of the church, who had slipped in late, was Mrs. Lestrange.

I need hardly say that Mrs. Price Ridley, Miss Hartnell, Miss Wetherby, and Miss Marple were there in full force. All the village people were there, with hardly a single exception. I don't know when we have had such a crowded congregation.

Crowds are queer things. There was a magnetic atmosphere that night, and the first person to feel its influence was myself.

As a rule, I prepare my sermons beforehand. I am careful and conscientious over them, but no one is better aware than myself of their deficiencies.

Tonight I was of necessity preaching *ex tempore*, and as I looked down on the sea of upturned faces, a sudden madness entered my brain. I ceased to be in any sense a minister of God. I became an actor. I had an audience before me and I wanted to move that audience—and more, I felt the power to move it.

I am not proud of what I did that night. I am an utter disbeliever in the emotional revivalist spirit. Yet that night I acted the part of a raving, ranting evangelist.

I gave out my text slowly.

"I am come to call not the righteous but the sinners to repentance."

I repeated it twice, and I heard my own voice, a resonant, ringing voice unlike the voice of the everyday Leonard Clement.

I saw Griselda from her front pew look up in surprise, and Dennis follow her example.

I held my breath for a moment or two, and then I let myself rip.

The congregation in that church were in a state of pent-up emotion, ripe to be played upon. I played upon them. I exhorted sinners to repentance. I lashed myself into a kind of emotional frenzy. Again and again I threw out a denouncing hand and reiterated the phrase:

"I am speaking to *you*."

And each time, from different parts of the church, a kind of sighing gasp went up.

Mass emotion is a strange and terrible thing.

I finished up with those beautiful and poignant words—perhaps the most poignant words in the whole Bible: *"This very night shall thy soul be required of thee."*

It was a strange, brief possession. When I got back to the Vicarage I was my usual faded, indeterminate self. I found Griselda rather pale. She slipped her arm through mine.

"Len," she said. "You were rather terrible tonight. I—I didn't like it. I've never heard you preach like that before."

"I don't suppose you ever will again," I said, sinking down wearily on the sofa. I was tired.

"What made you do it?"

"A sudden madness came over me."

"Oh! It—it wasn't something special?"

"What do you mean—something special?"

"I wondered—that was all. You're very unexpected, Len. I never feel I really know you."

We sat down to cold supper, Mary being out.

"There's a note for you in the hall," said Griselda. "Get it, will you, Dennis?"

Dennis, who had been very silent, obeyed.

I took it and groaned. Across the top left-hand corner was written: *By hand—Urgent.*

"This," I said, "must be from Miss Marple. There's no one else left."

I had been perfectly correct in my assumption.

Dear Mr. Clement, I should so much like to have a little chat with you about one or two things that have occurred to me. I feel we should all try and help in elucidating this sad mystery. I will come over about half past nine, if I may, and tap on your study window. Perhaps dear Griselda would be so very kind as to run over here and cheer up my nephew. And Mr. Dennis, too, of course, if he cares to come. If I do not hear, I will expect them and will come over myself at the time I have stated. Yours very sincerely, Jane Marple.

I handed the note to Griselda.

"Oh! We'll go," she said cheerfully. "A glass or two of home-made liqueur is just what one needs on Sunday evening. I think it's Mary's blanc mange that is so frightfully depressing. It's like something out of a mortuary."

Dennis seemed less charmed at the prospect.

"It's all very well for you," he grumbled. "You can talk all this high-brow stuff about art and books. I always feel a perfect fool sitting and listening to you."

"That's good for you," said Griselda serenely. "It puts you in your place. Anyway I don't think Mr. Raymond West is so frightfully clever as he pretends to be."

"Very few of us are," I said.

I wondered very much what exactly it was that Miss Marple wished to talk over. Of all the ladies in my congregation, I consider her by far the shrewdest. Not only does she see and hear practically everything that goes on, but she draws amazingly neat and apposite deductions from the facts that come under her notice.

If I were at any time to set out on a career of deceit, it would be of Miss Marple that I should be afraid.

What Griselda called the Nephew Amusing Party started off at a little after nine, and while I was waiting for Miss Marple to arrive I amused myself by drawing up a kind of schedule of the facts connected with the crime. I arranged them so far as possible in chronological order. I am not a punctual person, but I am a neat one, and I like things jotted down in a methodical fashion.

At half past nine punctually, there was a little tap on the window, and I rose and admitted Miss Marple.

She had a very fine Shetland shawl thrown over her head and shoulders, and was looking rather old and frail. She came in full of little fluttering remarks.

"So good of you to let me come—and so good of dear Griselda—Raymond admires her so much—the perfect Greuze he always calls her. Shall I sit here? I am not taking your chair? Oh! Thank you. No, I won't have a footstool."

I deposited the Shetland shawl on a chair and returned to take a chair facing my guest. We looked at each other, and a little deprecating smile broke out on her face.

"I feel that you must be wondering why—why I am so interested in all this. You may possibly think it's very unwomanly. No—please—I should like to explain if I may."

She paused a moment, a pink color suffusing her cheeks.

"You see," she began at last, "living alone as I do, in a rather out-of-the-way part of the world, one has to have a hobby. There is, of course, woolwork, and Guides, and Welfare, and sketching, but my hobby is—and always has been—Human Nature. So varied—and so very fascinating. And, of course, in a small village, with nothing to distract one, one has such ample opportunity for becoming what I might call proficient in one's study. One begins to class people, quite definitely, just as though they were birds or flowers, group so and so, genus this, species that. Sometimes, of course, one makes mistakes, but less and less as time goes on. And then, too, one tests oneself. One takes a little problem—for instance the gill of picked shrimps that amused dear Griselda so much—a quite unimportant mystery, but absolutely incomprehensible unless one solves it right. And then there was that matter of the changed cough drops, and the butcher's wife's umbrella—the last absolutely meaningless, unless on the assumption that the greengrocer was not behaving at all nicely with the chemist's wife—which, of course, turned out to be the case. It is so fascinating, you know, to apply one's judgment and find that one is right."

"You usually are, I believe," I said, smiling.

"That, I am afraid, is what has made me a little conceited," confessed Miss Marple. "But I have always wondered whether, if some day a really big mystery came along, I should be able to do the same thing. I mean—just solve it correctly. Logically, it ought to be exactly the same thing. After all, a tiny working model of a torpedo is just the same as a real torpedo."

"You mean it's all a question of relativity," I said slowly. "It should be—logically, I admit. But I don't know whether it really is."

"Surely it must be the same," said Miss Marple. "The—what one used to call the factors at school—are the same. There's money, and mutual attraction between people of an—er—opposite sex—and there's queerness, of course—so many people are a little queer, aren't they?—in fact, most people are when you know them well. And normal people do such astonishing things sometimes, and abnormal people are sometimes so very sane and ordinary. In fact, the only way is to compare people with other people you have known or come across. You'd be surprised if you knew how very few distinct types there are in all."

"You frighten me," I said. "I feel I'm being put under the microscope."

"Of course, I wouldn't dream of saying any of this to Colonel Melchett—such an autocratic man, isn't he?—and poor Inspector Slack—well, he's exactly like the young lady in the boot shop who wants to sell you patent leather because she's got it in your size, and doesn't take any notice of the fact that you want brown calf."

That really is a very good description of Slack.

"But you, Mr. Clement, know, I'm sure, quite as much about the crime as Inspector Slack. I thought, if we could work together—"

"I wonder," I said. "I think each one of us in his secret heart fancies himself as Sherlock Holmes."

Then I told her of the three summonses I had received that afternoon. I told her of Anne's discovery of the picture with the slashed face. I also told her of Miss Cram's attitude at the police station, and I described Haydock's identification of the crystal I had picked up.

"Having found that myself," I finished up, "I should like it to be important. But it's probably got nothing to do with the case."

"I have been reading a lot of American detective stories from the library lately," said Miss Marple, "hoping to find them helpful."

"Was there anything in them about picric acid?"

"I'm afraid not. I do remember reading a story once, though, in which a man was poisoned by picric acid and lanoline being rubbed on him as an ointment."

"But as nobody has been poisoned here, that doesn't seem to enter into the question," I said.

Then I took up my schedule and handed it to her.

"I've tried," I said, "to recapitulate the facts of the case as clearly as possible."

MY SCHEDULE

THURSDAY, 21st inst.

12:30 p.m. *Colonel Protheroe alters his appointment from six to six-fifteen. Overheard by half village very probably.*

12:45. *Pistol seen in its proper place. (But this is doubtful as Mrs. Archer had previously said she could not remember.)*

5:30 (*approx.*) *Colonel and Mrs. Protheroe leave Old Hall for village in car.*

5:30. *Fake call put through to me from the North Lodge, Old Hall.*

6:15 (*or a minute or two earlier*) *Colonel Protheroe arrives at Vicarage. Is shown into study by Mary.*

6:20. *Mrs. Protheroe comes along back lane and across garden to study window. Colonel Protheroe not visible.*

6:29. *Call from Lawrence Redding's cottage put through to Mrs. Price Ridley (according to exchange).*

6:30-6:35. *Shot heard (accepting telephone call time as correct). Lawrence Redding, Anne Protheroe, and Dr. Stone's evidence seem to point to its being earlier, but Mrs. P. R. probably right.*

6:45. *Lawrence Redding arrives Vicarage and finds the body.*

6:48. *I meet Lawrence Redding.*

6:49. *Body discovered by me.*

6:55. *Haydock examines body.*

Note. *The only two people who have no kind of alibi for 6:30-6:35 are Miss Cram and Mrs. Lestrange. Miss Cram says she was at the barrow, but no confirmation. It seems reasonable, however, to dismiss her from case, as there seems nothing to connect her with it. Mrs. Lestrange left Dr. Haydock's house sometime after six to keep an appointment. Where was the appointment, and with whom? It could hardly have been with Colonel Protheroe, as he expected to be engaged with me. It is true that Mrs. Lestrange was near the spot at the time the crime was committed, but it seems doubtful what motive she could have had for murdering him. She did not gain by his death, and the Inspector's theory of blackmail I cannot accept. Mrs. Lestrange is not that kind of woman. Also, it seems unlikely that she should have got hold of Lawrence Redding's pistol.*

"Very clear," said Miss Marple nodding her head in approval. "Very clear, indeed. Gentlemen always make such excellent memoranda."

"You agree with what I have written?" I asked.

"Oh, yes—you have put it all beautifully."

I asked her the question then that I had been meaning to put all along.

"Miss Marple," I said. "Whom do you suspect? You once said that there were seven people."

"Quite that, I should think," said Miss Marple absently. "I expect everyone of us suspects someone different. In fact, one can see they do."

She didn't ask me whom I suspected.

"The point is," she said, "that one must provide an explanation for everything. Each thing has got to be explained away satisfactorily. If you have a theory that fits every fact—well, then it must be the right one. But that's extremely difficult. If it wasn't for that note—"

"The note?" I said surprised.

"Yes, you remember, I told you. That note has worried me all along. It's wrong, somehow."

"Surely," I said, "that is explained now. It was written at six thirty-five, and another hand—the murderer's—put the misleading six-twenty at the top. I think that is clearly established."

"But even then," said Miss Marple, "it's all wrong."

"But why?"

"Listen—" Miss Marple leaned forward eagerly. "Mrs. Protheroe passed my garden, as I told you, and she went as far as the study window and she looked in and she didn't see Colonel Protheroe."

"Because he was writing at the desk," I said.

"And that's what's all wrong. That was at twenty past six. We agreed that he wouldn't sit down to say he couldn't wait any longer until after half past six—so, why was he sitting at the writing table then?"

"I never thought of that," I said slowly.

"Let us, dear Mr. Clement, just go over it again. Mrs. Protheroe comes to the window and she thinks the room is empty—she must have thought so, because otherwise she would never have gone down to the studio to meet Mr. Redding. It wouldn't have been safe. The room must have been absolutely silent if she thought it was empty. And that leaves us three alternatives, doesn't it?"

"You mean—"

"Well, the first alternative would be that Colonel Protheroe was dead already—but I don't think that's the most likely one. To begin with, he'd only been there about five minutes, and she or I would have heard the shot; and, secondly, the same difficulty remains about his being at the writing table. The second alternative is, of course, that he was sitting at the writing table writing a note, but in that case it must have been a different note altogether. It can't have been to say he couldn't wait. And the third—"

"Yes?" I said.

"Well, the third is, of course, that Mrs. Protheroe was right, and that the room was actually empty."

"You mean that, after he had been shown in, he went out again and came back later?"

"Yes."

"But why should he have done that?"

Miss Marple spread out her hands in a little gesture of bewilderment.

"That would mean looking at the case from an entirely different angle," I said.

"One so often has to do that—about everything. Don't you think so?"

I did not reply. I was going over carefully in my mind the three alternatives that Miss Marple had suggested.

With a slight sigh, the old lady rose to her feet.

"I must be getting back. I am very glad to have had this little chat—though we haven't got very far, have we?"

"To tell you the truth," I said, as I fetched her shawl, "the whole thing seems to me a bewildering maze."

"Oh! I wouldn't say that. I think, on the whole, one theory fits nearly everything. That is, if you admit one coincidence—and I think one coincidence is allowable. More than one, of course, is unlikely."

"Do you really think that? About the theory, I mean?" I asked, looking at her.

"I admit that there is one flaw in my theory—one fact that I can't get over. Oh! If only that note had been something quite different—"

She sighed and shook her head. She moved toward the window and absent-mindedly reached up her hand and felt the rather depressed looking plant that stood in a stand.

"You know, dear Mr. Clement, this should be watered oftener. Poor thing, it needs it badly. Your maid should water it every day. I suppose it is she who attends to it?"

"As much," I said, "as she attends to anything."

"A little raw at present," suggested Miss Marple.

"Yes," I said. "And Griselda steadily refuses to attempt to cook her. Her idea is that only a thoroughly undesirable maid will remain with us. However, Mary herself gave us notice the other day."

"Indeed. I always imagined she was very fond of you both."

"I haven't noticed it," I said. "But as a matter of fact, it was Lettice Protheroe who upset her. Mary came back from the inquest in rather a temperamental state and found Lettice here and —well, they had words."

"Oh!" said Miss Marple. She was just about to step through the window when she stopped suddenly, and a bewildering series of changes passed over her face.

"Oh, dear," she muttered to herself. "I *have* been stupid. So that was it! Perfectly possible all the time."

"I beg your pardon?"

She turned a worried face upon me.

"Nothing. An idea that has just occurred to me. I must go home and think things out thoroughly. Do you know, I believe I have been extremely stupid—almost incredibly so."

"I find that hard to believe," I said gallantly.

I escorted her through the window and across the lawn.

"Can you tell me what it is that has occurred to you so suddenly?" I asked.

"I would rather not—just at present. You see, there is still a possibility that I may be mistaken. But I do not think so. Here we are at my garden gate. Thank you so much. Please do not come any farther."

"Is the note still a stumbling block?" I asked as she passed through the gate and latched it behind her.

She looked at me abstractedly.

"The note? Oh! Of course that wasn't the real note. I never thought it was. Good night, Mr. Clement."

She went rapidly up the path to the house, leaving me staring after her.

I didn't know what to think.

CHAPTER TWENTY-SEVEN

GRISELDA AND DENNIS had not yet returned. I realized that the most natural thing would have been for me to go up to the house with Miss Marple and fetch them home. Both she and I had been so entirely taken up with our preoccupation over the mystery that we had forgotten anybody existed in the world except ourselves.

I was just standing in the hall, wondering whether I would not even now go over and join them, when the doorbell rang.

I crossed over to it. I saw there was a letter in the box and, presuming that this was the cause of the ring, I took it out.

As I did so, however, the bell rang again, and I shoved the letter hastily into my pocket and opened the front door.

It was Colonel Melchett.

"Hullo, Clement. I'm on my way home from town in the car. Thought I'd just look in and see if you could give me a drink."

"Delighted," I said. "Come into the study."

He pulled off the leather coat that he was wearing and followed me into the study. I fetched the whisky and soda and two glasses. Melchett was standing in front of the fireplace, legs wide apart, stroking his closely clipped mustache.

"I've got one bit of news for you, Clement. Most astounding thing you've ever heard. But let that go for the minute. How are things going down here? Any more old ladies hot on the scent?"

"They're not doing so badly," I said. "One of them, at all events, thinks she's got there."

"Our friend, Miss Marple, eh?"

"Our friend Miss Marple."

"Women like that always think they know everything," said Colonel Melchett.

He sipped his whisky and soda appreciatively.

"It's probably unnecessary interference on my part asking," I said, "but I suppose somebody has questioned the fish boy. I mean, if the murderer left by the front door, there's a chance the boy may have seen him."

"Slack questioned him right enough," said Melchett, "but the boy says he didn't meet anybody. Hardly likely he would. The murderer wouldn't be exactly courting observation. Lots of cover by your front gate. He would have taken a look to see if the road was clear. The boy had to call at the Vicarage, at Haydock's and at Mrs. Price Ridley's. Easy enough to dodge him."

"Yes," I said. "I suppose it would be."

"On the other hand," went on Melchett, "if by any chance that rascal Archer did the job, and young Fred Jackson saw him about the place, I doubt very much whether he'd let on. Archer is a cousin of his."

"Do you seriously suspect Archer?"

"Well, you know, old Protheroe had his knife into Archer pretty badly. Lots of bad blood between them. Leniency wasn't Protheroe's strong point."

"No," I said. "He was a very ruthless man."

"What I say is," said Melchett, "live and let live. Of course, the law's the law, but it never hurts to give a man the benefit of the doubt. That's what Protheroe never did."

"He prided himself on it," I said. There was a pause and then I asked, "What is this 'astounding bit of news' you promised me?"

"Well, it *is* astounding. You know that unfinished letter that Protheroe was writing when he was killed?"

"Yes."

"We got an expert on it—to say whether the six-twenty was added by a different hand. Naturally we sent up samples of Protheroe's handwriting. And do you know the verdict? *That letter was never written by Protheroe at all.*"

"You mean a forgery?"

"It's a forgery. The six-twenty they think is written in a different hand again—but they're not sure about that. The heading is in a different ink, but the letter itself is a forgery. Protheroe never wrote it."

"Are they certain?"

"Well, they're as certain as experts ever are. You know what an expert is! Oh! But they're sure enough."

"Amazing," I said.

Then a memory assailed me.

"Why," I said, "I remember at the time Mrs. Protheroe said it wasn't like her husband's handwriting at all, and I took no notice."

"Really?"

"I thought it one of those silly remarks women will make. If there seemed one thing sure on earth it was that Protheroe had written that note."

We looked at each other.

"It's curious," I said slowly. "Miss Marple was saying this evening that that note was all wrong."

"Confound the woman, she couldn't know more about it if she had committed the murder herself."

At that moment the telephone bell rang. There is a queer kind of psychology about a telephone bell. It rang now persistently and with a kind of sinister significance.

I went over and took up the receiver.

"This is the Vicarage," I said. "Who's speaking?"

A strange, high-pitched, hysterical voice came over the wire.

"*I want to confess*," it said. "*My God, I want to confess.*"

"Hullo," I said. "Hullo. Look here, you've cut me off. What number was that?"

A languid voice said it didn't know. It added that it was sorry I had been troubled.

I put down the receiver, and turned to Melchett.

"You once said," I remarked, "that you would go mad if anyone else accused themselves of the crime."

"What about it?"

"That was someone who wanted to confess—and the exchange has cut us off."

Melchett dashed over and took up the receiver.

"I'll speak to them."

"Do," I said. "You may have some effect. I'll leave you to it. I'm going out. I've a fancy I recognized that voice."

CHAPTER TWENTY-EIGHT

I HURRIED down the village street. It was eleven o'clock, and at eleven o'clock on a Sunday night the whole village of St. Mary Mead might be dead. I saw, however, a light in a first-floor window as I passed, and, realizing that Hawes was still up, I stopped and rang the doorbell.

After what seemed a long time, Hawes's landlady, Mrs. Sadler, laboriously unfastened two bolts, a chain, and turned a key, and peered out at me suspiciously.

"Why, it's Vicar!" she exclaimed.

"Good evening," I said. "I want to see Mr. Hawes. I see there's a light in the window, so he's up still."

"That may be. I've not seen him since I took up his supper. He's had a quiet evening—no one to see him, and he's not been out."

I nodded and, passing her, went quickly up the stairs. Hawes has a bedroom and sitting-room on the first floor.

I passed into the latter. Hawes was lying back in a long chair asleep. My entrance did not wake him. An empty cachet box and a glass of water, half full, stood beside him.

On the floor, by his left foot, was a crumpled sheet of paper with writing on it. I picked it up and straightened it out.

It began: *My dear Clement—*

I read it through, uttered an exclamation, and shoved it into my pocket. Then I bent over Hawes and studied him attentively.

Next, reaching for the telephone which stood by his elbow, I gave the number of the Vicarage. Melchett must have been still trying to trace the call, for I was told that the number was engaged. Asking them to call me, I put the instrument down again.

I put my hand into my pocket to look at the paper I had picked up once more. With it, I drew out the note that I had found in the letter box, and which was still unopened.

Its appearance was horribly familiar. It was the same handwriting as the anonymous letter that had come that afternoon.

I tore it open.

I read it once—twice—unable to realize its contents.

I was beginning to read it a third time when the telephone rang. Like a man in a dream I picked up the receiver and spoke.

"Hullo?"

"Hullo."

"Is that you, Melchett?"

"Yes, where are you? I've traced that call. The number is—"

"I know the number."

"Oh! Good. Is that where you are speaking from?"

"Yes."

"What about that confession?"

"I've got the confession, all right."

"You mean you've got the murderer?"

I had then the strongest temptation of my life. I looked at Hawes. I looked at the crumpled letter. I looked at the anonymous scrawl. I looked at the empty cachet box with the name of Cherubim on it. I remembered a certain casual conversation.

I made an immense effort.

"I—don't know," I said. "You'd better come round."

And I gave him the address.

Then I sat down in the chair opposite Hawes to think.

I had two clear minutes in which to do so.

In two minutes' time, Melchett would have arrived.

I took up the anonymous letter and read it through again for the third time.

Then I closed my eyes and thought. . . .

CHAPTER TWENTY-NINE

I DON'T KNOW how long I sat there—only a few minutes in reality, I suppose. Yet it seemed as though an eternity had passed when I heard the door open and, turning my head, looked up to see Melchett entering the room.

He stared at Hawes asleep in his chair, then turned to me.

"What's this, Clement? What does it all mean?"

Of the two letters in my hand I selected one and passed it to him. He read it aloud in a low voice.

"'My dear Clement: It is a peculiarly unpleasant thing that I have to say. After all, I think I prefer writing it. We can discuss it at a later date. It concerns the recent peculations. I am sorry to say that I have satisfied myself beyond any possible doubt as to the identity of the culprit. Painful as it is for me to have to accuse an ordained priest of the church, my duty is only too painfully clear. An example must be made and—'"

He looked at me questioningly. At this point the writing tailed off in an undistinguishable scrawl where death had overtaken the writer's hand.

Melchett drew a deep breath, then looked at Hawes.

"So that's the solution! The one man we never even considered. And remorse drove him to confess!"

"He's been very queer lately," I said.

Suddenly Melchett strode across to the sleeping man with a sharp exclamation. He seized him by the shoulder and shook him, at first gently, then with increasing violence.

"He's not asleep! He's drugged! What's the meaning of this?"

His eye went to the empty cachet box. He picked it up.

"Has he—"

"I think so," I said. "He showed me these the other day. Told me he'd been warned against an overdose. It's his way out, poor chap. Perhaps the best way. It's not for us to judge him."

But Melchett was Chief Constable of the County before anything else. The arguments that appealed to me had no weight with him. He had caught a murderer and he wanted his murderer hanged.

In one second he was at the telephone, jerking the receiver up and down impatiently until he got a reply. He asked for Haydock's number. Then there was a further pause during which he stood, his ear to the telephone and his eyes on the limp figure in the chair.

"Hullo—Hullo—Hullo—is that Doctor Haydock's? Will the doctor come around at once to High Street? Mr. Hawes's. It's urgent—what's that? Well, what number is it, then? Oh! Sorry."

He rang off, fuming.

"Wrong number, wrong number—always wrong numbers! And a man's life hanging on it. HULLO—you gave me the wrong number—yes—don't waste time—give me three nine—*nine*, not five."

Another period of impatience—shorter this time.

"Hullo—is that you, Haydock? Melchett speaking. Come to Nineteen High Street at once, will you? Hawes has taken some kind of overdose. At once, man, it's vital."

He rang off, strode impatiently up and down the room.

"Why on earth you didn't get hold of the doctor at once, Clement, I cannot think. Your wits must have all gone wool-gathering."

Fortunately it never occurs to Melchett that anyone can possibly have any different ideas on conduct from those he holds himself. I said nothing, and he went on.

"Where did you find this letter?"

"Crumpled on the floor—where it had fallen from his hand."

"Extraordinary business—that old maid was right about its being the wrong note we found. Wonder how she tumbled to that? But what an ass the fellow was not to destroy this one. Fancy keeping it—the most damaging evidence you can imagine!"

"Human nature is full of inconsistencies."

"If it weren't, I doubt if we should ever catch a murderer! Sooner or later they always do some fool things. You're looking very under the weather, Clement. I suppose this has been the most awful shock to you?"

"It has. As I say, Hawes has been queer in his manner for some time, but I never dreamed—"

"Who would? Hullo, that sounds like a car." He went across to the window, pushing up the sash and leaning out. "Yes, it's Haydock, all right."

A moment later the doctor entered the room.

In a few succinct words, Melchett explained the situation.

Haydock is not a man who ever shows his feelings. He merely raised his eyebrows, nodded, and strode across to his patient. He felt his pulse, raised the eyelid, and looked intently at the eye.

The he turned to Melchett.

"Want me to save him for the gallows?" he asked. "He's pretty far gone, you know. It will be touch and go anyway. I doubt if I can bring him round."

"Do everything possible."

"Right."

He busied himself with the case he had brought with him, preparing a hypodermic injection which he injected into Hawes's arm. Then he stood up.

"Best thing is to run him into Much Benham—to the hospital there. Give me a hand to get him down to the car."

We both lent our assistance. As Haydock climbed into the driving seat, he threw a parting remark over his shoulder.

"You won't be able to hang him, you know, Melchett."

"You mean he won't recover?"

"May or may not. I didn't mean that. I mean that even if he does recover—well, the poor devil wasn't responsible for his actions. I shall give evidence to that effect."

"What did he mean by that?" asked Melchett as we went upstairs again.

I explained that Hawes had been a victim of *encephalitis lethargica*.

"Sleeping sickness, eh? Always some good reason nowadays for every dirty action that's done. Don't you agree?"

"Science is teaching us a lot."

"Science be damned—I beg your pardon, Clement—but all this namby-pambyism annoys me. I'm a plain man. Well, I suppose we'd better have a look round here."

But at this moment there was an interruption—and a most amazing one. The door opened, and Miss Marple walked into the room.

She was pink and somewhat flustered, and seemed to realize our condition of bewilderment.

"So sorry—so very sorry—to intrude—good evening, Colonel Melchett. As I say, I am so sorry, but hearing that Mr. Hawes was taken ill, I felt I must come round and see if I couldn't do something."

She paused. Colonel Melchett was regarding her in a somewhat disgusted fashion.

"Very kind of you, Miss Marple," he said dryly. "But no need to trouble. How did you know, by the way?"

It was the question I had been yearning to ask!

"The telephone," explained Miss Marple. "So careless with their wrong numbers, aren't they? You spoke to me first, thinking I was Doctor Haydock. My number is three five."

"So that was it!" I exclaimed.

There is always some perfectly good and reasonable explanation for Miss Marple's omniscience.

"And so," she continued, "I just came round to see if I could be of any use."

"Very kind of you," said Melchett again, even more dryly this time. "But nothing to be done. Haydock's taken him off to hospital."

"Actually to hospital? Oh, that's a great relief! I am so very glad to hear it. He'll be quite safe there. When you say nothing to be done, you don't mean that there's nothing to be done for him, do you? You don't mean that he won't recover?"

"It's very doubtful," I said.

Miss Marple's eyes had gone to the cachet box.

"I suppose he took an overdose?" she said.

Melchett, I think, was in favor of being reticent. Perhaps I might have been under other circumstances. But my discussion of the case with Miss Marple was too fresh in my mind for me to have the same view, though I must admit that her rapid appearance on the scene and eager curiosity repelled me slightly.

"You had better look at this," I said, and handed her Protheroe's unfinished letter.

She took it and read it without any appearance of surprise.

"You had already deduced something of the kind, had you not?" I asked.

"Yes—yes, indeed. May I ask you, Mr. Clement, what made you come here this evening? That is a point which puzzles me. You and Colonel Melchett—not at all what I should have expected."

I explained the telephone call, and that I believed I had recognized Hawes's voice. Miss Marple nodded thoughtfully.

"Very interesting. Very providential—if I may use the term. Yes, it brought you here in the nick of time."

"In the nick of time for what?" I said bitterly.

Miss Marple looked surprised.

"To save Mr. Hawes's life, of course."

"Don't you think," I said, "that it might be better if Hawes didn't recover? Better for him—better for everyone. We know the truth now and—"

I stopped—for Miss Marple was nodding her head with such a peculiar vehemence that it made me lose the thread of what I was saying.

"Of course," she said. "Of course! That's what he wants you to think! That you know the truth—and that it's best for everyone as it is. Oh, yes, it all fits in—the letter, and the overdose, and poor Mr. Hawes's state of mind and his confession. It all fits in—*but it's wrong.*"

We stared at her.

"That's why I am so glad Mr. Hawes is safe—in the hospital—where no one can get at him. If he recovers, he'll tell you the truth."

"The truth?"

"Yes—that he never touched a hair of Colonel Protheroe's head."

"But the telephone call," I said. "The letter—the overdose. It's all so clear."

"That's what he wants you to think. Oh, he's very clever! Keeping the letter and using it this way was very clever indeed."

"Who do you mean," I said, "by 'he'?"

"I mean the murderer," said Miss Marple.

She added very quietly, "I mean Mr. Lawrence Redding."

CHAPTER THIRTY

We stared at her. I really think that for a moment or two we really believed she was out of her mind. The accusation seemed so utterly preposterous.

Colonel Melchett was the first to speak. He spoke kindly and with a kind of pitying tolerance.

"That is absurd, Miss Marple," he said. "Young Redding has been completely cleared."

"Naturally," said Miss Marple. "He saw to that."

"On the contrary," said Colonel Melchett dryly, "he did his best to get himself accused of the murder."

"Yes," said Miss Marple. "He took us all in that way—myself as much as anyone else. You will remember, dear Mr. Clement, that I was quite taken aback when I heard Mr. Redding had confessed to the crime. It upset all my ideas and made me think him innocent—when up to then I had felt convinced that he was guilty."

"Then it was Lawrence Redding you suspected?"

"I know that in books it is always the most unlikely person. But I never find that rule applies in real life. There it is so often the obvious that is true. Much as I have always liked Mrs. Protheroe, I could not avoid coming to the conclusion that she was completely under Mr. Redding's thumb and would do anything he told her, and of course he is not the kind of young man who would dream of running away with a penniless woman. From his point of view it was necessary that Colonel Protheroe should be removed—and so he removed him. One of those charming young men who have *no* moral sense."

Colonel Melchett had been snorting impatiently for some time. Now he broke out.

"Absolute nonsense—the whole thing! Redding's time is fully accounted for up to six forty-five, and Haydock says positively Protheroe couldn't have been shot then. I suppose you think you know better than a doctor. Or do you suggest that Haydock is deliberately lying—the Lord knows why?"

"I think Doctor Haydock's evidence was absolutely truthful. He is a very upright man. And, of course, it was Mrs. Protheroe who actually shot Colonel Protheroe—not Mr. Redding."

Again we stared at her. Miss Marple arranged her lace fichu, pushed back the fleecy shawl that draped her shoulders, and began to deliver a gentle, old-maidish lecture comprising the most astounding statements in the most natural way in the world.

"I have not thought it right to speak until now. One's own belief—even so strong as to amount to knowledge—is not the same as proof. And unless one has an explanation that will fit all the facts—as I was saying to dear Mr. Clement this evening—one cannot advance it with any real conviction. And my own explanation was not quite complete—it lacked just one thing—but suddenly, just as I was leaving Mr. Clement's study, I noticed the palm in the pot by the window—and—well—there the whole thing was—clear as daylight!"

"Mad—quite mad," murmured Melchett to me.

But Miss Marple beamed on us serenely and went on in her gentle ladylike voice.

"I was very sorry to believe what I did—very sorry. Because I liked them both. But you know what human nature is. And to begin with, when first he and then she both confessed in the most foolish way—well, I was more relieved than I could say. I had been wrong. And I began to think of other people who had a possible motive for wishing Colonel Protheroe out of the way."

"The seven suspects!" I murmured.

She smiled at me.

"Yes, indeed. There was that man Archer—not likely, but primed with drink—so inflaming—you never know. And, of course, there was your Mary. She's been walking out with Archer a long time, and she's a queer-tempered girl. Motive *and* opportunity—why, she was alone in the house! Old Mrs. Archer could easily have got the pistol from Mr. Redding's house for either of those two. And then, of course, there was Lettice—wanting freedom and money to do as she liked. I've known many cases where the most beautiful and ethereal girls have shown next to no moral scruple—though, of course, gentlemen never wish to believe it of them."

I winced.

"And then there was the tennis racket," continued Miss Marple.

"The tennis racket?"

"Yes, the one Mrs. Price Ridley's Clara saw lying on the grass by the Vicarage gate. That looked as though Mr. Dennis had got back earlier from his tennis party than he said. Boys of sixteen are so very susceptible and so very unbalanced. Whatever the motive—for Lettice's sake or for yours—it was a possibility. And then, of course, there was poor Mr. Hawes and you—not both of you naturally, but alternatively, as the lawyers say."

"Me?" I exclaimed in lively astonishment.

"Well, yes. I do apologize—and, indeed, I never really thought—But there was the question of these disappearing sums of money. Either you or Mr. Hawes must be guilty, and Mrs. Price Ridley was going about everywhere hinting that you were the person in fault—principally because you objected so vigorously to any kind of inquiry into the matter. Of course, I myself was always convinced it was Mr. Hawes—he reminded me so much of that unfortunate organist I mentioned—but all the same one couldn't be absolutely *sure*—'

"Human nature being what it is," I ended grimly.

"Exactly. And then, of course, there was dear Griselda."

"But Mrs. Clement was completely out of it," interruped Melchett. "She returned by the six-fifty train."

"That's what she *said*," retorted Miss Marple. "One should never go by what people say. The six-fifty was half an hour late that night. But at a quarter past seven I saw her with my own eyes starting for Old Hall. So it followed that she must have come by the earlier train. Indeed she was seen—but perhaps you know that?"

She looked at me inquiringly.

Some magnetism in her glance impelled me to hold out the last anonymous letter, the one I had opened so short a time ago. It set out in detail that Griselda had been seen leaving Lawrence Redding's cottage by the back window at half past six on the fatal day.

I said nothing then or at any time of the dreadful suspicion that had for one moment assailed my mind. I had seen it in nightmare terms—past intrigue between Lawrence and Griselda, the knowledge of it coming to Protheroe's ears, his decision to make me acquainted with the facts—and Griselda, desperate, stealing the pistol and silencing Protheroe. As I say—a nightmare only—but invested for a few long minutes with a dreadful appearance of reality.

I don't know whether Miss Marple had any inkling of all this. Very probably she had. Few things are hidden from her.

She handed me back the note with a little nod.

"That's been all over the village," she said. "And it did look rather suspicious, didn't it? Especially with Mrs. Archer swearing at the inquest that the pistol was still in the cottage when she left at midday."

She paused a minute and then went on.

"But I'm wandering terribly from the point. What I want to say—and I believe it my duty—is to put my own explanation of the mystery before you. If you don't believe it—well, I shall have done my best. Even as it is, my wish to be quite sure before I spoke may have cost poor Mr. Hawes his life."

Again she paused, and when she resumed, her voice held a different note. It was less apologetic, more decided.

"This is my own explanation of the facts. By Thursday afternoon the crime had been fully planned down to the smallest detail. Lawrence Redding first called on the Vicar, knowing him to be out. He had with him the pistol which he concealed in that pot in the stand by the window. When the Vicar came in, Lawrence explained his visit by a statement that he had made up his mind to go away. At five-thirty, Lawrence Redding telephoned from the North Lodge to the Vicar, adopting a woman's voice. You remember what a good amateur actor he was.

"Mrs. Protheroe and her husband had just started for the village. And—a very curious thing (though no one happened to think of it that way)—Mrs. Protheroe took no handbag with her. Really a *most* unusual thing for a woman to do. Just before twenty past six she passes my garden and stops and speaks, so as to give me every opportunity of noticing that she has no weapon with her, and also that she is quite her normal self. They realized, you see, that I am a noticing kind of person. She disappears round the corner of the house to the study window. The poor Colonel is sitting at the desk writing his letter to you. He is deaf as we all know. She takes the pistol from the bowl, where it is waiting for her, comes up behind him and shoots him through the head, throws down the pistol and is out again like a flash, and going down the garden to the studio. Nearly anyone would swear that there couldn't have been time!"

"But the shot?" objected the Colonel. "You didn't hear the shot?"

"There is, I believe, an invention called a Maxim silencer. So I gather from detective stories. I wonder if, possibly, the sneeze that the maid Clara heard might have actually been the shot? But no matter. Mrs. Protheroe is met at the studio by Mr. Redding. They go in together—and—human nature being what it is—I'm afraid they realize that I shan't leave the garden till they come out again!"

I had never liked Miss Marple better than at this moment, with her humorous perception of her own weakness.

"When they do come out, their demeanor is gay and natural. And there, in reality, they make a mistake. Because if they had really said good-by to each other, as they pretended, they would have looked very different. But you see, that was their weak point. They simply *dare* not appear upset in any way. For the next ten minutes they are careful to provide themselves with what is called an alibi, I believe. Finally Mr. Redding goes to the Vicarage, leaving it as late as he dares. He probably saw you on the footpath from far away and was able to time matters nicely. He picks up the pistol and the silencer, leaves the forged letter with the time on it written in a different ink and apparently in a different handwriting. When the forgery is discovered it will look like a clumsy attempt to incriminate Anne Protheroe.

"But when he leaves the letter, he finds the one actually written by Colonel Protheroe—something quite unexpected. And, being a very intelligent young man, and seeing that this letter many come in very useful to him, he takes it away with him. He alters the hands of the clock to the same time as the letter—knowing that it is always kept a quarter of an hour fast. The same idea—attempt to throw suspicion on Mrs. Protheroe. Then he leaves, meeting you outside the gate, and acting the part of someone nearly distraught. As I say, he is really most intelligent. What would a murderer who had committed a crime try to do? Behave naturally, of course. So that is just what Mr. Redding does not do. He gets rid of the silencer, but marches into the police station with the pistol and makes a perfectly ridiculous self-accusation which takes everybody in."

There was something fascinating in Miss Marple's résumé of the case. She spoke with such certainty that we both felt that in this way and in no other could the crime have been committed.

"What about the shot heard in the woods?" I asked. "Was that the coincidence to which you were referring earlier this evening?"

"Oh, dear, no." Miss Marple shook her head briskly. "*That*

wasn't a coincidence—very far from it. It was absolutely necessary that a shot should be heard—otherwise suspicion of Mrs. Protheroe might have continued. How Mr. Redding arranged it, I don't quite know. But I understand that picric acid explodes if you drop a weight on it, and you will remember, dear Vicar, that you met Mr. Redding carrying a large stone just in the part of the woods where you picked up that crystal later. Gentlemen are so clever at arranging things—the stone suspended above the crystals and then a time fuse—or do I mean a slow match? Something that would take about twenty minutes to burn through—so that the explosion would come about six-thirty when he and Mrs. Protheroe had come out of the studio and were in full view. A very safe device because what would there be to find afterward—only a big stone! But even that he tried to remove—when you came upon him."

"I believe you are right," I exclaimed, remembering the start of surprise Lawrence had given on seeing me that day. It had seemed natural enough at the time, but now— Miss Marple seemed to read my thoughts, for she nodded her head shrewdly.

"Yes," she said, "it must have been a very nasty shock for him to come across you just then. But he turned it off very well—pretending he was bringing it to me for my rock gardens. Only—" Miss Marple became suddenly very emphatic. *"It was the wrong sort of stone for my rock gardens!* And that put me on the right track!"

All this time Colonel Melchett had sat like a man in a trance. Now he showed signs of coming to. He snorted once or twice, blew his nose in a bewildered fashion, and said, "Upon my word! Well, upon my word!"

Beyond that, he did not commit himself. I think that he, like myself, was impressed with the logical certainty of Miss Marple's conclusions. But for the moment he was not willing to admit it.

Instead, he stretched out a hand, picked up the crumpled letter, and barked out, "All very well. But how do you account for this fellow Hawes? Why, he actually rang up and confessed."

"Yes—that was what was so providential. The Vicar's sermon, doubtless. You know, dear Mr. Clement, you really preached a most remarkable sermon. It must have affected Mr. Hawes deeply. He could bear it no longer, and felt he must confess—about the misappropriations of the church funds."

"What?"

"Yes—and that, under Providence, is what has saved his life. For I hope and trust it *is* saved. Doctor Haydock is so clever. As I see the matter, Mr. Redding kept this letter—a risky thing to do, but I expect he hid it in some safe place—and waited till he found out for certain to whom it referred. He soon made quite sure that it was Mr. Hawes. I understand he came back here with Mr. Hawes last night and spent a long time with him. I suspect that he then substituted a cachet of his own for one of Mr. Hawes's and slipped this letter in the pocket of Mr. Hawes's dressing gown. The poor young man would swallow the fatal cachet in all innocence—after his death his things would be gone through and the letter found and everyone would jump to the conclusion that he had shot Colonel Protheroe and taken his own life out of remorse. I rather fancy Mr. Hawes must have found that letter to-night just after taking the fatal cachet. In his disordered state, it must have seemed like something supernatural, and, coming on top of the Vicar's sermon, it must have impelled him to confess the whole thing."

"Upon my word," said Colonel Melchett. "Upon my word! *Most* extraordinary! I—I—don't believe a word of it."

He had never made a statement that sounded more unconvincing. It must have sounded so in his own ears for he went on.

"And can you explain the other telephone call—the one from Mr. Redding's cottage to Mrs. Price Ridley?"

"Ah!" said Miss Marple. "That is what I call the coincidence. Dear Griselda sent that call—she and Mr. Dennis between them, I fancy. They had heard the rumors Mrs. Price Ridley was circulating about the Vicar, and they thought of this—perhaps rather childish—way of silencing her. The coincidence lies in the fact that the call should have been put through at exactly the same time as the fake shot from the wood. It led one to believe that the two must be connected."

I suddenly remembered how everyone who spoke of the shot had described it as different from the usual shot. They had been right. Yet how hard to explain just in what way the difference of the shot consisted.

Colonel Melchett cleared his throat.

"Your solution is a very plausible one, Miss Marple," he said.

"But you will allow me to point out that there is not a shadow of proof."

"I know," said Miss Marple. "But you believe it to be true, don't you?"

There was a pause, then the Colonel said almost reluctantly, "Yes, I do. Dash it all, it's the only way the thing could have happened. But there's no proof—not an atom."

Miss Marple coughed. "That is why I thought perhaps—under the circumstances—"

"Yes?"

"A little trap might be permissible."

CHAPTER THIRTY-ONE

Colonel Melchett and I both stared at her.

"A trap? What kind of a trap?"

Miss Marple was a little diffident, but it was clear that she had a plan fully outlined.

"Supposing Mr. Redding were to be rung up on the telephone and warned."

Colonel Melchett smiled.

"'All is discovered. Fly!' That's an old wheeze, Miss Marple. Not that it isn't often successful! But I think in this case young Redding is too downy a bird to be caught that way."

"It would have to be something specific. I quite realize that," said Miss Marple. "I would suggest—this is just a mere suggestion—that the warning should come from somebody who is known to have rather unusual views on these matters. Doctor Haydock's conversation would lead anyone to suppose that he might view such a thing as murder from an unusual angle. If he were to hint that somebody—Mrs. Sadler—or one of her children—had actually happened to see the transposing of the cachets—well—of course, if Mr. Redding is an innocent man, that statement will mean nothing to him, but if he isn't—"

"If he isn't?"

"Well—he might just possibly do something foolish."

"And deliver himself into our hands. It's possible. Very ingenious, Miss Marple. But will Haydock stand for it? As you say his views—"

Miss Marple interrupted him brightly. "Oh, but that's theory! So very different from practice, isn't it? But anyway here he is, so we can ask him."

Haydock was, I think, rather astonished to find Miss Marple with us. He looked tired and haggard.

"It's been a near thing," he said. "A very near thing. But he's going to pull through. It's a doctor's business to save his patient, and I've saved him, but I'd have been just as glad if I hadn't pulled it off."

"You may think differently," said Melchett, "when you have heard what we have to tell you."

And briefly and succinctly he put Miss Marple's theory of the crime before the doctor, ending up with her final suggestion.

We were then privileged to see exactly what Miss Marple meant by the difference between theory and practice.

Haydock's views appeared to have undergone complete transformation. He would, I think, have liked Lawrence Redding's head on a charger. It was not, I imagine, the murder of Colonel Protheroe that so stirred his rancor. It was the assault on the unlucky Hawes.

"The damned scoundrel," said Haydock. "The damned scoundrel! That poor devil Hawes. He's got a mother and a sister, too. The stigma of being the mother and sister of a murderer would have rested on them for life, and think of their mental anguish. Of all the cowardly dastardly tricks!"

For sheer primitive rage, commend me to a thorough-going humanitarian when you get him well roused.

"If this thing's true," he said, "you can count on me. The fellow's not fit to live. A defenseless chap like Hawes."

A lame dog of any kind can always count on Haydock's sympathy.

He was eagerly arranging details with Melchett when Miss Marple rose and I insisted on seeing her home.

"It is most kind of you, Mr. Clement," said Miss Marple as we walked down the deserted street. "Dear me, past twelve o'clock. I hope Raymond has gone to bed and not waited up."

"He should have accompanied you," I said.

"I didn't let him know I was going," said Miss Marple.

I smiled suddenly as I remembered Raymond West's subtle psychological analysis of the crime.

"If your theory turns out to be the truth—which I for one do not doubt for a minute," I said, "you will have a very good score over your nephew."

Miss Marple smiled also—an indulgent smile.

"I remember a saying of my Great Aunt Fanny's. I was sixteen at the time and thought it particularly foolish."

"Yes?" I inquired.

"She used to say, 'The young people think the old people are fools—but the old people *know* the young people are fools!' "

CHAPTER THIRTY-TWO

THERE IS LITTLE MORE to be told. Miss Marple's plan succeeded. Lawrence Redding was not an innocent man, and the hint of a witness of the change of capsule did indeed cause him to do "something foolish." Such is the power of an evil conscience.

He was, of course, peculiarly placed. His first impulse, I imagine, must have been to cut and run. But there was his accomplice to consider. He could not leave without getting word to her, and he dared not wait till morning. So he went up to Old Hall that night—and two of Colonel Melchett's most efficient officers followed him. He threw gravel at Anne Protheroe's window, aroused her, and an urgent whisper brought her down to speak with him. Doubtless they felt safer outside than in—with the possibility of Lettice waking. But as it happened, the two police officers were able to overhear their conversation in full. It left the matter in no doubt. Miss Marple had been right on every count.

The trial of Lawrence Redding and Anne Protheroe is a matter of public knowledge. I do not propose to go into it. I will only mention that great credit was reflected upon Inspector Slack, whose zeal and intelligence had resulted in the criminals being brought to justice. Naturally, nothing was said of Miss Marple's share in the business. She herself would have been horrified at the thought of such a thing.

Lettice came to see me just before the trial took place. She drifted through my study window, wraithlike as ever. She told me then that she had all along been convinced of her stepmother's complicity. The loss of the yellow beret had been a mere excuse for searching the study. She hoped against hope that she might find something the police had overlooked.

"You see," she said in her dreamy voice, "they didn't hate her like I did. And hate makes things easier for you."

Disappointed in the result of her search, she had deliberately dropped Anne's earring by the desk.

"Since I *knew* she had done it, what did it matter? One way was as good as another. She *had* killed him."

I sighed a little. There are always some things that Lettice will never see. In some respects she is morally color blind.

"What are you going to do, Lettice?" I asked.

"When—when it's all over, I am going abroad." She hesitated and then went on. "I am going abroad with my mother."

I looked up, startled.

She nodded.

"Didn't you ever guess? Mrs. Lestrange is my mother. She is—is dying, you know. She wanted to see me, and so she came down here under an assumed name. Doctor Haydock helped her. He's a very old friend of hers—he was keen about her once—you can see that! In a way, he still is. Men always went batty about Mother, I believe. She's awfully attractive, even now. Anyway, Doctor Haydock did everything he could to help her. She didn't come down here under her own name, because of the disgusting way people talk and gossip. She went to see Father that night, and told him she was dying and had a great longing to see something of me. Father was a beast. He said she'd forfeited all claim, and that I thought she was dead—as though I had ever swallowed that story! Men like Father never see an inch before their noses!

"But Mother is not the sort to give in. She thought it only decent to go to Father first, but when he turned her down so brutally she sent a note to me, and I arranged to leave the tennis party early and meet her at the end of the footpath at a quarter past six. We just had a hurried meeting and arranged when to meet again. We left each other before half past six. Afterward, I was terrified that she would be suspected of having killed Father. After all, she *had* got a grudge against him. That's why I got hold of that old picture of her up in the attic and slashed it about. I was afraid the police might go nosing about and get hold of it and recognize it. Doctor Haydock was frightened, too. Sometimes, I believe, he really thought she had done it! Mother is rather a—desperate kind of person. She doesn't count consequences."

She paused.

"It's queer. She and I belong to each other. Father and I didn't. But Mother— Well, anyway, I'm going abroad with her. I shall be with her till—till the end."

She got up, and I took her hand.

"God bless you both," I said. "Some day, I hope, there is a lot of happiness coming to you, Lettice."

"There should be," she said, with an attempt at a laugh. "There hasn't been much so far—has there? Oh, well, I don't suppose it matters. Good-by, Mr. Clement. You've been frightfully decent to me always—you and Griselda."

Griselda!

I had to own to her how terribly the anonymous letter had upset me, and first she laughed, and then solemnly read me a lecture.

"However," she added, "I'm going to be very sober and godfearing in future—quite like the Pilgrim Fathers."

I did not see Griselda in the role of a Pilgrim Father.

She went on.

"You see, Len, I have a steadying influence coming into my life. It's coming into your life, too, but in your case it will be a kind of—of rejuvenating one—at least, I hope so! You can't call me a dear child half so much when we have a real child of our own. And, Len, I've decided that, now I'm going to be a real 'wife and mother' as they say in books; I must be a housekeeper, too. I've bought two books on Household Management and one on Mother Love and if that doesn't turn me out a pattern, I don't know what will! They are all simply screamingly funny—not intentionally, you know. Especially the one about bringing up children."

"You haven't bought a book on How To Treat a Husband, have you?" I asked with sudden apprehension as I drew her to me.

"I don't need to," said Griselda. "I'm a very good wife. I love you dearly. What more do you want?"

"Nothing," I said.

"Could you say, just for once, that you love me madly?"

"Griselda," I said, "I adore you! I worship you! I am wildly, hopelessly, and quite unclerically crazy about you!"

My wife gave a deep and contented sigh.

Then she drew away suddenly.

"Bother! Here's Miss Marple coming. Don't let her suspect, will you? I don't want everyone offering me cushions and urging me to put my feet up. Tell her I've gone down to the golf links. That will put her off the scent—and it's quite true because I left my yellow pullover there and I want it."

Miss Marple came to the window, halted apologetically, and asked for Griselda.

"Griselda," I said, "has gone to the golf links."

An expression of concern leaped into Miss Marple's eyes.

"Oh, but surely," she said, "that is most unwise—just now."

And then in a nice, old-fashioned, ladylike, maiden-lady way, she blushed.

And to cover the moment's confusion, we talked hurriedly of the Protheroe case, and of "Dr. Stone," who had turned out to be a well-known cracksman with several different aliases. Miss Cram, by the way, had been cleared of all complicity. She had at last admitted taking the suitcase to the woods, but had done so in all good faith, Dr. Stone having told her that he feared the rivalry of other archaeologists who would not stick at burglary to gain their object of discrediting his theories. The girl apparently swallowed this not very plausible story. She is now, according to the village, looking out for a more genuine article in the line of an elderly bachelor requiring a secretary.

As we talked, I wondered very much how Miss Marple had discovered our latest secret. But presently, in a discreet fashion, Miss Marple herself supplied me with a clue.

"I hope dear Griselda is not overdoing it," she murmured, and added after a discreet pause, "I was in the bookshop in Much Benham yesterday—"

Poor Griselda—that book on Mother Love has been her undoing!

"I wonder, Miss Marple," I said suddenly, "if you were to commit a murder whether you would ever be found out."

"What a terrible idea," said Miss Marple, shocked. "I hope I could never do such a wicked thing."

"But human nature being what it is," I murmured.

Miss Marple acknowledged the hit with a pretty old-ladyish laugh.

"How naughty of you, Mr. Clement." She rose. "But naturally you are in good spirits."

She paused by the window.

"My love to dear Griselda—and tell her—that any little secret is quite safe with me."

Really Miss Marple is rather a dear.